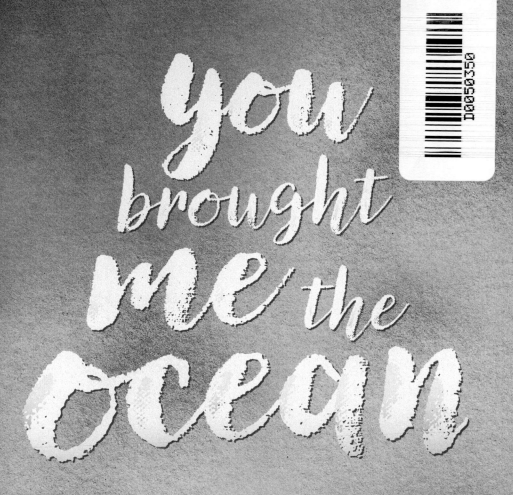

you brought me the ocean

WRITTEN BY
ALEX SANCHEZ

ART BY
JULIE MAROH

LETTERED BY
DERON BENNETT

SARA MILLER Editor
STEVE COOK Design Director – Books
AMIE BROCKWAY-METCALF Publication Design

BOB HARRAS Senior VP – Editor-in-Chief, DC Comics
MICHELE R. WELLS VP & Executive Editor, Young Reader

DAN DiDIO Publisher
JIM LEE Publisher & Chief Creative Officer
BOBBIE CHASE VP – New Publishing Initiatives
DON FALLETTI VP – Manufacturing Operations & Workflow Management
LAWRENCE GANEM VP – Talent Services
ALISON GILL Senior VP – Manufacturing & Operations
HANK KANALZ Senior VP – Publishing Strategy & Support Services
DAN MIRON VP – Publishing Operations
NICK J. NAPOLITANO VP – Manufacturing Administration & Design
NANCY SPEARS VP – Sales
JONAH WEILAND VP – Marketing & Creative Services

YOU BROUGHT ME THE OCEAN

DC Comics, 2900 West Alameda Ave., Burbank,
CA 91505
Printed by LSC Communications, Crawfordsville,
IN, USA. 5/1/20.
First Printing.
ISBN: 978-1-4012-9081-8

Library of Congress Cataloging-in-Publication Data

Names: Sanchez, Alex, writer. | Maroh, Julie, 1985- artist. | Bennett,
    Deron, letterer.
Title: You brought me the ocean / Alex Sanchez, writer ; Julie Maroh,
    artist ; Deron Bennett, letterer.
Description: Burbank, CA : DC Comics, [2020] | Audience: Ages 13-17 |
    Audience: Grades 7-9 | Summary: Jake Hyde yearns for the ocean and is
    determined to leave his hometown in New Mexico for a college on the
    coast, and while his family and friends encourage him to stay, he must
    deal with his secrets of being gay and some strange new blue markings on
    his skin giving him a glow when he touches water.
Identifiers: LCCN 2020000813 | ISBN 9781401290818 (trade paperback)
Subjects: LCSH: Graphic novels. | CYAC: Graphic novels. | Coming out
    (Sexual orientation)--Fiction. | Identity--Fiction. | Gays--Fiction. |
    Love--Fiction. | Ability--Fiction.
Classification: LCC PZ7.7.S1524 Yo 2020 | DDC 741.5/973--dc23

FROM
ALEX SANCHEZ

When I was a boy, some of my favorite comics heroes possessed superpowers and wore iconic capes. Others, however, were monsters: Casper the Friendly Ghost, Wendy the Good Little Witch, and Hot Stuff the Little Devil. In their subversive story lines, these so-called "monsters" were good, but even so, people were scared of them. I loved those misunderstood characters. I knew how they felt.

From as far back as I can remember, I had romantic yearnings toward guys. And with some of my first elementary-school boy crushes, I discovered we loved to kiss and hold each other. But I also understood from adult whisperings and classmates' hateful comments that people who had feelings like my friends and I did were equal to monsters. So I hid that part of me until years later, when I felt safe and strong enough to share my true self—first personally and later publicly in my books.

When DC asked me to write a graphic novel about a super-powered teen confronting his sexuality, I remembered those beloved monster comics that had given me so much needed hope and understanding. And I tried to capture their timeless message: "It's okay to be who you are, even if you're different; you're not a monster."

The world has changed a lot since I was a boy, and yet too often people of a different sexuality, gender identity, ethnicity, religion, or nationality are still treated like monsters. My wish is that *You Brought Me the Ocean* will help remind us that we're all equal human beings with the same yearnings to love and be loved. And for those who need courage, I hope Jake, Kenny, and Maria will give you the inspiration to be who you are!

My huge thanks go to Julie Maroh for bringing these characters to life in such an expressive and stunning way, to the rest of the tremendously creative team involved in this project, and to you, dear reader.

Wishing you peace in your journey,

Alex Sanchez

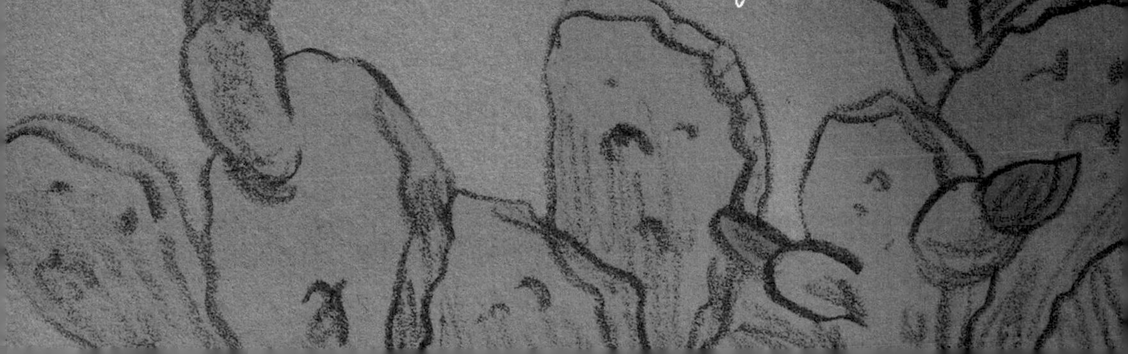

CHAPTER 1

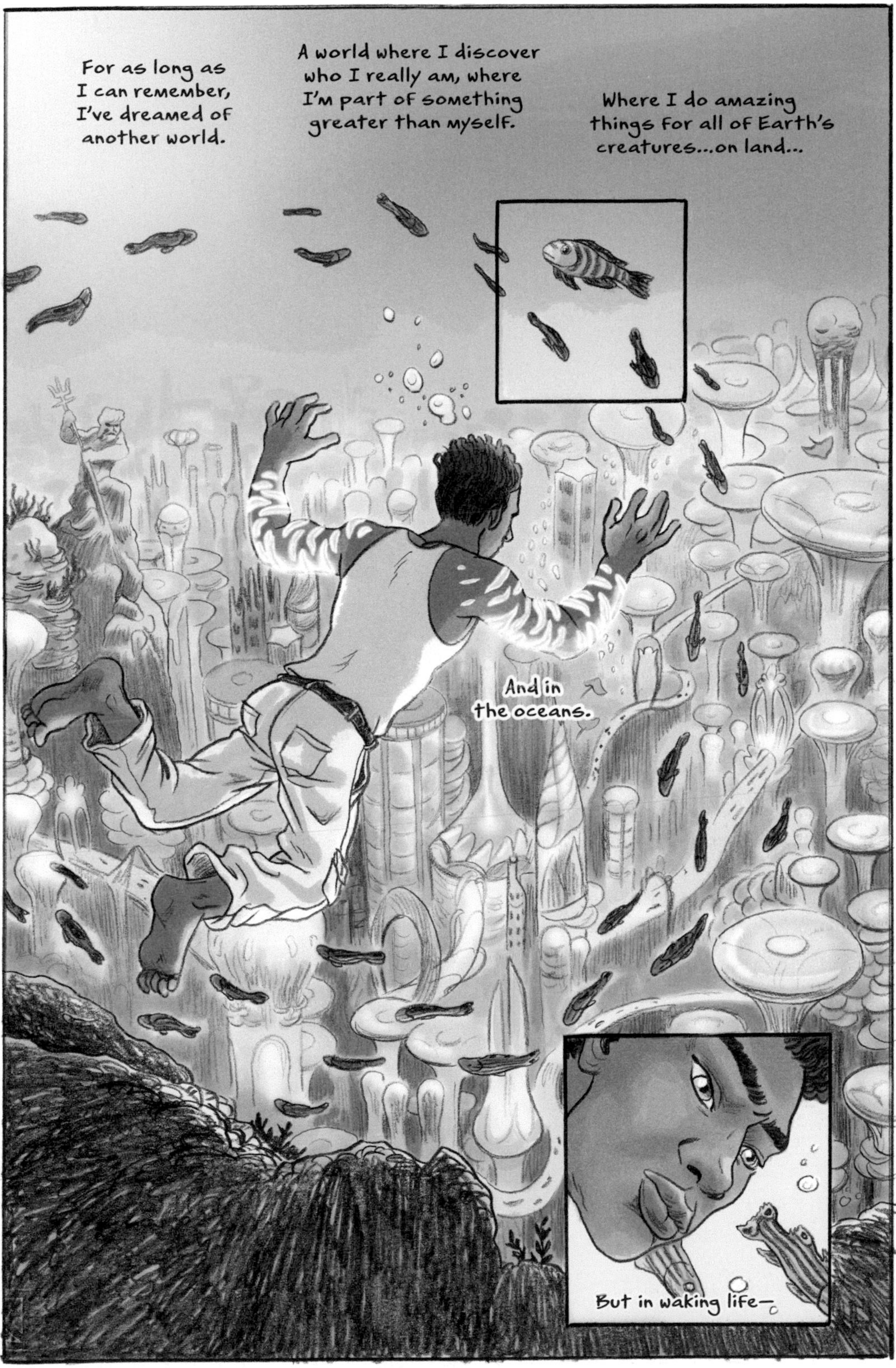
For as long as I can remember, I've dreamed of another world.
A world where I discover who I really am, where I'm part of something greater than myself.
Where I do amazing things for all of Earth's creatures...on land...
And in the oceans.
But in waking life—

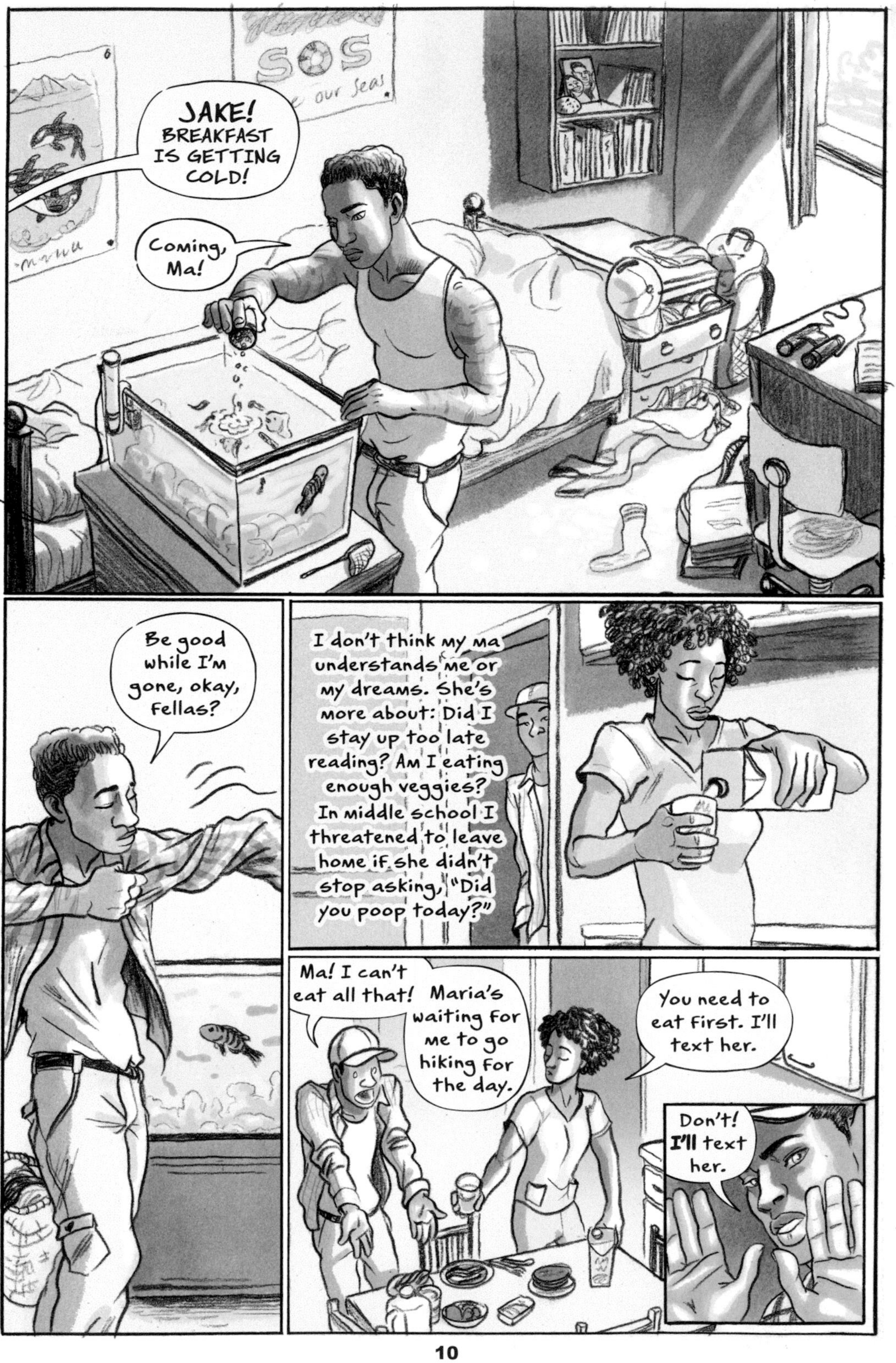
SOS
JAKE! BREAKFAST IS GETTING COLD!
Coming, Ma!
Be good while I'm gone, okay, fellas?
I don't think my ma understands me or my dreams. She's more about: Did I stay up too late reading? Am I eating enough veggies? In middle school I threatened to leave home if she didn't stop asking, "Did you poop today?"
Ma! I can't eat all that!
Maria's waiting for me to go hiking for the day.
You need to eat first. I'll text her.
Don't! **I'll** text her.

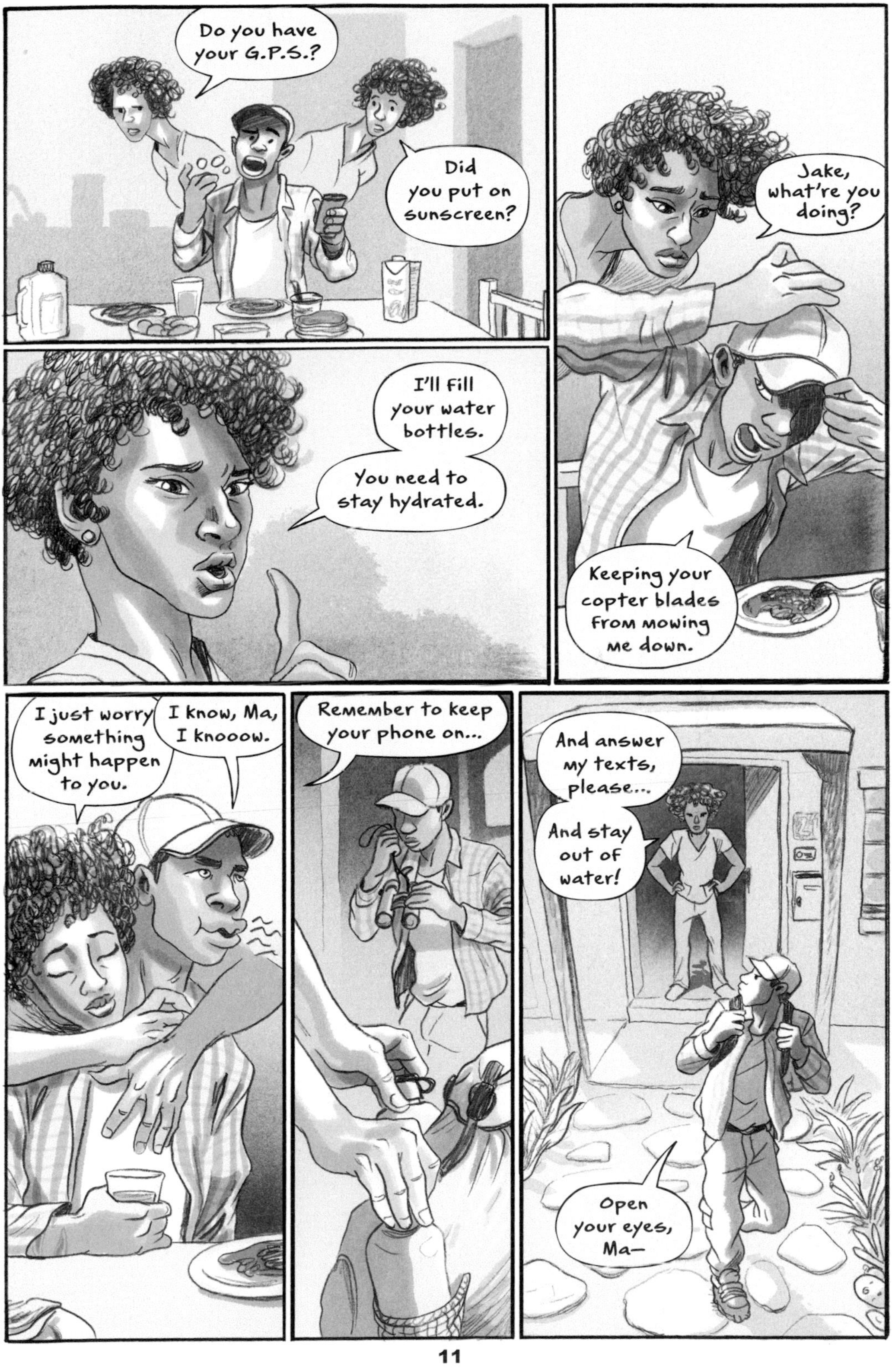
Do you have your G.P.S.?
Did you put on sunscreen?
Jake, what're you doing?
Keeping your copter blades from mowing me down.
I'll fill your water bottles.
You need to stay hydrated.
I just worry something might happen to you.
I know, Ma, I knooow.
Remember to keep your phone on...
And answer my texts, please...
And stay out of water!
Open your eyes, Ma—

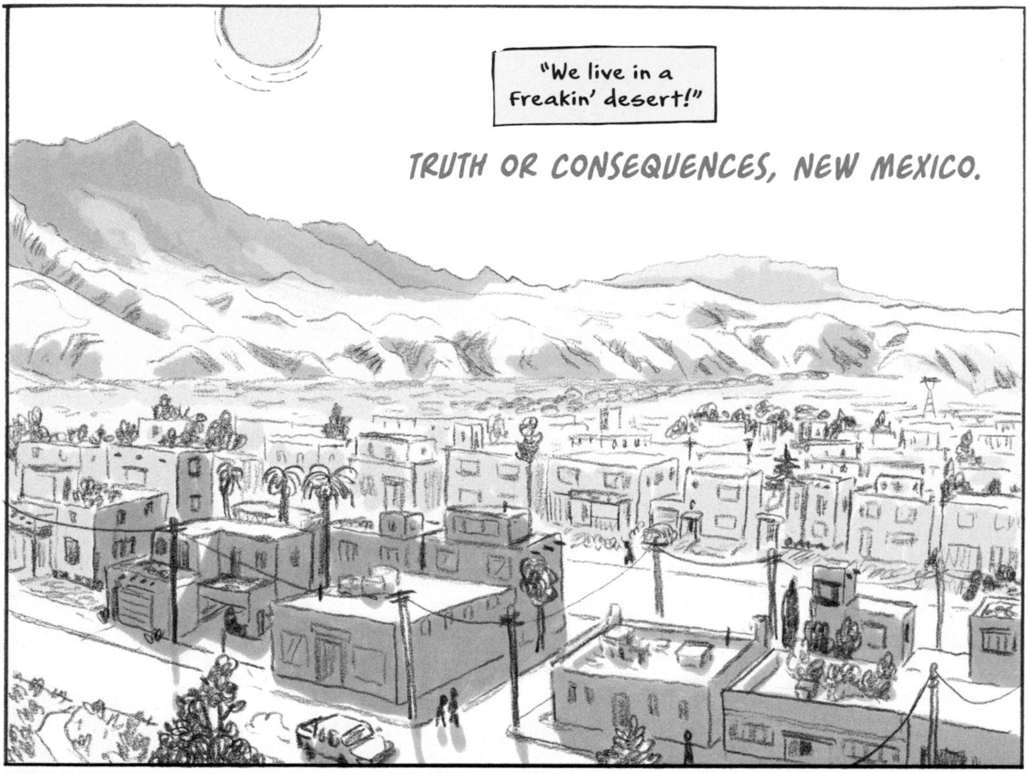
"We live in a Freakin' desert!"
TRUTH OR CONSEQUENCES, NEW MEXICO.

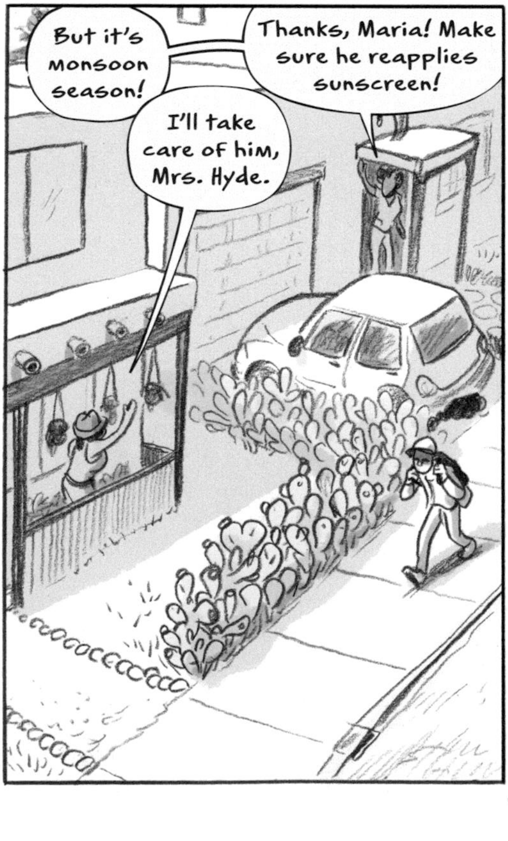
But it's monsoon season!
Thanks, Maria! Make sure he reapplies sunscreen!
I'll take care of him, Mrs. Hyde.

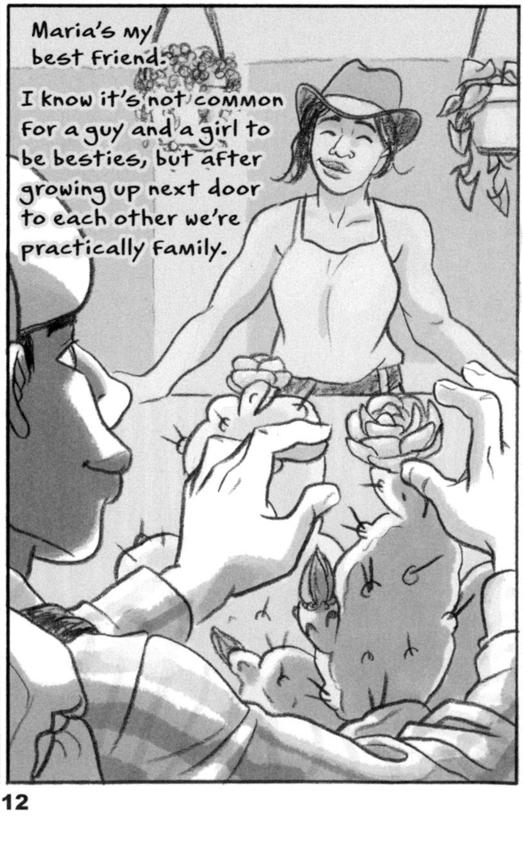
Maria's my best friend.
I know it's not common for a guy and a girl to be besties, but after growing up next door to each other we're practically family.

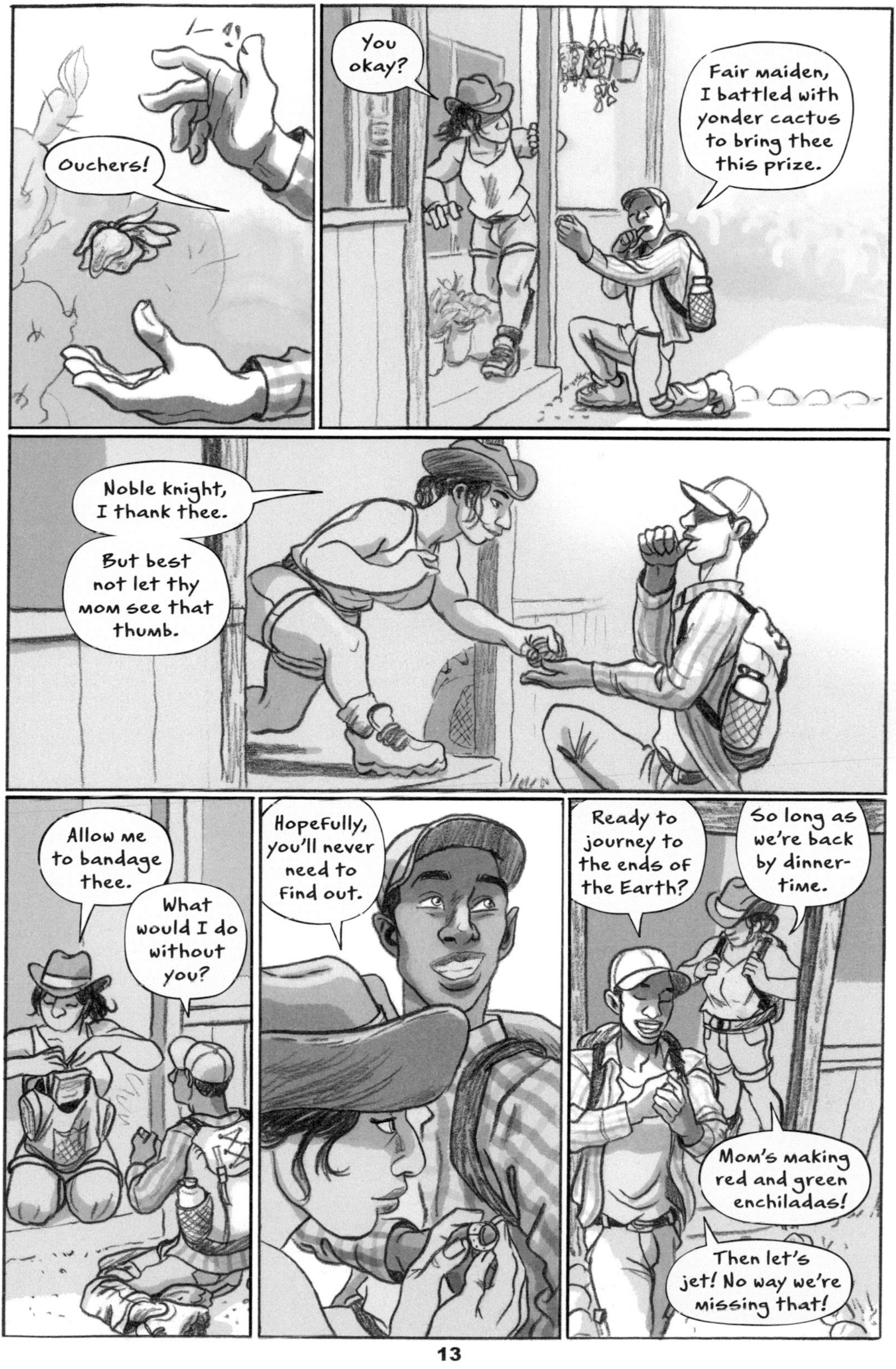
Ouchers!
You okay?
Fair maiden, I battled with yonder cactus to bring thee this prize.
Noble knight, I thank thee.
But best not let thy mom see that thumb.
Allow me to bandage thee.
What would I do without you?
Hopefully, you'll never need to find out.
Ready to journey to the ends of the Earth?
So long as we're back by dinner-time.
Mom's making red and green enchiladas!
Then let's jet! No way we're missing that!

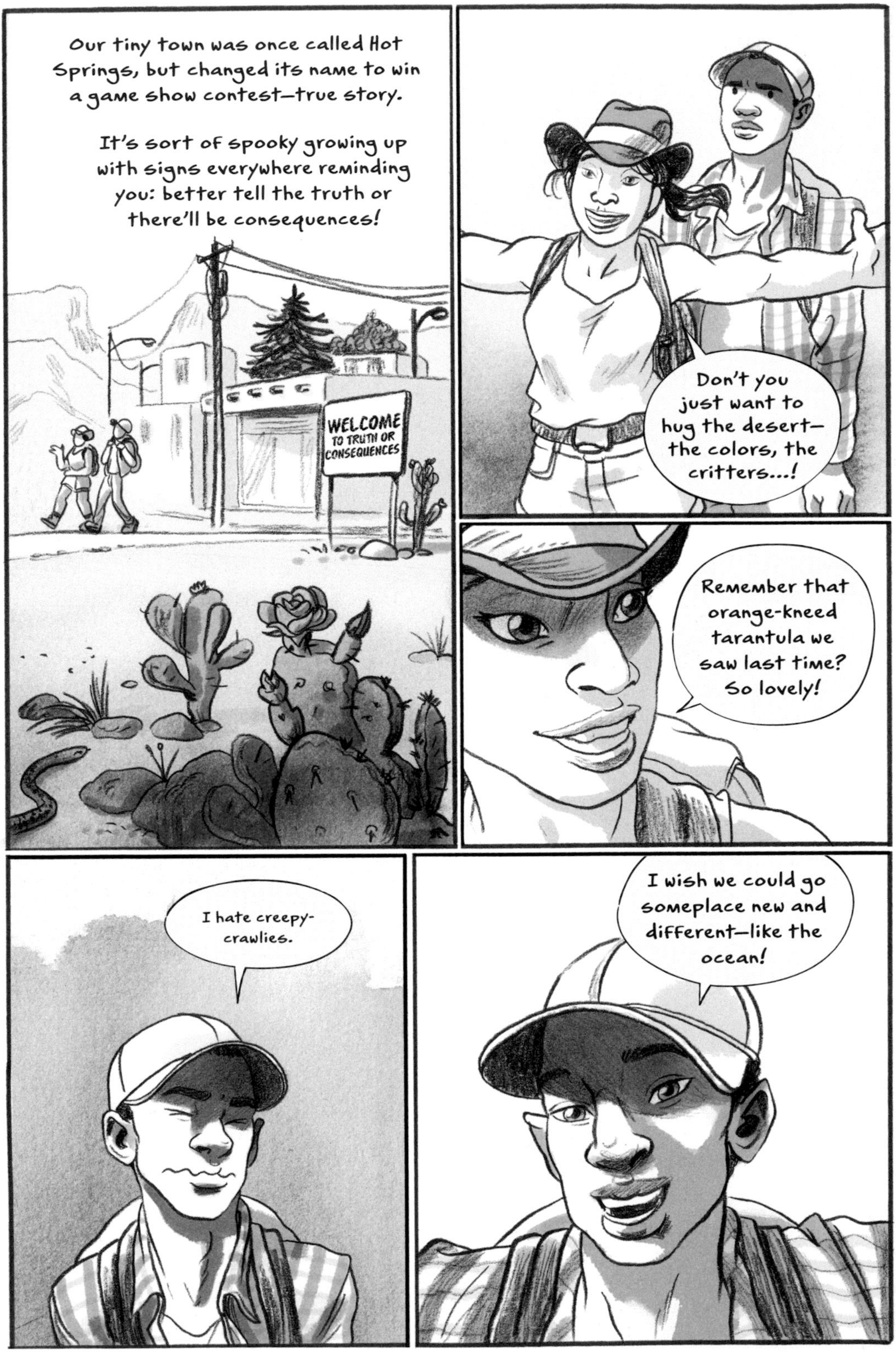
Our tiny town was once called Hot Springs, but changed its name to win a game show contest—true story.
It's sort of spooky growing up with signs everywhere reminding you: better tell the truth or there'll be consequences!
WELCOME TO TRUTH OR CONSEQUENCES
Don't you just want to hug the desert—the colors, the critters...!
Remember that orange-kneed tarantula we saw last time? So lovely!
I hate creepy-crawlies.
I wish we could go someplace new and different—like the ocean!

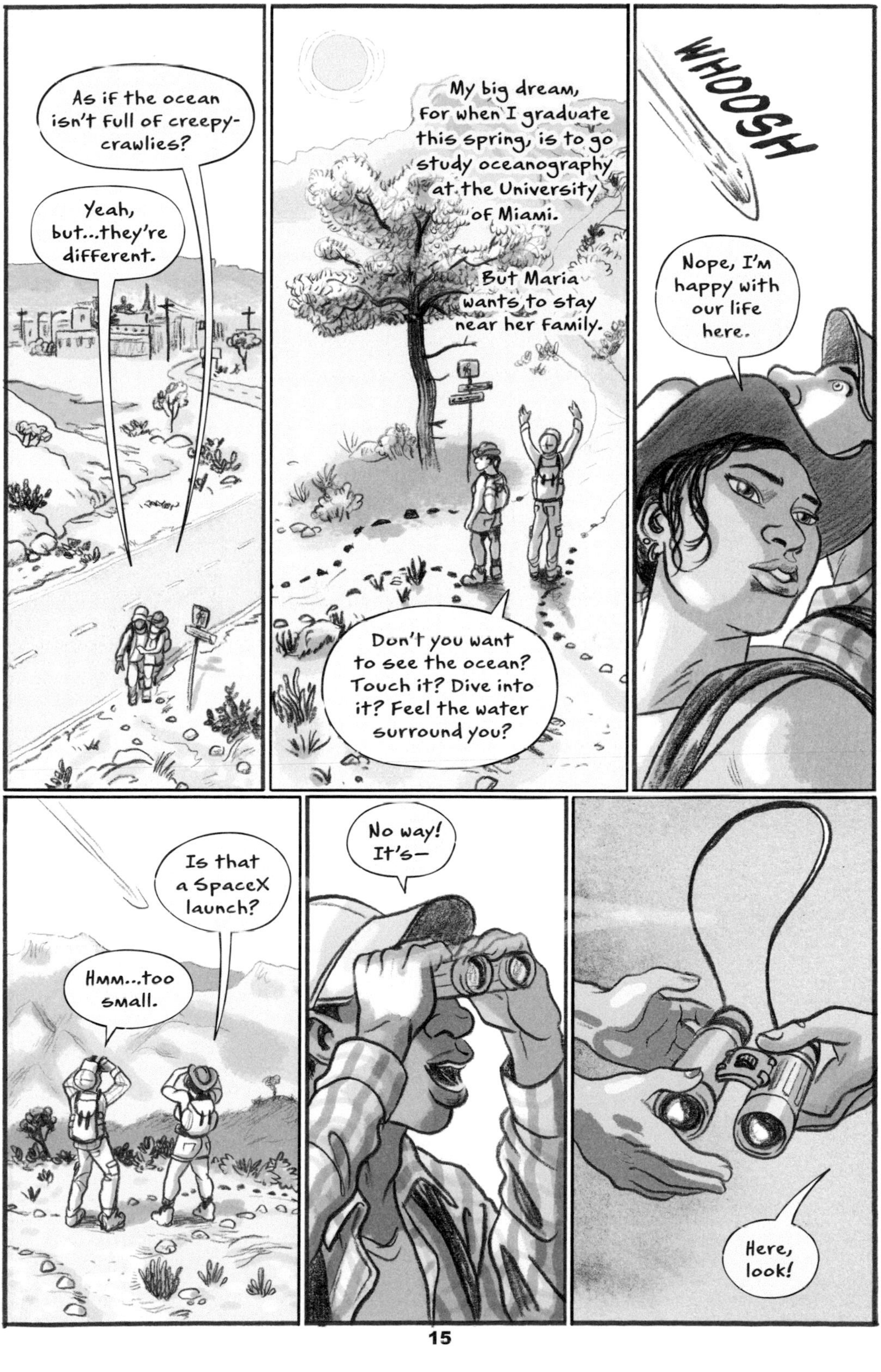
As if the ocean isn't full of creepy-crawlies?
Yeah, but...they're different.
My big dream, for when I graduate this spring, is to go study oceanography at the University of Miami.
But Maria wants to stay near her family.
Don't you want to see the ocean? Touch it? Dive into it? Feel the water surround you?
WHOOSH
Nope, I'm happy with our life here.
Is that a SpaceX launch?
Hmm...too small.
No way! It's—
Here, look!

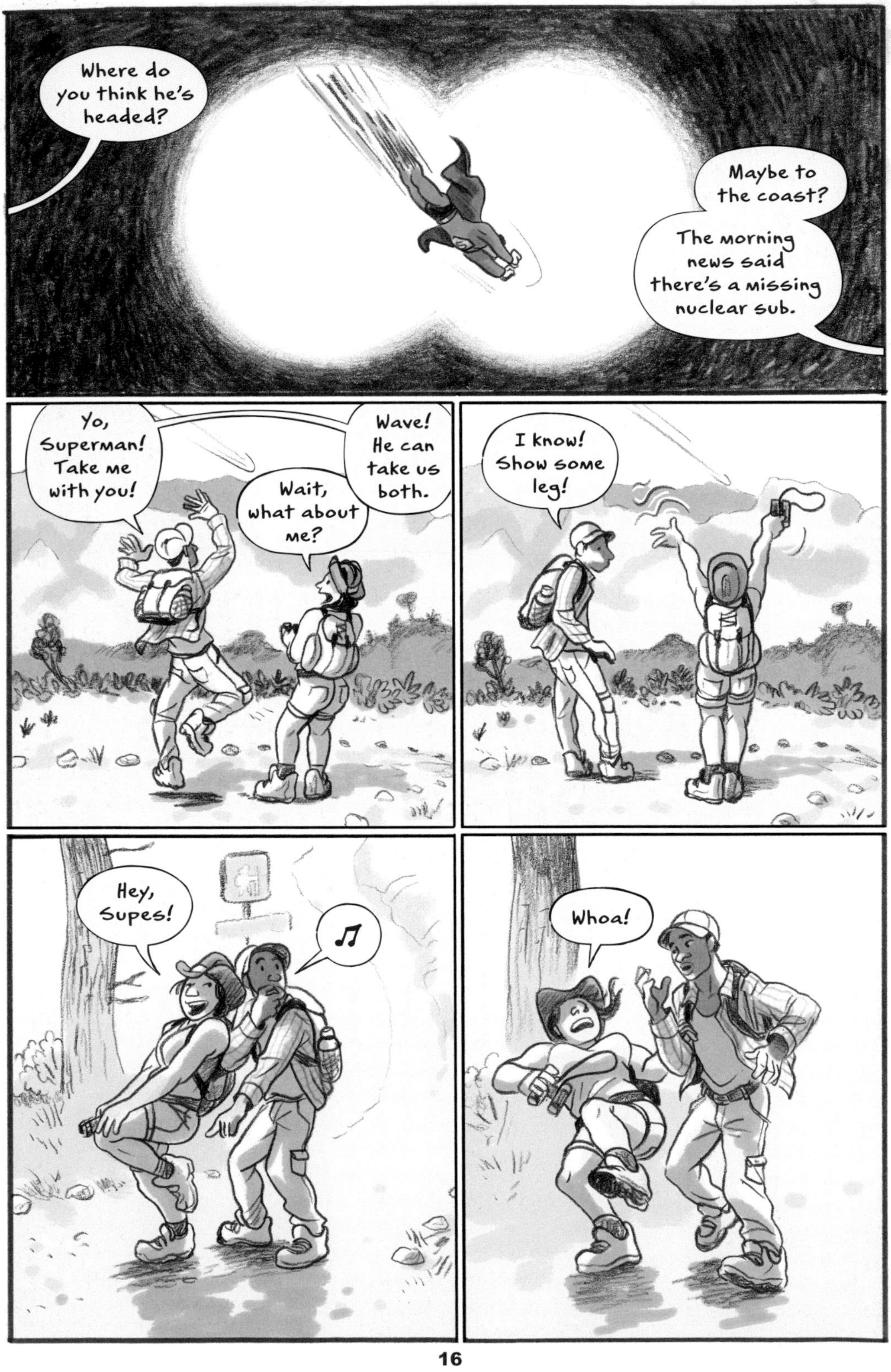
Where do you think he's headed?
Maybe to the coast?
The morning news said there's a missing nuclear sub.
Yo, Superman! Take me with you!
Wait, what about me?
Wave! He can take us both.
I know! Show some leg!
Hey, Supes!
♫
Whoa!

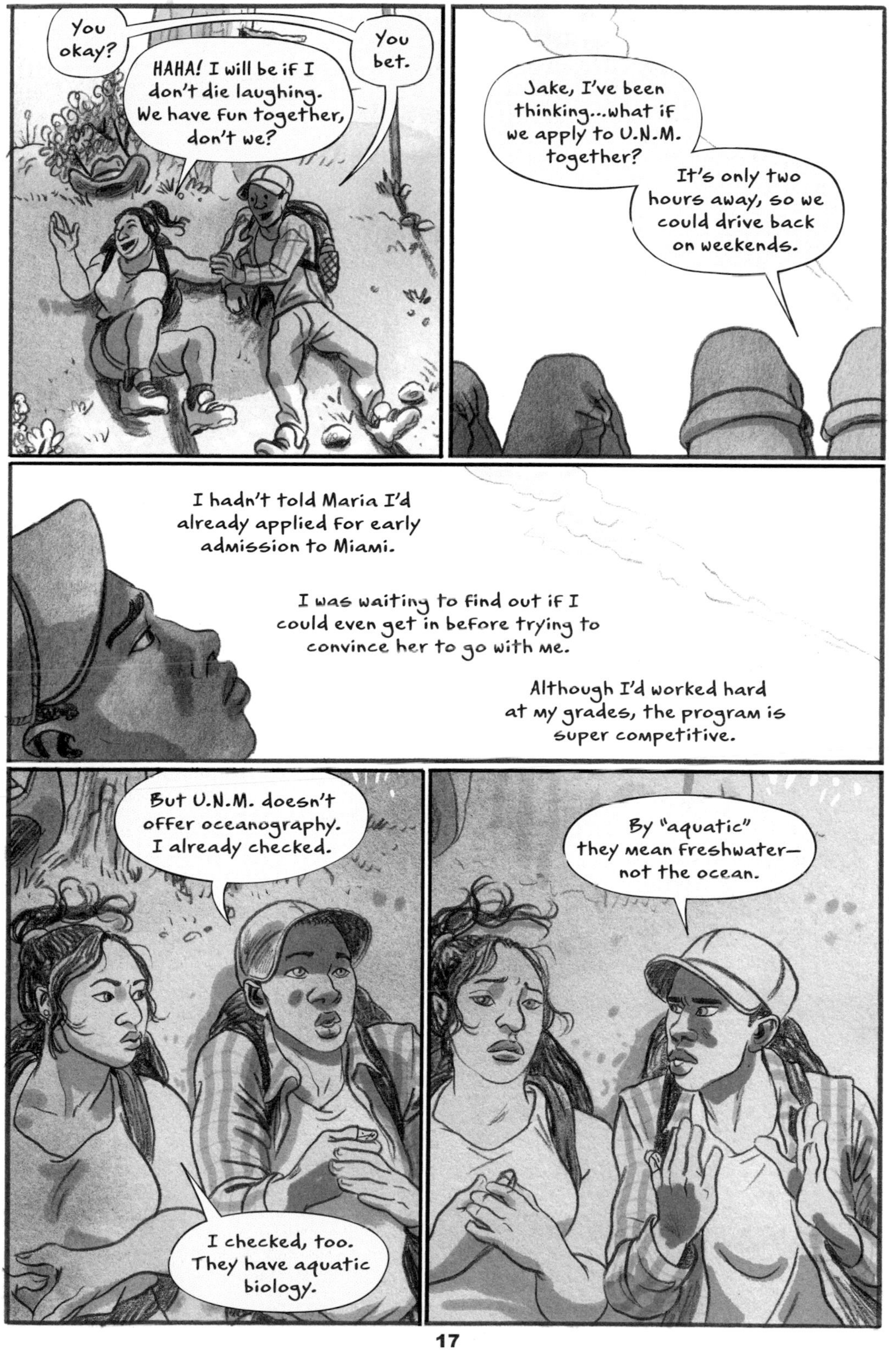

You okay?
HAHA! I will be if I don't die laughing. We have fun together, don't we?
You bet.
Jake, I've been thinking...what if we apply to U.N.M. together?
It's only two hours away, so we could drive back on weekends.
I hadn't told Maria I'd already applied for early admission to Miami.
I was waiting to find out if I could even get in before trying to convince her to go with me.
Although I'd worked hard at my grades, the program is super competitive.
But U.N.M. doesn't offer oceanography. I already checked.
I checked, too. They have aquatic biology.
By "aquatic" they mean freshwater—not the ocean.

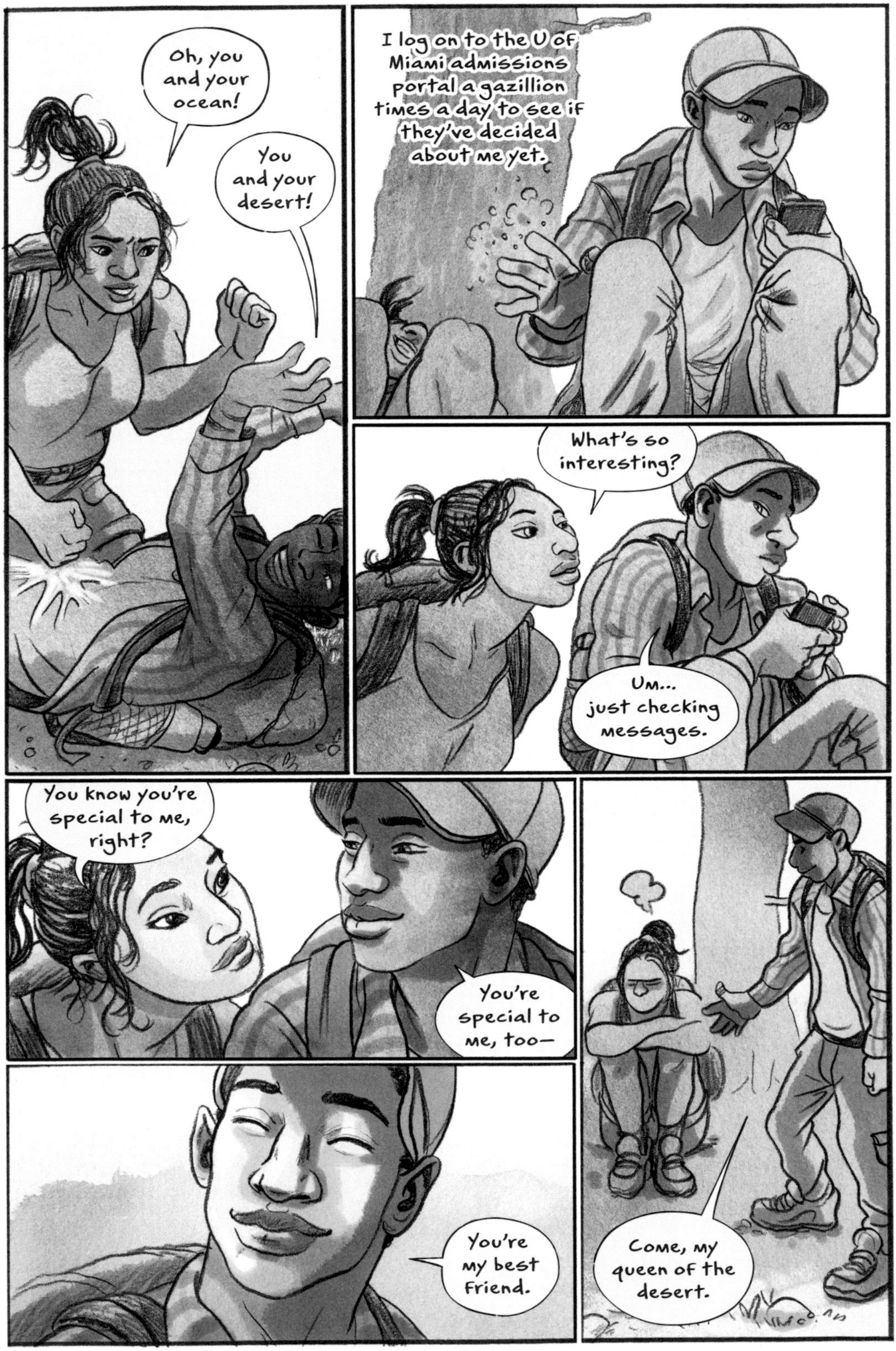
Oh, you and your ocean!
You and your desert!
I log on to the U of Miami admissions portal a gazillion times a day to see if they've decided about me yet.
What's so interesting?
Um... just checking messages.
You know you're special to me, right?
You're special to me, too—
You're my best friend.
Come, my queen of the desert.

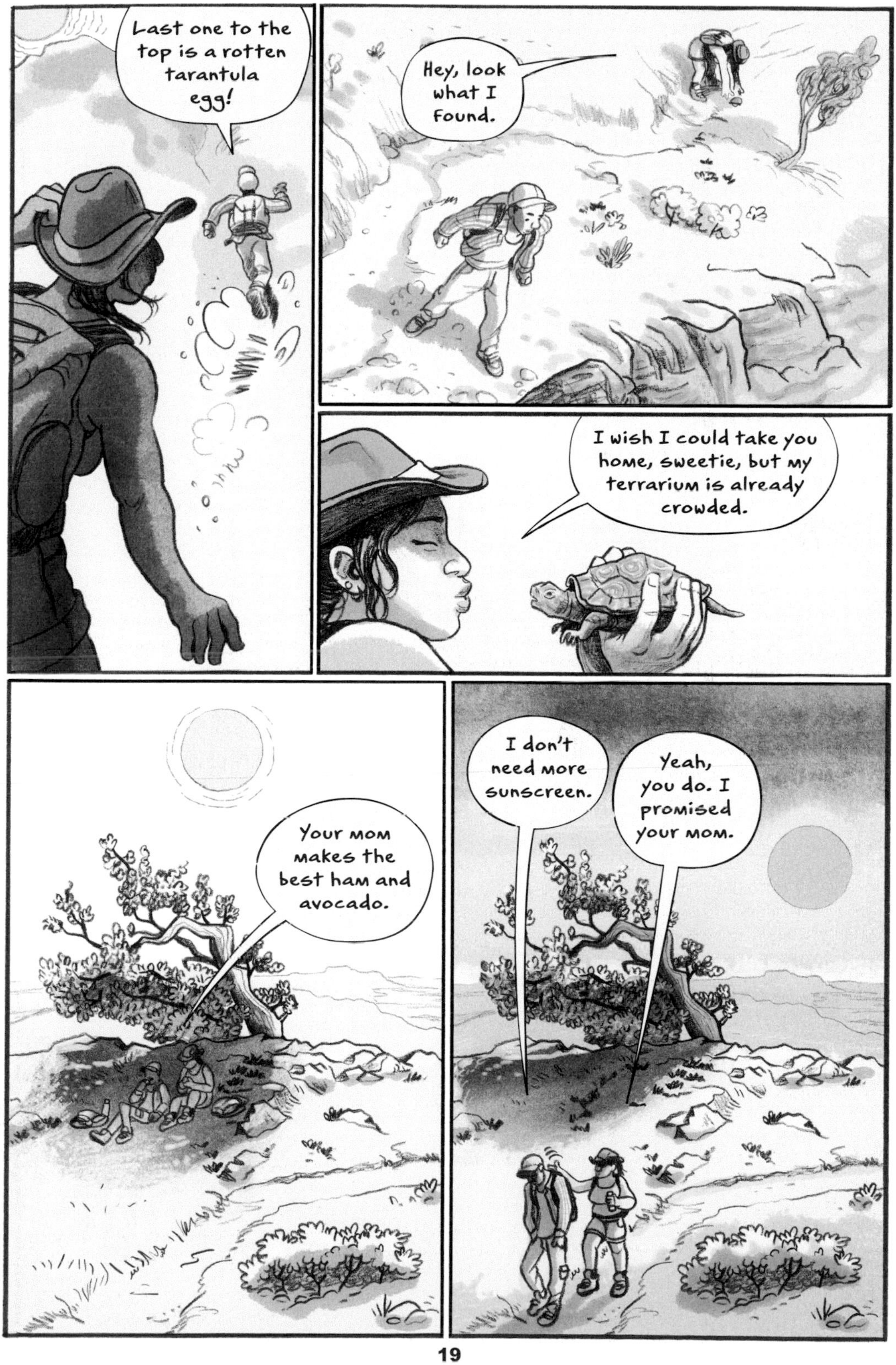

Last one to the top is a rotten tarantula egg!
Hey, look what I found.
I wish I could take you home, sweetie, but my terrarium is already crowded.
Your mom makes the best ham and avocado.
I don't need more sunscreen.
Yeah, you do. I promised your mom.

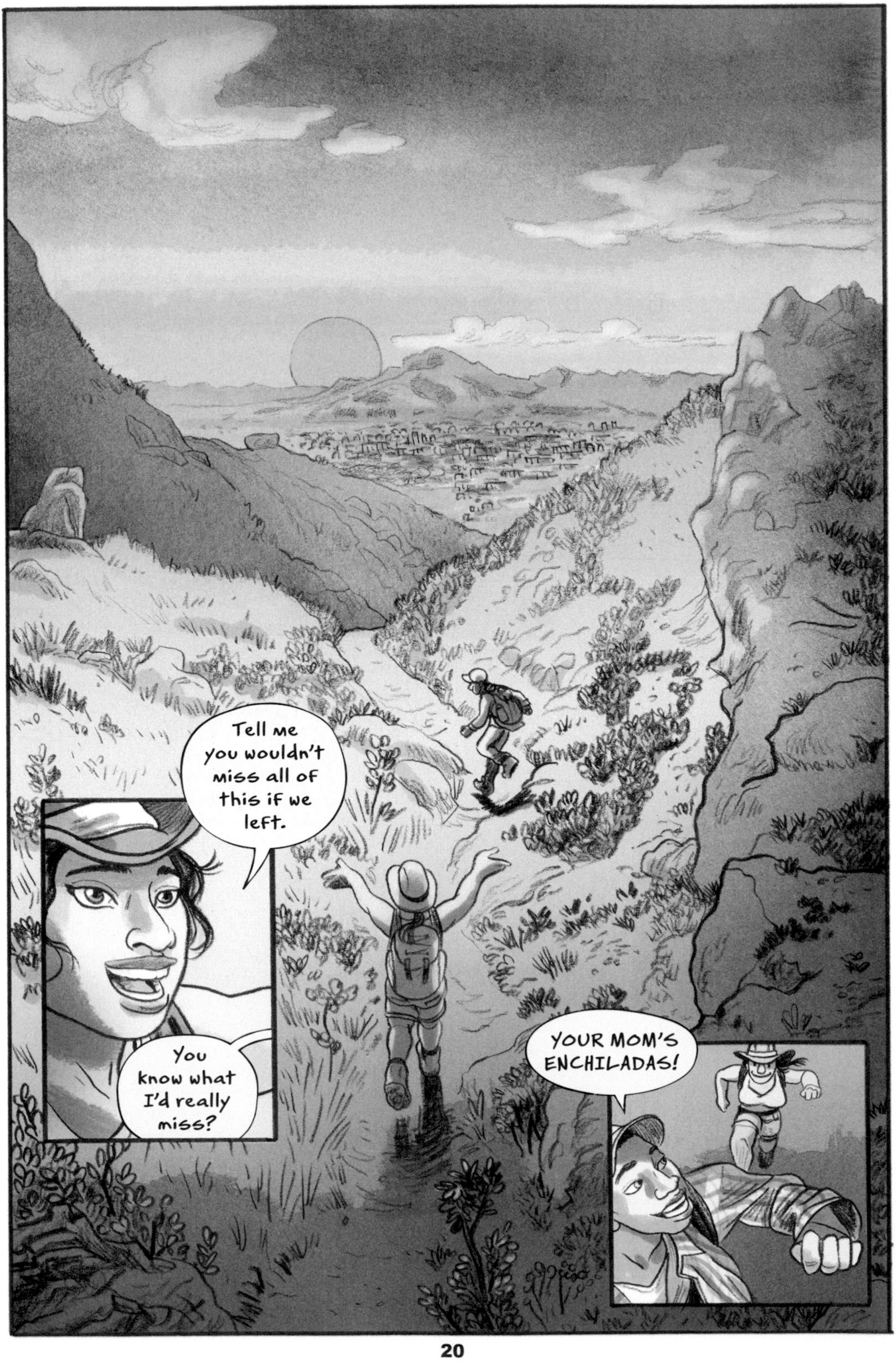
Tell me you wouldn't miss all of this if we left.
You know what I'd really miss?
YOUR MOM'S ENCHILADAS!

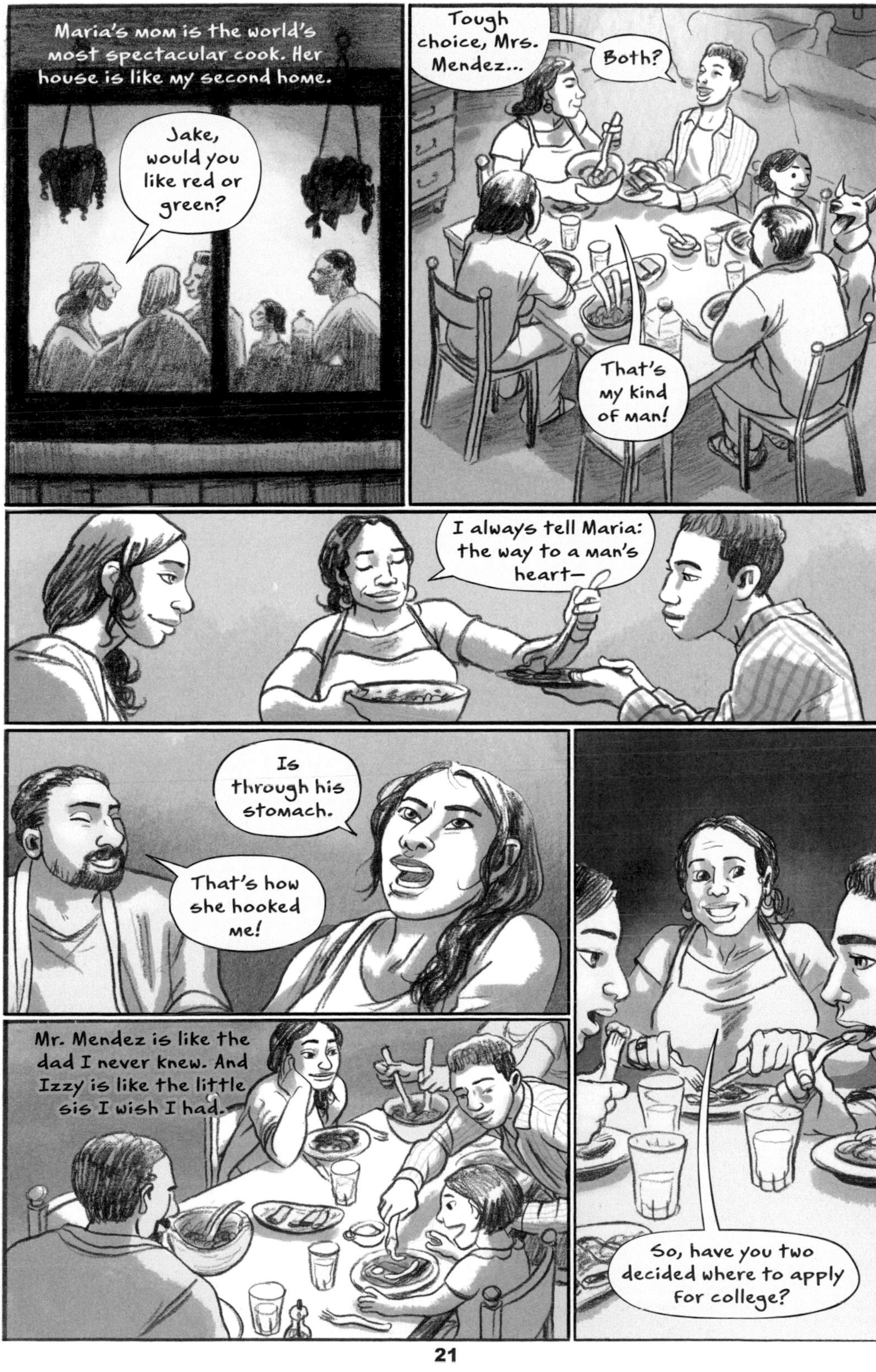

Maria's mom is the world's most spectacular cook. Her house is like my second home.
Jake, would you like red or green?
Tough choice, Mrs. Mendez...
Both?
That's my kind of man!
I always tell Maria: the way to a man's heart—
Is through his stomach.
That's how she hooked me!
Mr. Mendez is like the dad I never knew. And Izzy is like the little sis I wish I had.
So, have you two decided where to apply for college?

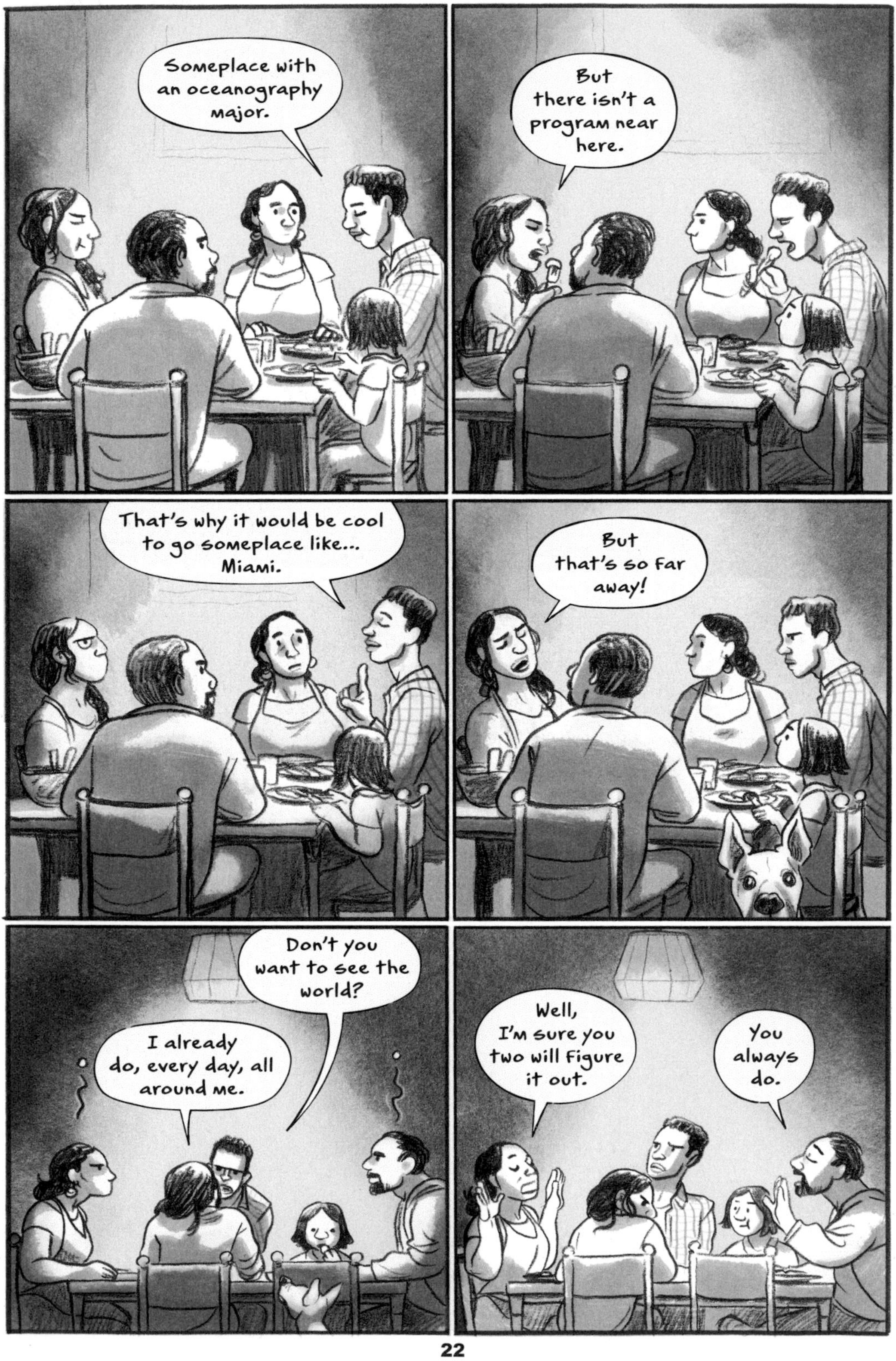
Someplace with an oceanography major.
But there isn't a program near here.
That's why it would be cool to go someplace like... Miami.
But that's so far away!
Don't you want to see the world?
I already do, every day, all around me.
Well, I'm sure you two will figure it out.
You always do.

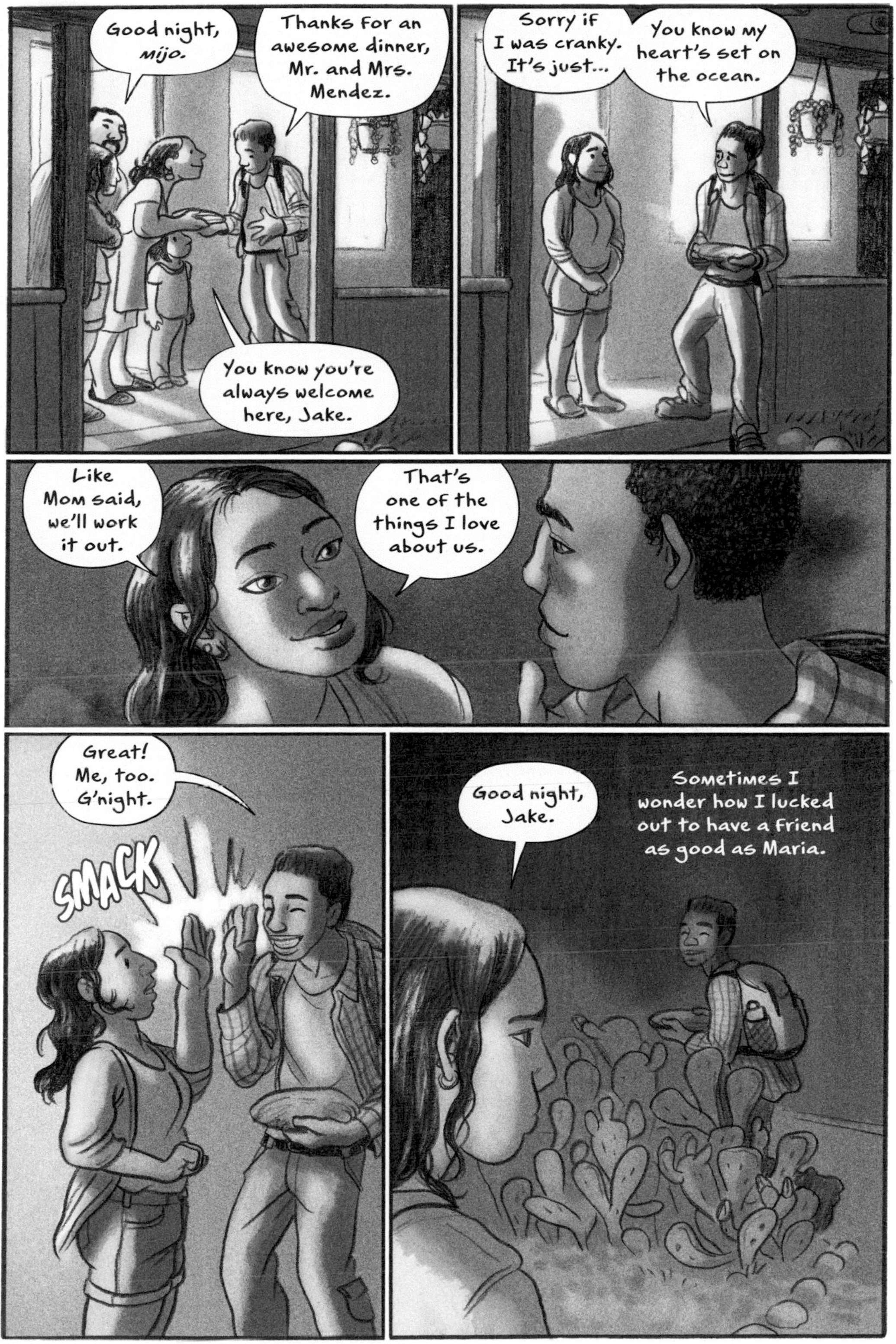
Good night, *mijo.*
Thanks for an awesome dinner, Mr. and Mrs. Mendez.
You know you're always welcome here, Jake.
Sorry if I was cranky. It's just...
You know my heart's set on the ocean.
Like Mom said, we'll work it out.
That's one of the things I love about us.
Great! Me, too. G'night.
SMACK
Good night, Jake.
Sometimes I wonder how I lucked out to have a friend as good as Maria.

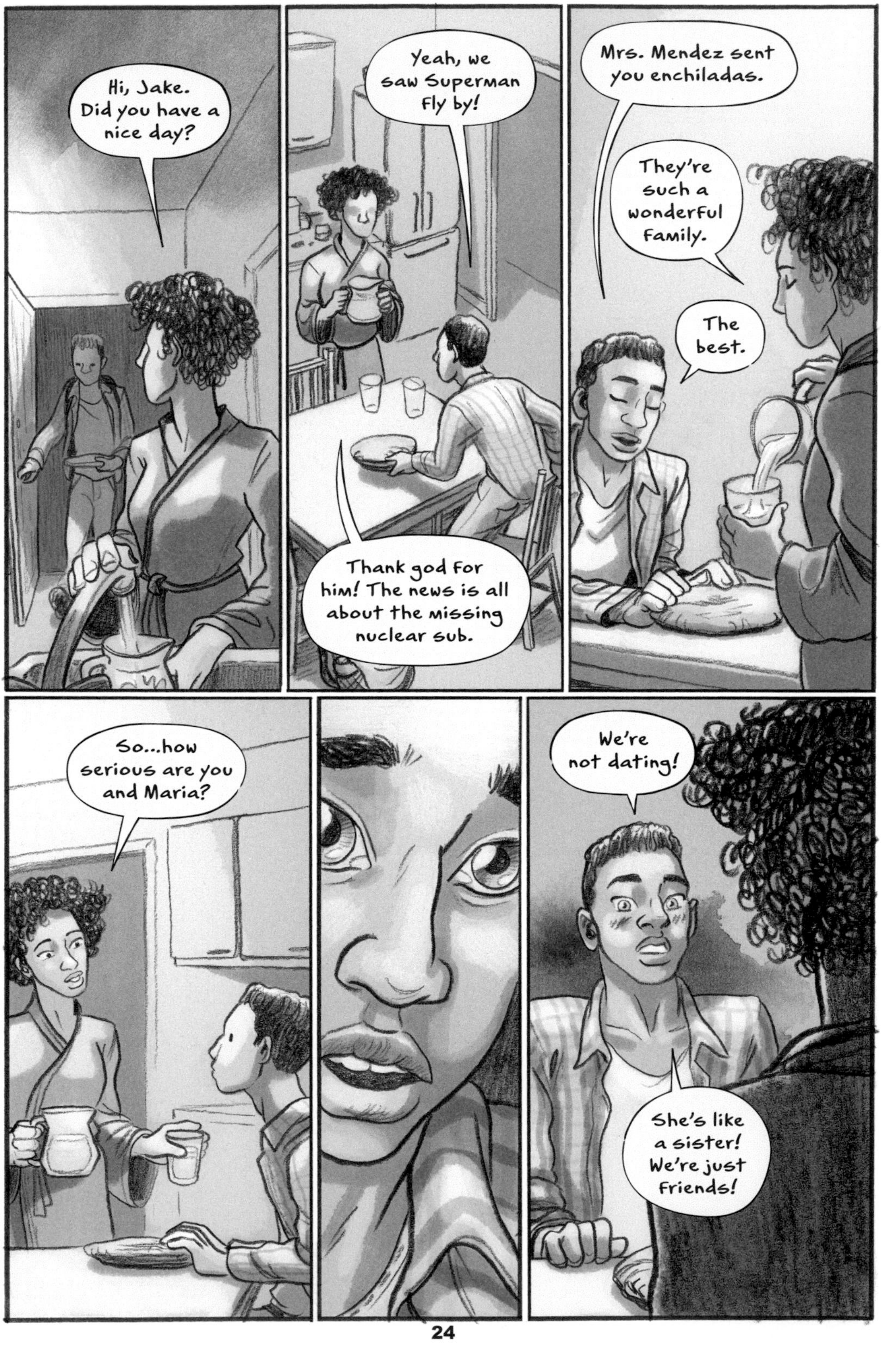
Hi, Jake. Did you have a nice day?
Yeah, we saw Superman fly by!
Thank god for him! The news is all about the missing nuclear sub.
Mrs. Mendez sent you enchiladas.
They're such a wonderful family.
The best.
So...how serious are you and Maria?
We're not dating!
She's like a sister! We're just friends!

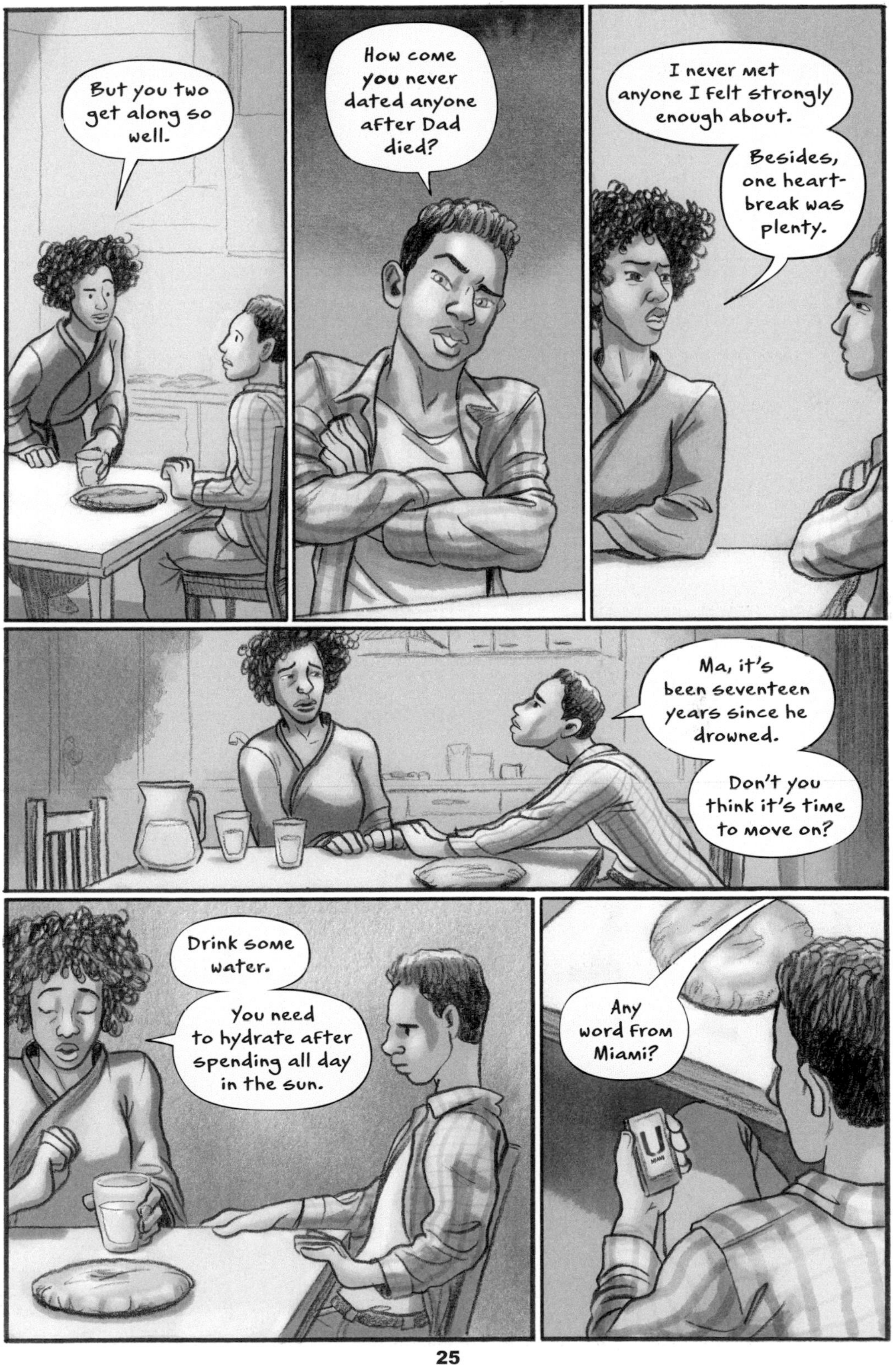
But you two get along so well.
How come you never dated anyone after Dad died?
I never met anyone I felt strongly enough about.
Besides, one heart-break was plenty.
Ma, it's been seventeen years since he drowned.
Don't you think it's time to move on?
Drink some water.
You need to hydrate after spending all day in the sun.
Any word from Miami?

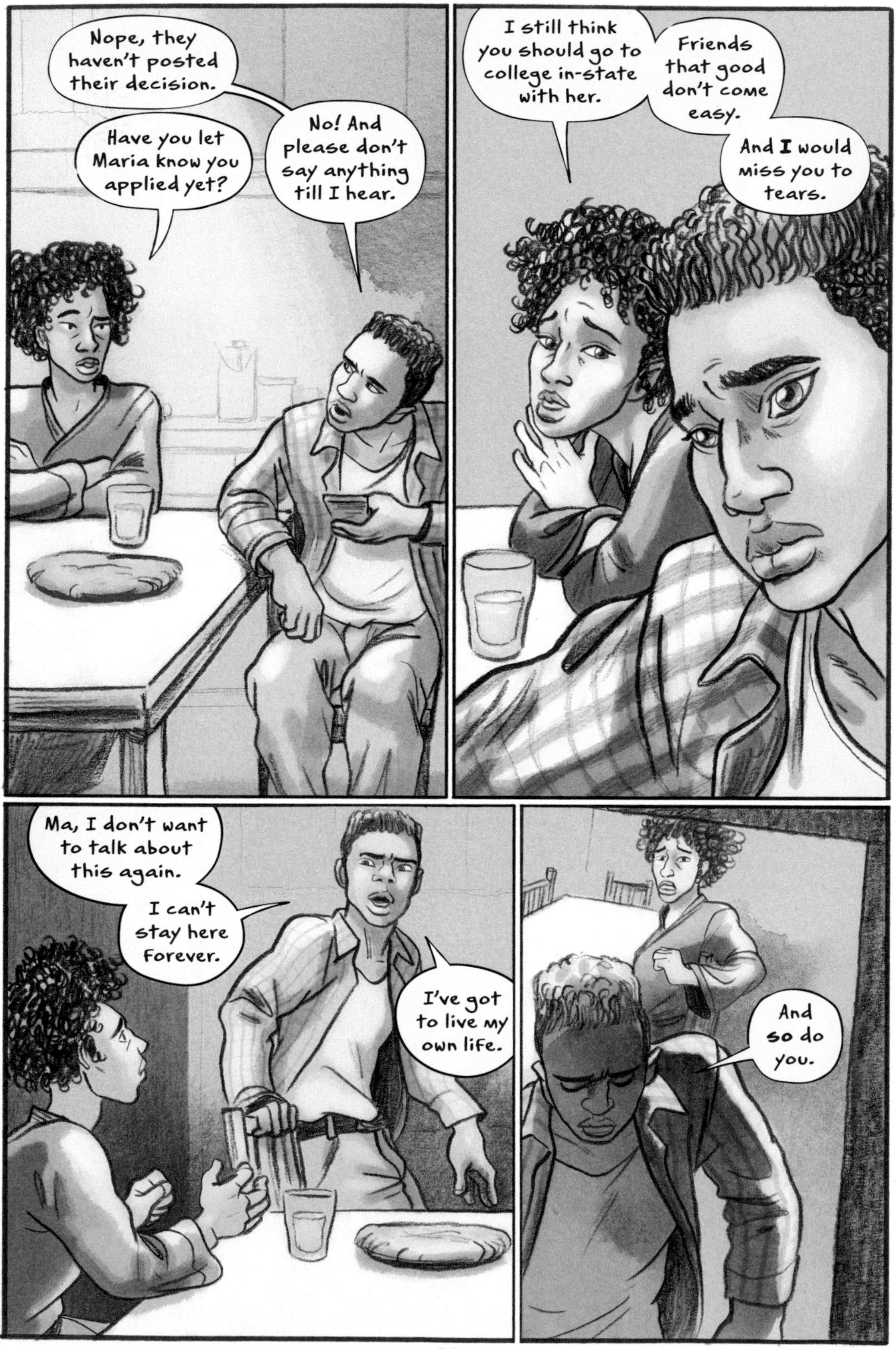
Nope, they haven't posted their decision.
Have you let Maria know you applied yet?
No! And please don't say anything till I hear.
I still think you should go to college in-state with her.
Friends that good don't come easy.
And **I** would miss you to tears.
Ma, I don't want to talk about this again.
I can't stay here forever.
I've got to live my own life.
And so do you.

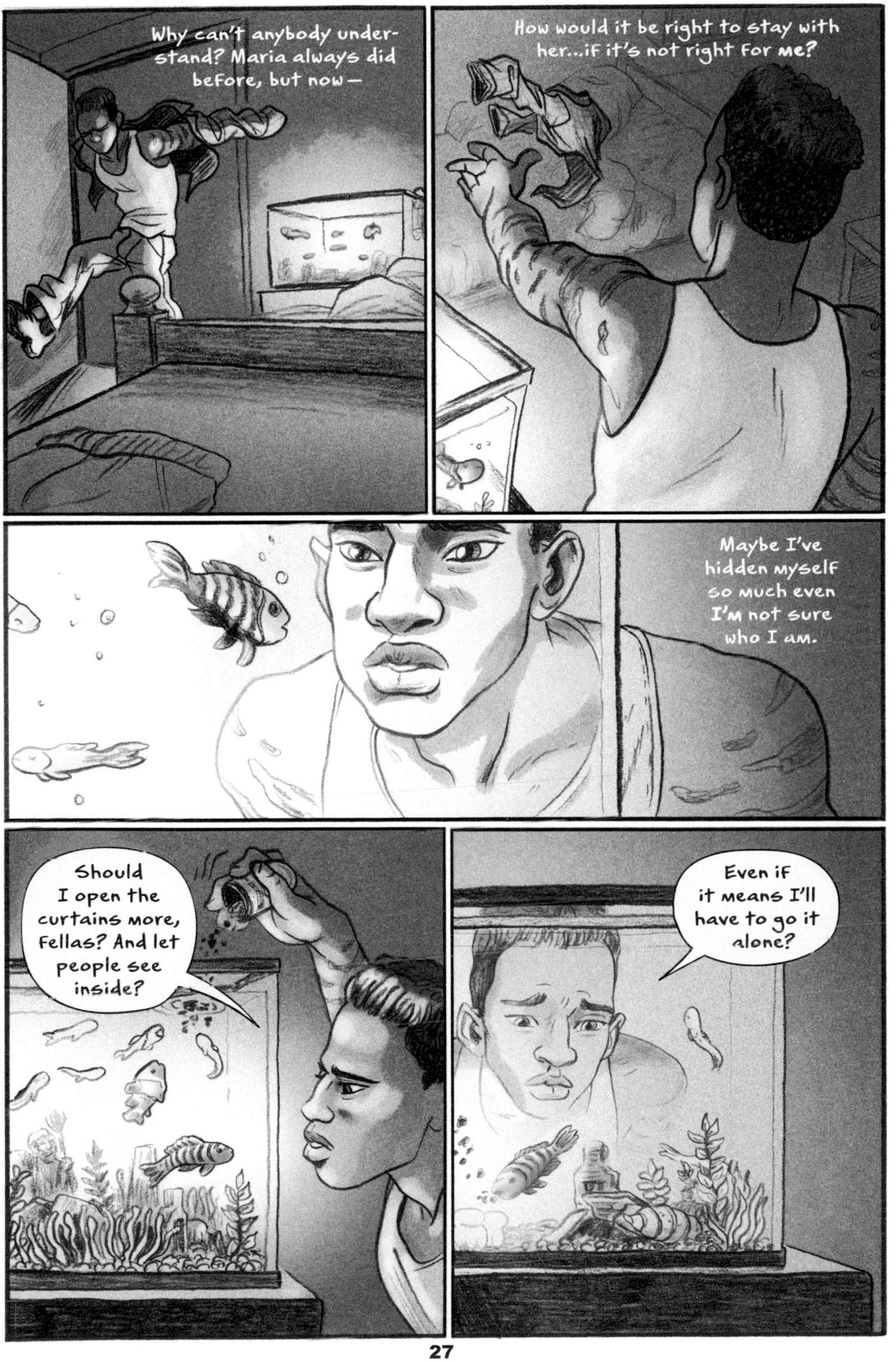

Why can't anybody understand? Maria always did before, but now—
How would it be right to stay with her...if it's not right for me?
Maybe I've hidden myself so much even I'm not sure who I am.
Should I open the curtains more, fellas? And let people see inside?
Even if it means I'll have to go it alone?

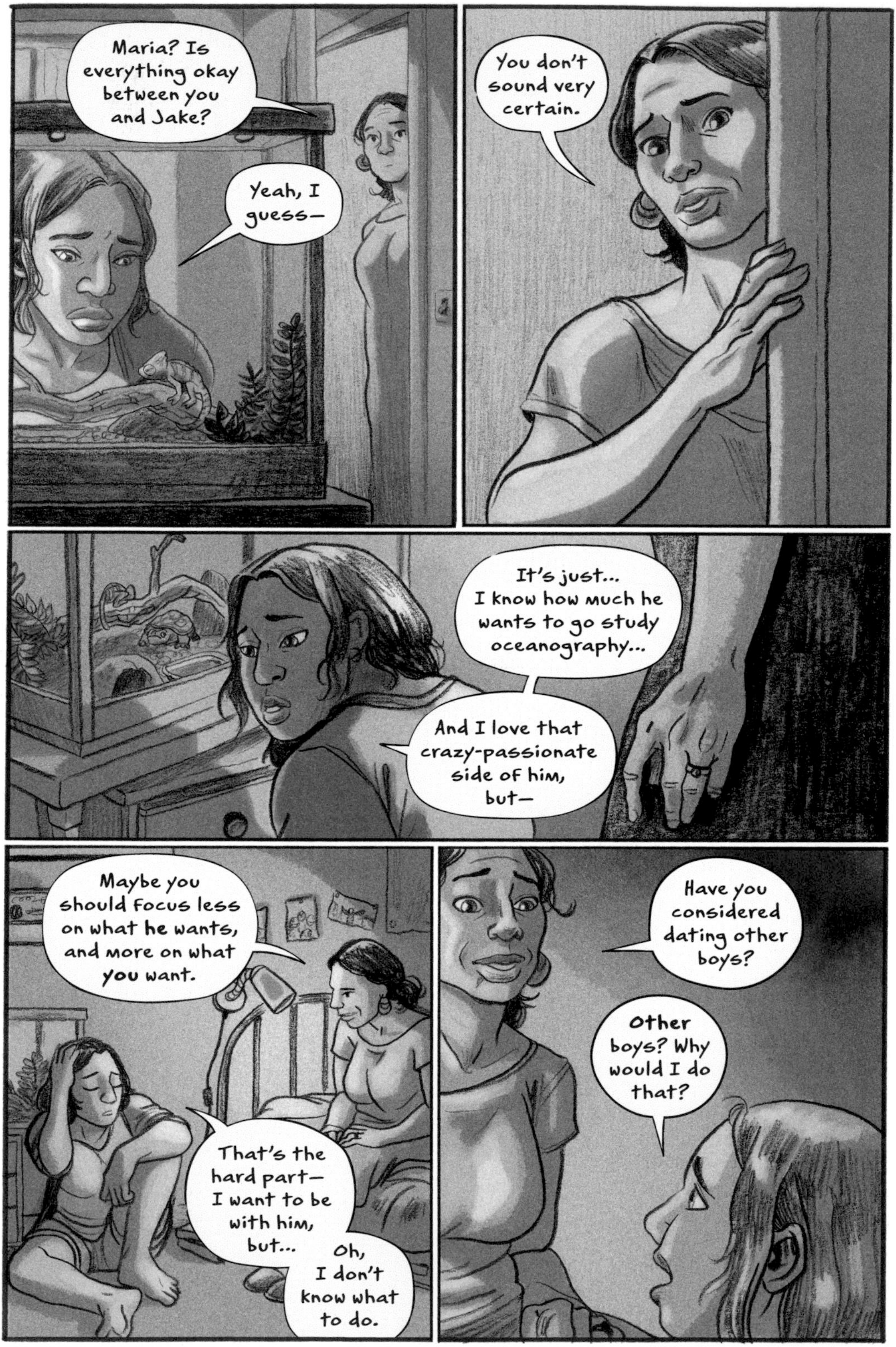
Maria? Is everything okay between you and Jake?
Yeah, I guess—
You don't sound very certain.
It's just... I know how much he wants to go study oceanography...
And I love that crazy-passionate side of him, but—
Maybe you should focus less on what **he** wants, and more on what **you** want.
That's the hard part— I want to be with him, but...
Oh, I don't know what to do.
Have you considered dating other boys?
Other boys? Why would I do that?

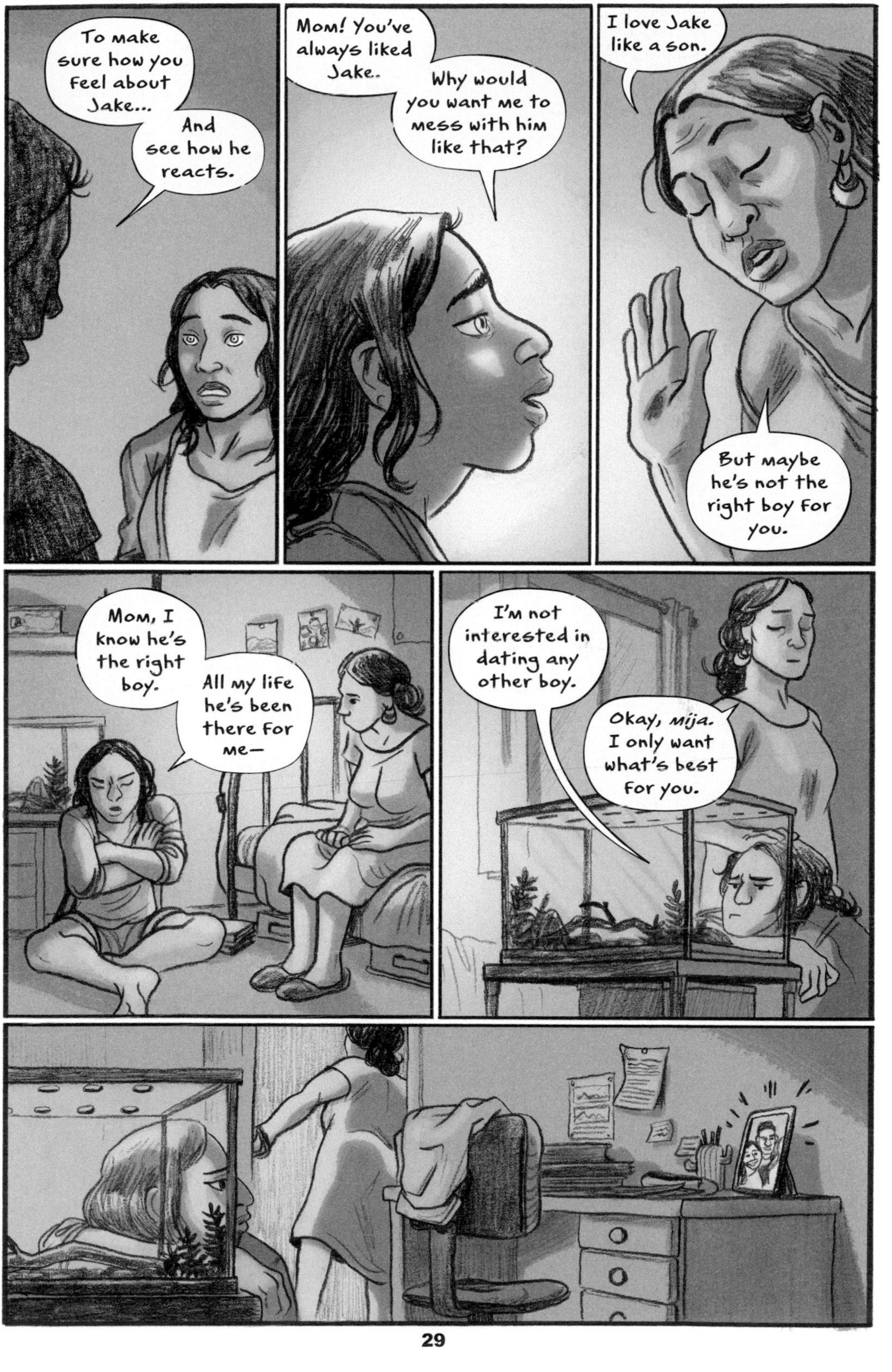
To make sure how you feel about Jake...
And see how he reacts.
Mom! You've always liked Jake.
Why would you want me to mess with him like that?
I love Jake like a son.
But maybe he's not the right boy for you.
Mom, I know he's the right boy.
All my life he's been there for me—
I'm not interested in dating any other boy.
Okay, *mija*. I only want what's best for you.

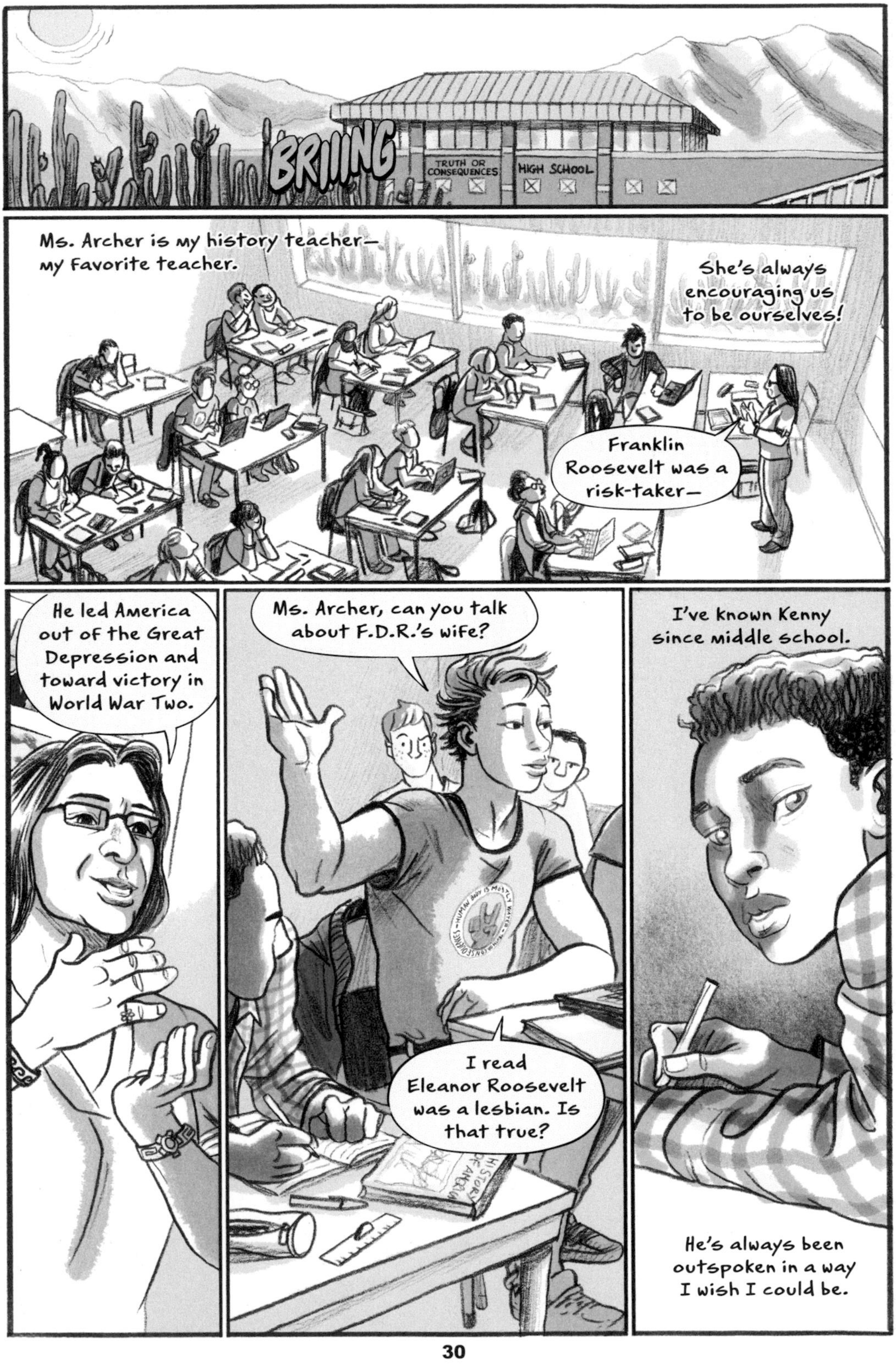
BRIIING
TRUTH OR CONSEQUENCES
HIGH SCHOOL
Ms. Archer is my history teacher— my favorite teacher.
She's always encouraging us to be ourselves!
Franklin Roosevelt was a risk-taker—
He led America out of the Great Depression and toward victory in World War Two.
Ms. Archer, can you talk about F.D.R.'s wife?
I read Eleanor Roosevelt was a lesbian. Is that true?
I've known Kenny since middle school.
He's always been outspoken in a way I wish I could be.

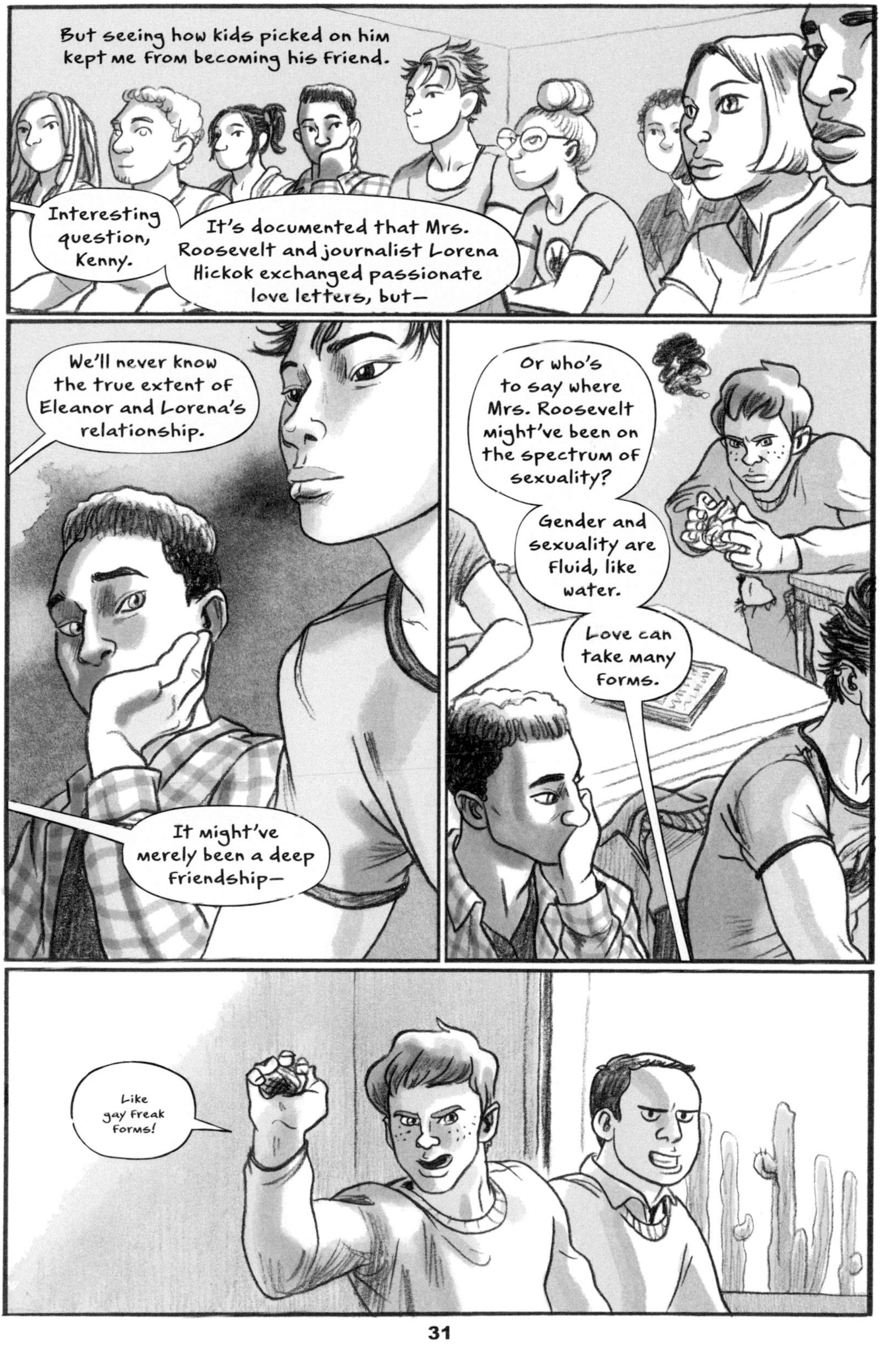
But seeing how kids picked on him kept me from becoming his friend.
Interesting question, Kenny.
It's documented that Mrs. Roosevelt and journalist Lorena Hickok exchanged passionate love letters, but—
We'll never know the true extent of Eleanor and Lorena's relationship.
It might've merely been a deep friendship—
Or who's to say where Mrs. Roosevelt might've been on the spectrum of sexuality?
Gender and sexuality are fluid, like water.
Love can take many forms.
Like gay freak forms!

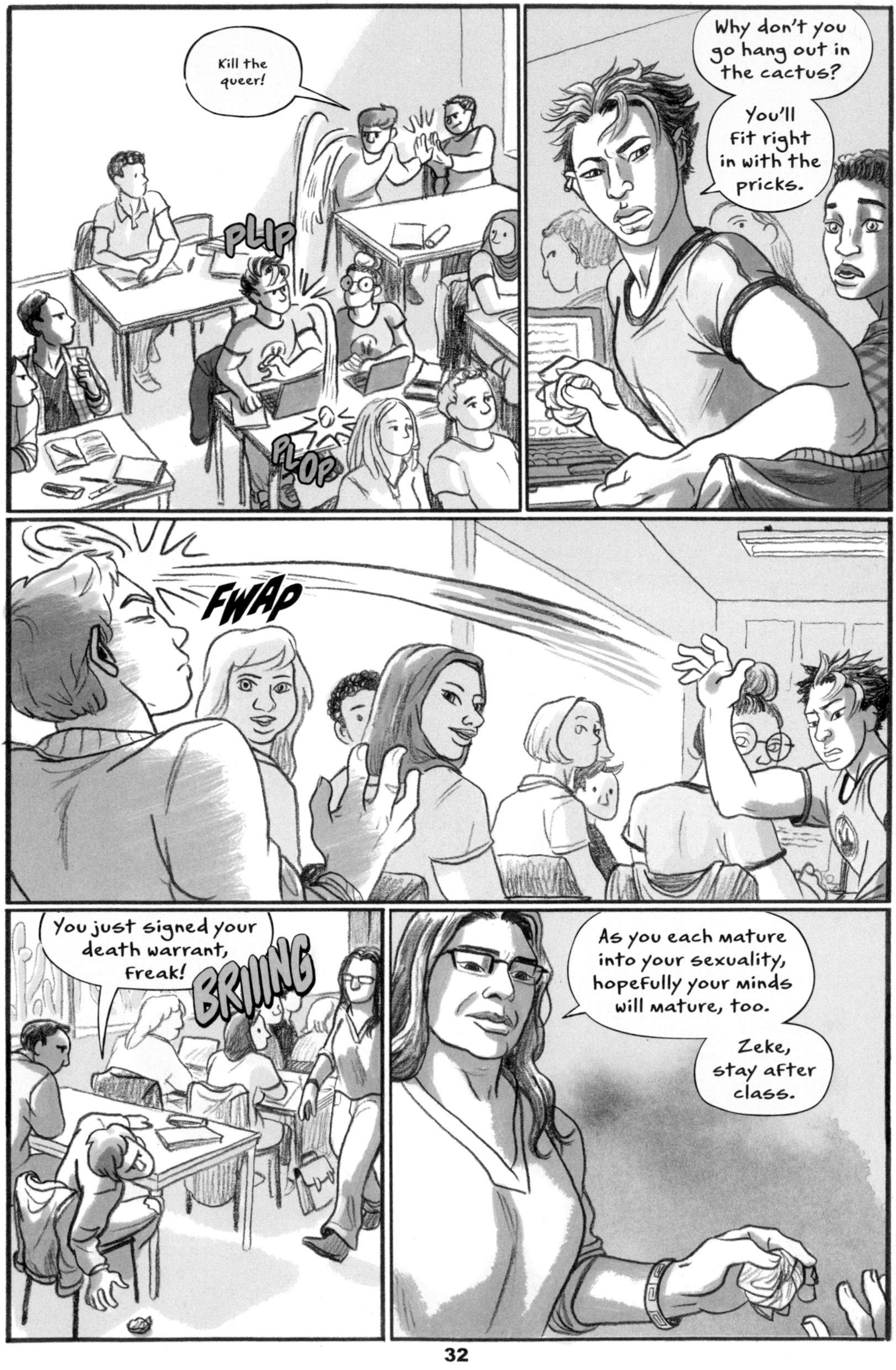
Kill the queer!
PLIP
PLOP
Why don't you go hang out in the cactus?
You'll fit right in with the pricks.
FWAP
You just signed your death warrant, Freak!
BRIIING
As you each mature into your sexuality, hopefully your minds will mature, too.
Zeke, stay after class.

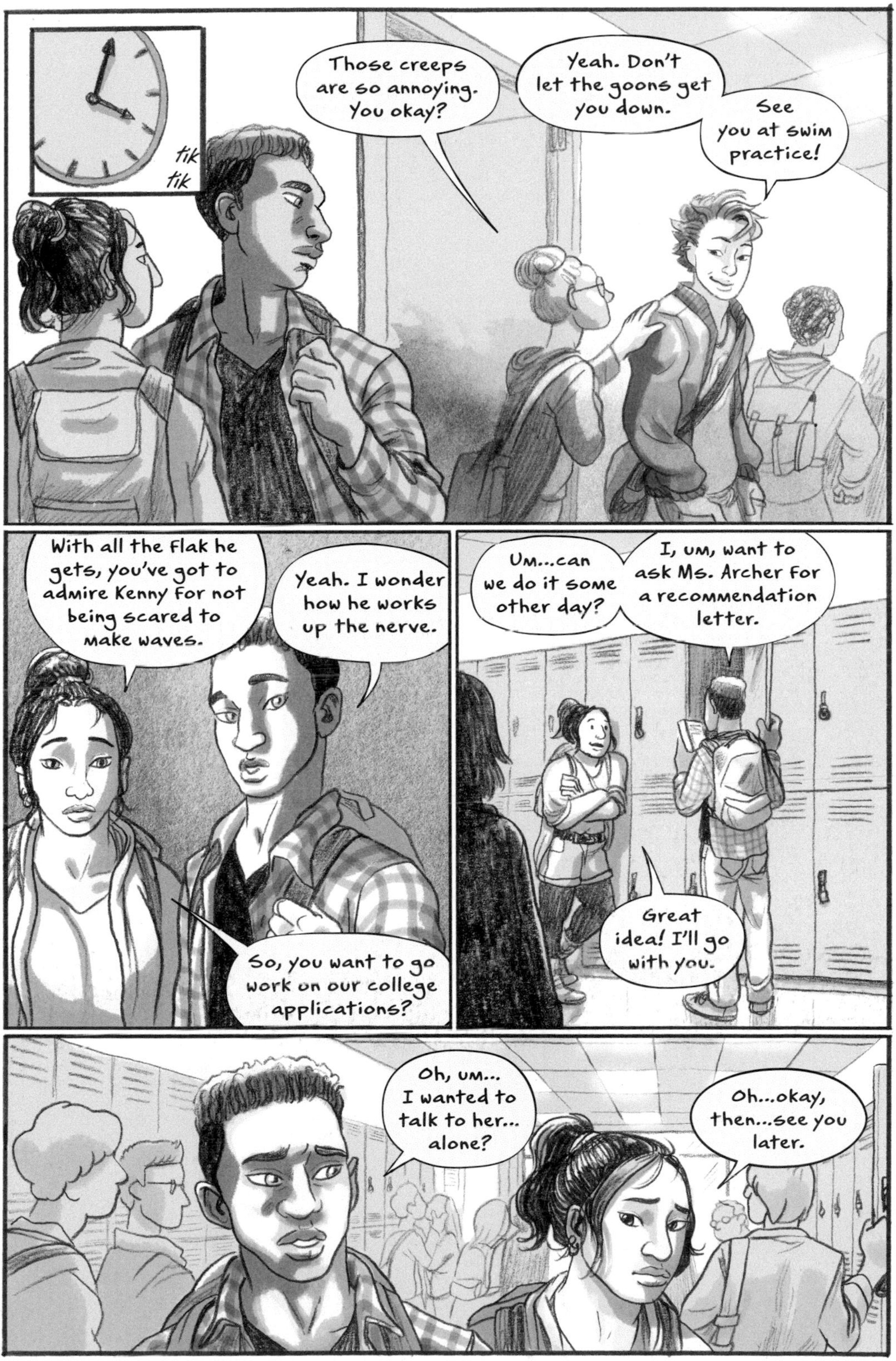
tik
tik
Those creeps are so annoying. You okay?
Yeah. Don't let the goons get you down.
See you at swim practice!
With all the flak he gets, you've got to admire Kenny for not being scared to make waves.
Yeah. I wonder how he works up the nerve.
So, you want to go work on our college applications?
Um...can we do it some other day?
I, um, want to ask Ms. Archer for a recommendation letter.
Great idea! I'll go with you.
Oh, um... I wanted to talk to her... alone?
Oh...okay, then...see you later.

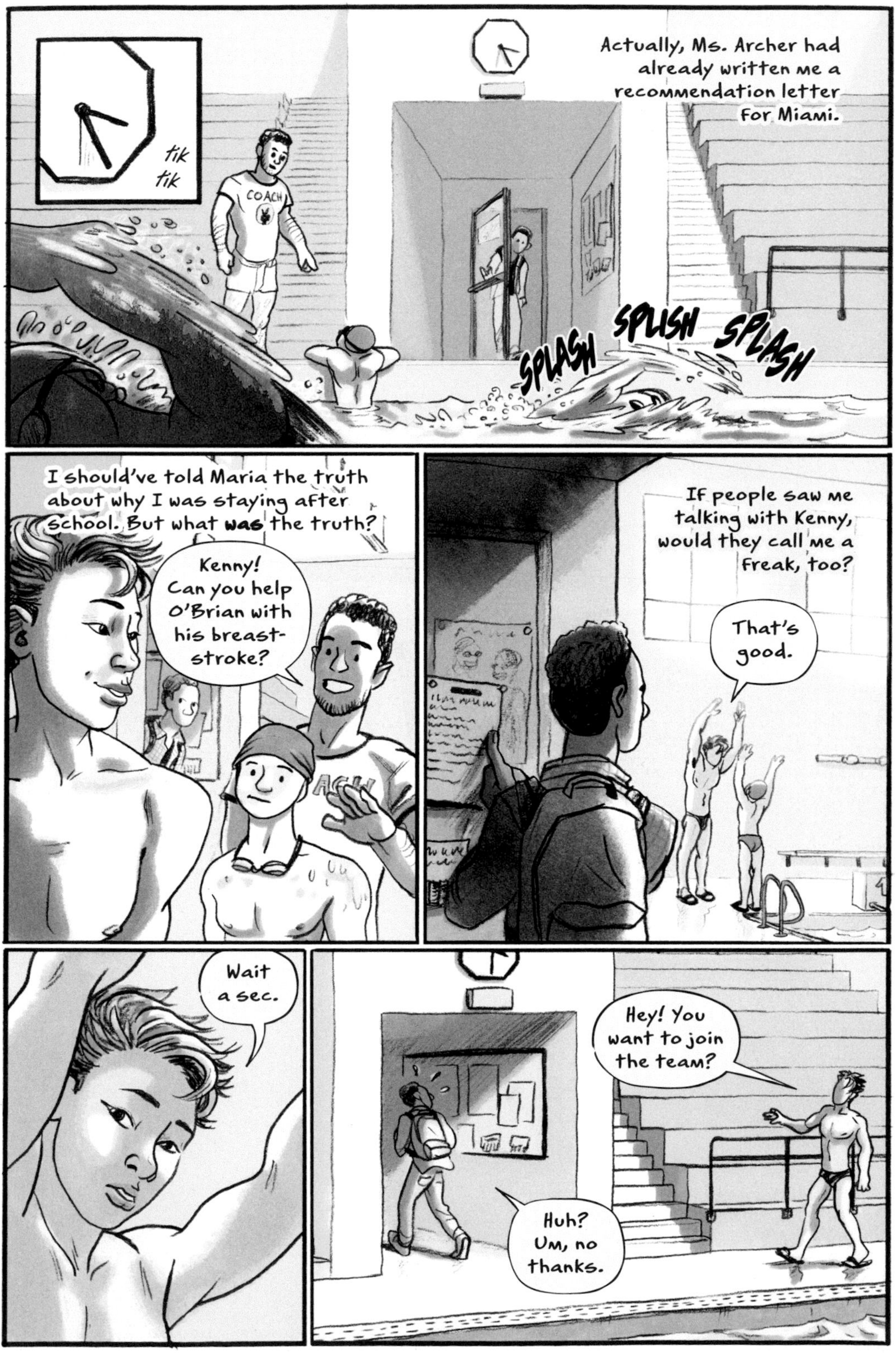

Actually, Ms. Archer had already written me a recommendation letter for Miami.
tik
tik
SPLASH
SPLISH
SPLASH
I should've told Maria the truth about why I was staying after school. But what **was** the truth?
Kenny! Can you help O'Brian with his breast-stroke?
If people saw me talking with Kenny, would they call me a freak, too?
That's good.
Wait a sec.
Hey! You want to join the team?
Huh? Um, no thanks.

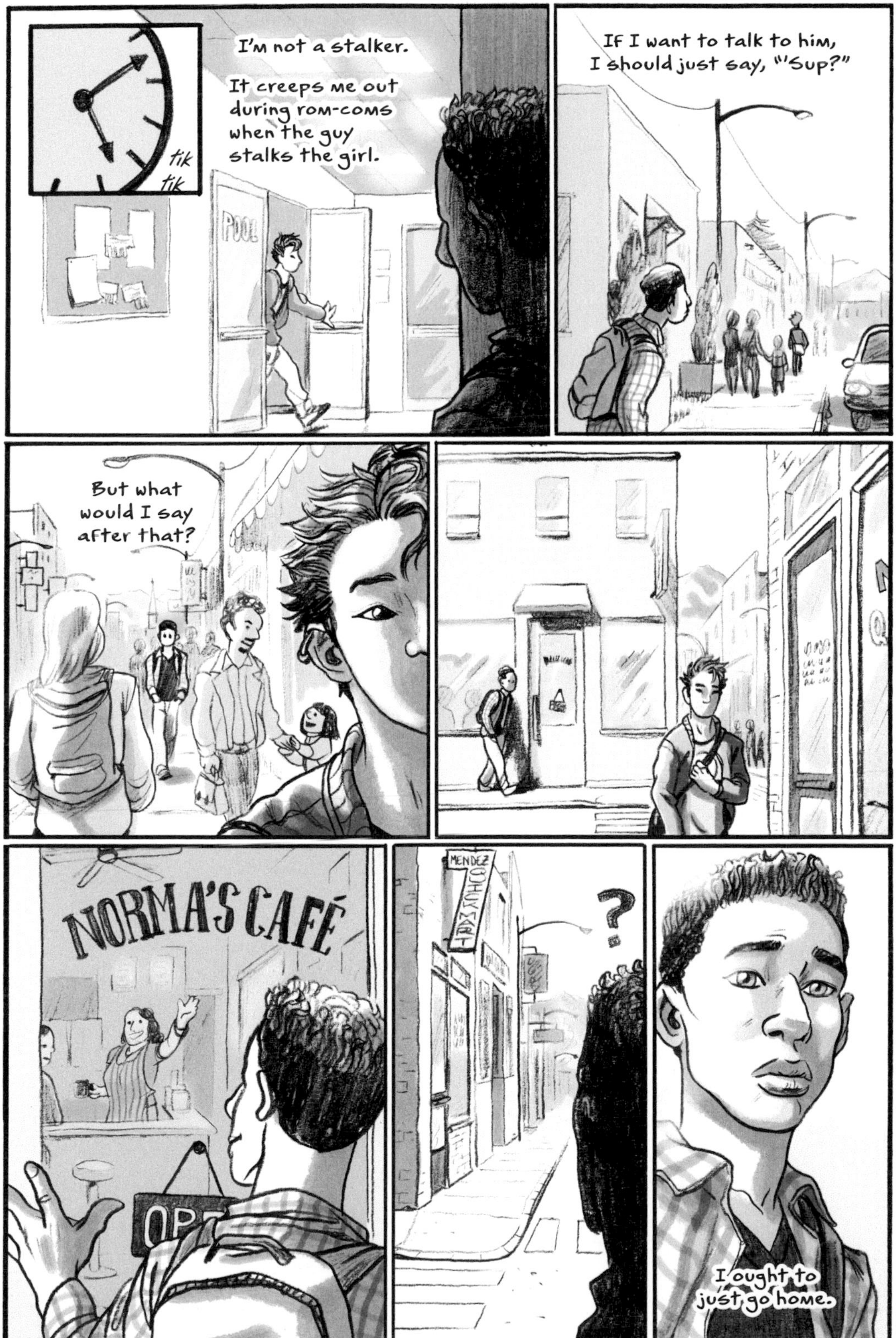
tik
tik
I'm not a stalker.
It creeps me out during rom-coms when the guy stalks the girl.
POOL
If I want to talk to him, I should just say, "'Sup?"
But what would I say after that?
NORMA'S CAFÉ
OP
MENDEZ
?
I ought to just go home.

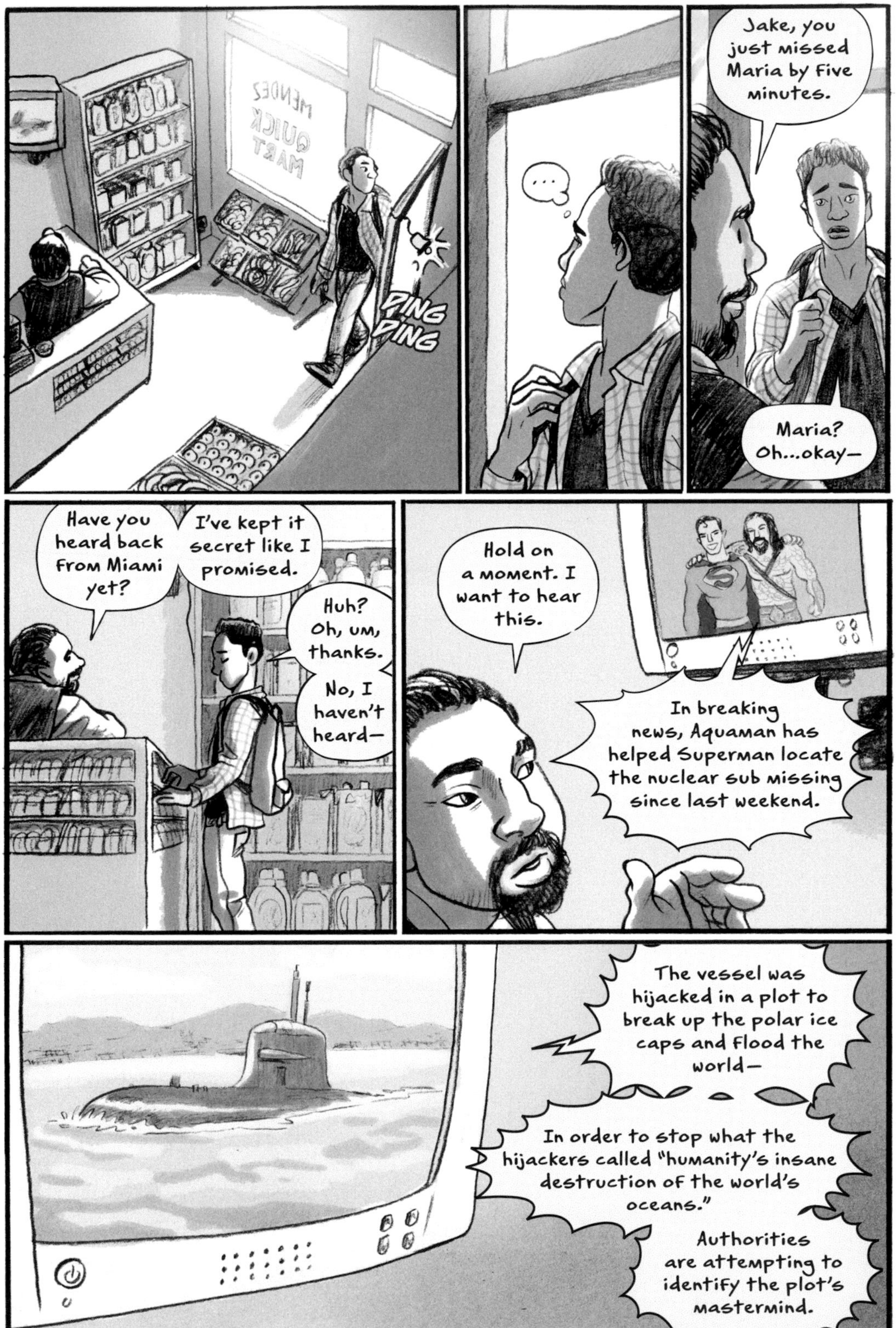
MENDEZ QUICK MART
DING DING
...
Jake, you just missed Maria by five minutes.
Maria? Oh...okay—
Have you heard back from Miami yet?
I've kept it secret like I promised.
Huh? Oh, um, thanks.
No, I haven't heard—
Hold on a moment. I want to hear this.
In breaking news, Aquaman has helped Superman locate the nuclear sub missing since last weekend.
The vessel was hijacked in a plot to break up the polar ice caps and flood the world—
In order to stop what the hijackers called "humanity's insane destruction of the world's oceans."
Authorities are attempting to identify the plot's mastermind.

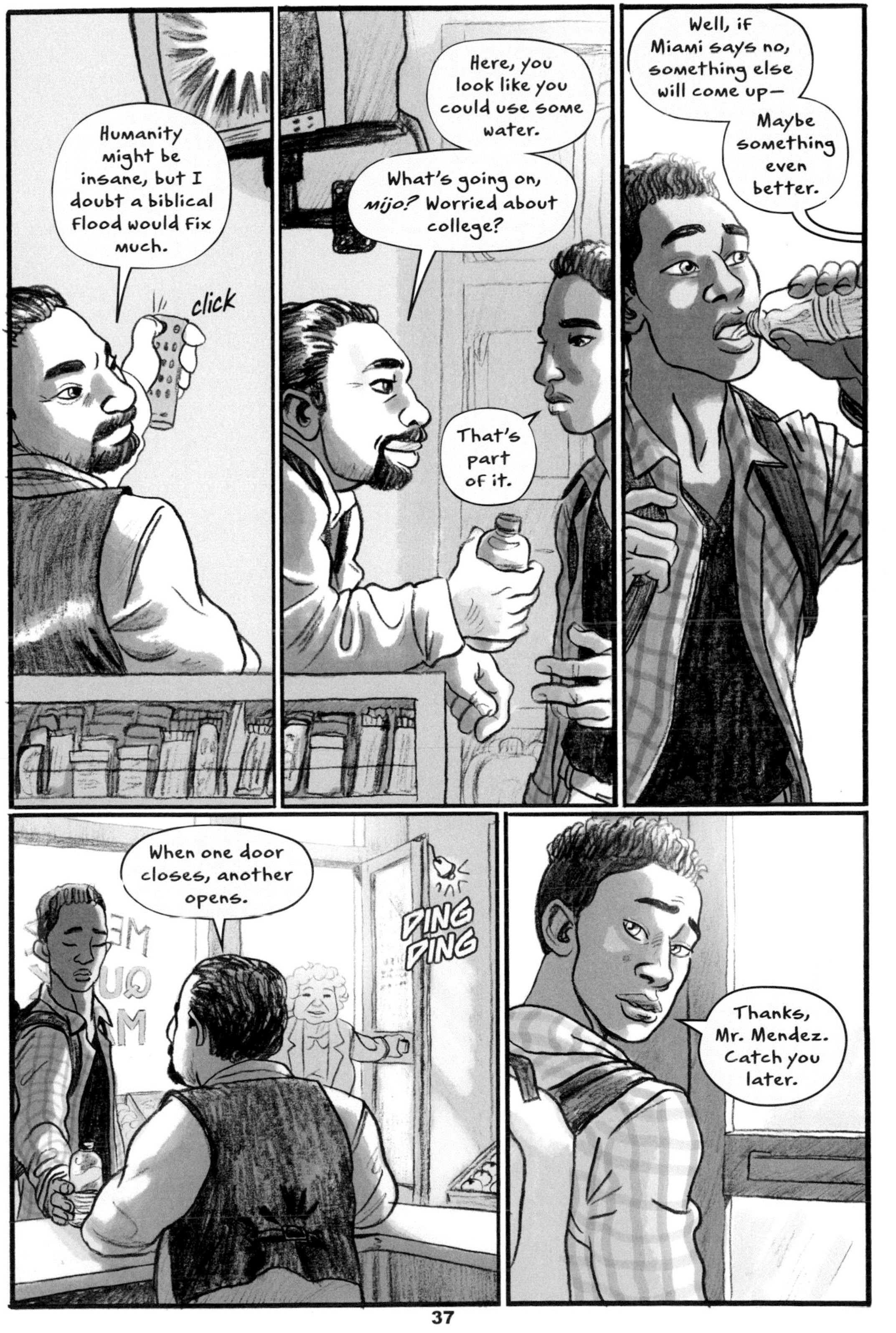
Humanity might be insane, but I doubt a biblical flood would fix much.
click
Here, you look like you could use some water.
What's going on, *mijo?* Worried about college?
That's part of it.
Well, if Miami says no, something else will come up—
Maybe something even better.
When one door closes, another opens.
DING DING
Thanks, Mr. Mendez. Catch you later.

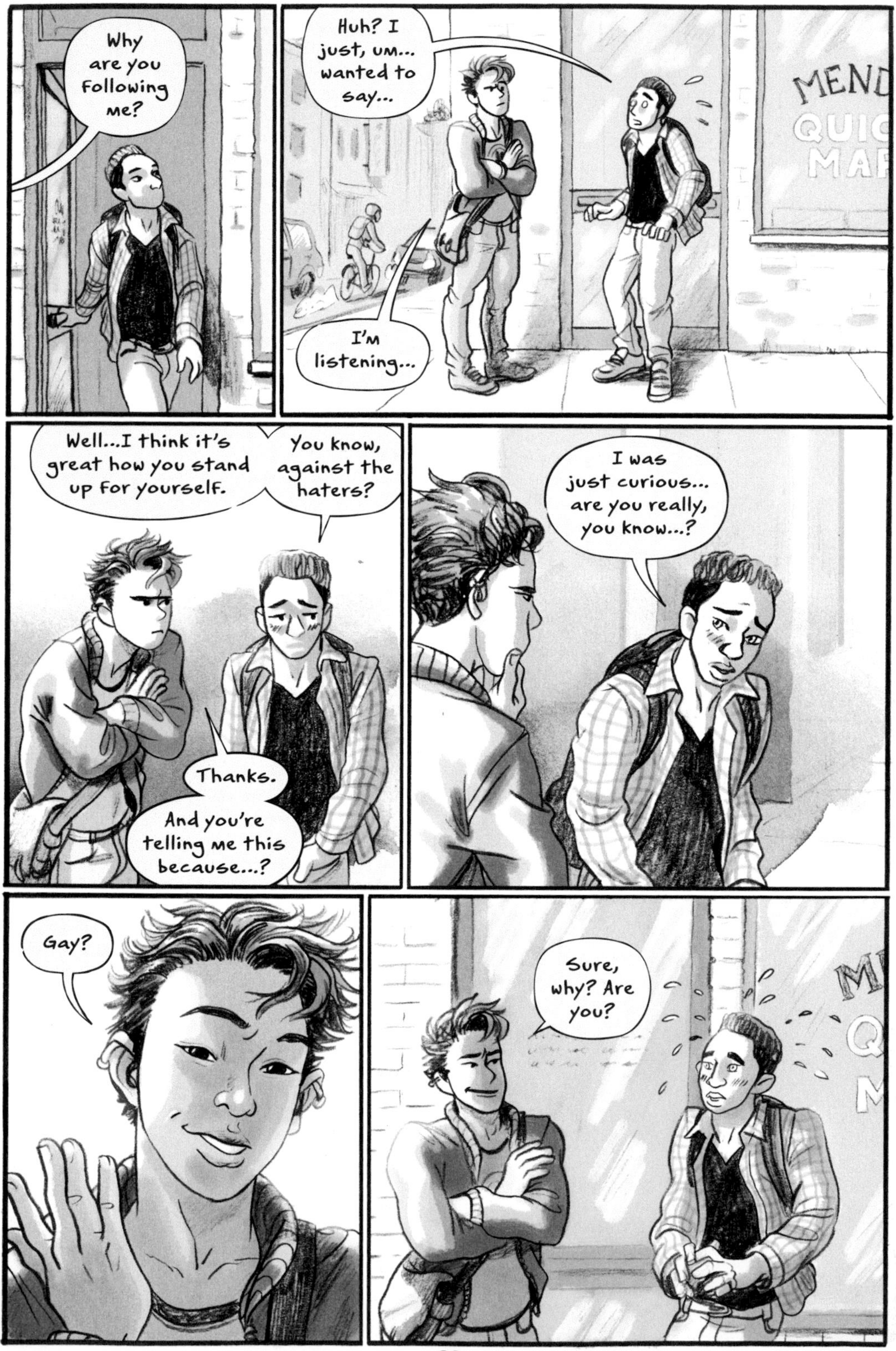
Why are you following me?
Huh? I just, um... wanted to say...
I'm listening...
MEND
QUIC
MAR
Well...I think it's great how you stand up for yourself.
You know, against the haters?
Thanks.
And you're telling me this because...?
I was just curious... are you really, you know...?
Gay?
Sure, why? Are you?

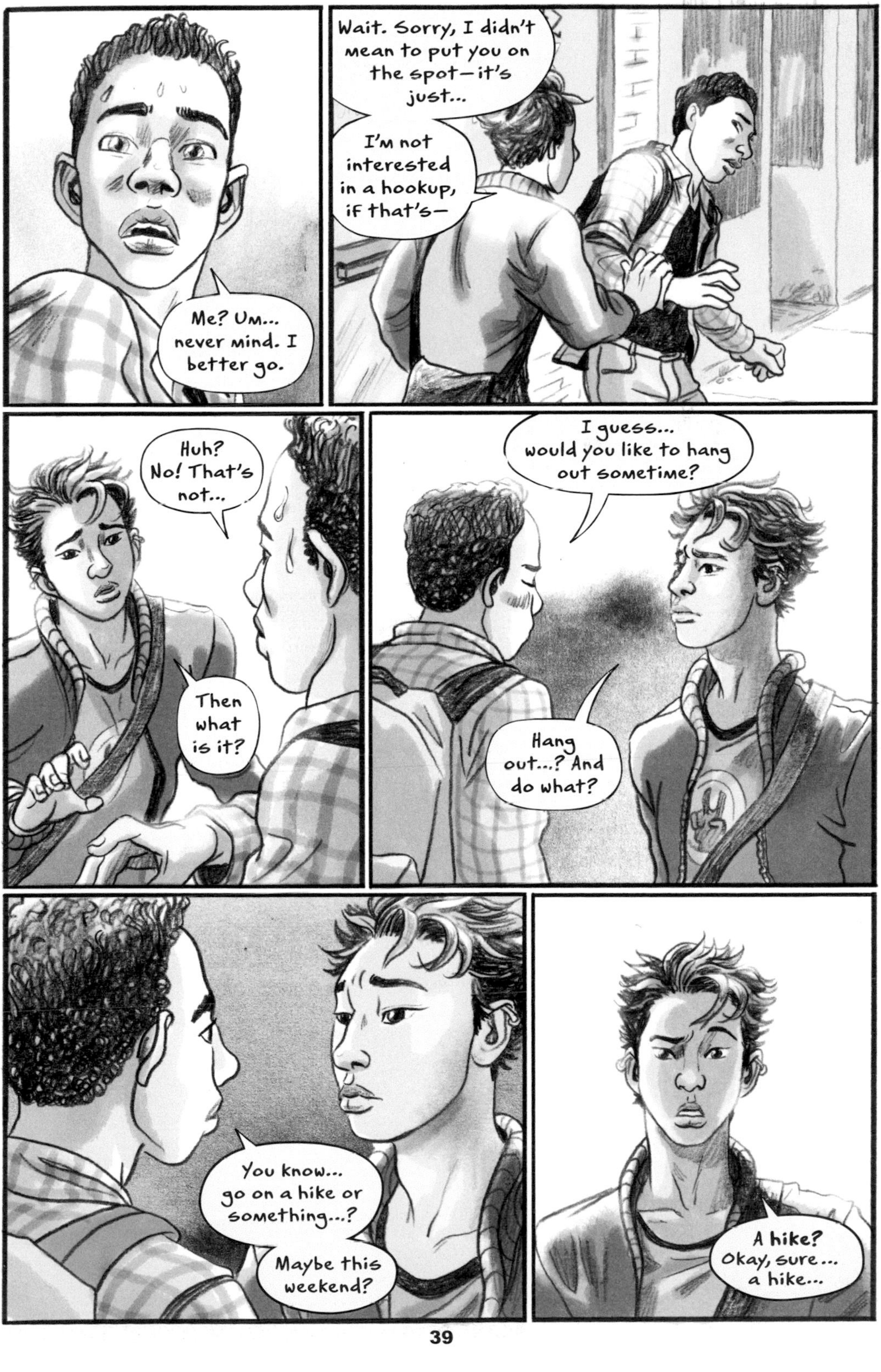
Me? Um... never mind. I better go.
Wait. Sorry, I didn't mean to put you on the spot—it's just...
I'm not interested in a hookup, if that's—
Huh? No! That's not...
Then what is it?
I guess... would you like to hang out sometime?
Hang out...? And do what?
You know... go on a hike or something...?
Maybe this weekend?
A hike? Okay, sure... a hike...

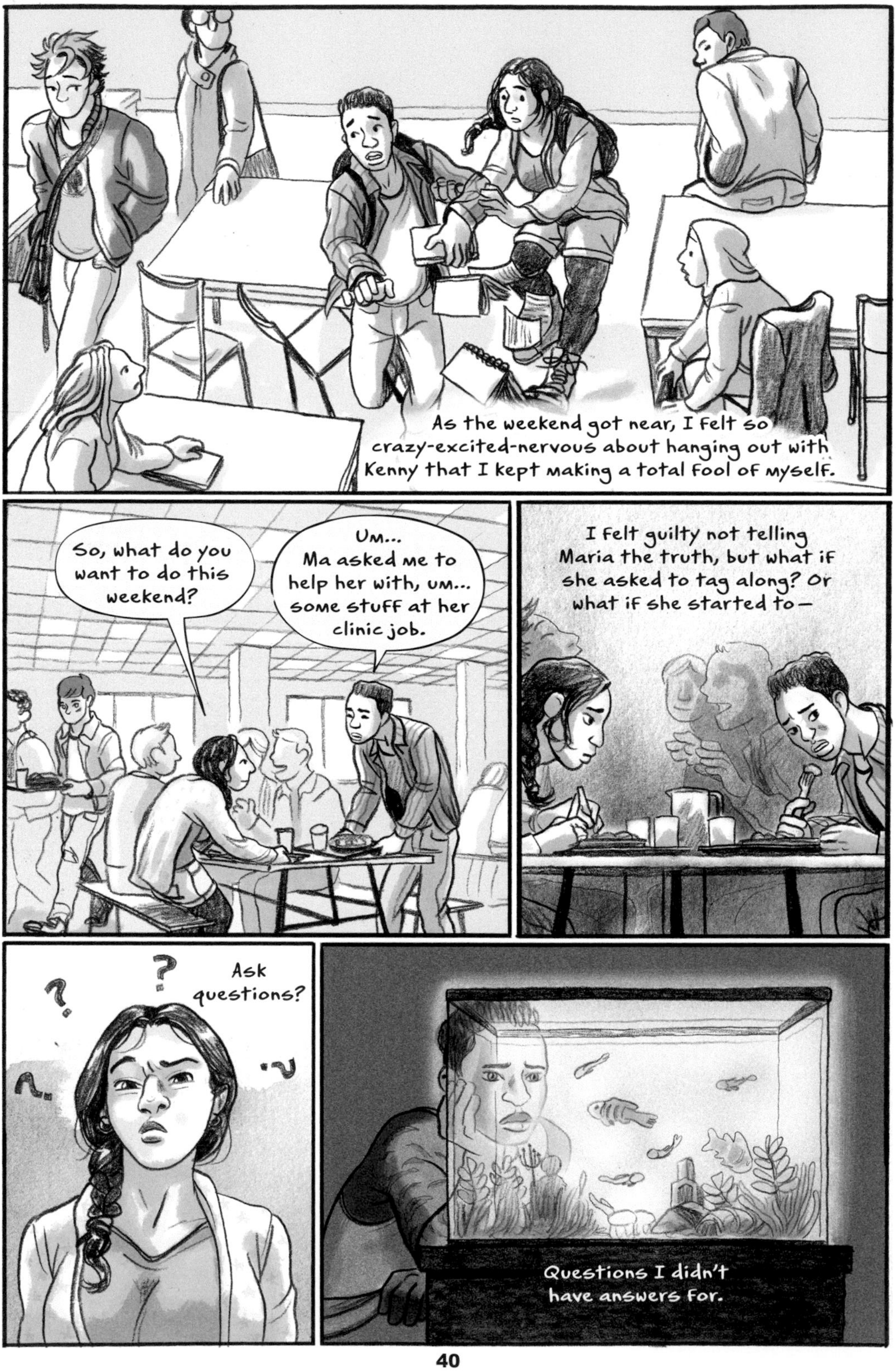

As the weekend got near, I felt so crazy-excited-nervous about hanging out with Kenny that I kept making a total fool of myself.
So, what do you want to do this weekend?
Um... Ma asked me to help her with, um... some stuff at her clinic job.
I felt guilty not telling Maria the truth, but what if she asked to tag along? Or what if she started to—
Ask questions?
Questions I didn't have answers for.

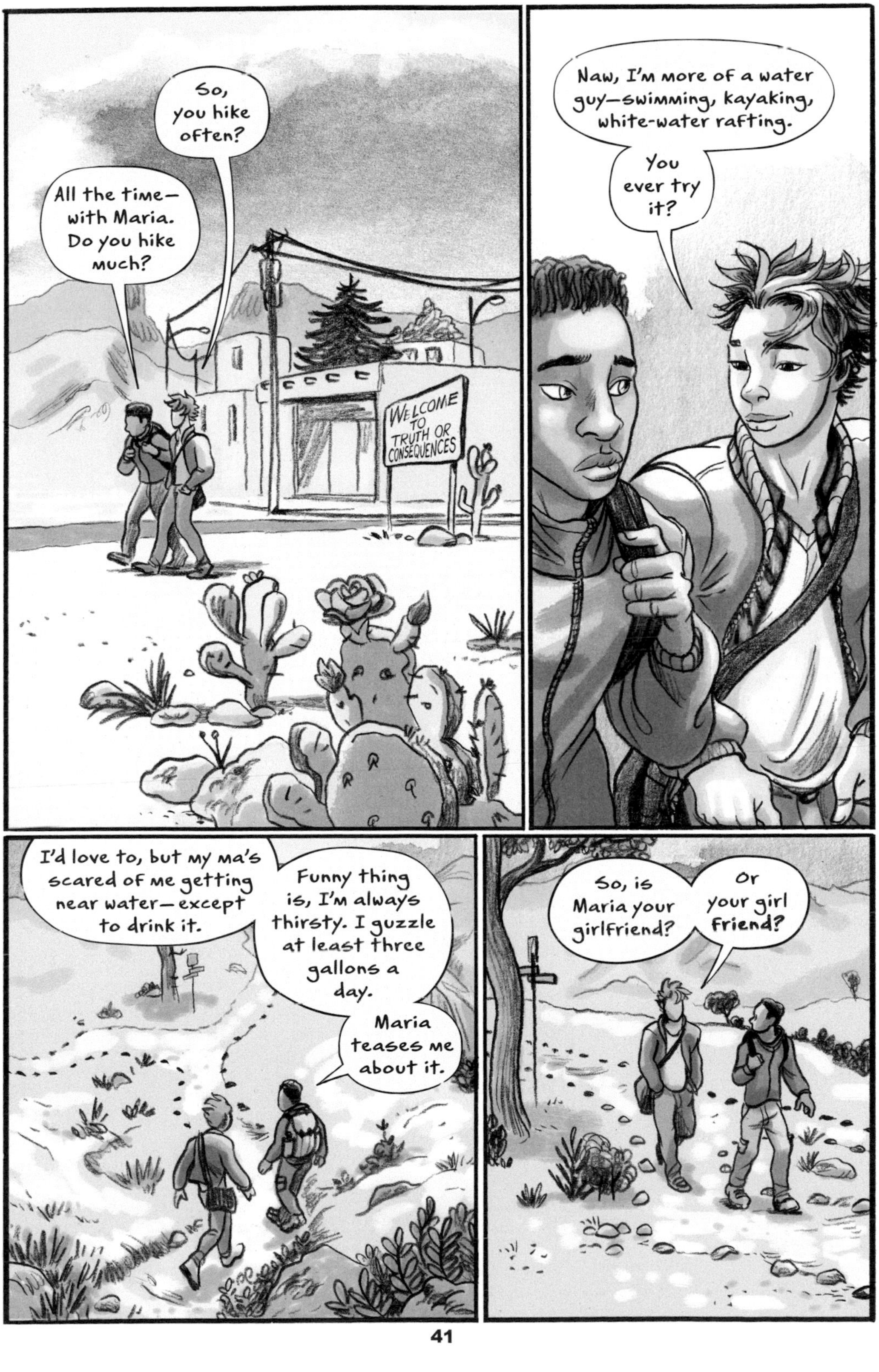

So, you hike often?
All the time— with Maria. Do you hike much?
WELCOME TO TRUTH OR CONSEQUENCES
Naw, I'm more of a water guy—swimming, kayaking, white-water rafting.
You ever try it?
I'd love to, but my ma's scared of me getting near water— except to drink it.
Funny thing is, I'm always thirsty. I guzzle at least three gallons a day.
Maria teases me about it.
So, is Maria your girlfriend?
Or your girl friend?

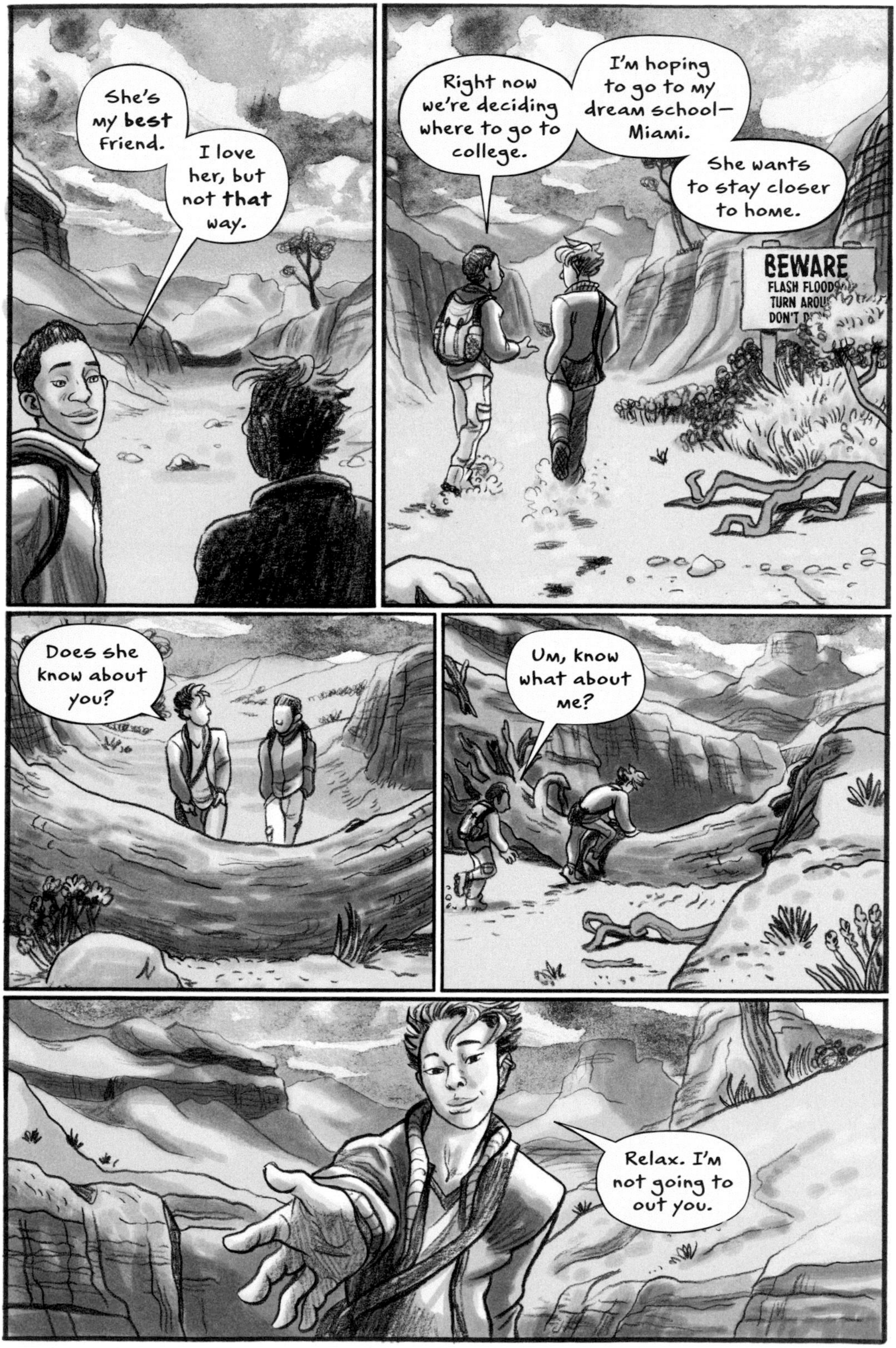
She's my **best** friend.
I love her, but not **that** way.
Right now we're deciding where to go to college.
I'm hoping to go to my dream school—Miami.
She wants to stay closer to home.
BEWARE
FLASH FLOODS
TURN AROU
DON'T D
Does she know about you?
Um, know what about me?
Relax. I'm not going to out you.

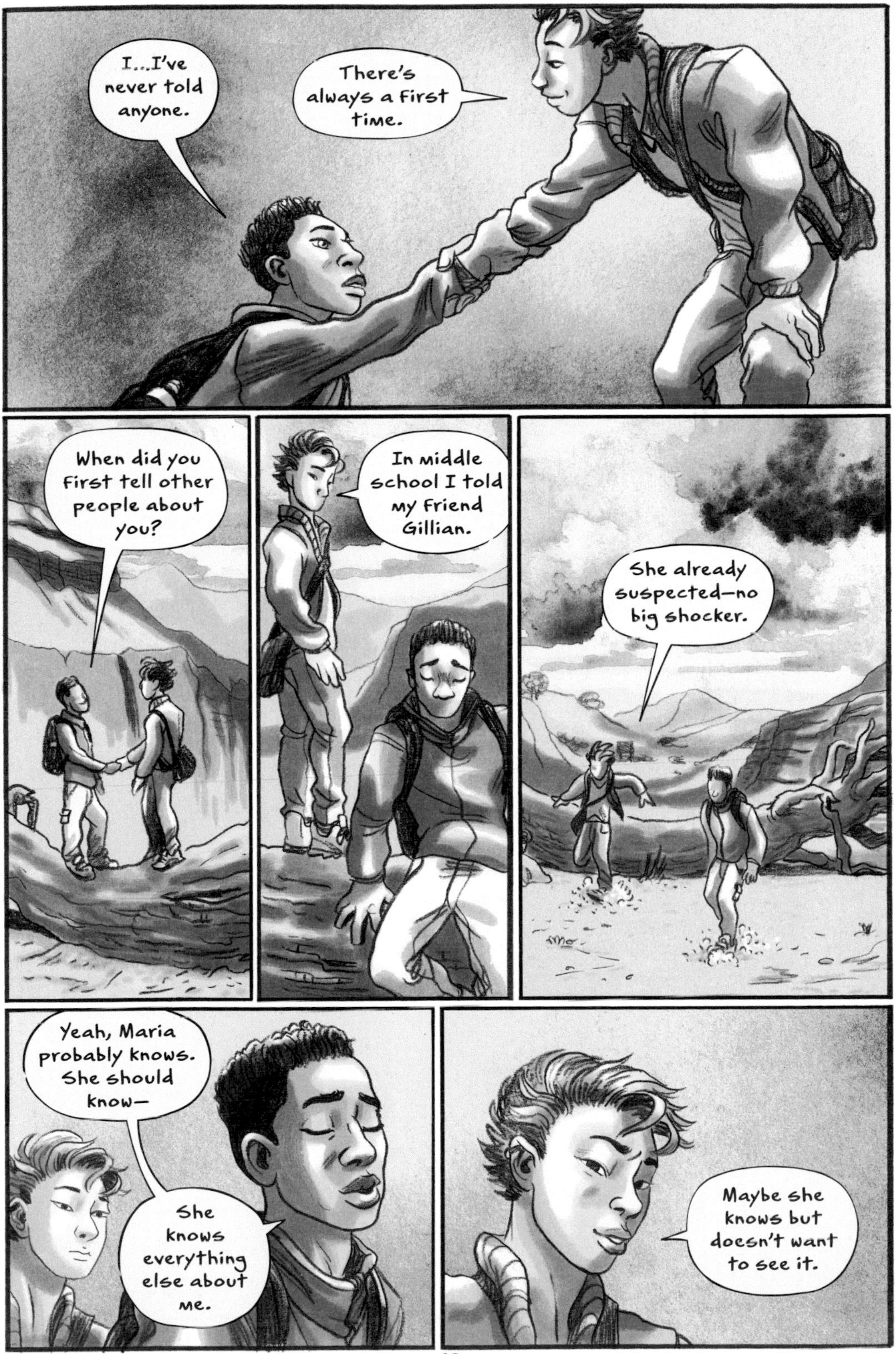
I...I've never told anyone.
There's always a first time.
When did you first tell other people about you?
In middle school I told my friend Gillian.
She already suspected—no big shocker.
Yeah, Maria probably knows. She should know—
She knows everything else about me.
Maybe she knows but doesn't want to see it.

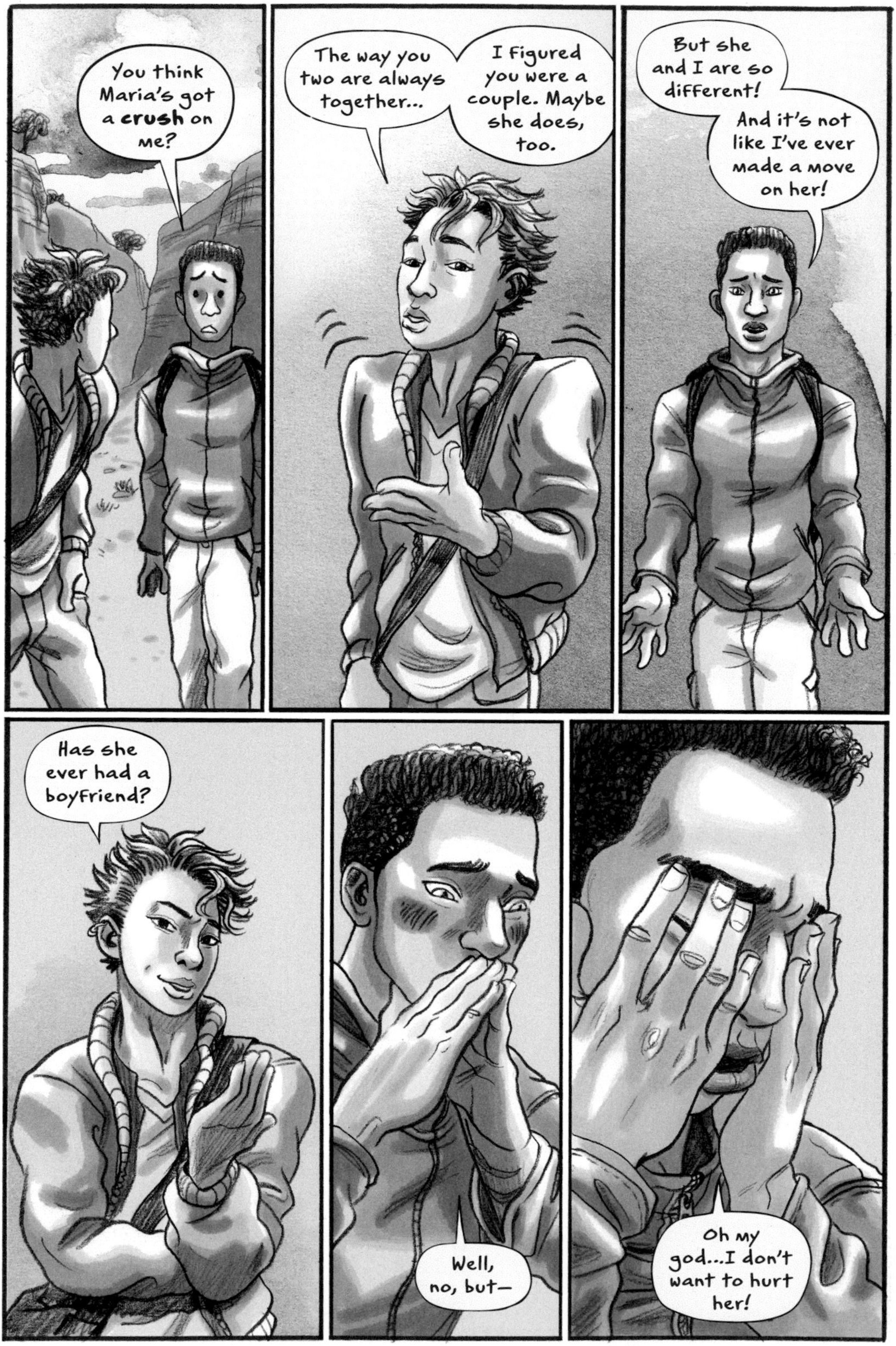
You think Maria's got a **crush** on me?
The way you two are always together...
I Figured you were a couple. Maybe she does, too.
But she and I are so different!
And it's not like I've ever made a move on her!
Has she ever had a boyfriend?
Well, no, but—
Oh my god...I don't want to hurt her!

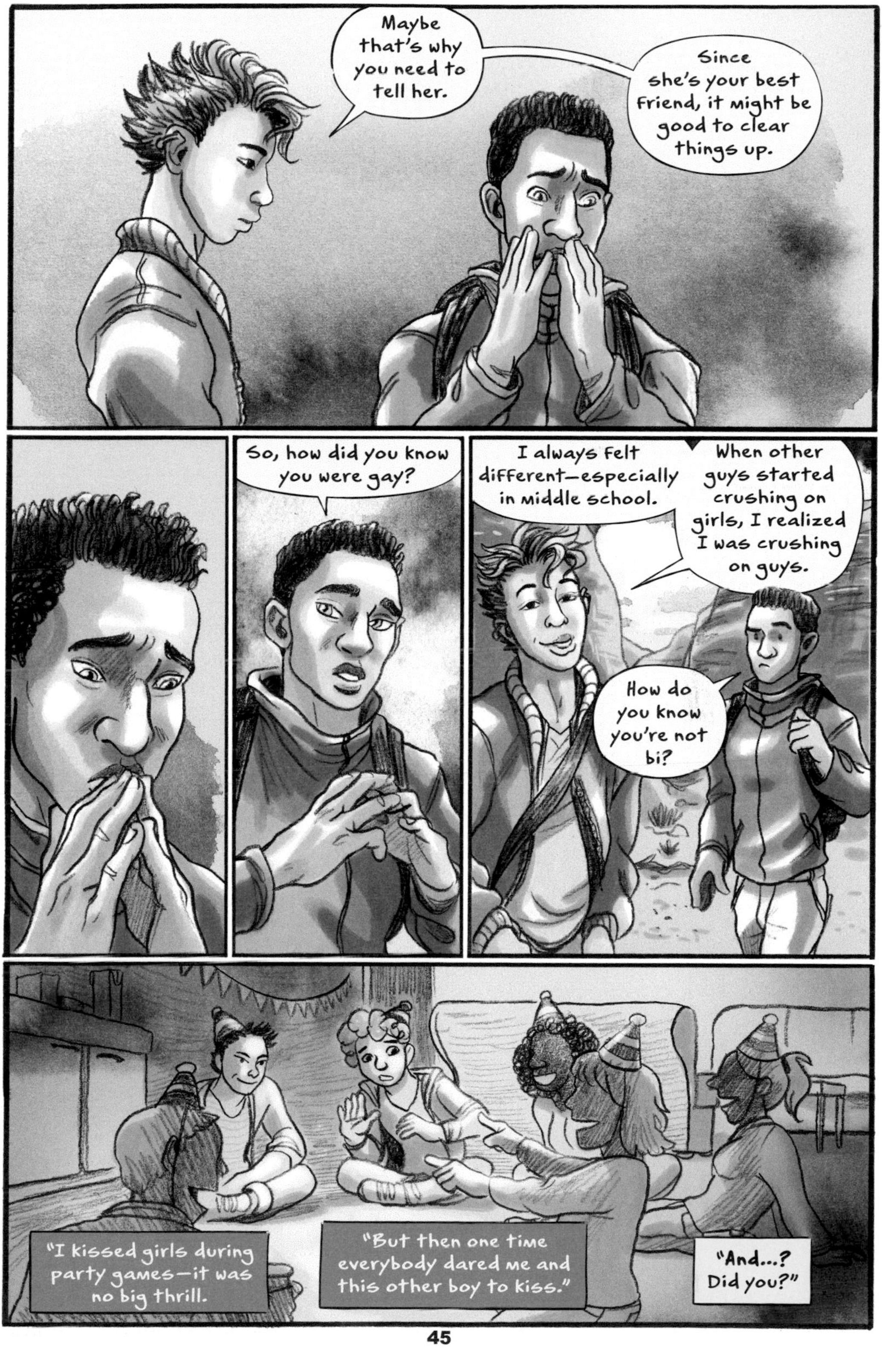
Maybe that's why you need to tell her.
Since she's your best friend, it might be good to clear things up.
So, how did you know you were gay?
I always felt different—especially in middle school.
When other guys started crushing on girls, I realized I was crushing on guys.
How do you know you're not bi?
"I kissed girls during party games—it was no big thrill.
"But then one time everybody dared me and this other boy to kiss."
"And...? Did you?"

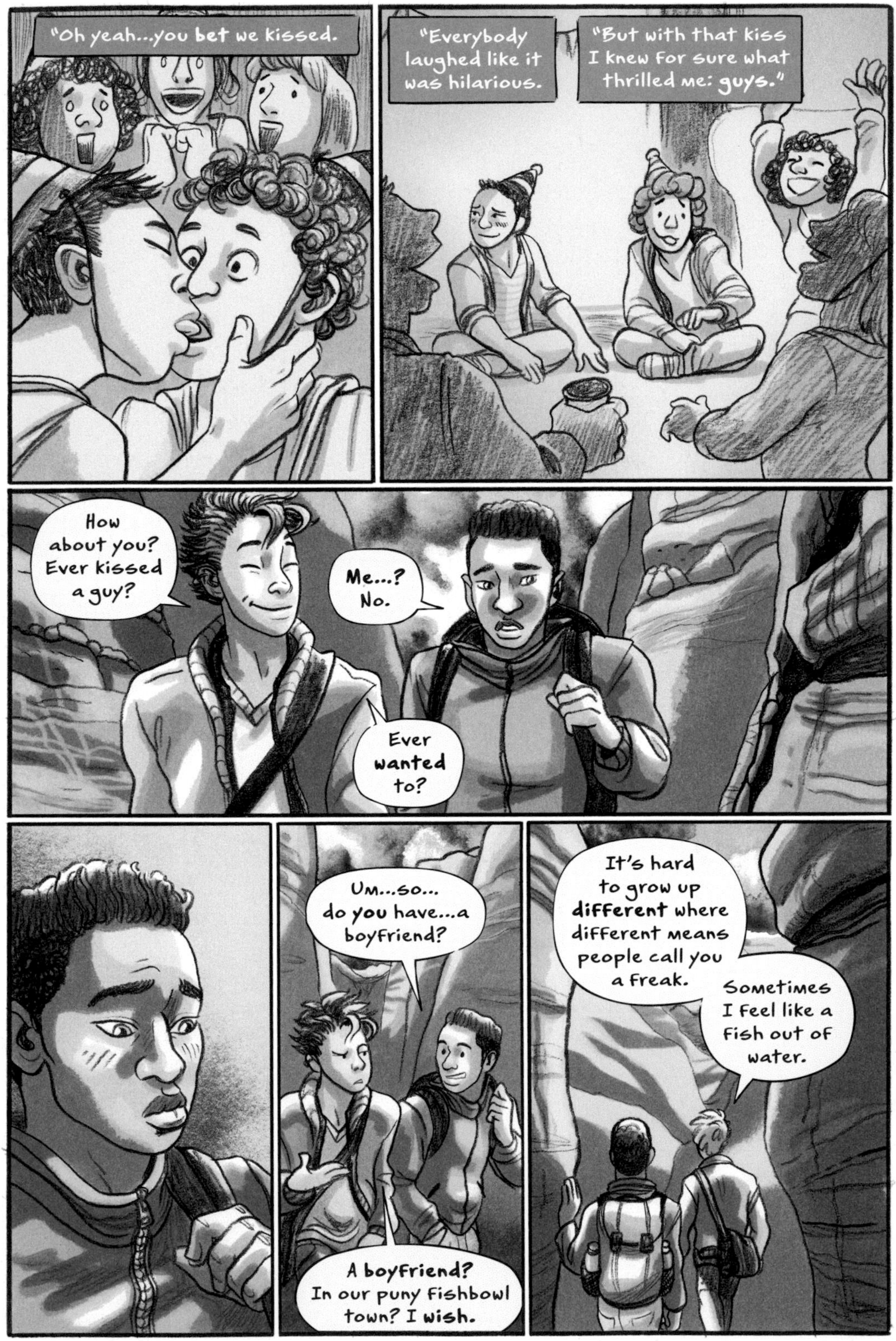
"Oh yeah...you bet we kissed.
"Everybody laughed like it was hilarious.
"But with that kiss I knew for sure what thrilled me: guys."
How about you? Ever kissed a guy?
Me...? No.
Ever wanted to?
Um...so... do you have...a boyfriend?
A boyfriend? In our puny fishbowl town? I wish.
It's hard to grow up different where different means people call you a freak.
Sometimes I feel like a fish out of water.

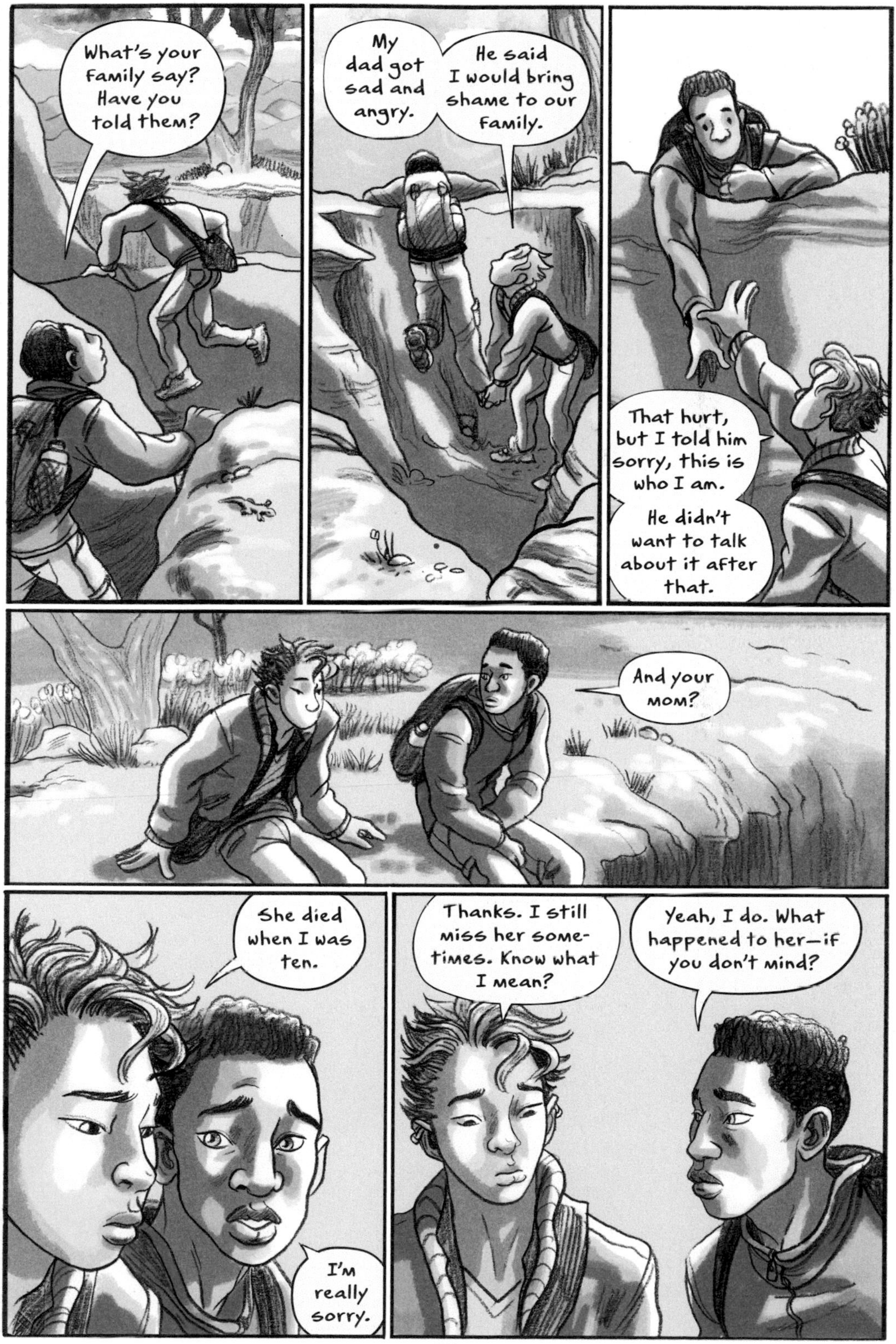
What's your family say? Have you told them?
My dad got sad and angry.
He said I would bring shame to our family.
That hurt, but I told him sorry, this is who I am.
He didn't want to talk about it after that.
And your mom?
She died when I was ten.
I'm really sorry.
Thanks. I still miss her some-times. Know what I mean?
Yeah, I do. What happened to her—if you don't mind?

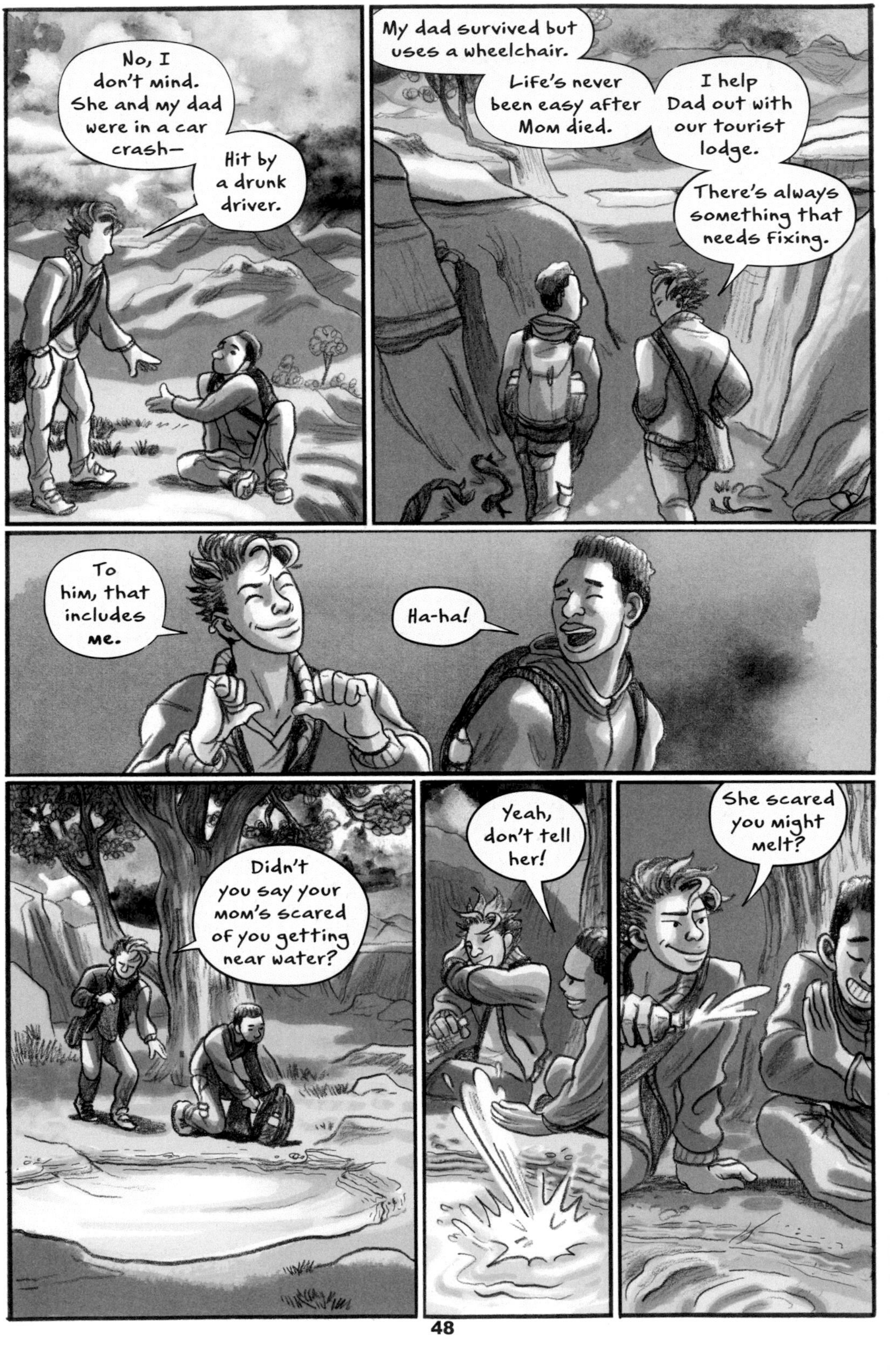
No, I don't mind. She and my dad were in a car crash—
Hit by a drunk driver.
My dad survived but uses a wheelchair.
Life's never been easy after Mom died.
I help Dad out with our tourist lodge.
There's always something that needs fixing.
To him, that includes **me.**
Ha-ha!
Didn't you say your mom's scared of you getting near water?
Yeah, don't tell her!
She scared you might melt?

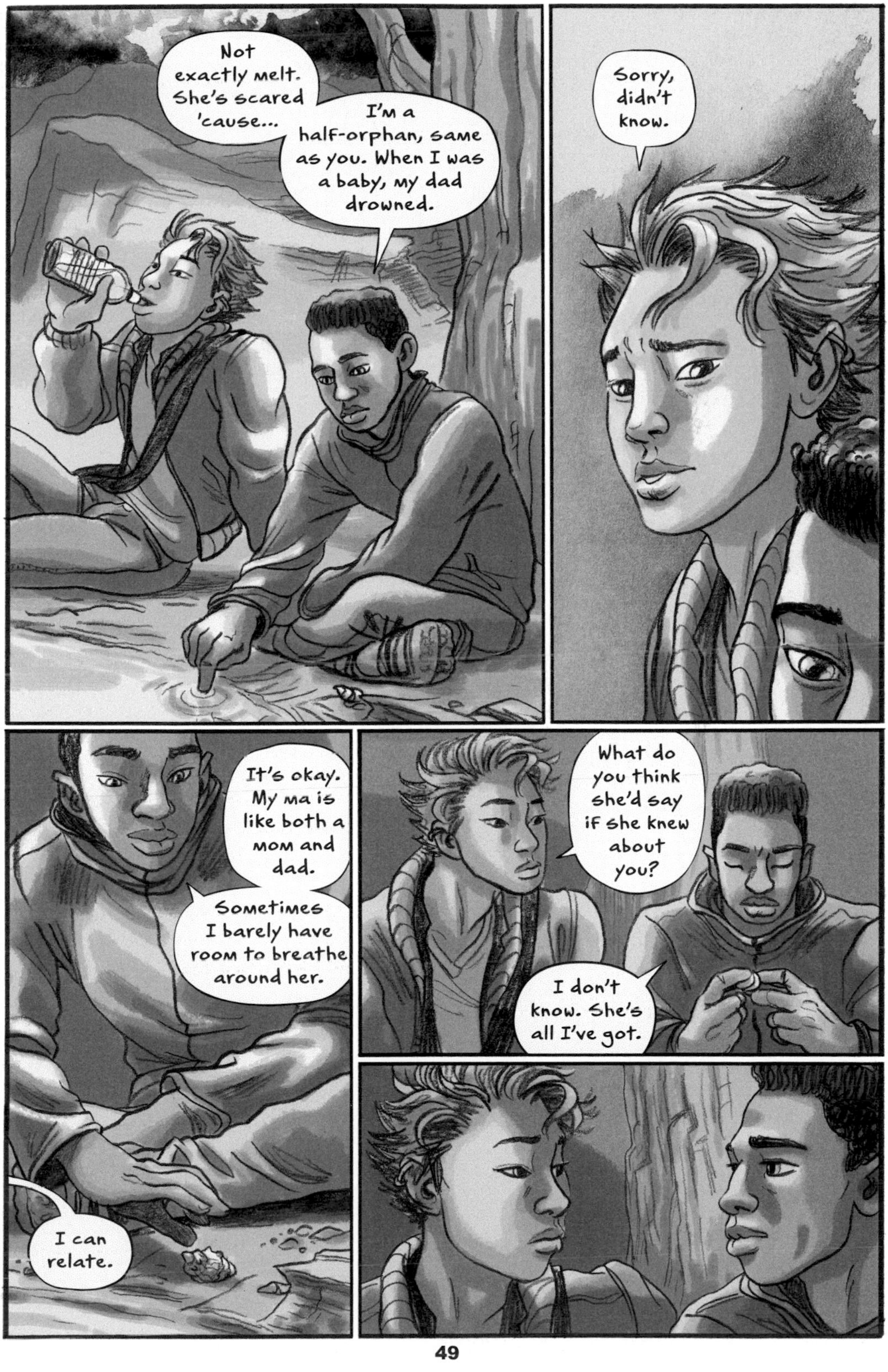
Not exactly melt. She's scared 'cause...
I'm a half-orphan, same as you. When I was a baby, my dad drowned.
Sorry, didn't know.
It's okay. My ma is like both a mom and dad.
Sometimes I barely have room to breathe around her.
I can relate.
What do you think she'd say if she knew about you?
I don't know. She's all I've got.

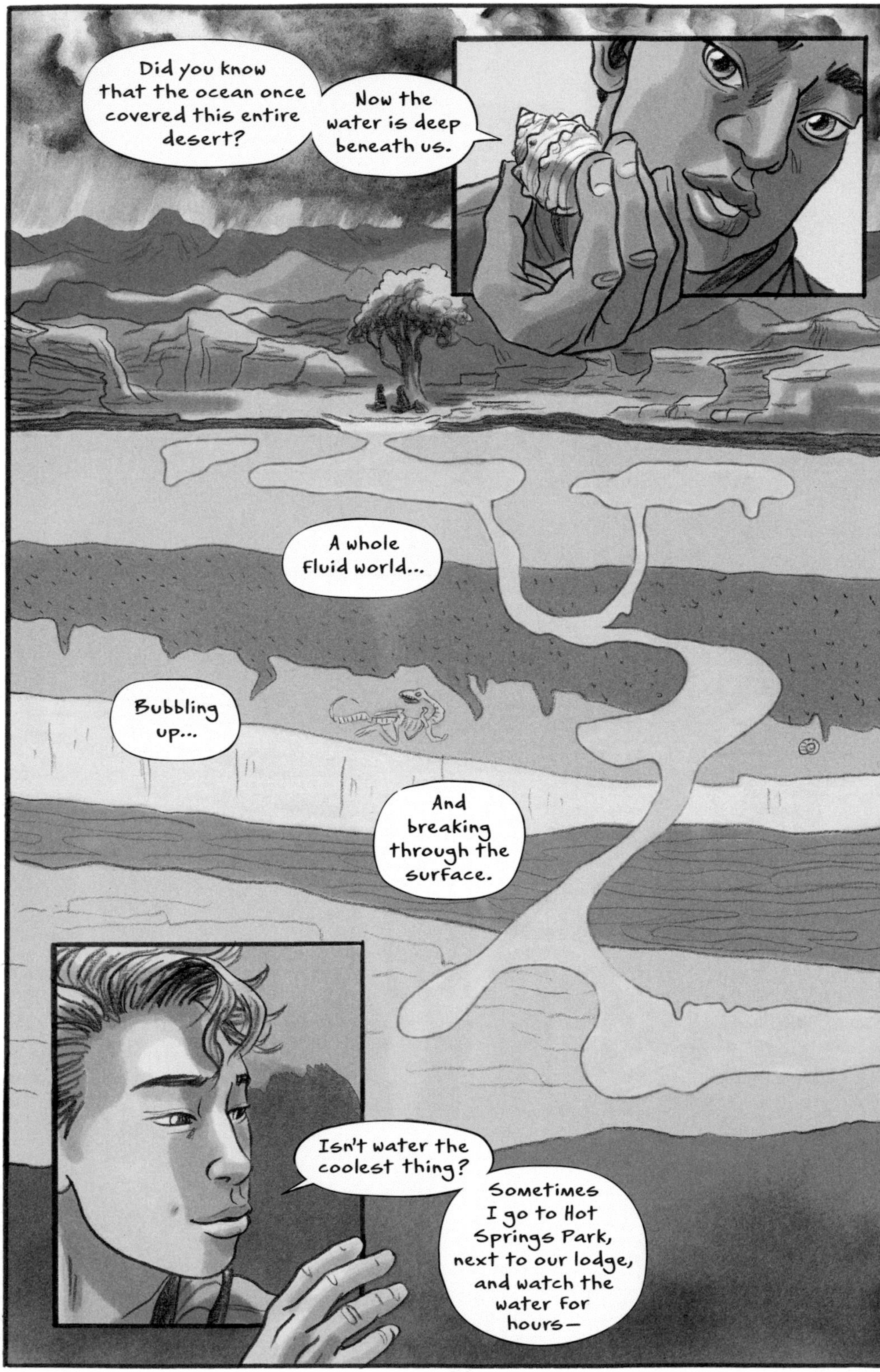
Did you know that the ocean once covered this entire desert?
Now the water is deep beneath us.
A whole fluid world...
Bubbling up...
And breaking through the surface.
Isn't water the coolest thing?
Sometimes I go to Hot Springs Park, next to our lodge, and watch the water for hours—

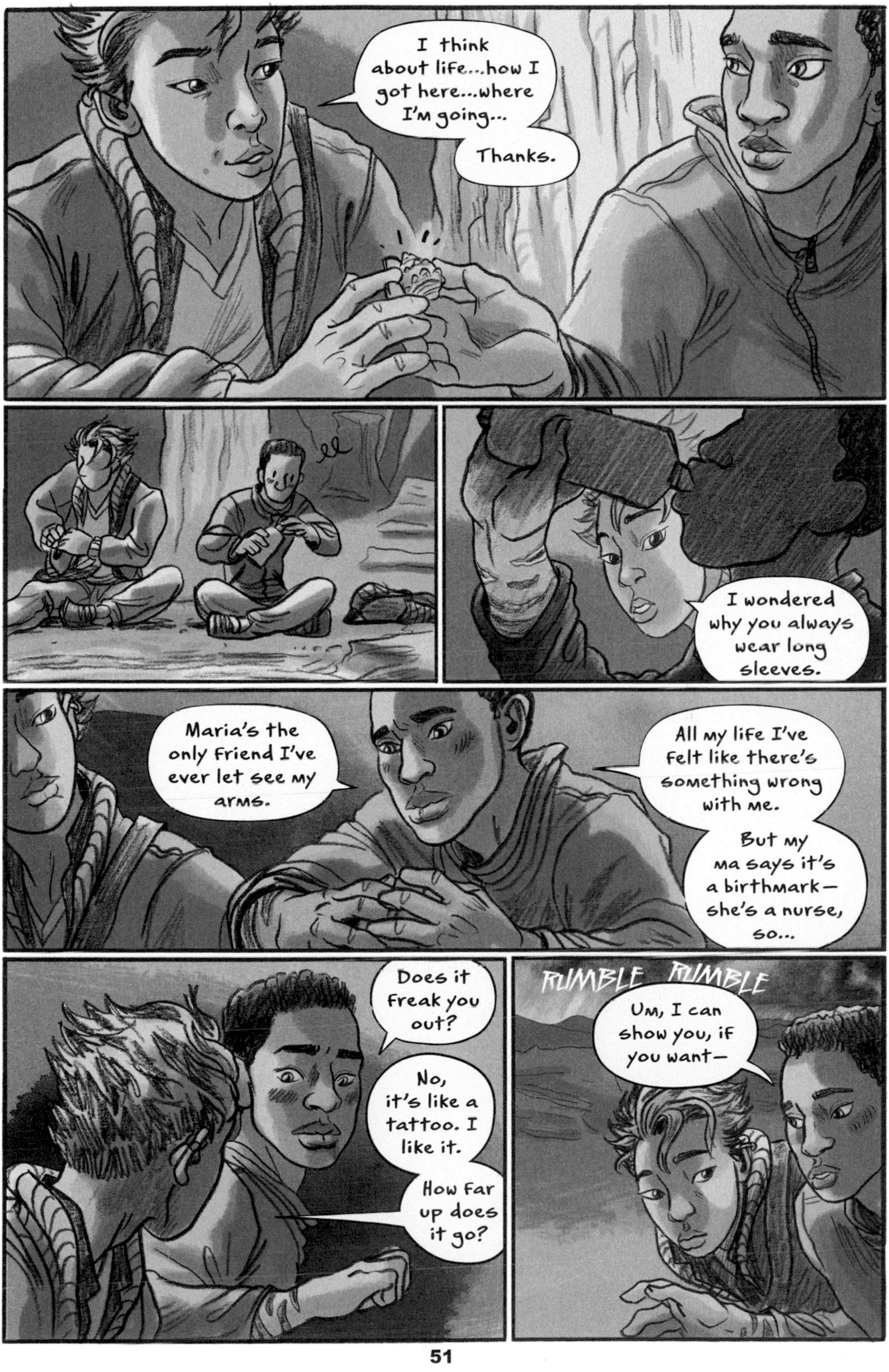
I think about life...how I got here...where I'm going...
Thanks.
I wondered why you always wear long sleeves.
Maria's the only friend I've ever let see my arms.
All my life I've felt like there's something wrong with me.
But my ma says it's a birthmark—she's a nurse, so...
Does it freak you out?
No, it's like a tattoo. I like it.
How far up does it go?
RUMBLE RUMBLE
Um, I can show you, if you want—

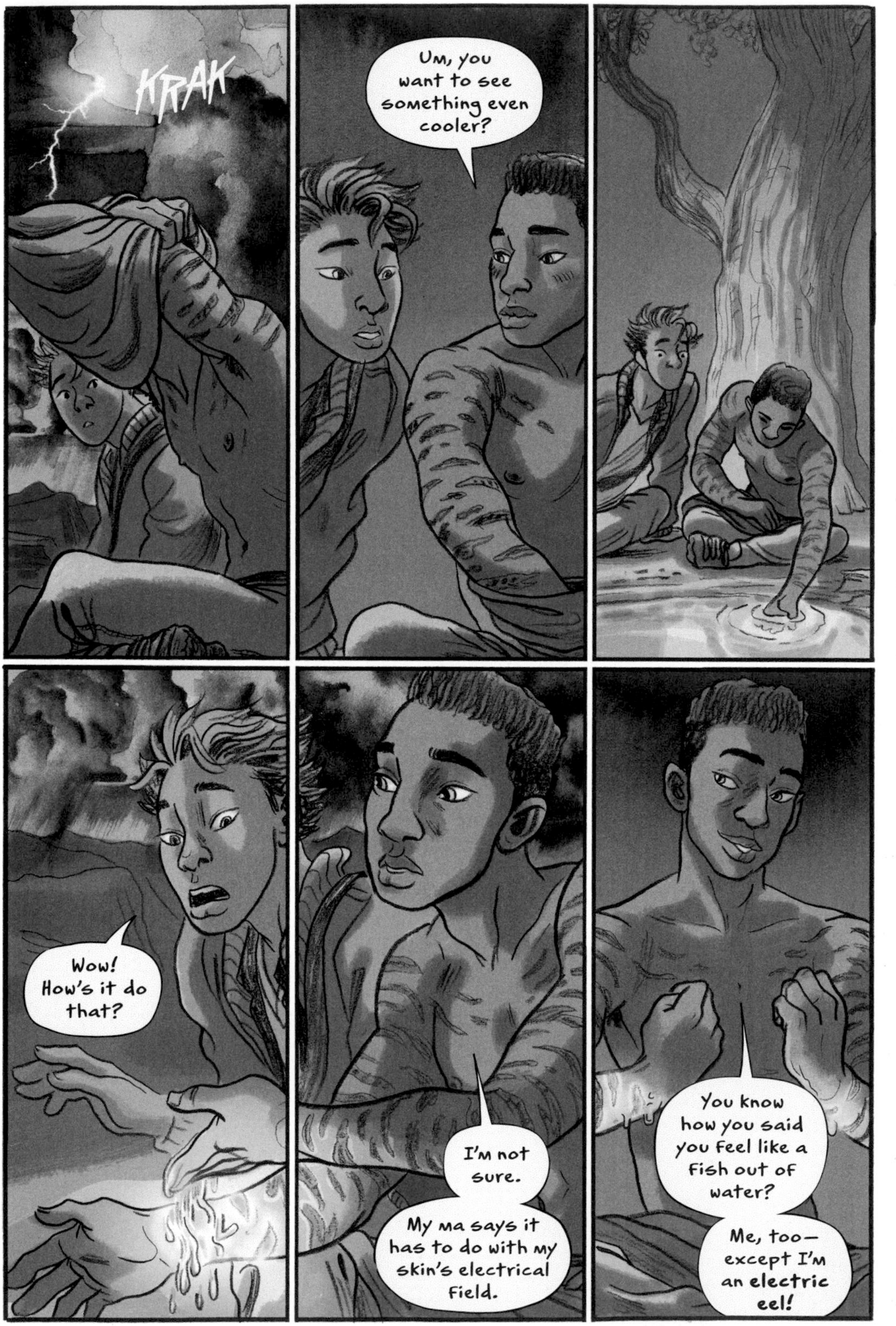
KRAK
Um, you want to see something even cooler?
Wow! How's it do that?
I'm not sure.
My ma says it has to do with my skin's electrical field.
You know how you said you feel like a fish out of water?
Me, too—except I'm an electric eel!

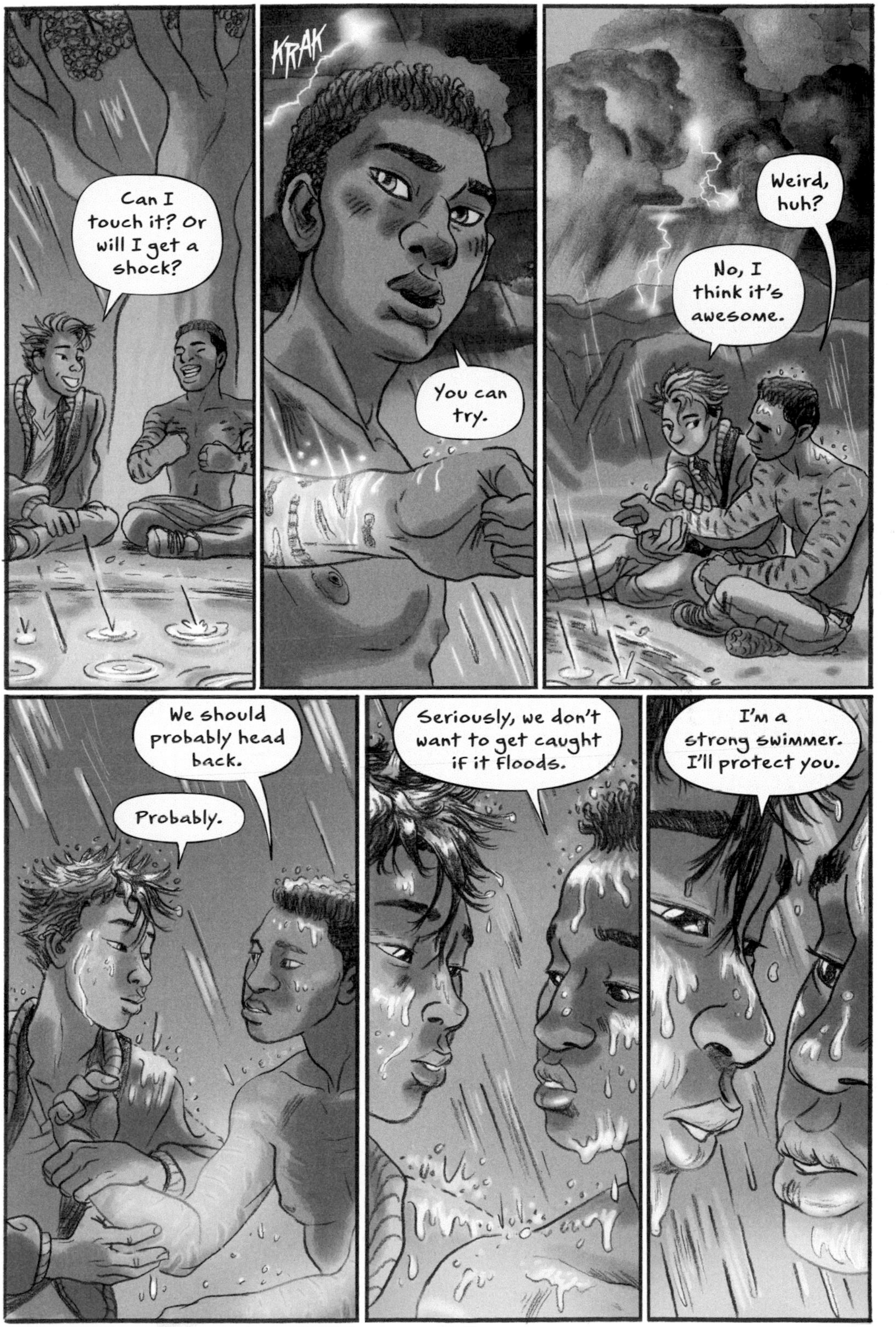
Can I touch it? Or will I get a shock?
KRAK
You can try.
Weird, huh?
No, I think it's awesome.
We should probably head back.
Probably.
Seriously, we don't want to get caught if it floods.
I'm a strong swimmer. I'll protect you.

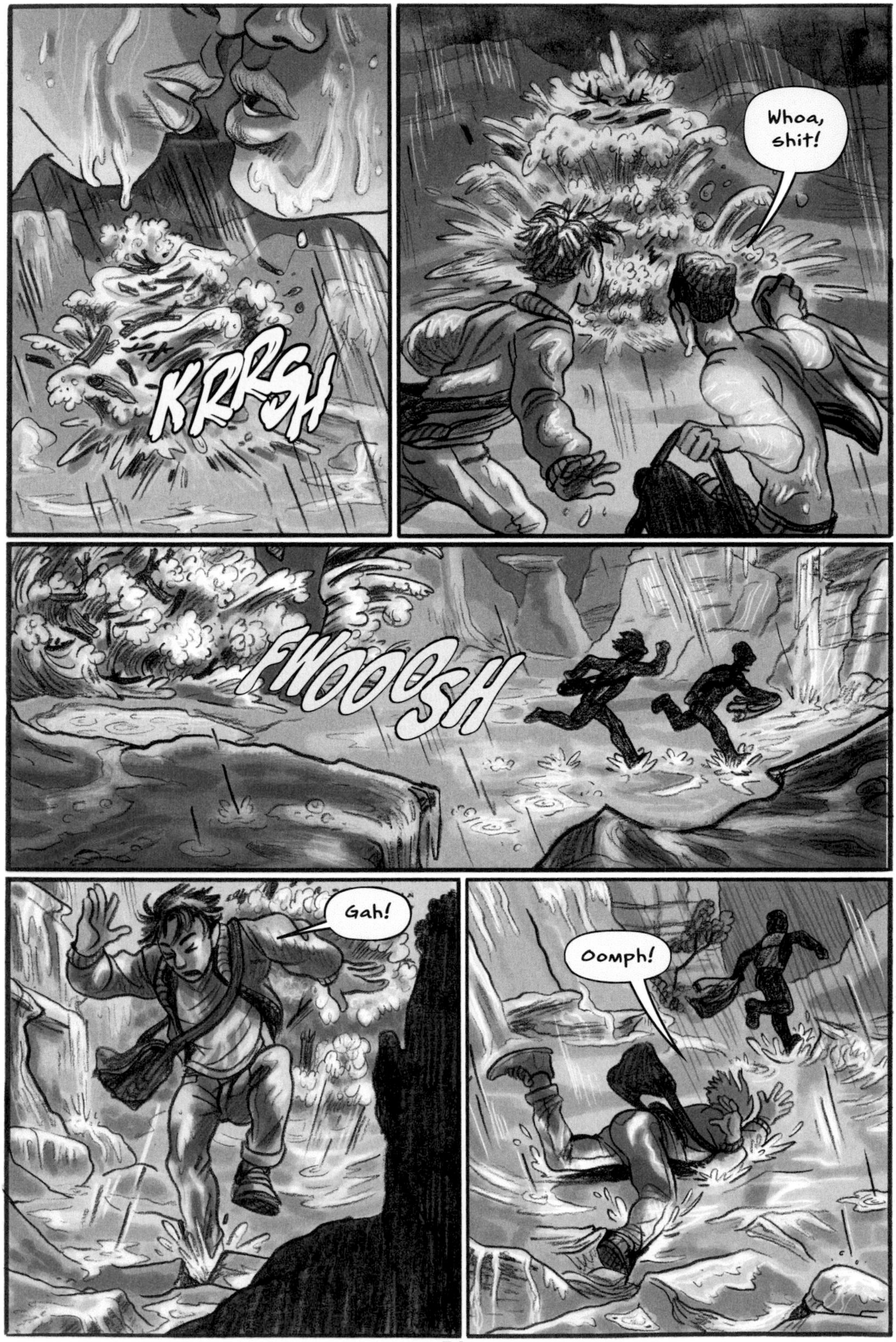
KRRSH
Whoa, shit!
FWOOOSH
Gah!
Oomph!

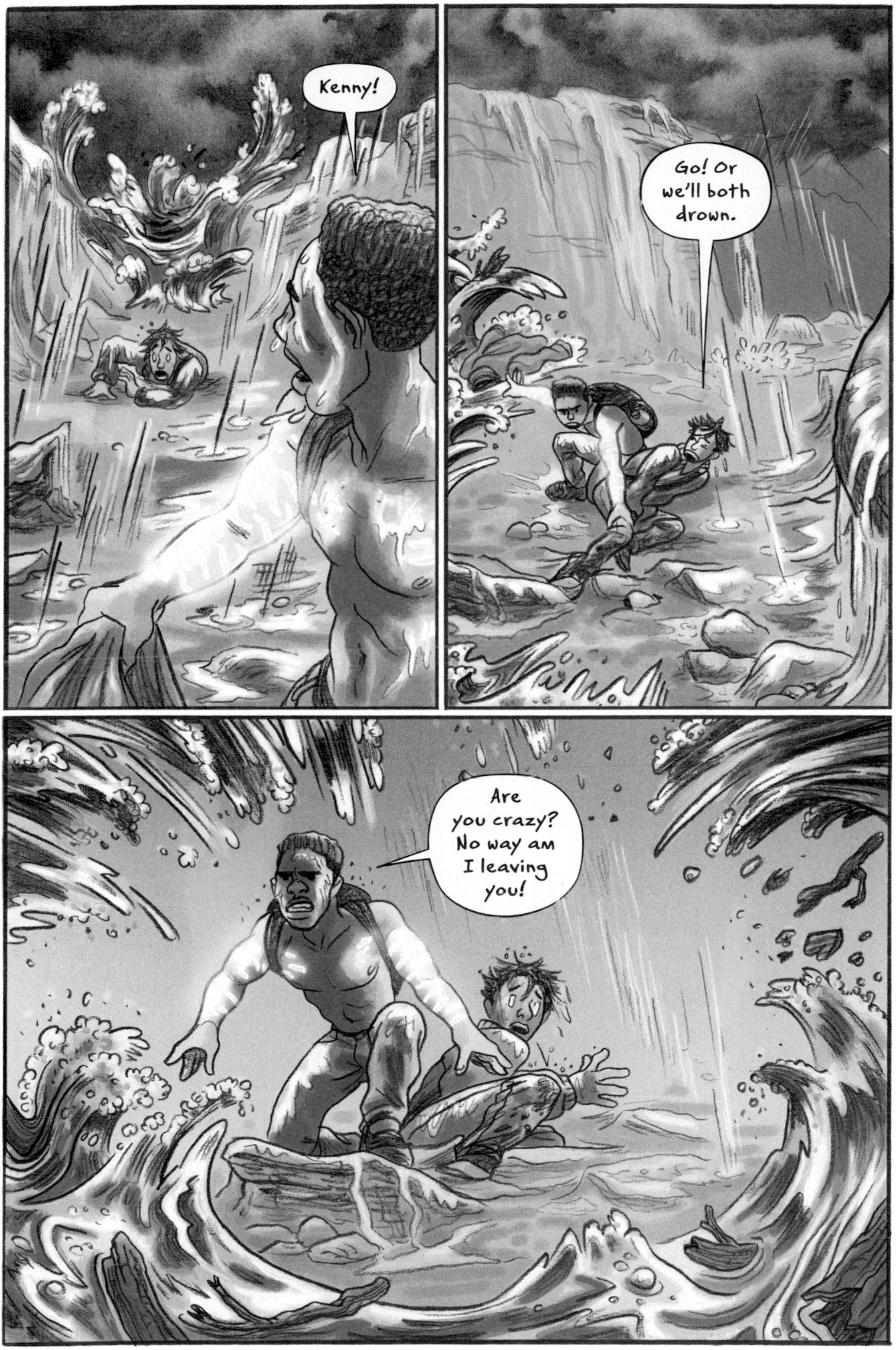
Kenny!
Go! Or we'll both drown.
Are you crazy? No way am I leaving you!

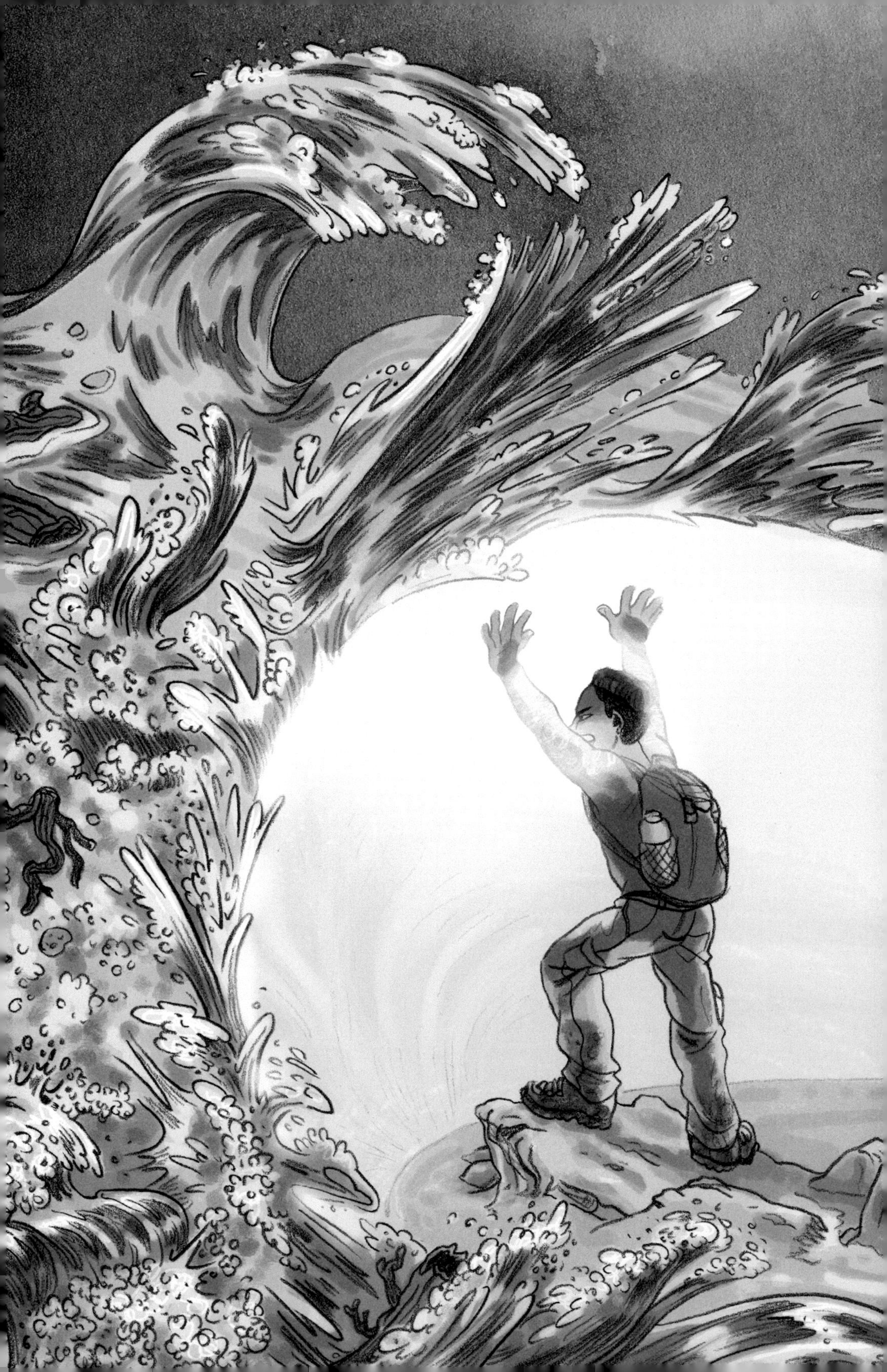

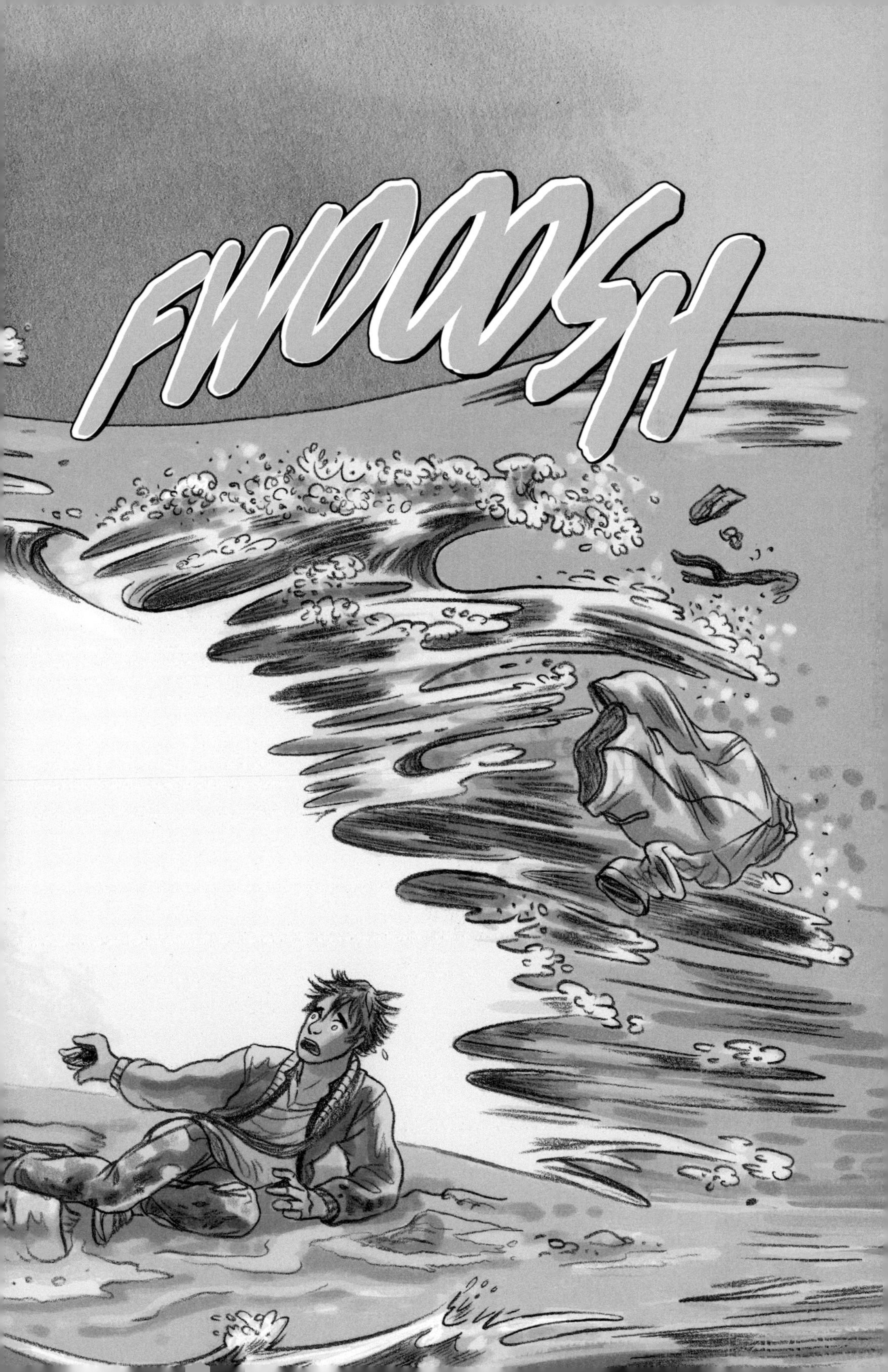
FWOOOSH

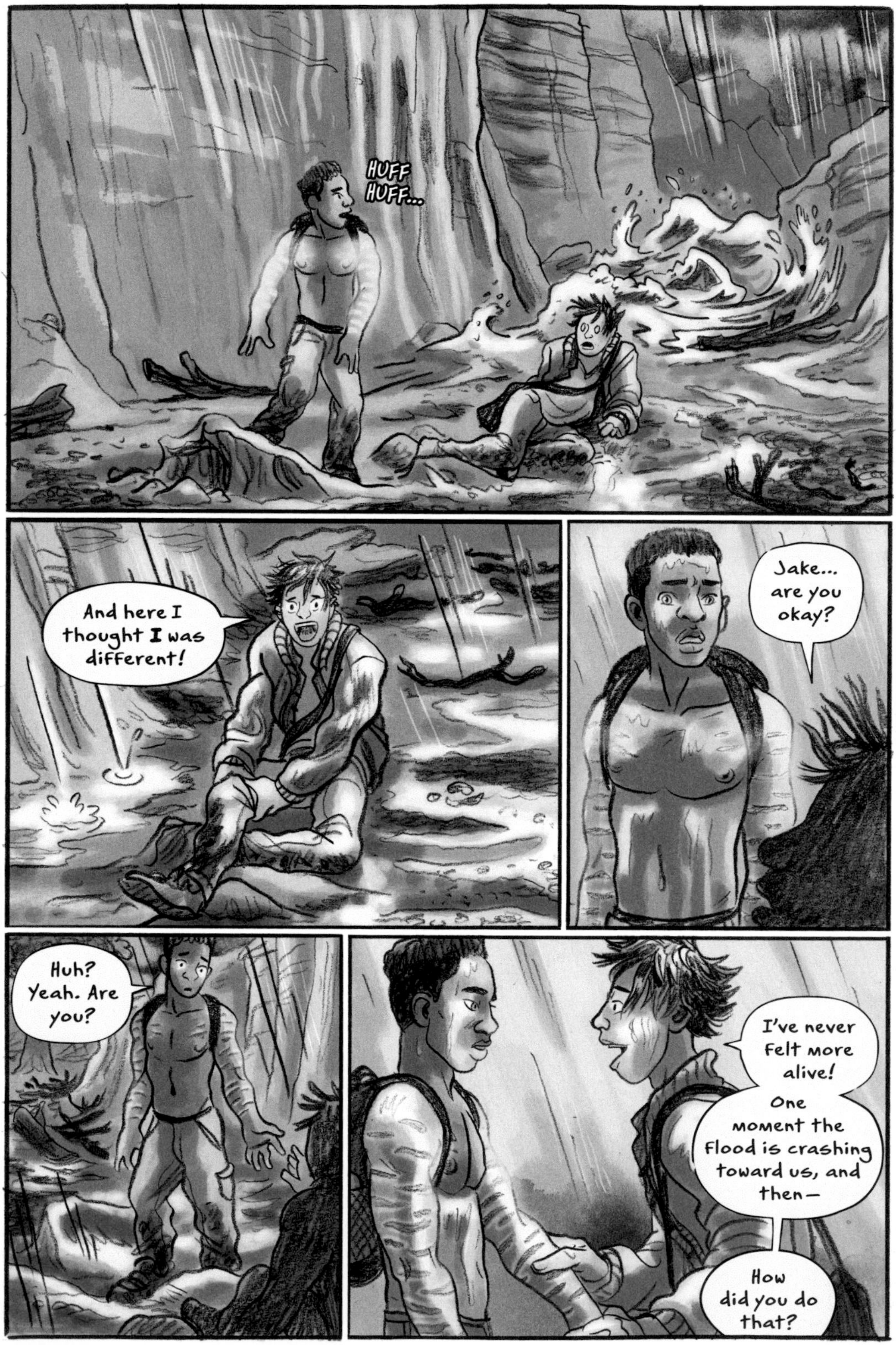
HUFF HUFF...
And here I thought I was different!
Jake... are you okay?
Huh? Yeah. Are you?
I've never felt more alive!
One moment the flood is crashing toward us, and then—
How did you do that?

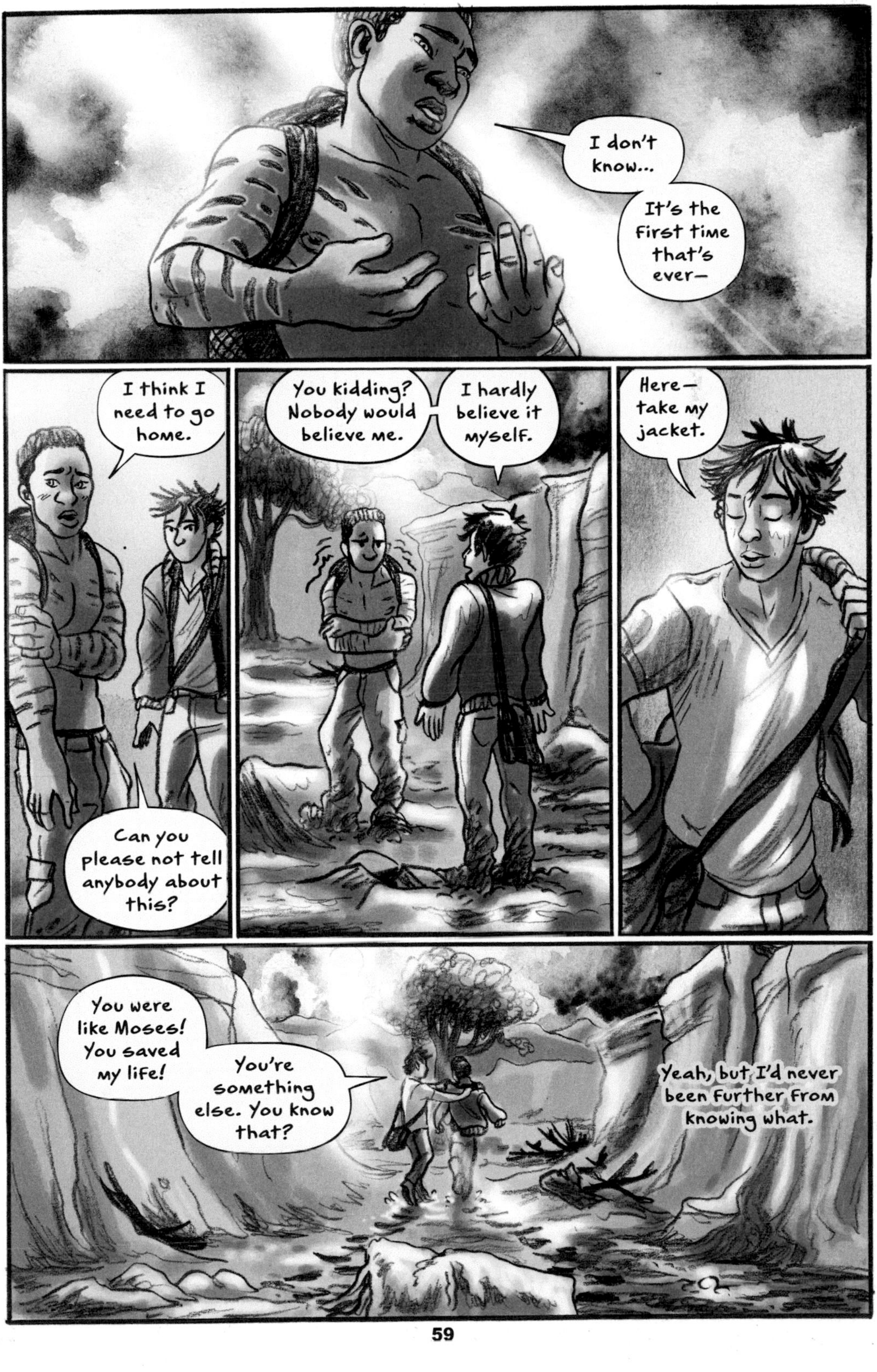
I don't know...
It's the first time that's ever—
I think I need to go home.
Can you please not tell anybody about this?
You kidding? Nobody would believe me.
I hardly believe it myself.
Here— take my jacket.
You were like Moses! You saved my life!
You're something else. You know that?
Yeah, but I'd never been further from knowing what.

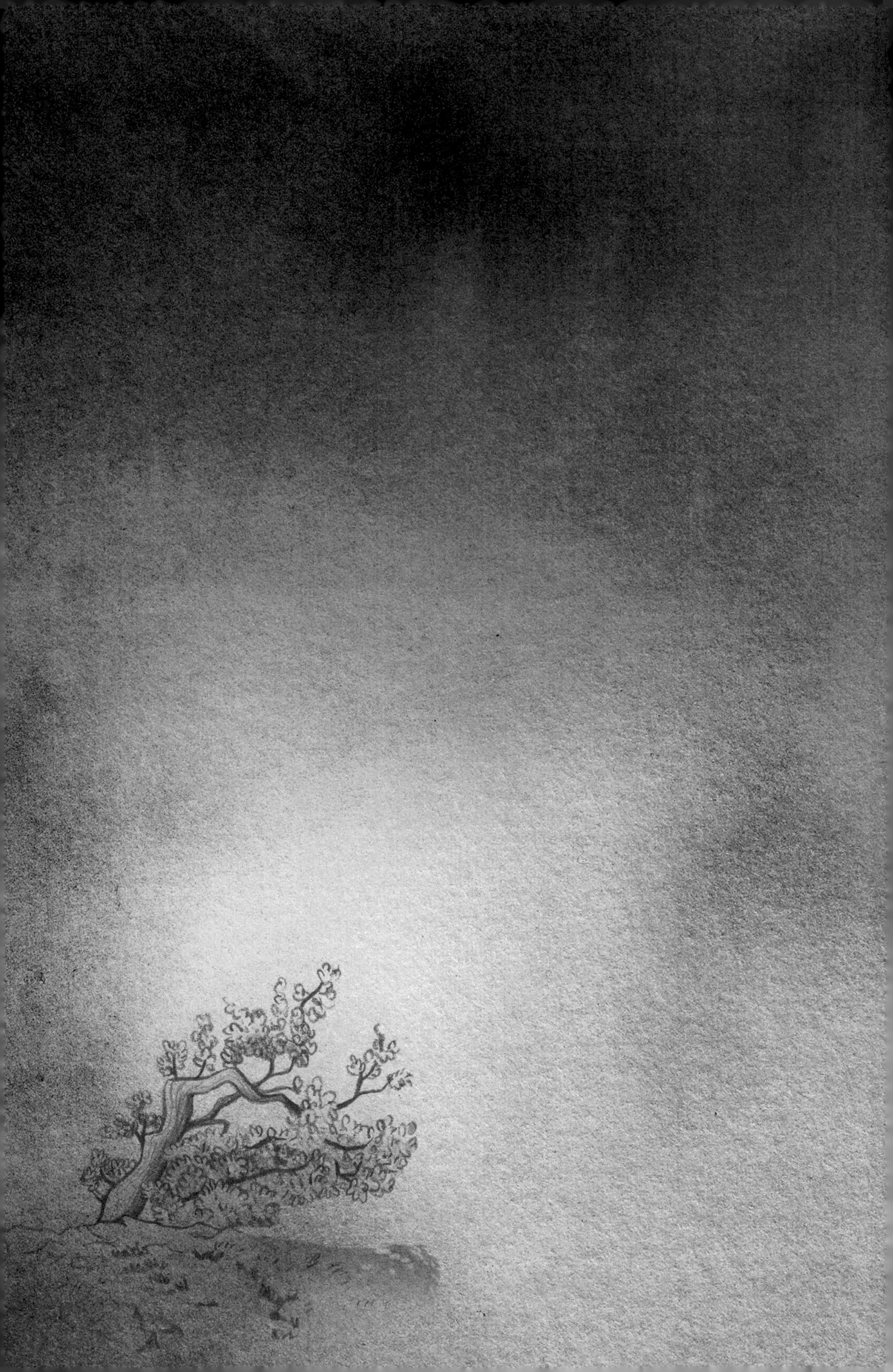

CHAPTER 2

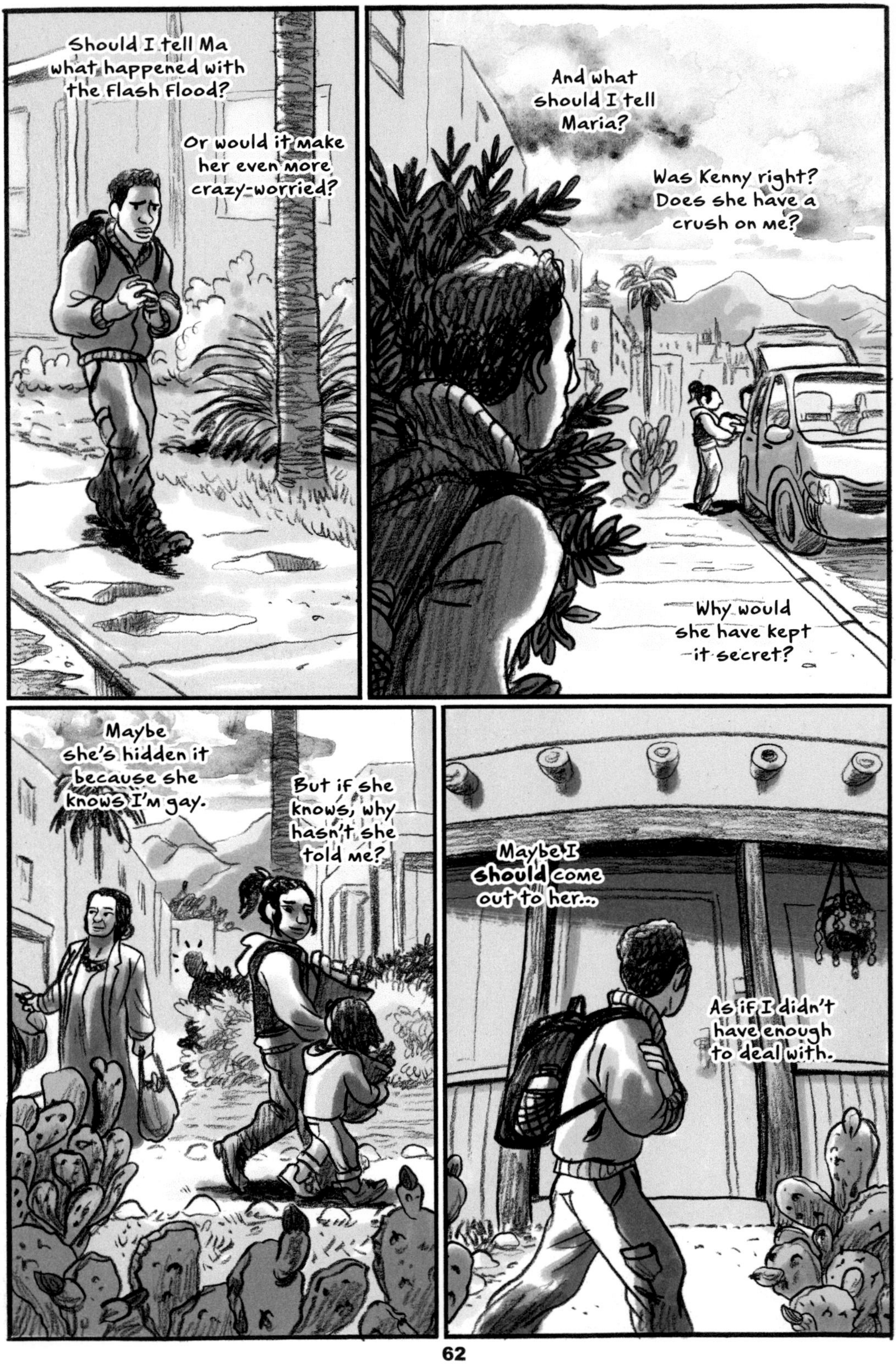
Should I tell Ma what happened with the Flash Flood?
Or would it make her even more crazy-worried?
And what should I tell Maria?
Was Kenny right? Does she have a crush on me?
Why would she have kept it secret?
Maybe she's hidden it because she knows I'm gay.
But if she knows, why hasn't she told me?
Maybe I **should** come out to her...
As if I didn't have enough to deal with.

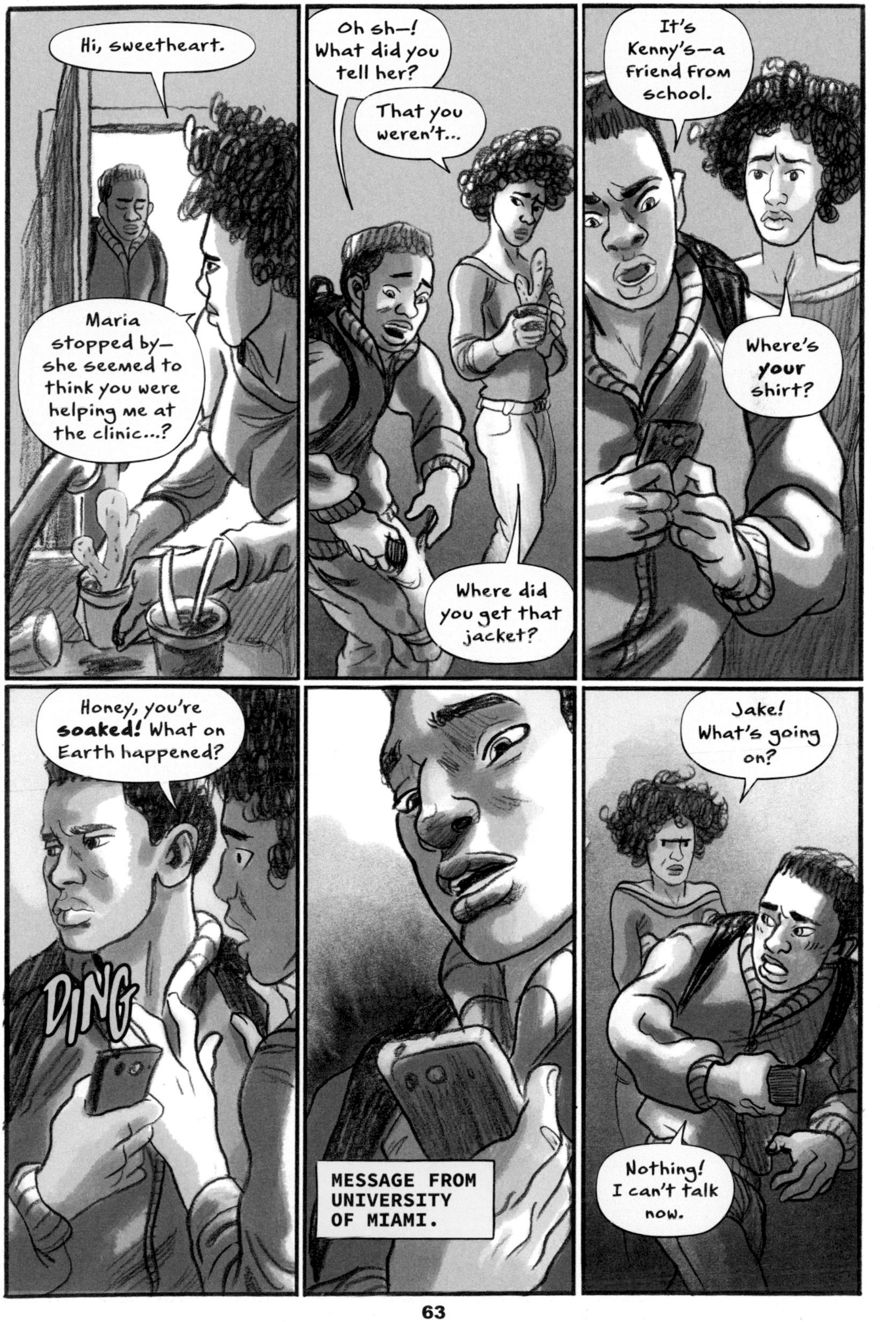
Hi, sweetheart.
Maria stopped by— she seemed to think you were helping me at the clinic...?
Oh sh—! What did you tell her?
That you weren't...
Where did you get that jacket?
It's Kenny's—a friend from school.
Where's **your** shirt?
Honey, you're **soaked!** What on Earth happened?
DING
MESSAGE FROM UNIVERSITY OF MIAMI.
Jake! What's going on?
Nothing! I can't talk now.

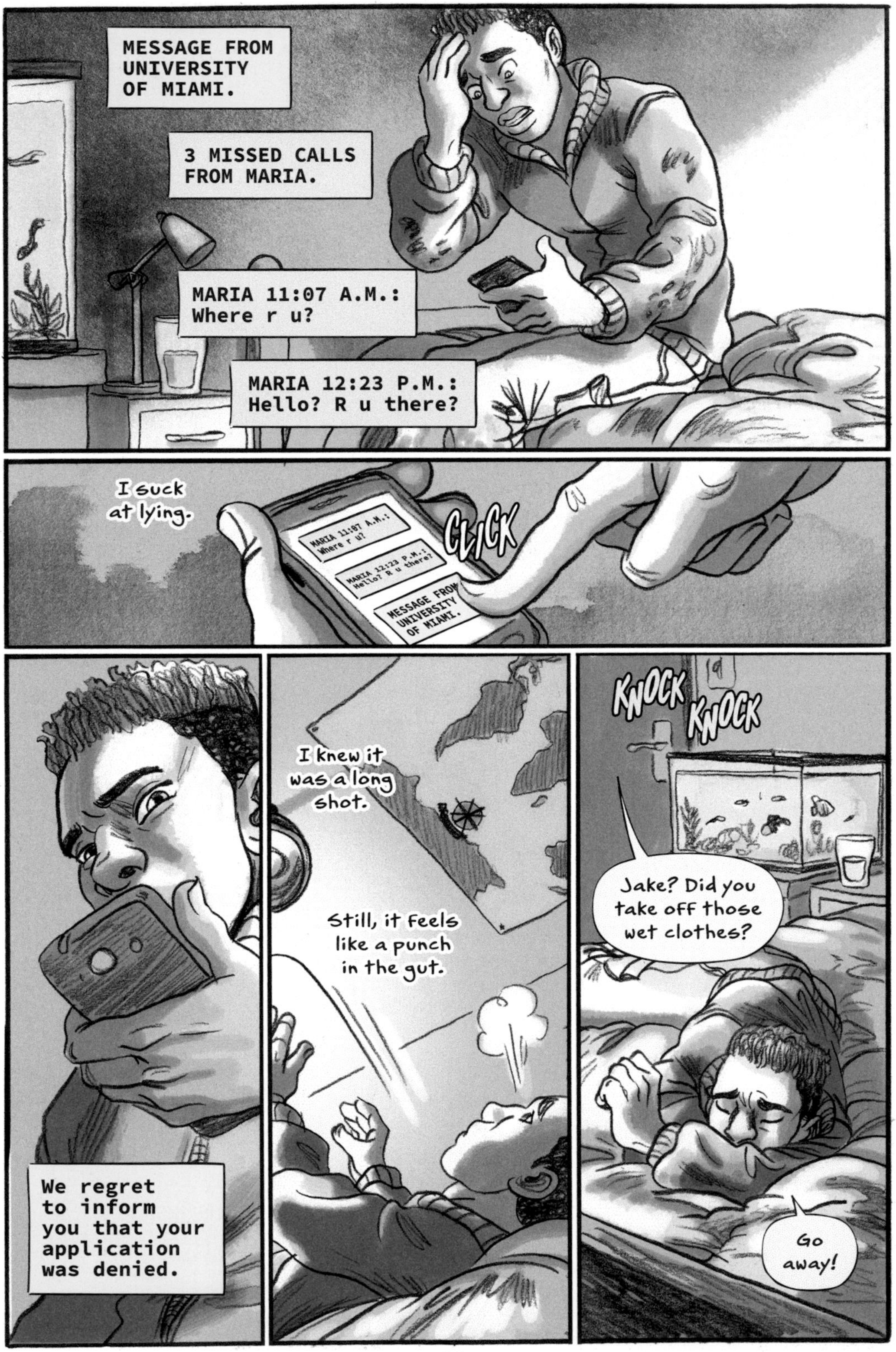
MESSAGE FROM UNIVERSITY OF MIAMI.
3 MISSED CALLS FROM MARIA.
MARIA 11:07 A.M.: Where r u?
MARIA 12:23 P.M.: Hello? R u there?
I suck at lying.
CLICK
MARIA 11:07 A.M.: Where r u?
MARIA 12:23 P.M.: Hello? R u there?
MESSAGE FROM UNIVERSITY OF MIAMI.
We regret to inform you that your application was denied.
I knew it was a long shot.
Still, it feels like a punch in the gut.
KNOCK KNOCK
Jake? Did you take off those wet clothes?
Go away!

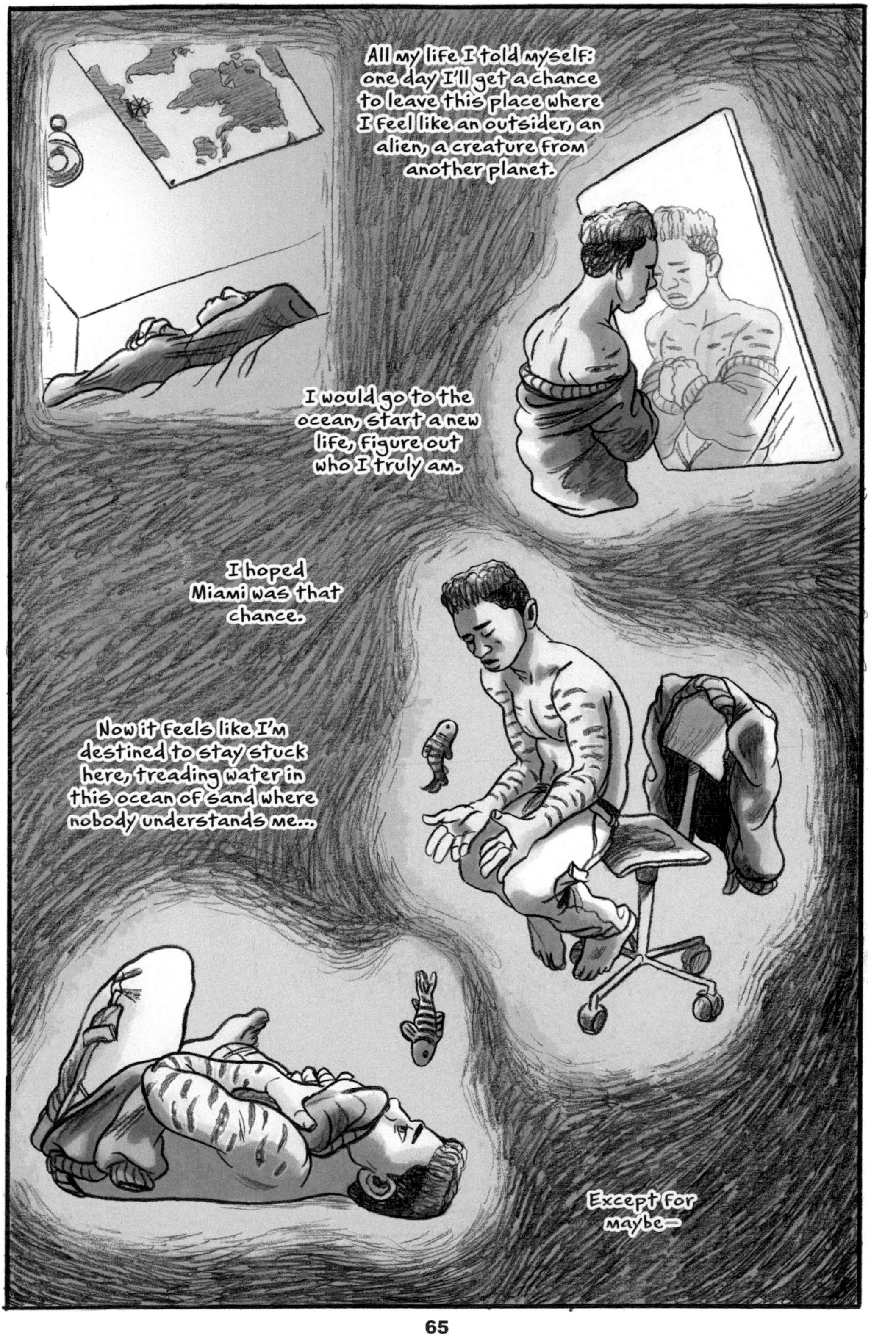
All my life I told myself: one day I'll get a chance to leave this place where I feel like an outsider, an alien, a creature from another planet.
I would go to the ocean, start a new life, figure out who I truly am.
I hoped Miami was that chance.
Now it feels like I'm destined to stay stuck here, treading water in this ocean of sand where nobody understands me...
Except for maybe—

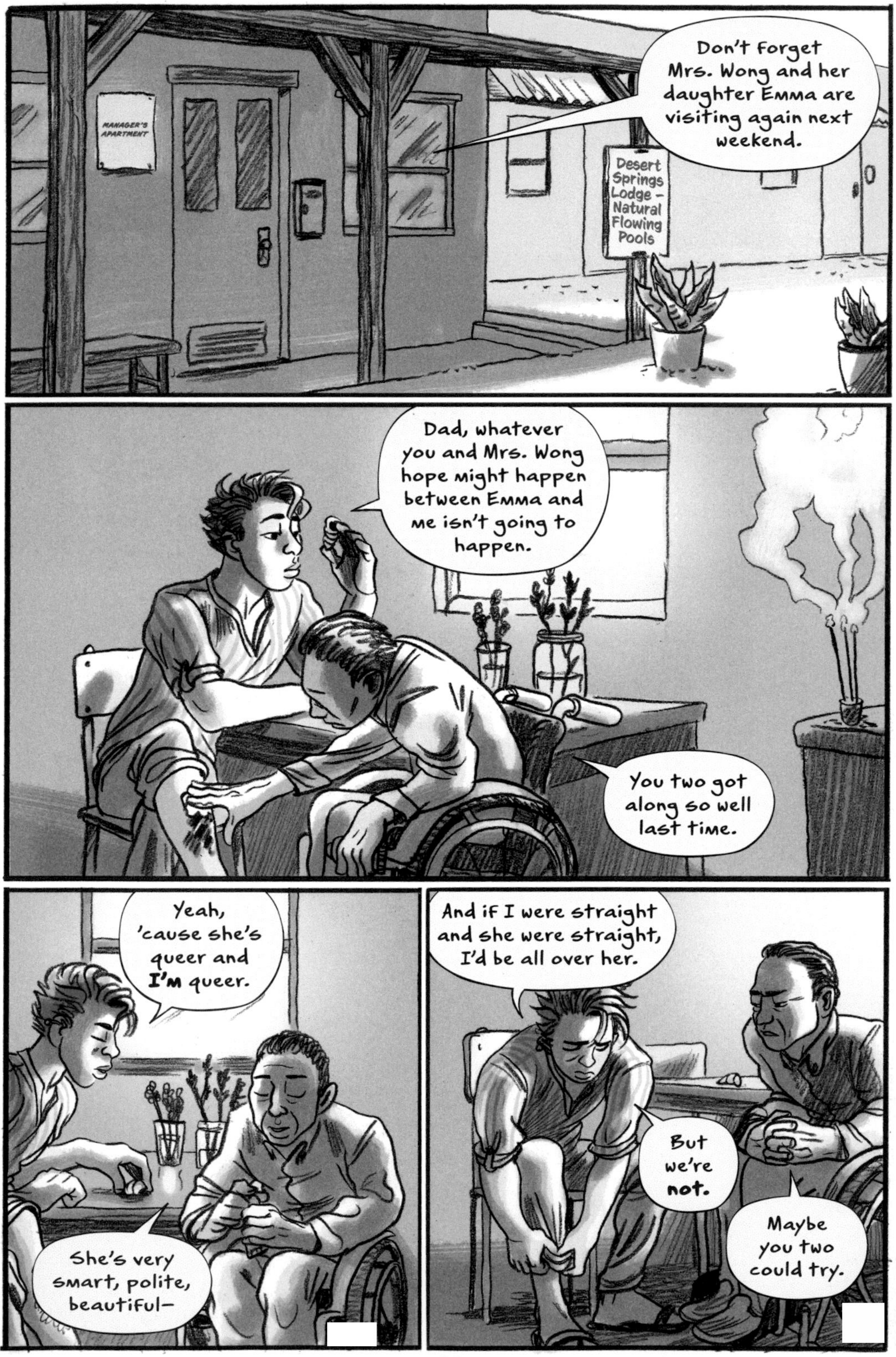
MANAGER'S APARTMENT
Don't forget Mrs. Wong and her daughter Emma are visiting again next weekend.
Desert Springs Lodge – Natural Flowing Pools
Dad, whatever you and Mrs. Wong hope might happen between Emma and me isn't going to happen.
You two got along so well last time.
Yeah, 'cause she's queer and **I'm** queer.
She's very smart, polite, beautiful–
And if I were straight and she were straight, I'd be all over her.
But we're **not**.
Maybe you two could try.

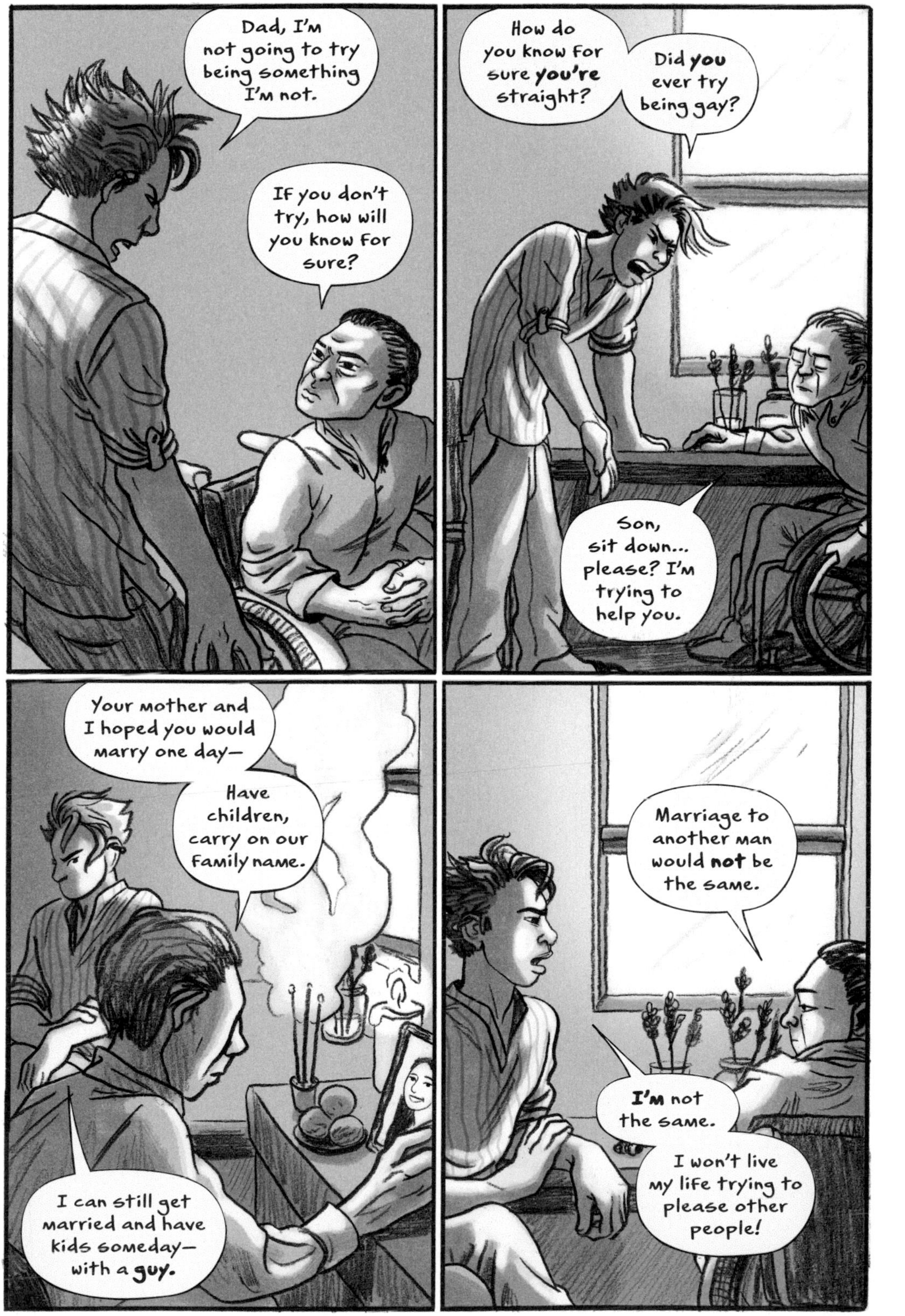
Dad, I'm not going to try being something I'm not.
If you don't try, how will you know for sure?
How do you know for sure **you're** straight?
Did **you** ever try being gay?
Son, sit down... please? I'm trying to help you.
Your mother and I hoped you would marry one day—
Have children, carry on our family name.
I can still get married and have kids someday— with a **guy.**
Marriage to another man would **not** be the same.
I'm not the same.
I won't live my life trying to please other people!

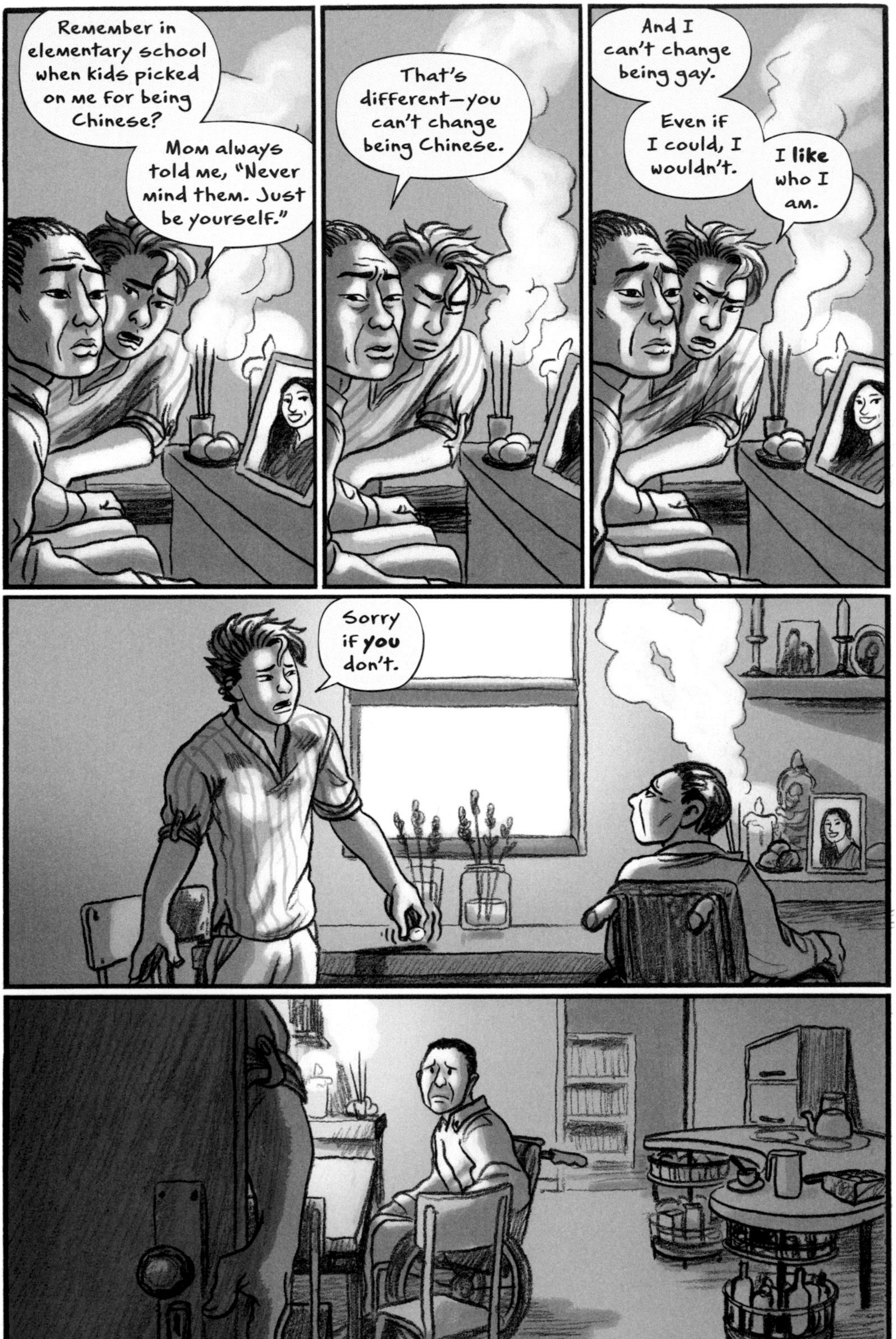
Remember in elementary school when kids picked on me for being Chinese?
Mom always told me, "Never mind them. Just be yourself."
That's different—you can't change being Chinese.
And I can't change being gay.
Even if I could, I wouldn't.
I **like** who I am.
Sorry if **you** don't.

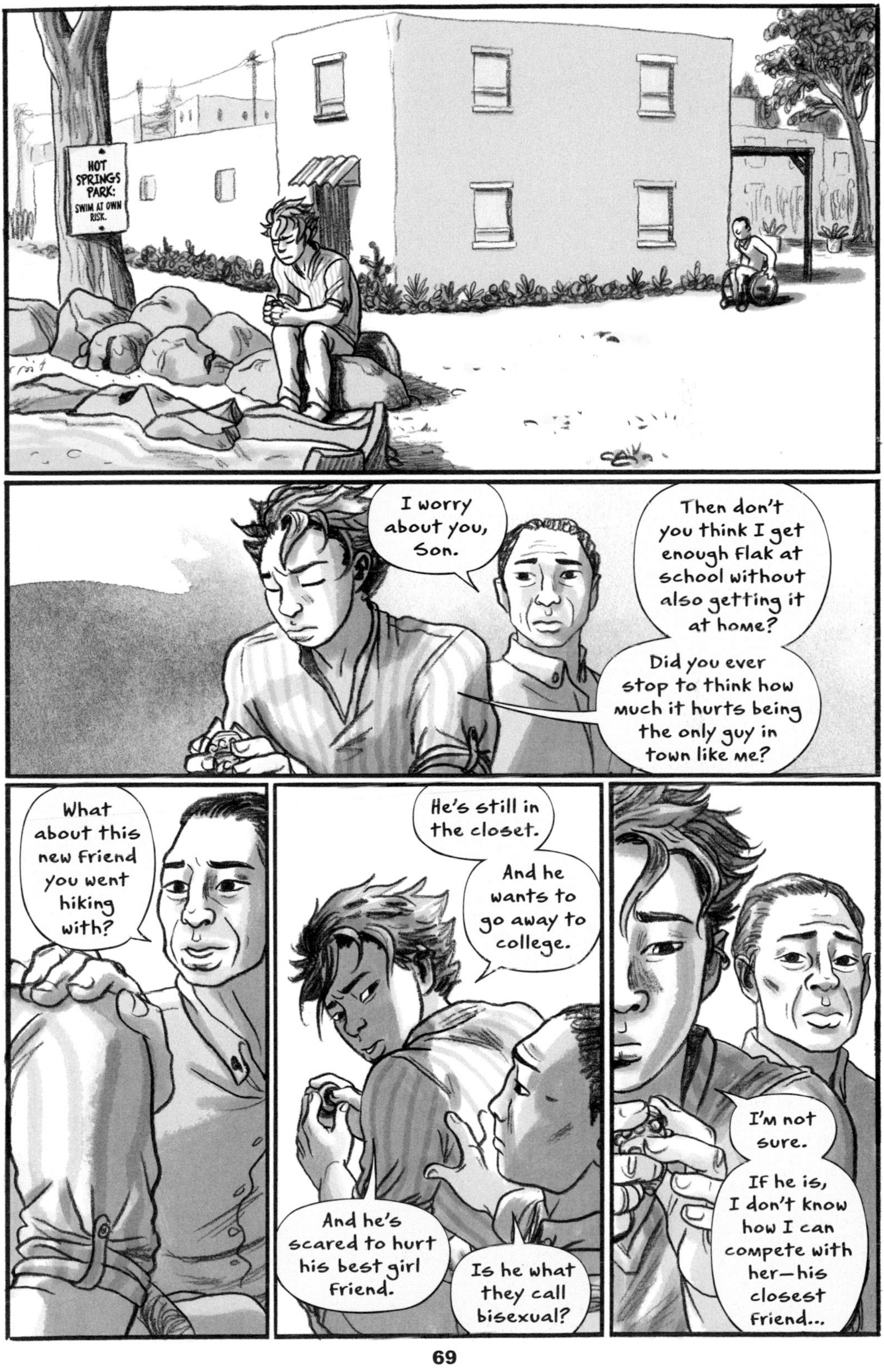
HOT SPRINGS PARK: SWIM AT OWN RISK.
I worry about you, Son.
Then don't you think I get enough flak at school without also getting it at home?
Did you ever stop to think how much it hurts being the only guy in town like me?
What about this new friend you went hiking with?
He's still in the closet.
And he wants to go away to college.
And he's scared to hurt his best girl friend.
Is he what they call bisexual?
I'm not sure.
If he is, I don't know how I can compete with her—his closest friend...

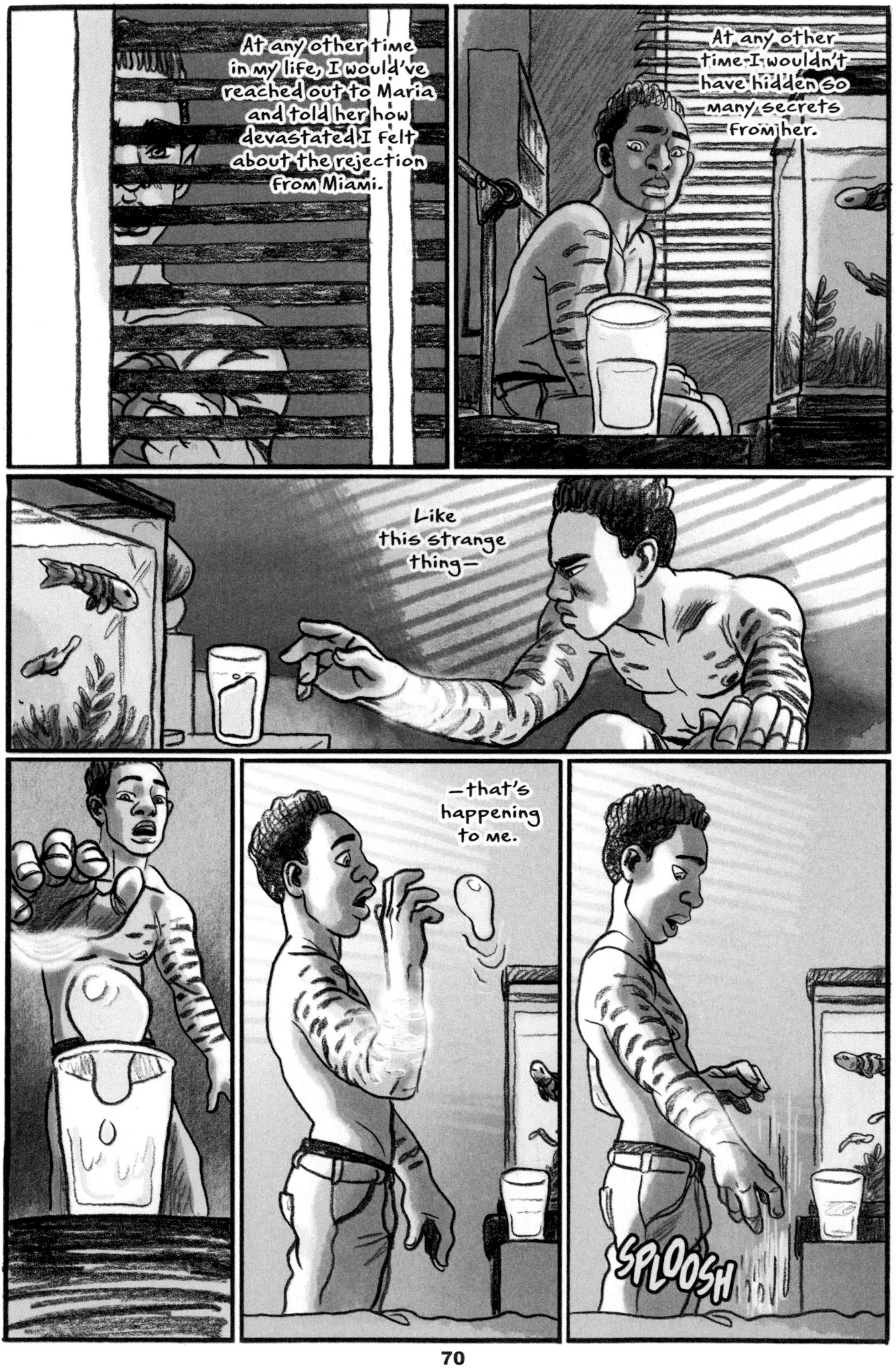
At any other time in my life, I would've reached out to Maria and told her how devastated I felt about the rejection from Miami.
At any other time I wouldn't have hidden so many secrets from her.
Like this strange thing—
—that's happening to me.
SPLOOSH

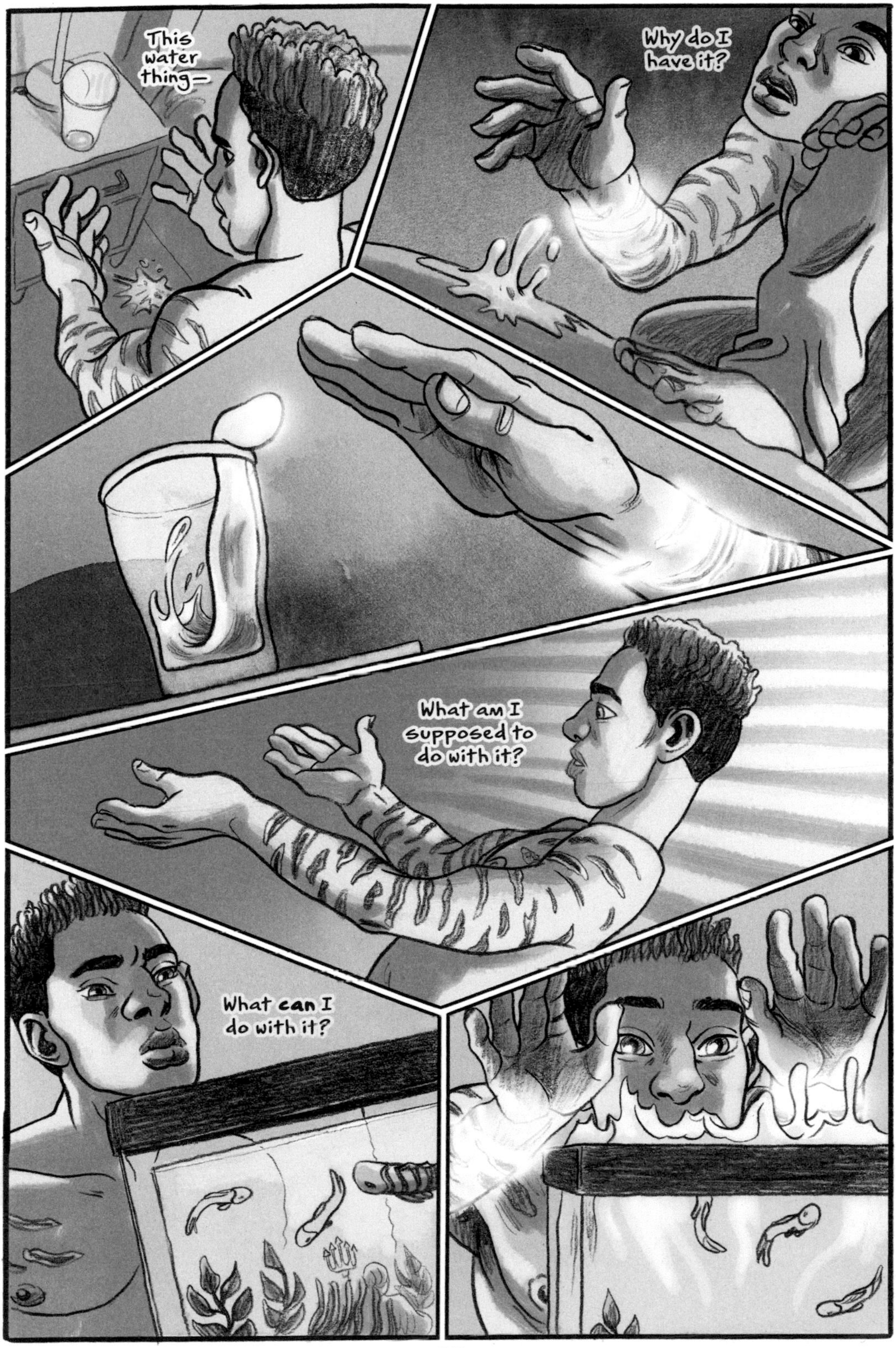
This water thing—
Why do I have it?
What am I supposed to do with it?
What **can** I do with it?

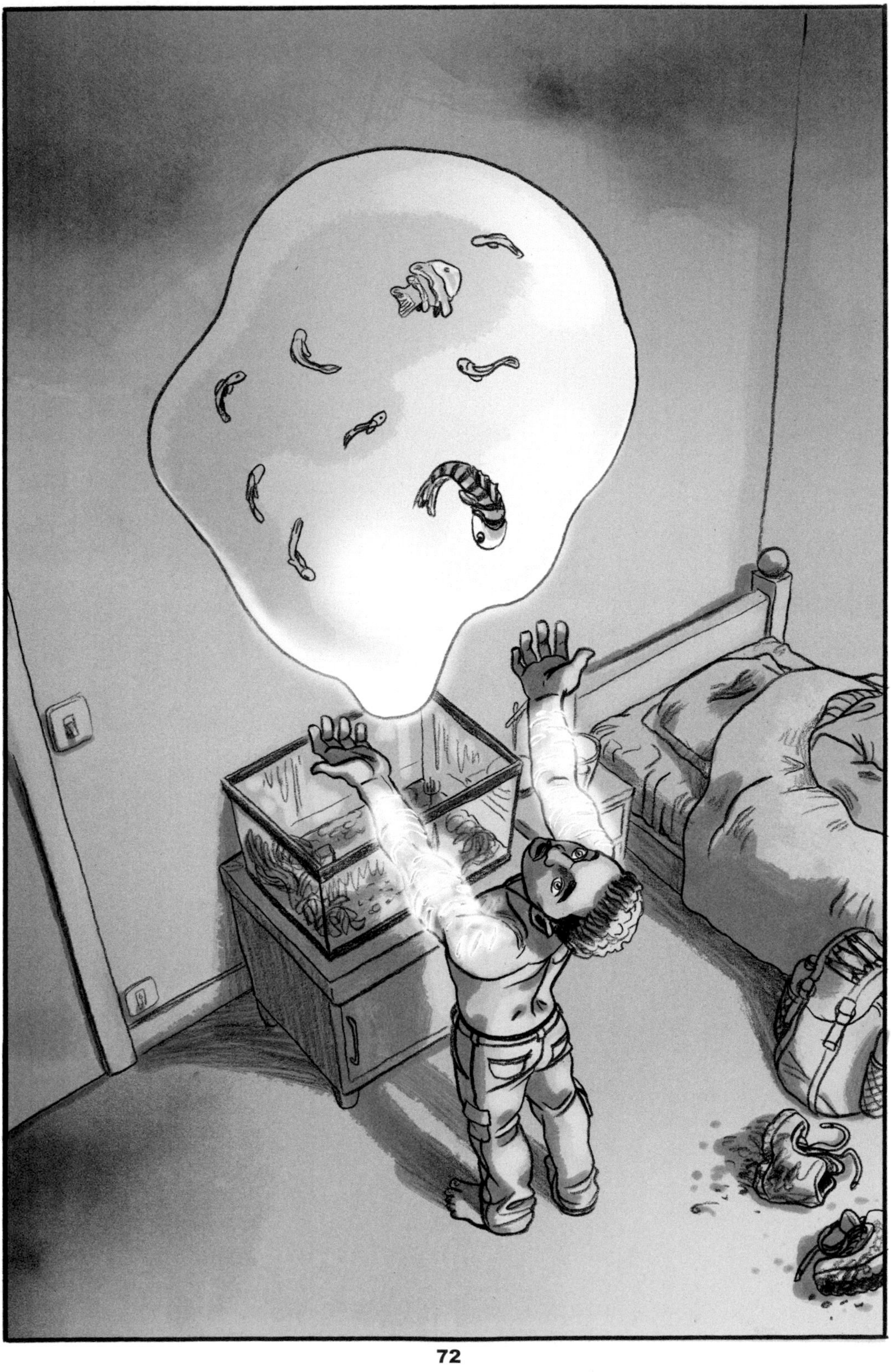

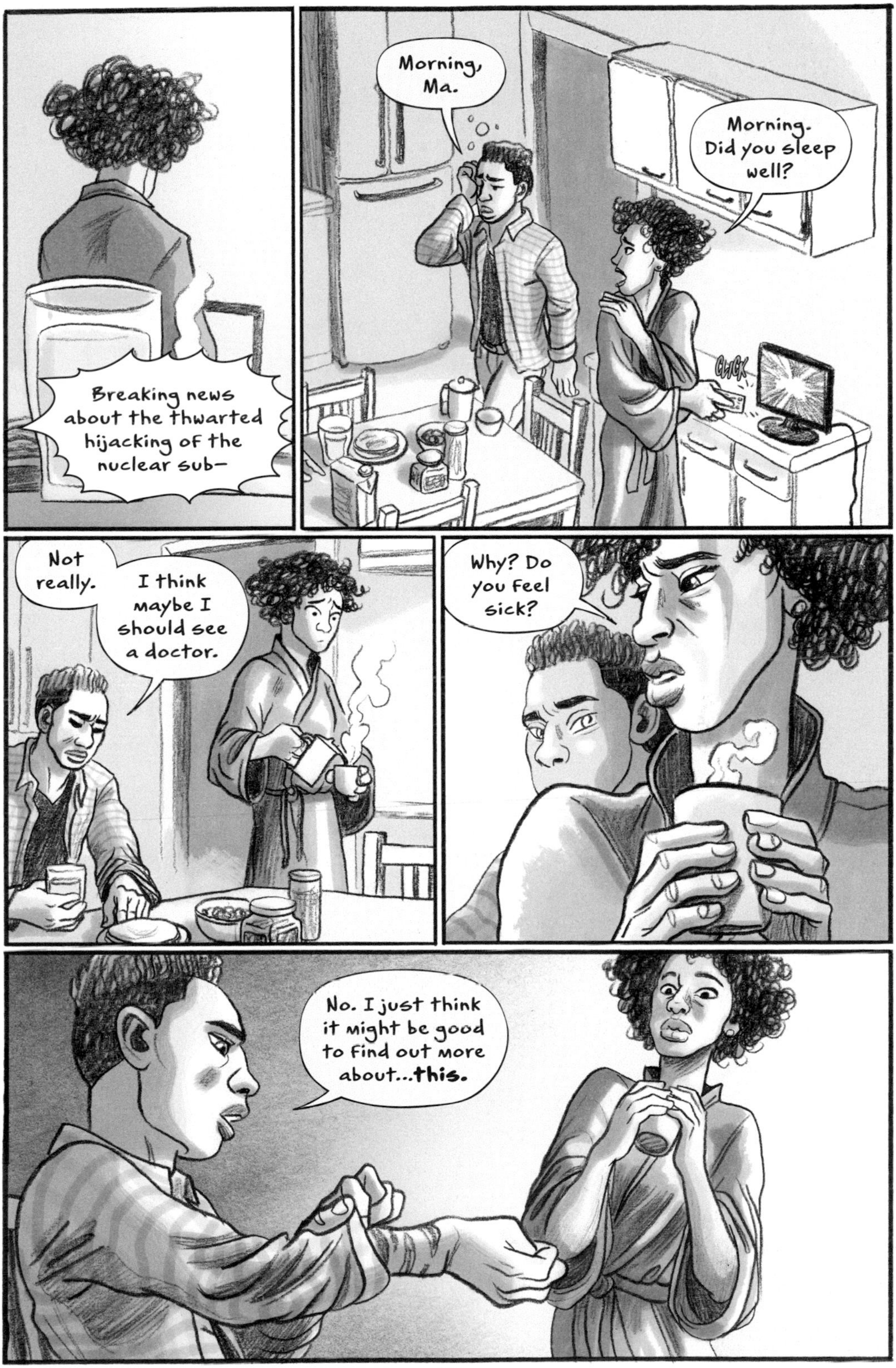

Breaking news about the thwarted hijacking of the nuclear sub—
Morning, Ma.
Morning. Did you sleep well?
CLICK
Not really.
I think maybe I should see a doctor.
Why? Do you feel sick?
No. I just think it might be good to find out more about...**this.**

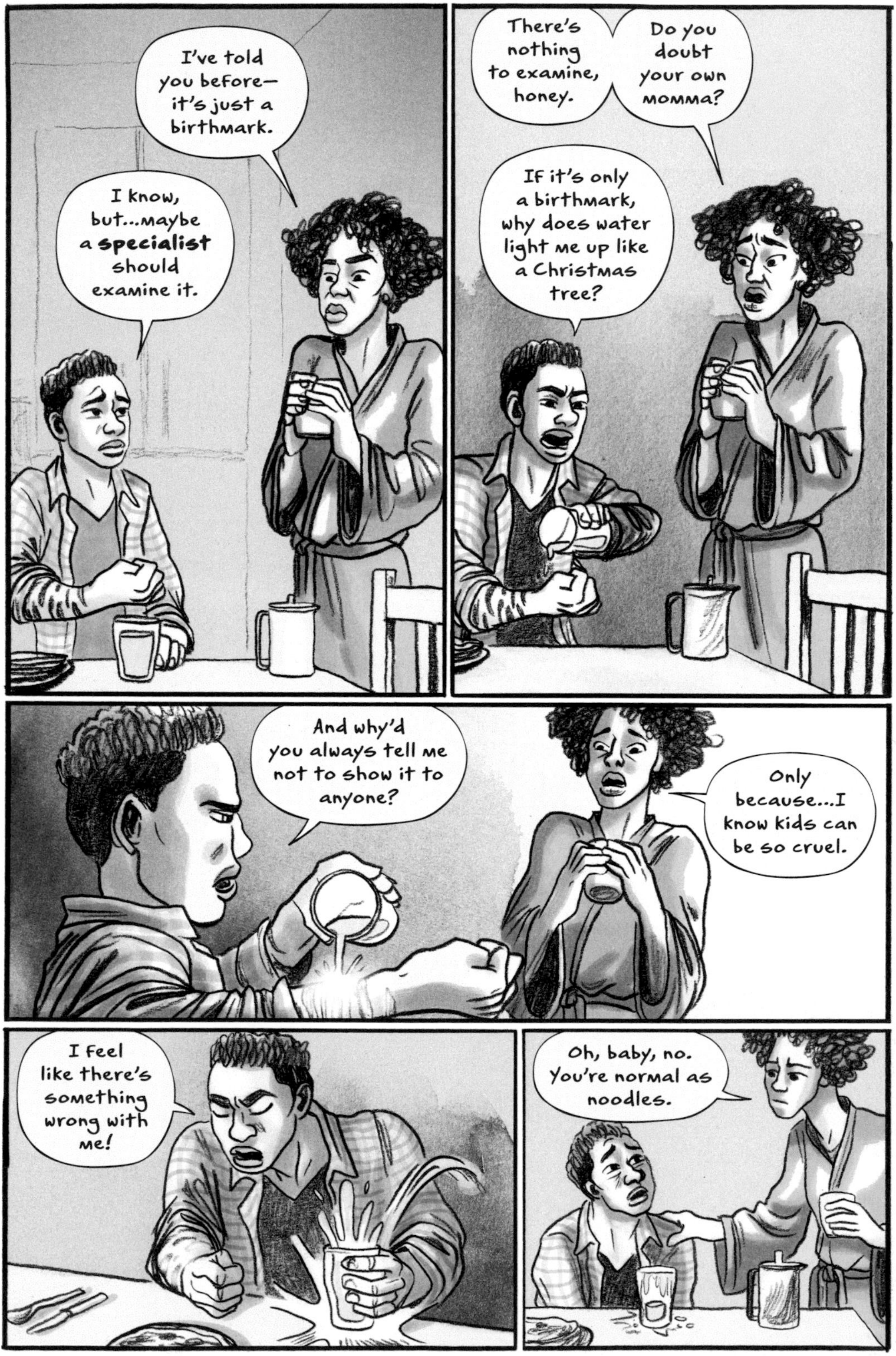
I know, but...maybe a **specialist** should examine it.
I've told you before— it's just a birthmark.
There's nothing to examine, honey.
Do you doubt your own momma?
If it's only a birthmark, why does water light me up like a Christmas tree?
And why'd you always tell me not to show it to anyone?
Only because...I know kids can be so cruel.
I Feel like there's something wrong with me!
Oh, baby, no. You're normal as noodles.

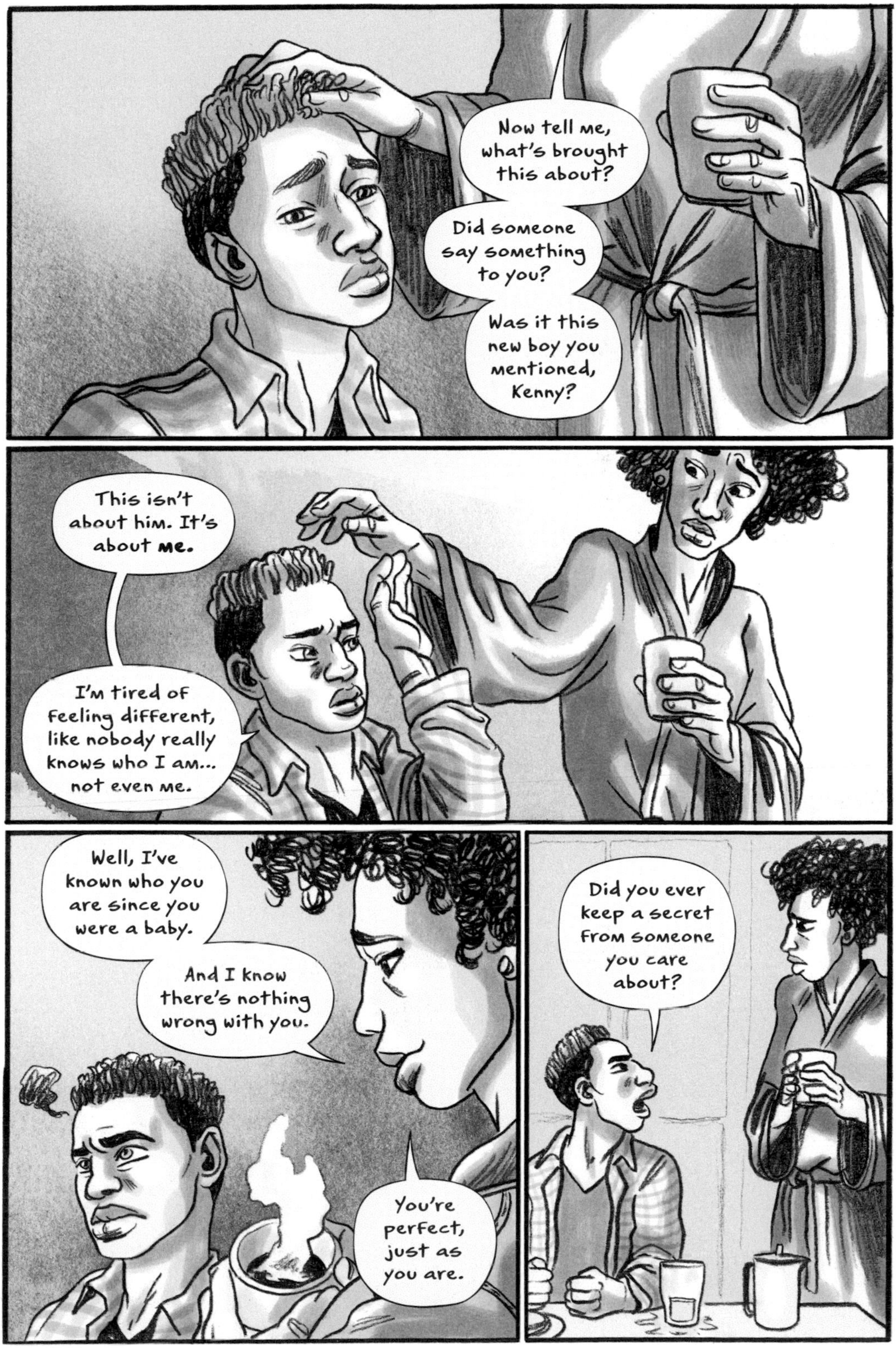
Now tell me, what's brought this about?
Did someone say something to you?
Was it this new boy you mentioned, Kenny?
This isn't about him. It's about **me.**
I'm tired of feeling different, like nobody really knows who I am... not even me.
Well, I've known who you are since you were a baby.
And I know there's nothing wrong with you.
You're perfect, just as you are.
Did you ever keep a secret from someone you care about?

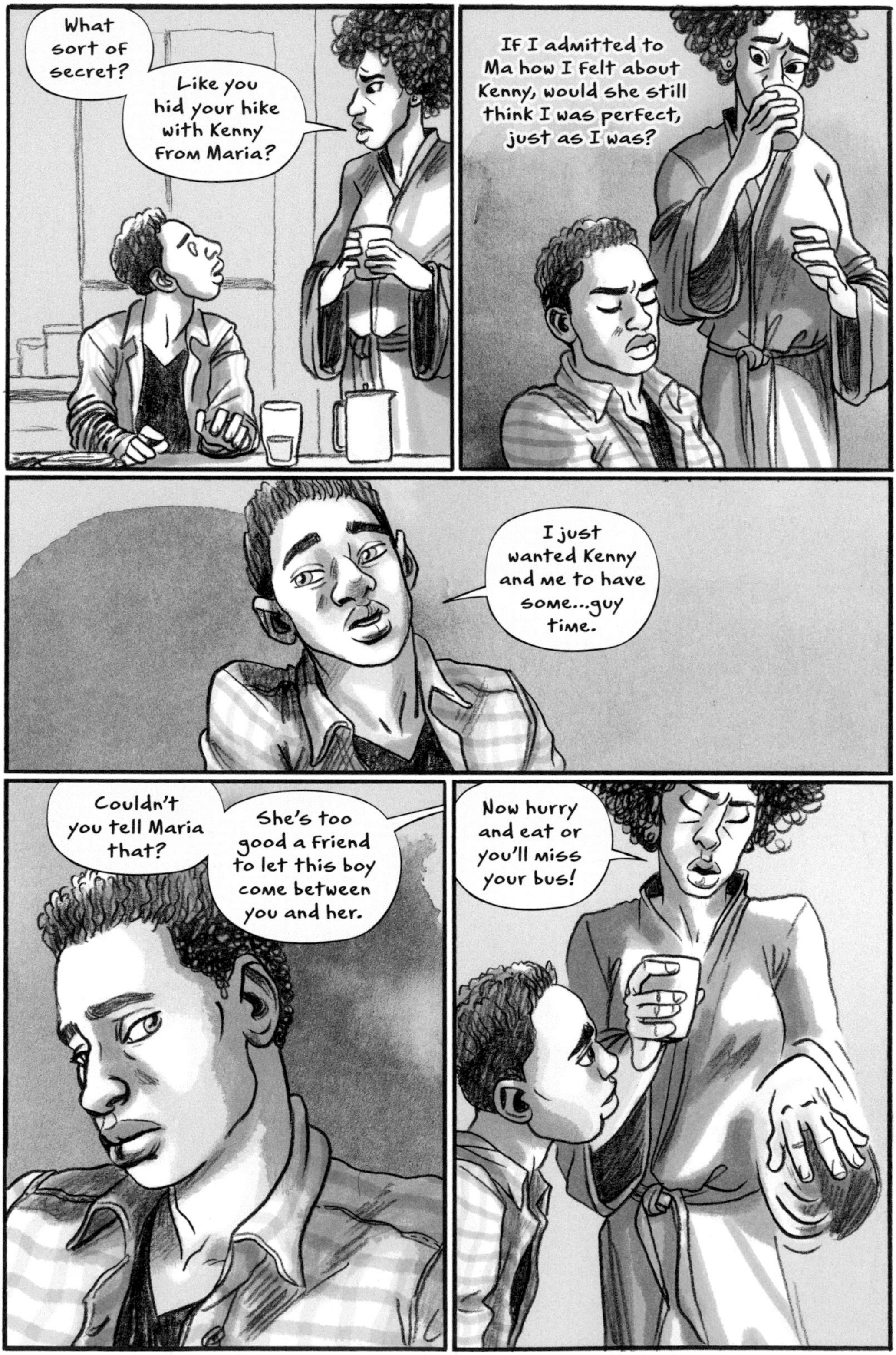
What sort of secret?
Like you hid your hike with Kenny from Maria?
If I admitted to Ma how I felt about Kenny, would she still think I was perfect, just as I was?
I just wanted Kenny and me to have some...guy time.
Couldn't you tell Maria that?
She's too good a friend to let this boy come between you and her.
Now hurry and eat or you'll miss your bus!

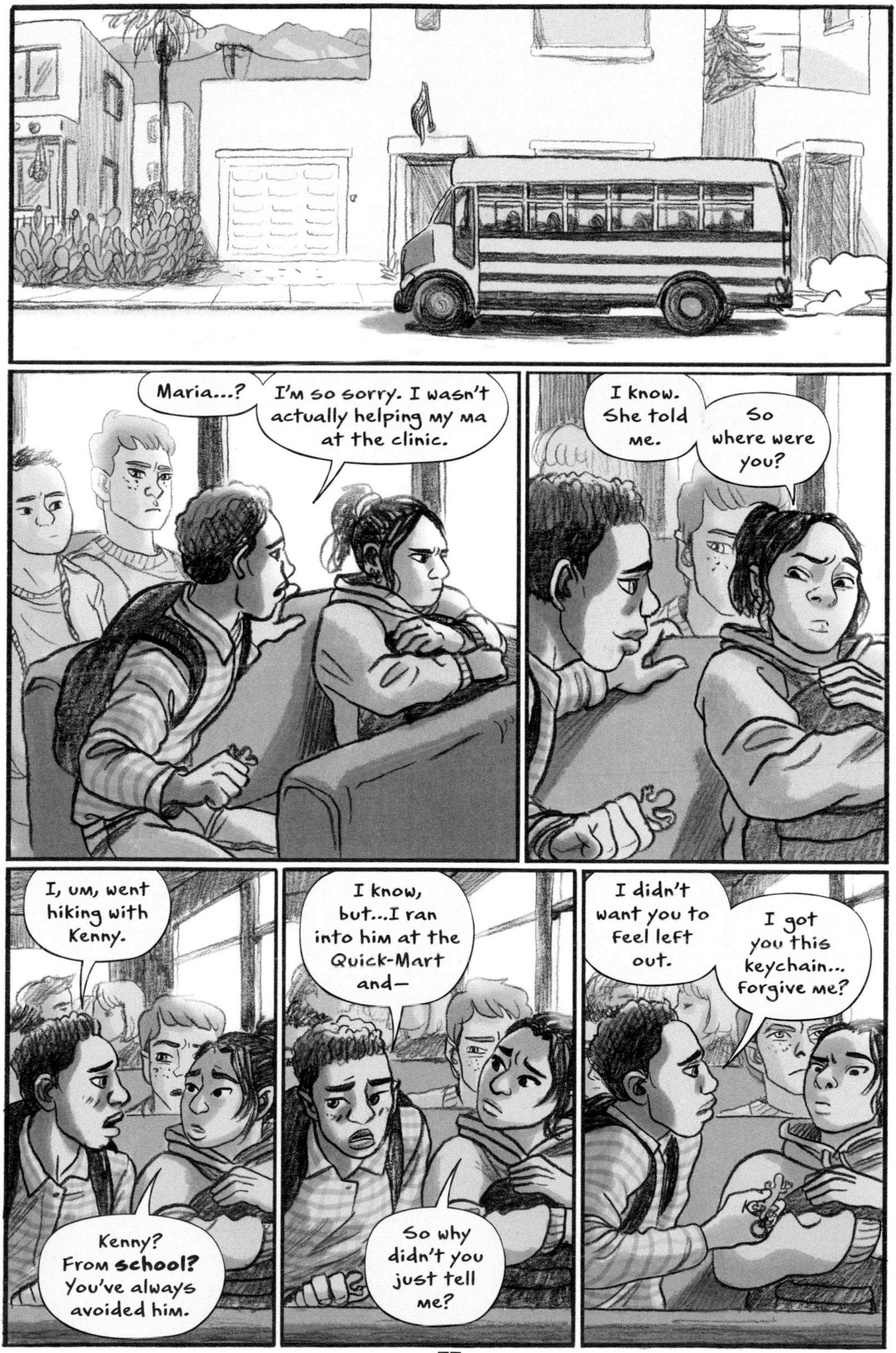
Maria...?
I'm so sorry. I wasn't actually helping my ma at the clinic.
I know. She told me.
So where were you?
I, um, went hiking with Kenny.
Kenny? From **school?** You've always avoided him.
I know, but...I ran into him at the Quick-Mart and—
So why didn't you just tell me?
I didn't want you to feel left out.
I got you this keychain... Forgive me?

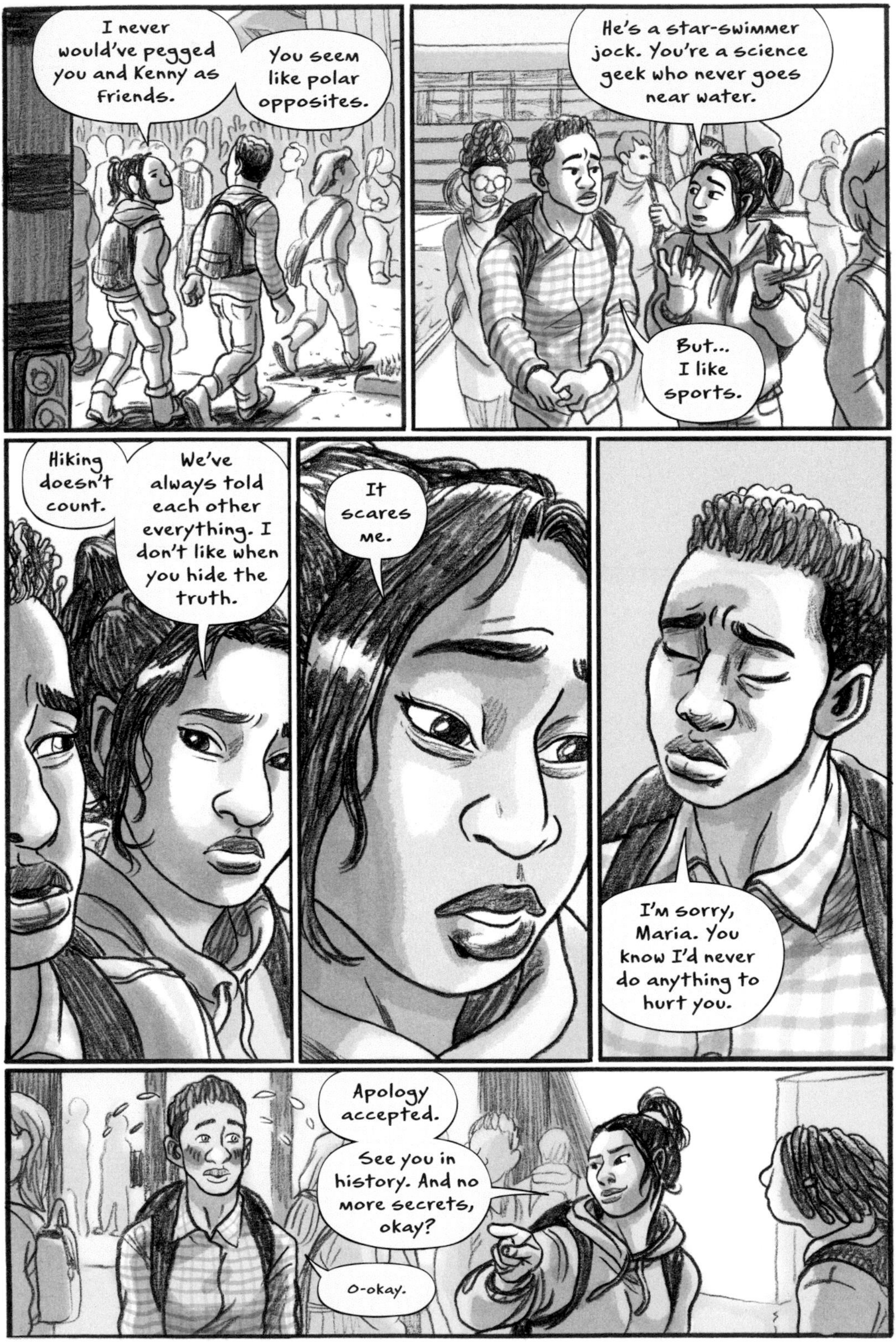
I never would've pegged you and Kenny as friends.
You seem like polar opposites.
He's a star-swimmer jock. You're a science geek who never goes near water.
But... I like sports.
Hiking doesn't count.
We've always told each other everything. I don't like when you hide the truth.
It scares me.
I'm sorry, Maria. You know I'd never do anything to hurt you.
Apology accepted.
See you in history. And no more secrets, okay?
O-okay.

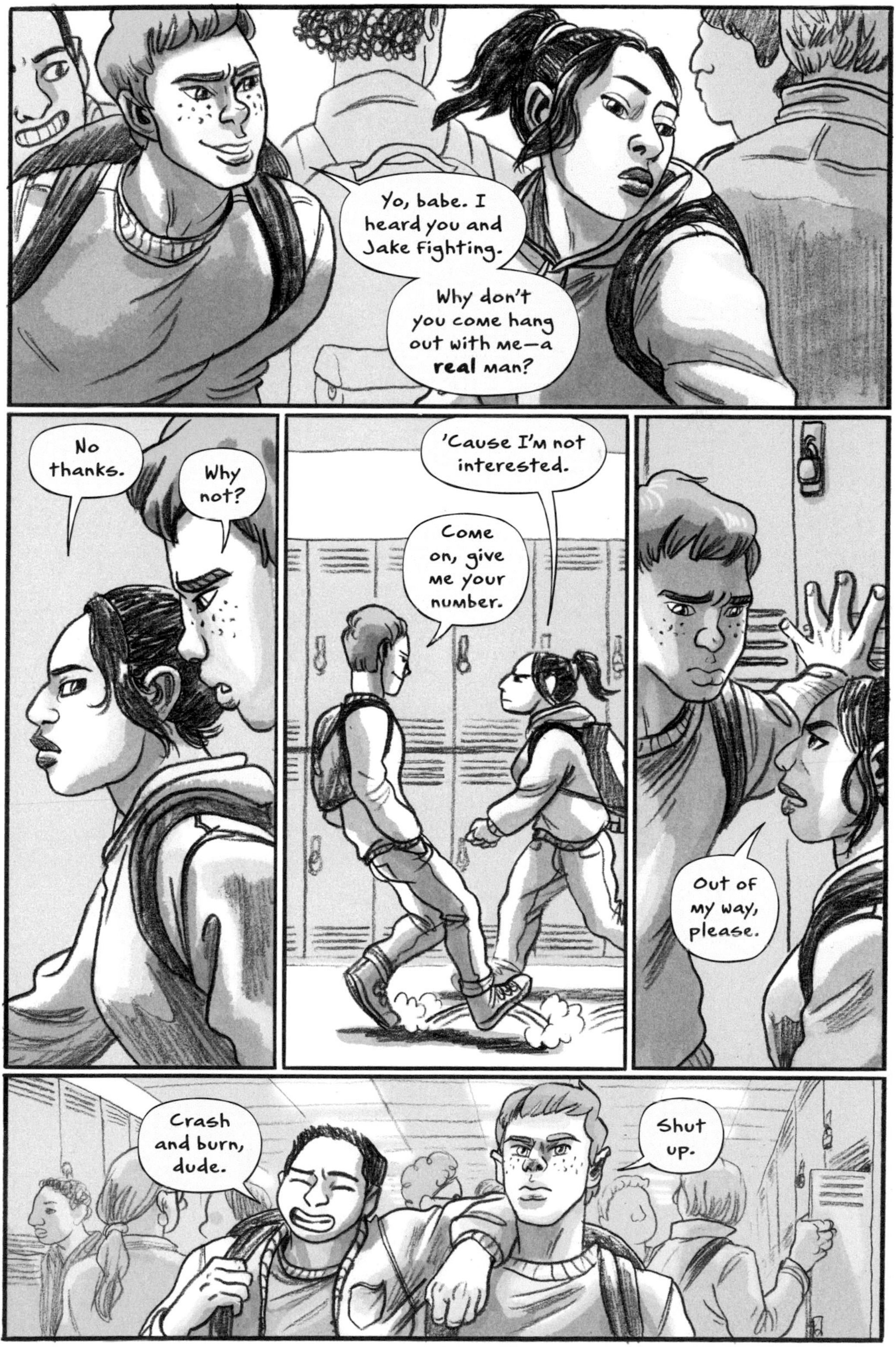
Yo, babe. I heard you and Jake fighting.
Why don't you come hang out with me—a **real** man?
No thanks.
Why not?
'Cause I'm not interested.
Come on, give me your number.
Out of my way, please.
Crash and burn, dude.
Shut up.

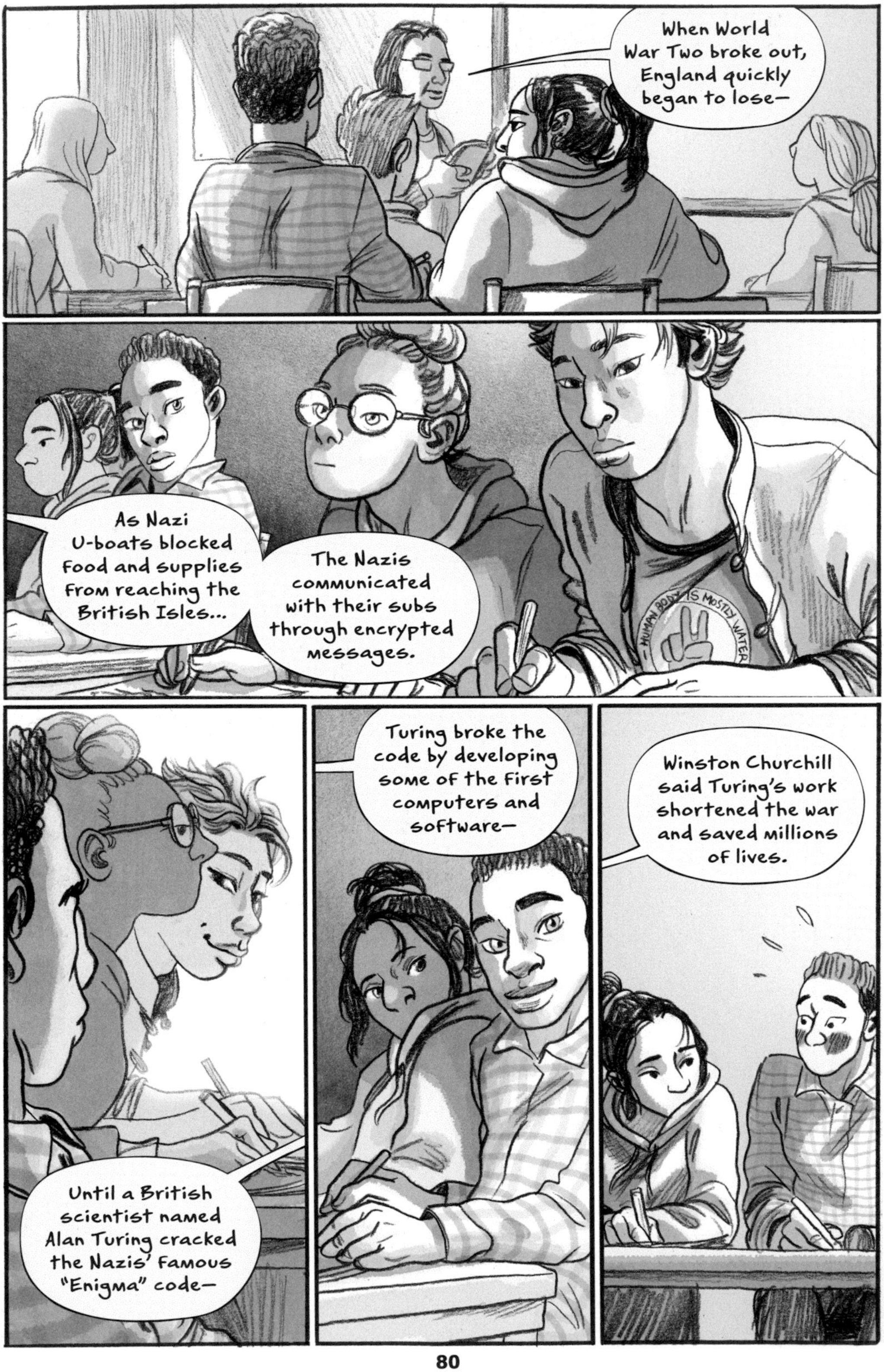
When World War Two broke out, England quickly began to lose—
As Nazi U-boats blocked food and supplies from reaching the British Isles...
The Nazis communicated with their subs through encrypted messages.
HUMAN BODY IS MOSTLY WATER
Until a British scientist named Alan Turing cracked the Nazis' famous "Enigma" code—
Turing broke the code by developing some of the first computers and software—
Winston Churchill said Turing's work shortened the war and saved millions of lives.

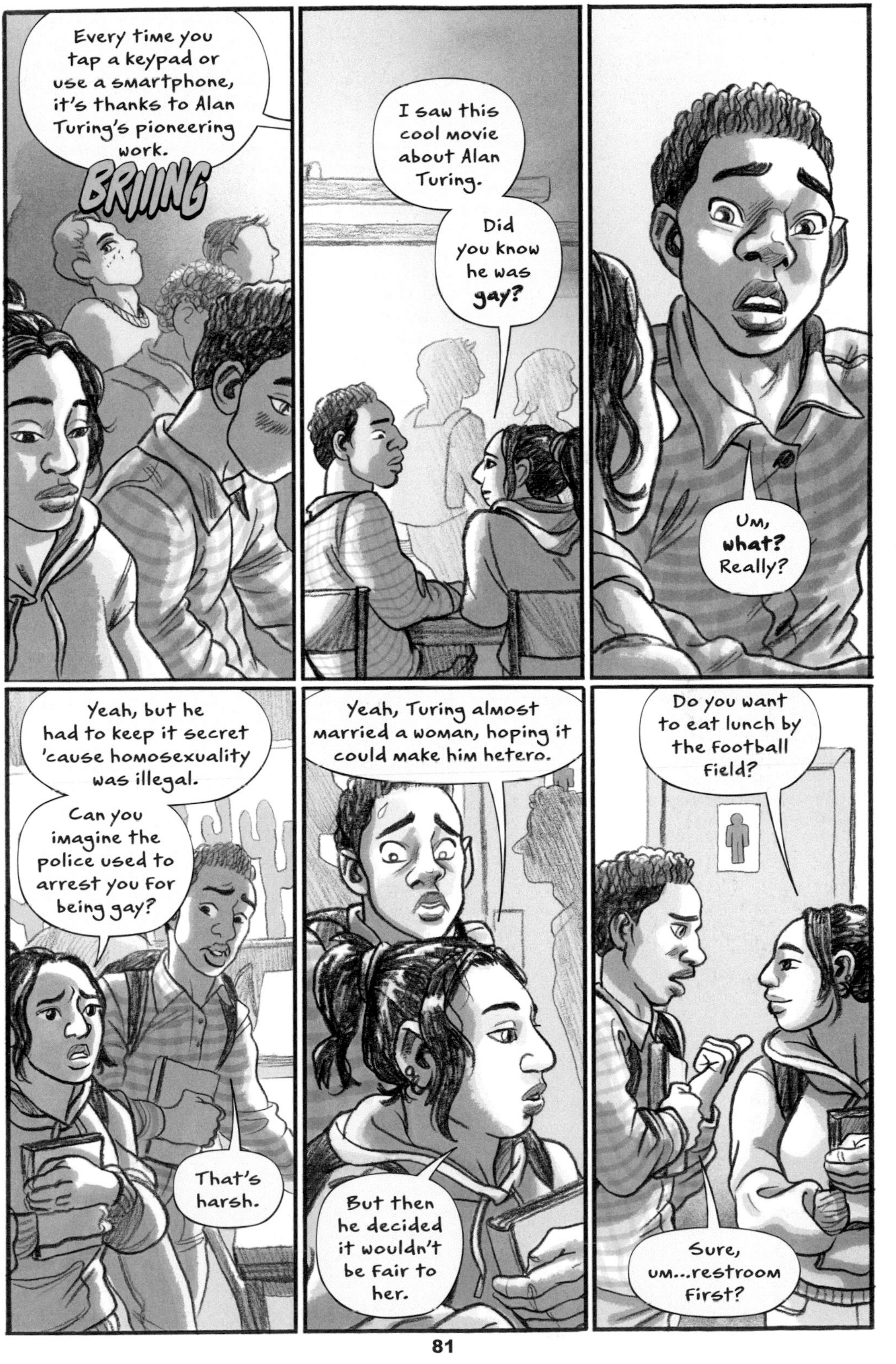

Every time you tap a keypad or use a smartphone, it's thanks to Alan Turing's pioneering work.
BRIIING
I saw this cool movie about Alan Turing.
Did you know he was gay?
Um, what? Really?
Yeah, but he had to keep it secret 'cause homosexuality was illegal.
Can you imagine the police used to arrest you for being gay?
That's harsh.
Yeah, Turing almost married a woman, hoping it could make him hetero.
But then he decided it wouldn't be fair to her.
Do you want to eat lunch by the football field?
Sure, um...restroom first?

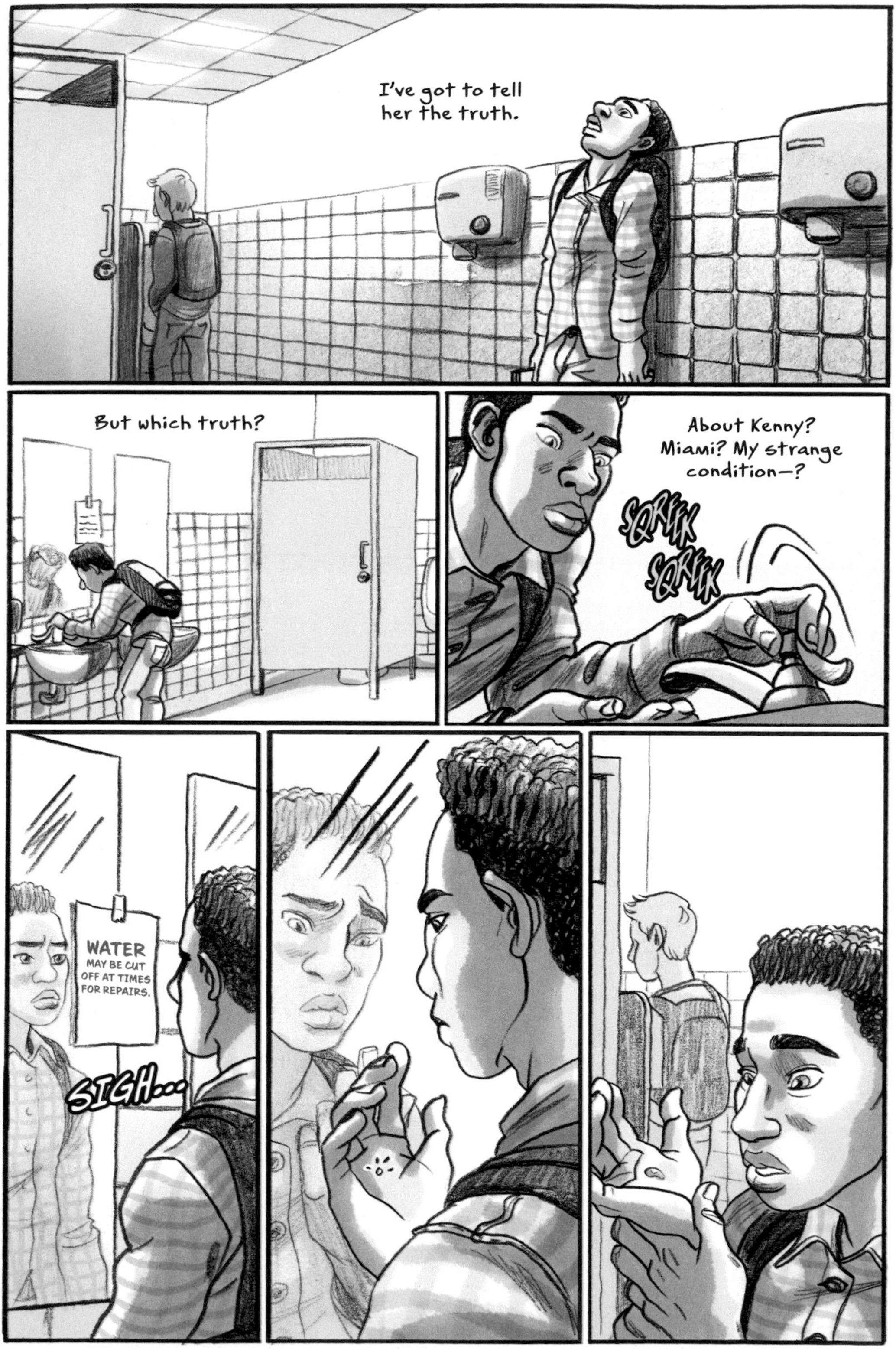
I've got to tell her the truth.
But which truth?
About Kenny? Miami? My strange condition—?
SQRKK
SQRKK
WATER MAY BE CUT OFF AT TIMES FOR REPAIRS.
SIGH...

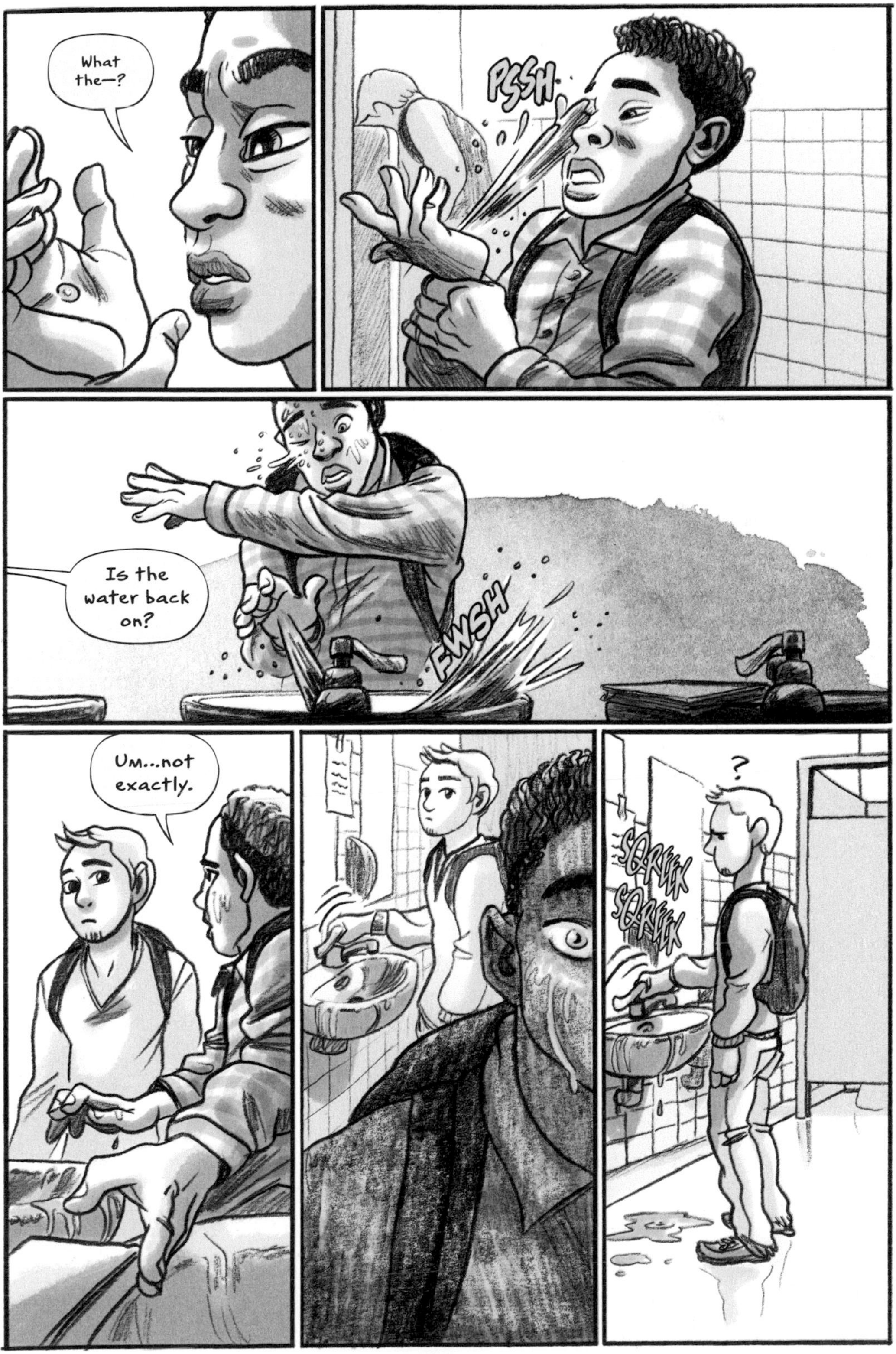

What the—?
PSSH
Is the water back on?
FWSH
Um...not exactly.
?
SQRUCK
SQRUCK

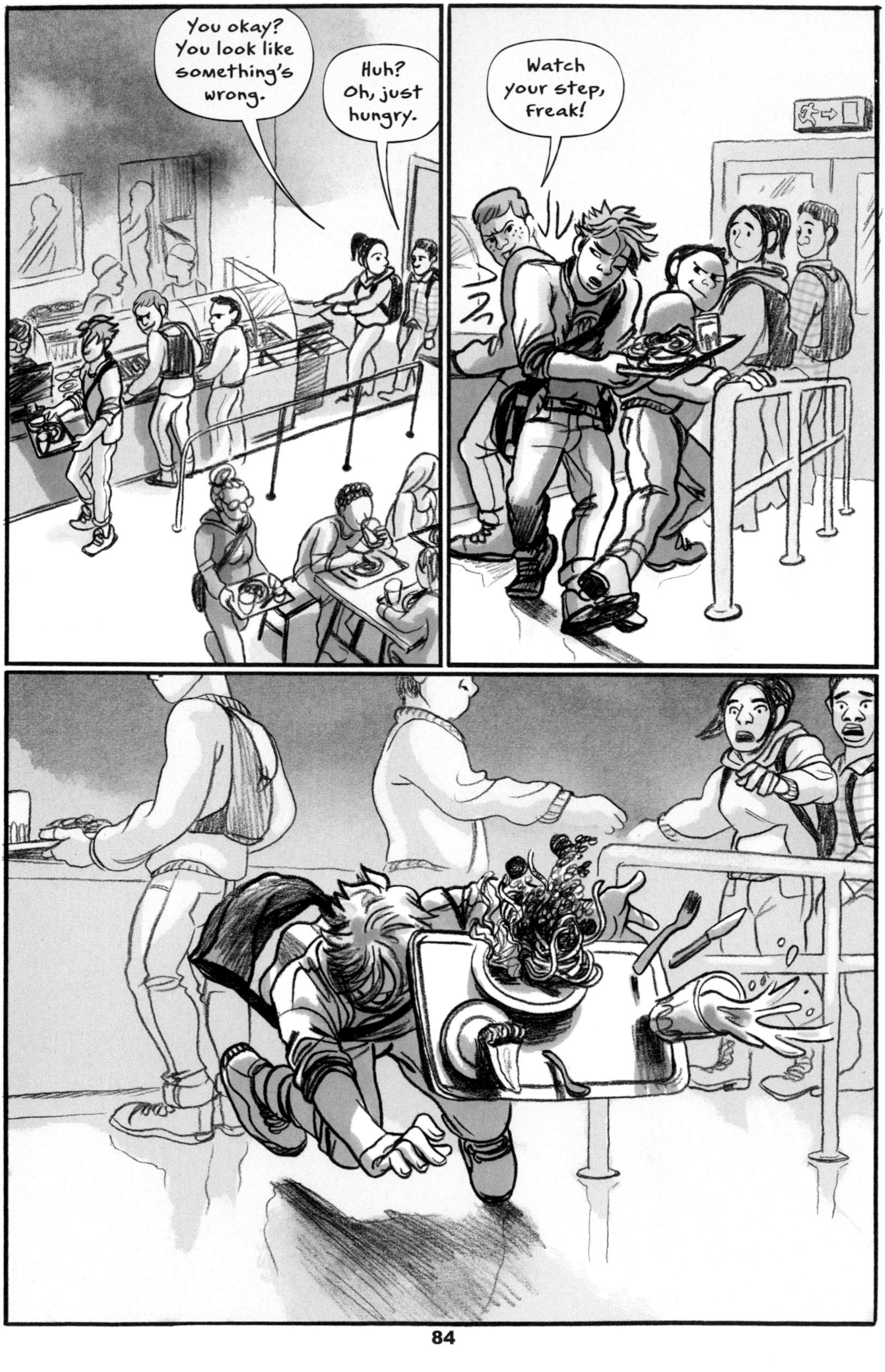

You okay? You look like something's wrong.
Huh? Oh, just hungry.
Watch your step, Freak!

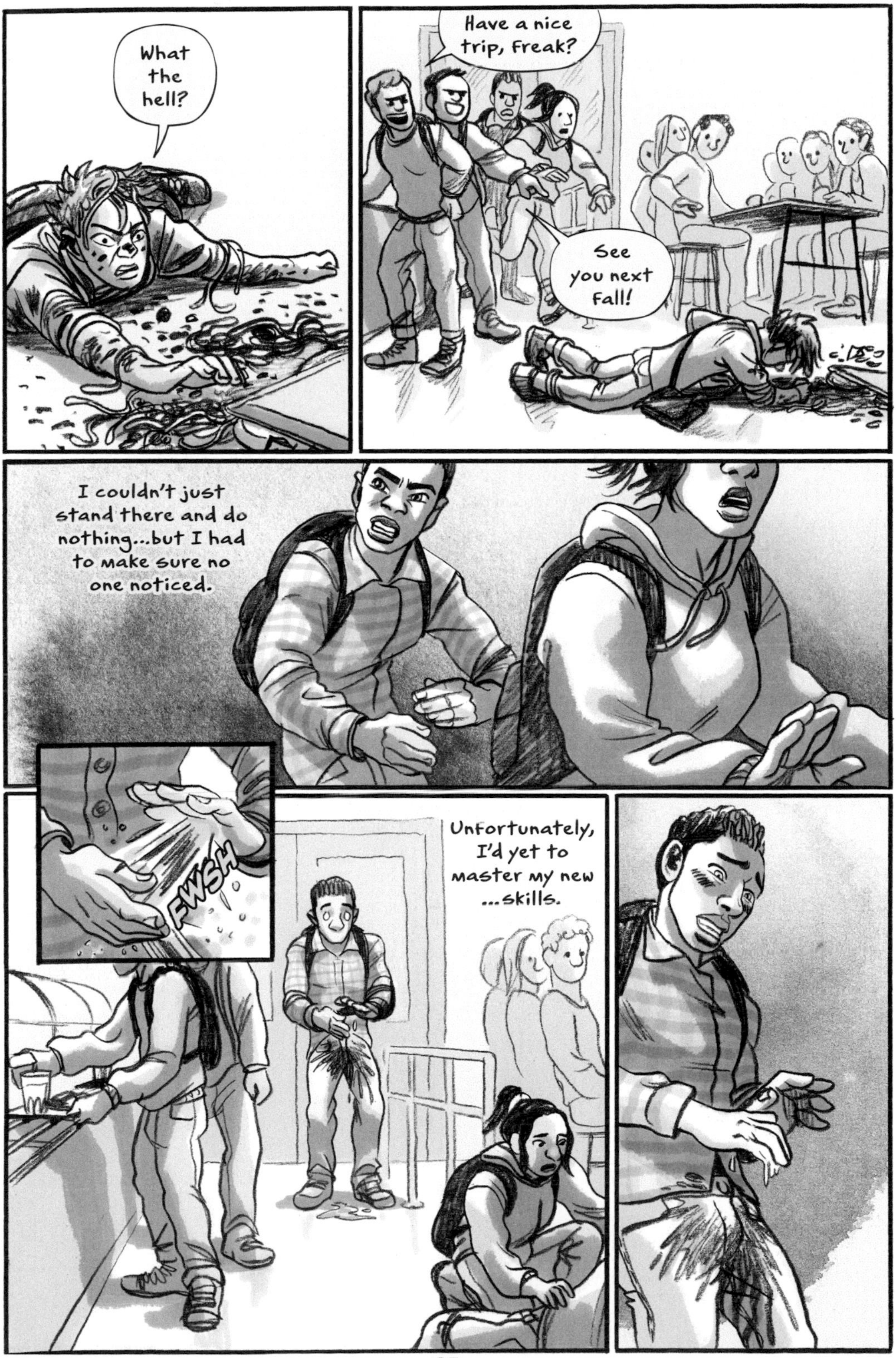
What the hell?
Have a nice trip, freak?
See you next fall!
I couldn't just stand there and do nothing...but I had to make sure no one noticed.
FWSH
Unfortunately, I'd yet to master my new ...skills.

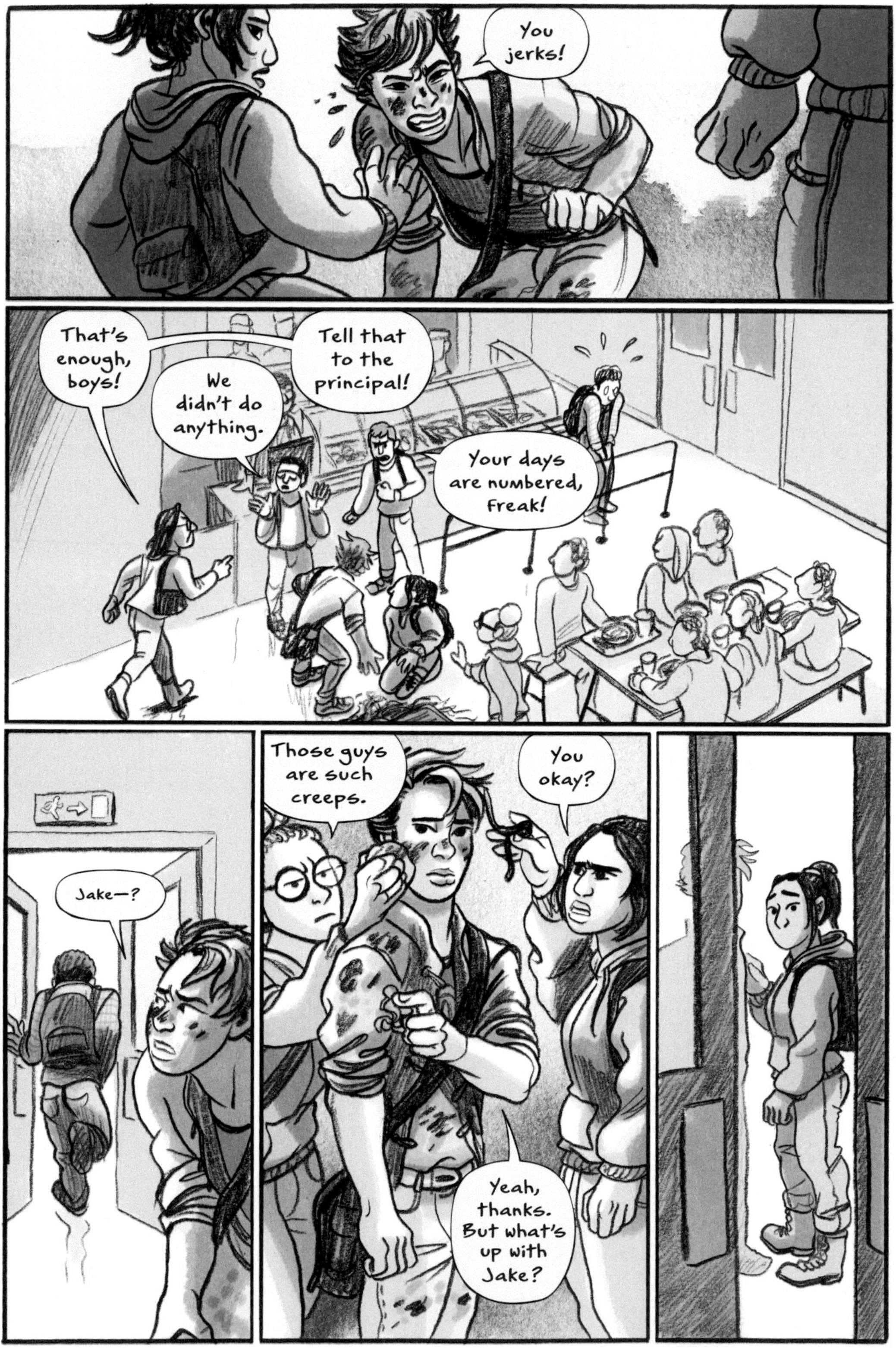
You jerks!
That's enough, boys!
Tell that to the principal!
We didn't do anything.
Your days are numbered, Freak!
Jake—?
Those guys are such creeps.
You okay?
Yeah, thanks. But what's up with Jake?

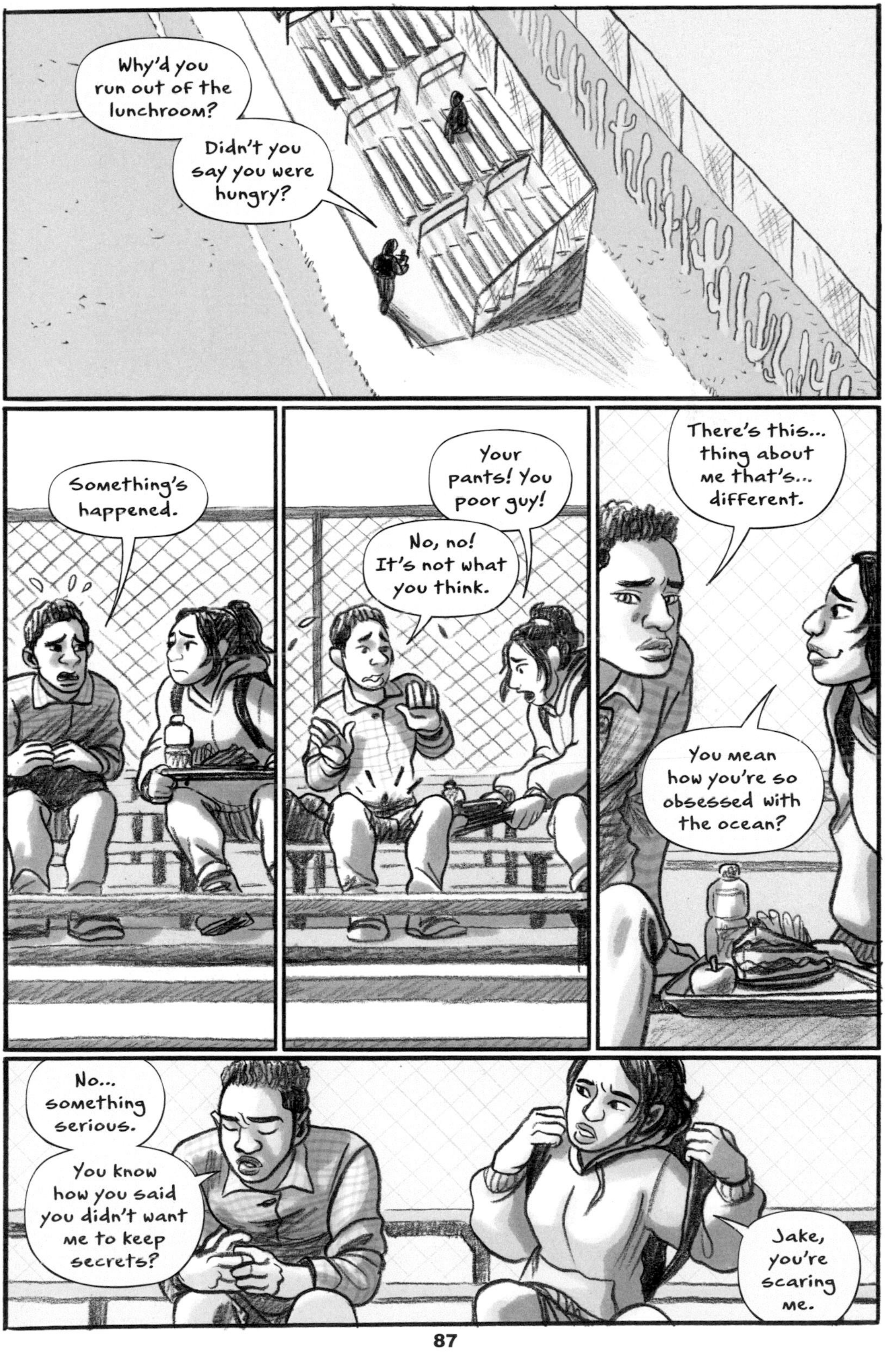

Why'd you run out of the lunchroom?
Didn't you say you were hungry?
Something's happened.
Your pants! You poor guy!
No, no! It's not what you think.
There's this... thing about me that's... different.
You mean how you're so obsessed with the ocean?
No... something serious.
You know how you said you didn't want me to keep secrets?
Jake, you're scaring me.

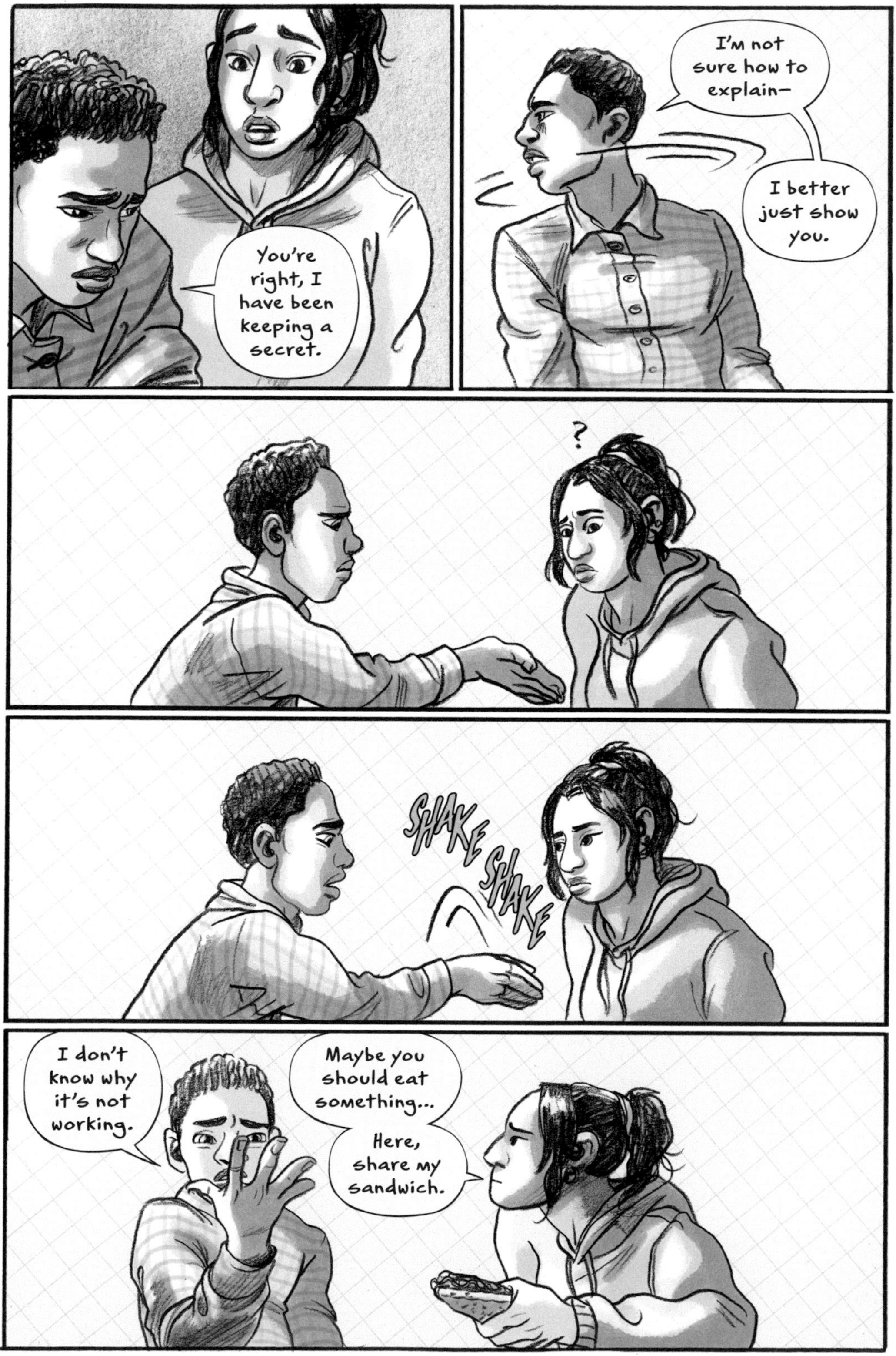
You're right, I have been keeping a secret.
I'm not sure how to explain—
I better just show you.
?
SHAKE SHAKE
I don't know why it's not working.
Maybe you should eat something...
Here, share my sandwich.

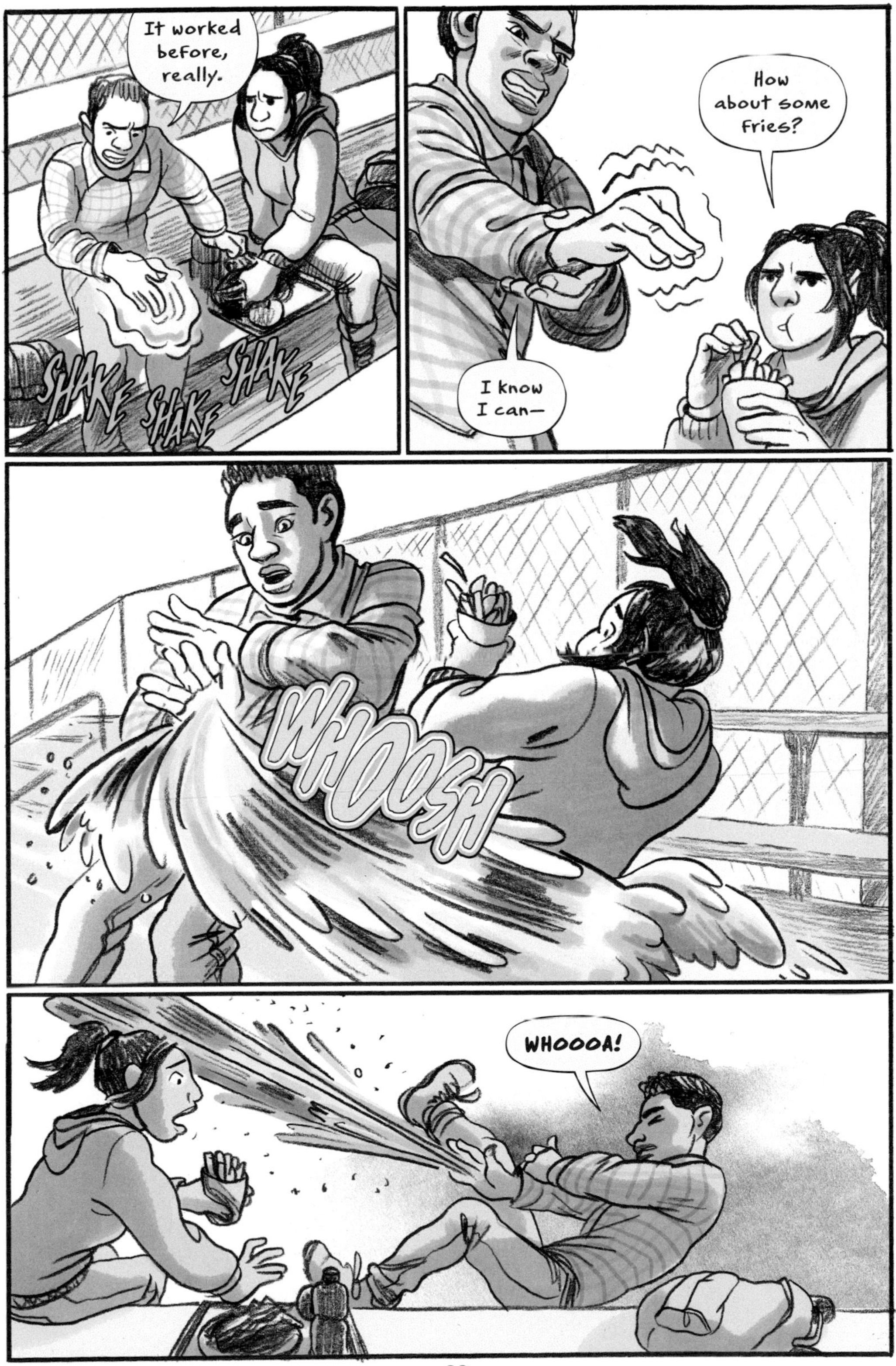
It worked before, really.
SHAKE SHAKE SHAKE
How about some fries?
I know I can—
WHOOSH
WHOOOA!

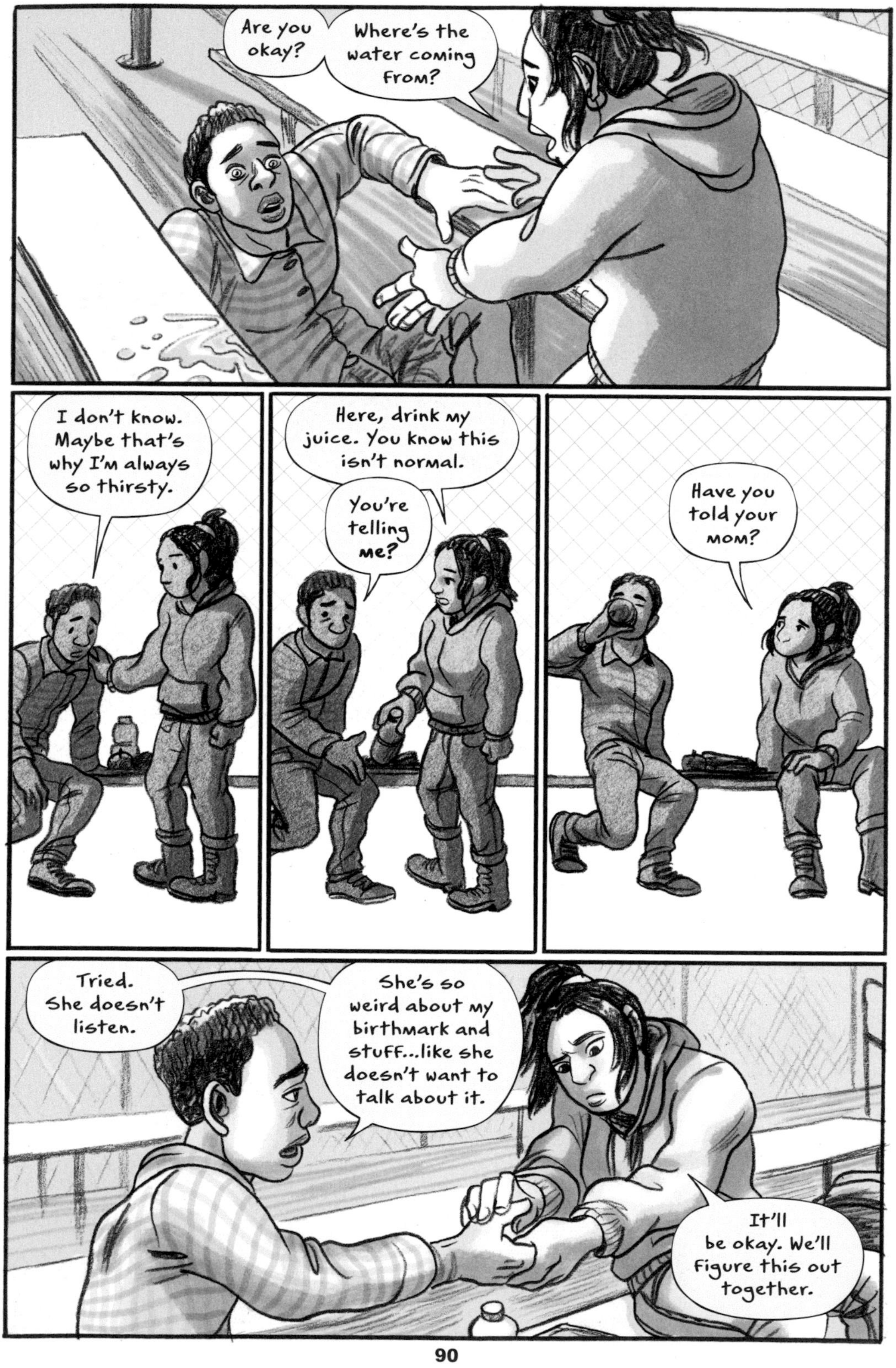
Are you okay?
Where's the water coming from?
I don't know. Maybe that's why I'm always so thirsty.
Here, drink my juice. You know this isn't normal.
You're telling me?
Have you told your mom?
Tried. She doesn't listen.
She's so weird about my birthmark and stuff...like she doesn't want to talk about it.
It'll be okay. We'll figure this out together.

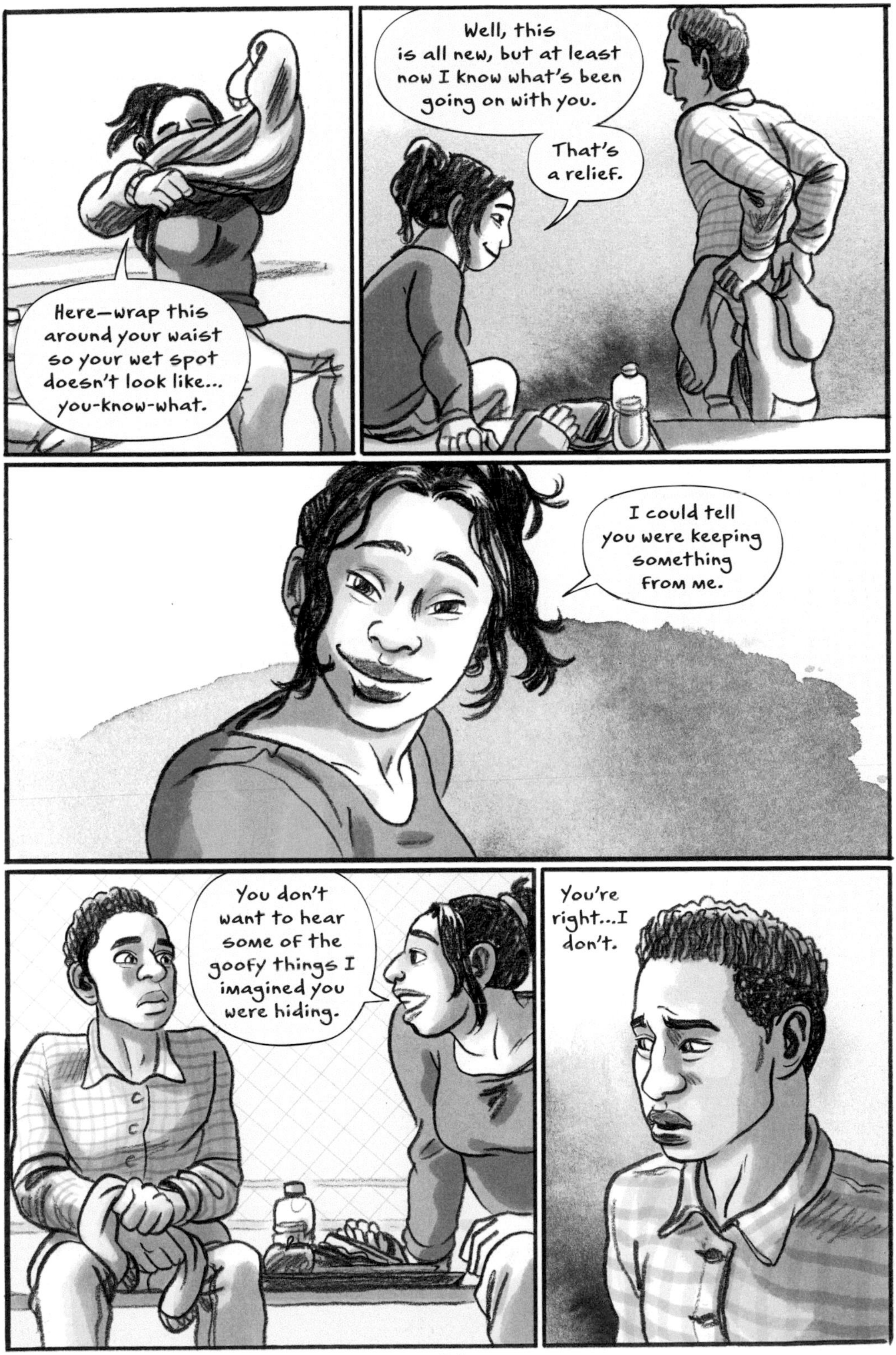
Here—wrap this around your waist so your wet spot doesn't look like... you-know-what.
Well, this is all new, but at least now I know what's been going on with you.
That's a relief.
I could tell you were keeping something from me.
You don't want to hear some of the goofy things I imagined you were hiding.
You're right...I don't.

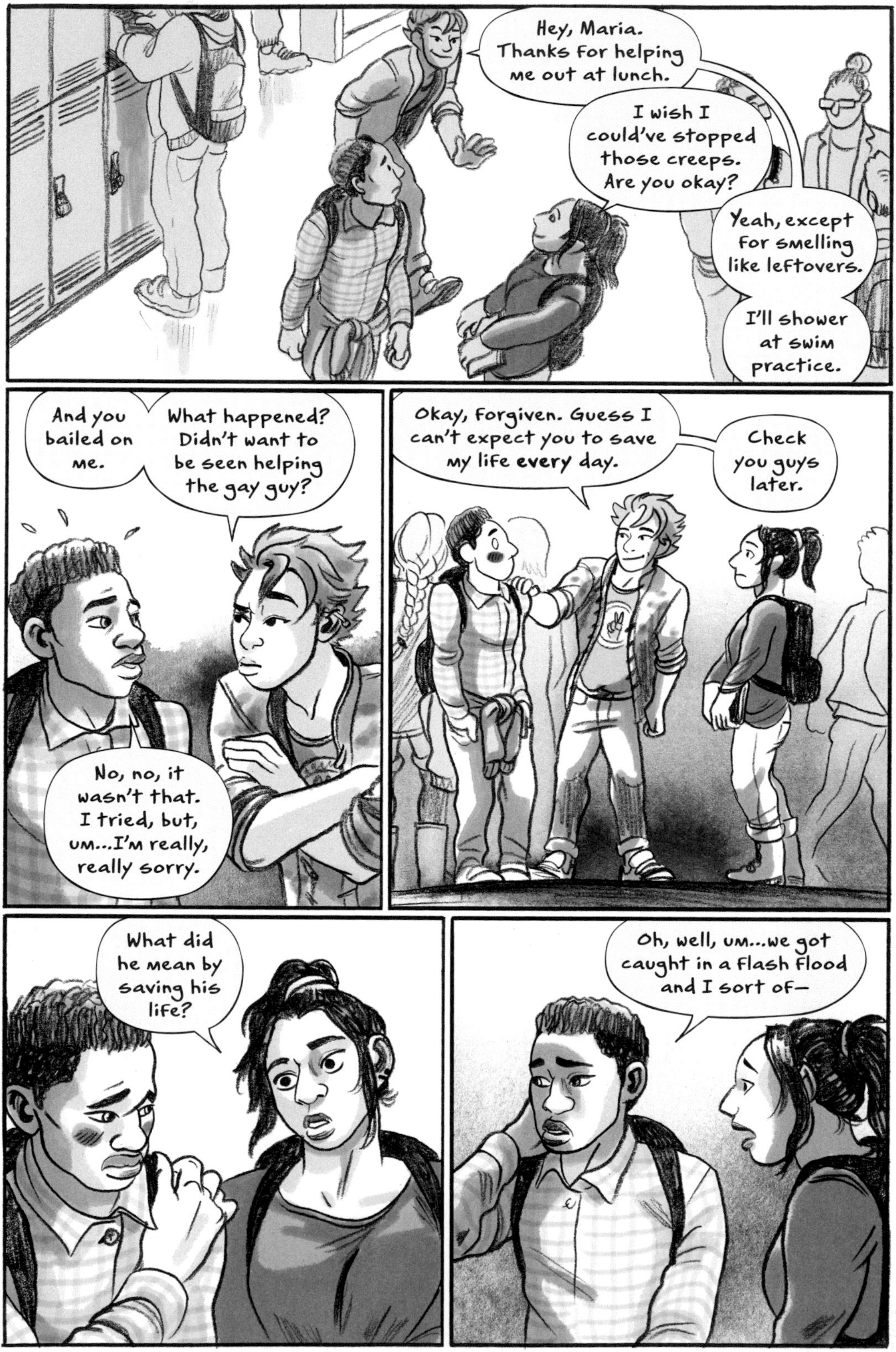
Hey, Maria. Thanks for helping me out at lunch.
I wish I could've stopped those creeps. Are you okay?
Yeah, except for smelling like leftovers.
I'll shower at swim practice.
And you bailed on me.
What happened? Didn't want to be seen helping the gay guy?
No, no, it wasn't that. I tried, but, um...I'm really, really sorry.
Okay, forgiven. Guess I can't expect you to save my life **every** day.
Check you guys later.
What did he mean by saving his life?
Oh, well, um...we got caught in a flash flood and I sort of—

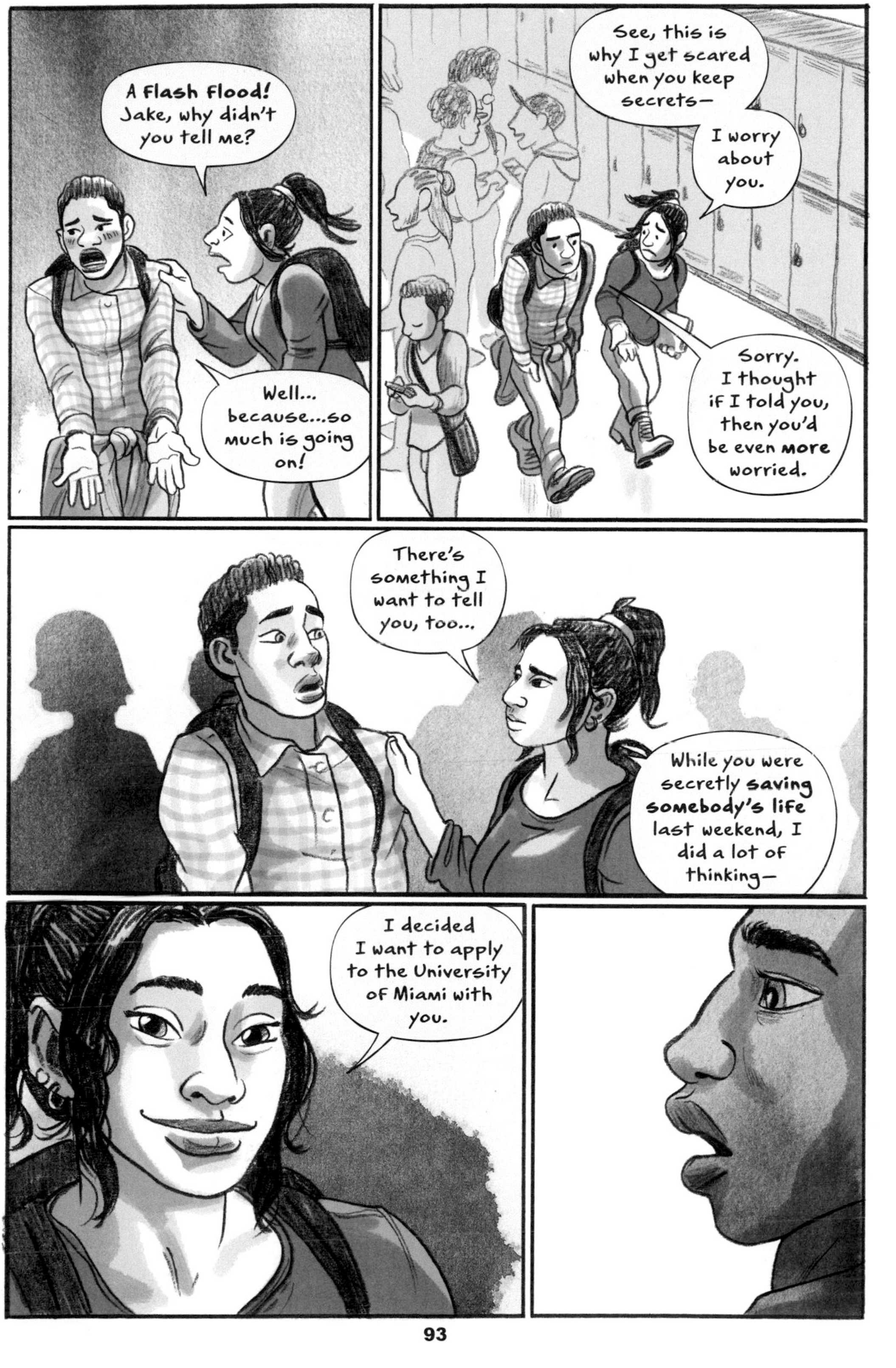
A Flash Flood! Jake, why didn't you tell me?
Well... because...so much is going on!
See, this is why I get scared when you keep secrets—
I worry about you.
Sorry. I thought if I told you, then you'd be even more worried.
There's something I want to tell you, too...
While you were secretly saving somebody's life last weekend, I did a lot of thinking—
I decided I want to apply to the University of Miami with you.

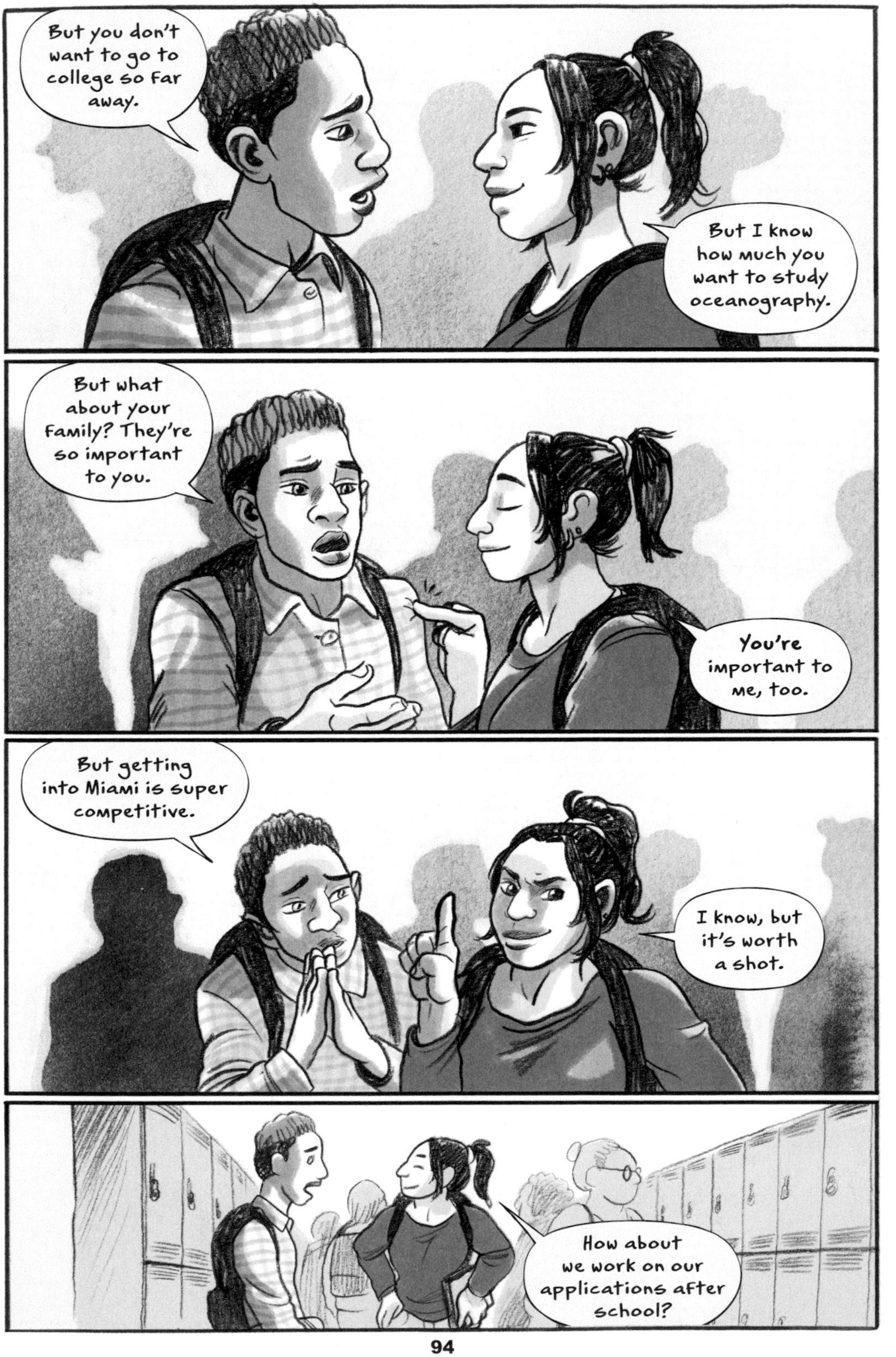

But you don't want to go to college so far away.
But I know how much you want to study oceanography.
But what about your family? They're so important to you.
You're important to me, too.
But getting into Miami is super competitive.
I know, but it's worth a shot.
How about we work on our applications after school?

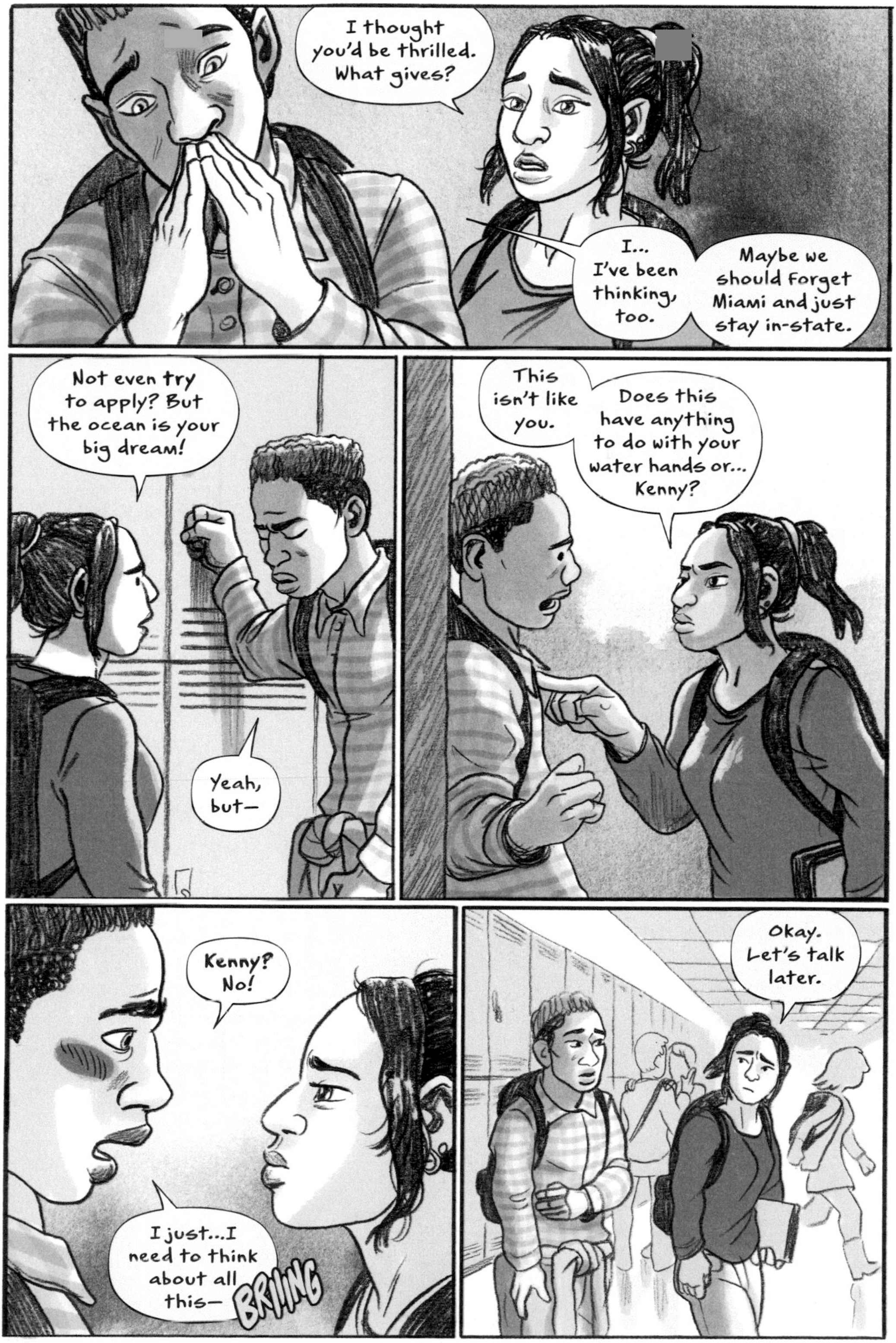
I thought you'd be thrilled. What gives?
I... I've been thinking, too.
Maybe we should forget Miami and just stay in-state.
Not even try to apply? But the ocean is your big dream!
Yeah, but—
This isn't like you.
Does this have anything to do with your water hands or... Kenny?
Kenny? No!
I just...I need to think about all this—
BRIIING
Okay. Let's talk later.

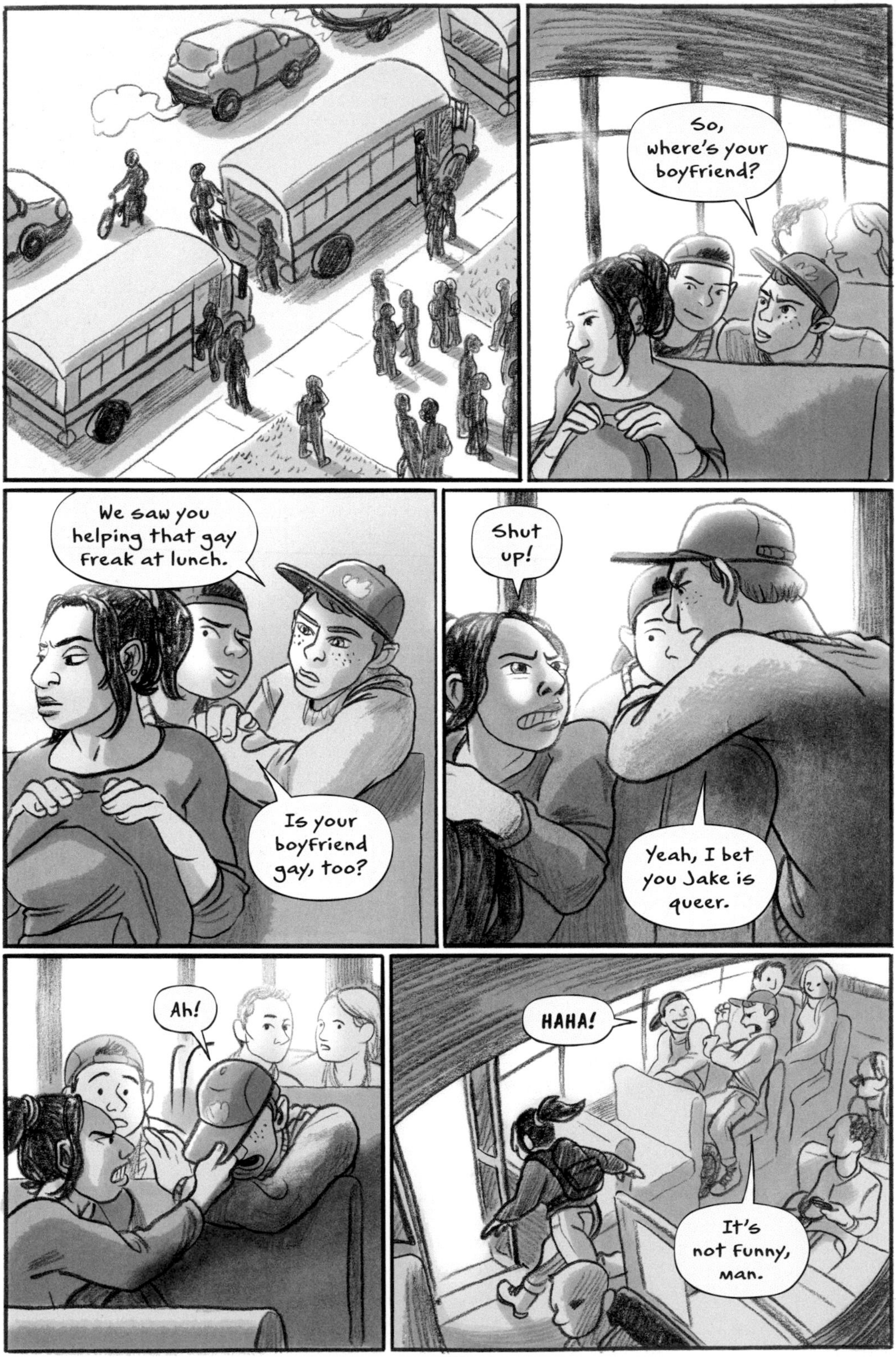
So, where's your boyfriend?
We saw you helping that gay freak at lunch.
Is your boyfriend gay, too?
Shut up!
Yeah, I bet you Jake is queer.
Ah!
HAHA!
It's not funny, man.

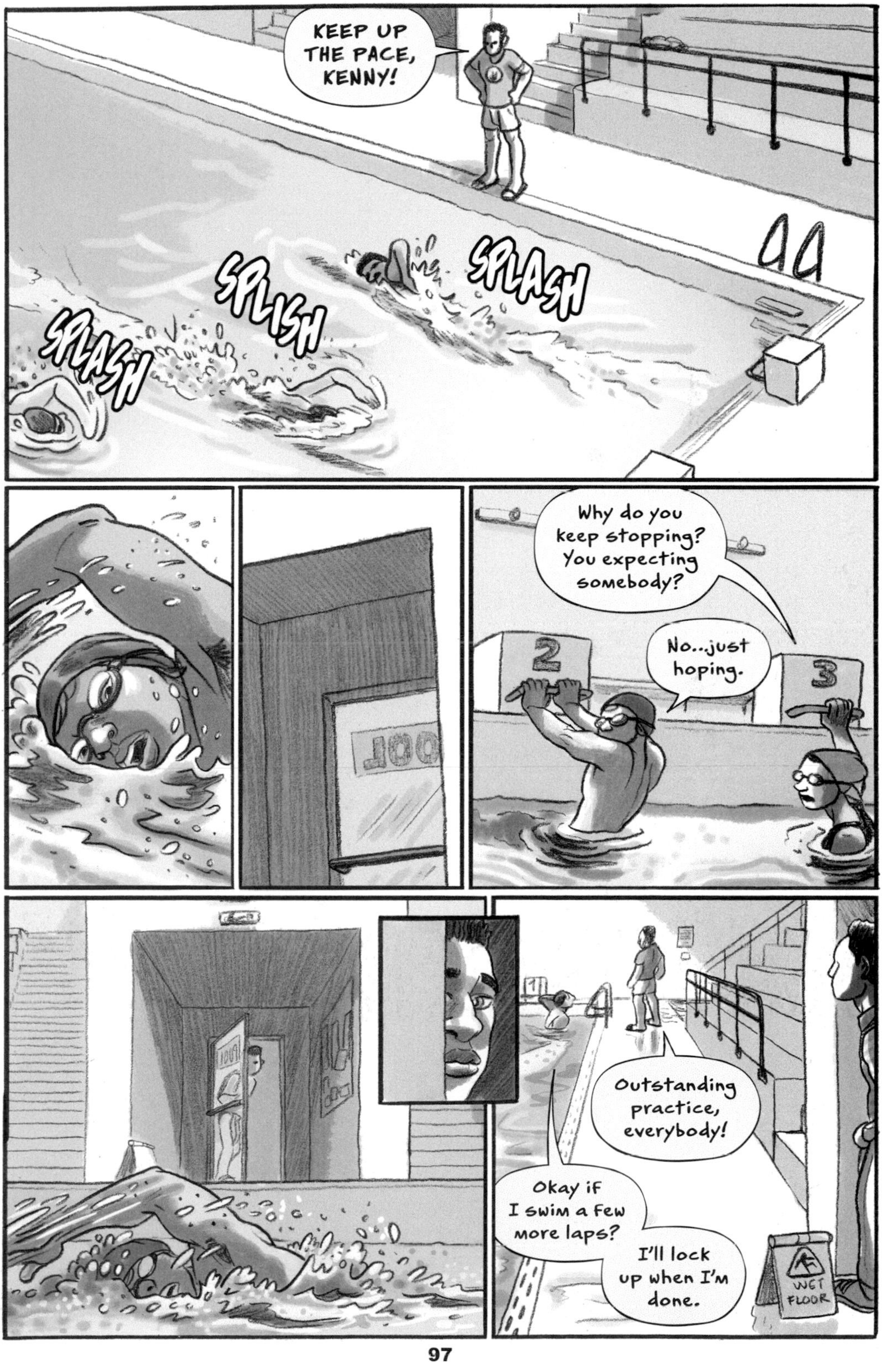
KEEP UP THE PACE, KENNY!
SPLASH
SPLISH
SPLASH
Why do you keep stopping? You expecting somebody?
No...just hoping.
Outstanding practice, everybody!
Okay if I swim a few more laps?
I'll lock up when I'm done.
WET FLOOR

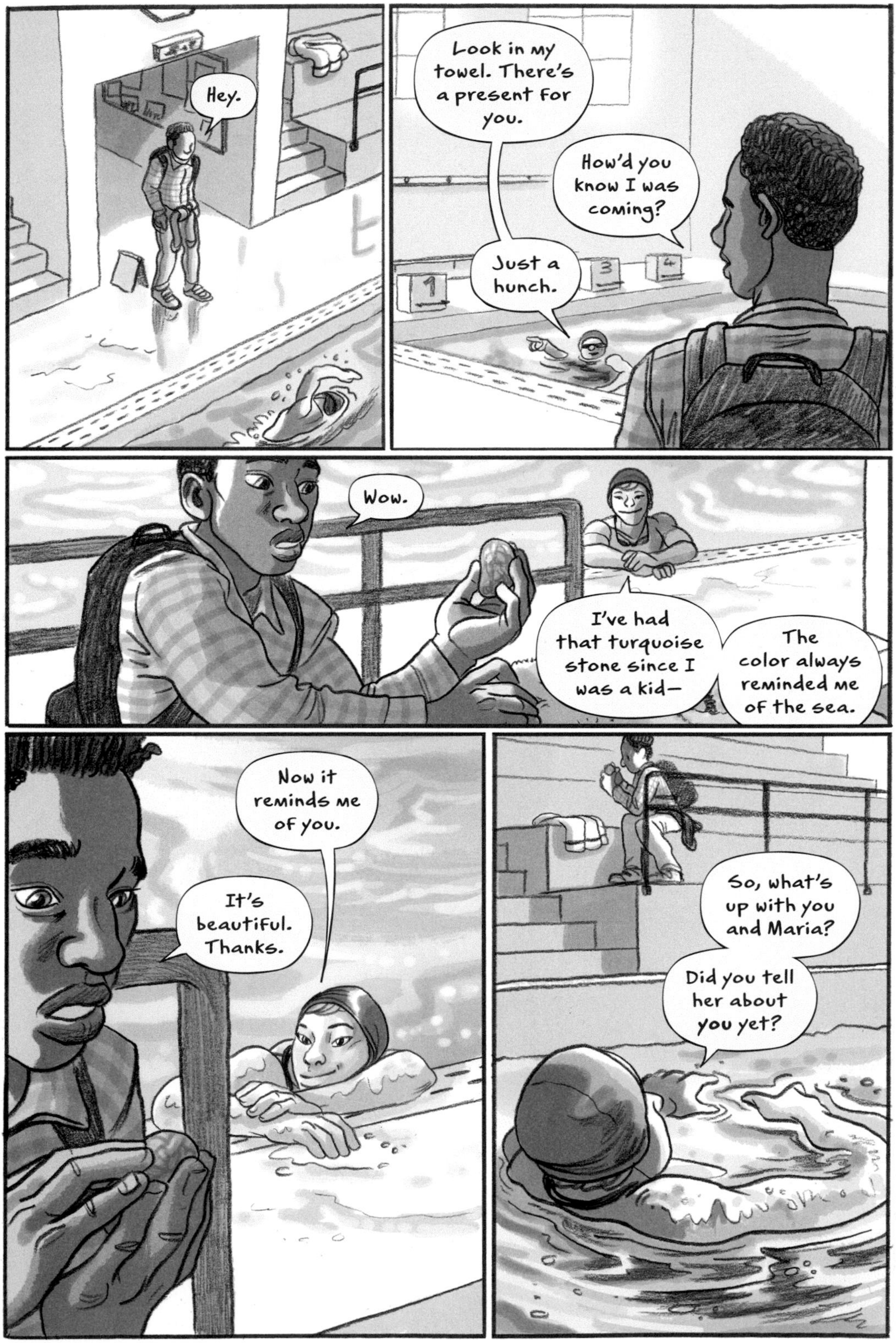
Hey.
Look in my towel. There's a present for you.
How'd you know I was coming?
Just a hunch.
Wow.
I've had that turquoise stone since I was a kid—
The color always reminded me of the sea.
Now it reminds me of you.
It's beautiful. Thanks.
So, what's up with you and Maria?
Did you tell her about you yet?

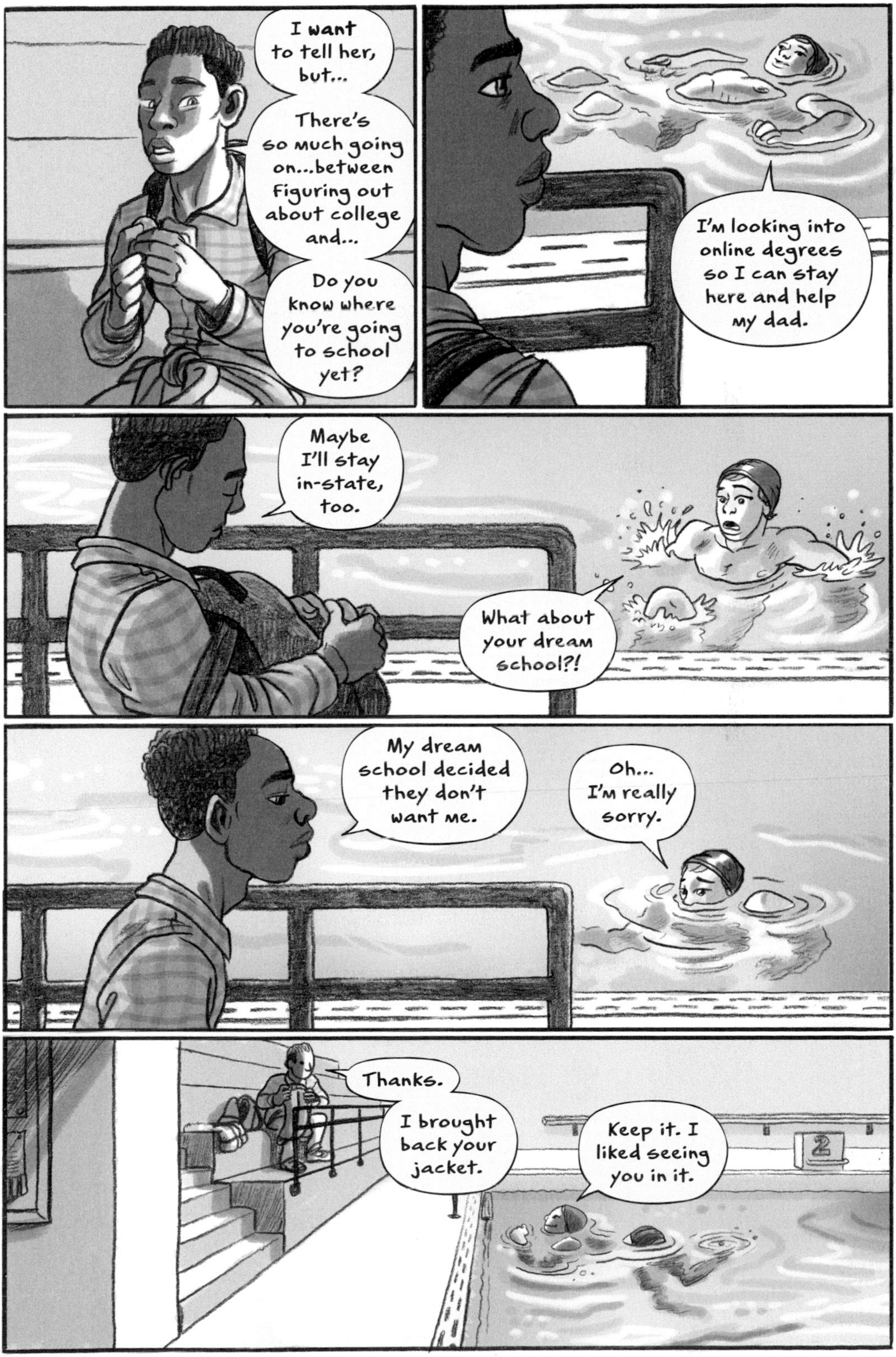
I want to tell her, but...
There's so much going on...between figuring out about college and...
Do you know where you're going to school yet?
I'm looking into online degrees so I can stay here and help my dad.
Maybe I'll stay in-state, too.
What about your dream school?!
My dream school decided they don't want me.
Oh... I'm really sorry.
Thanks.
I brought back your jacket.
Keep it. I liked seeing you in it.

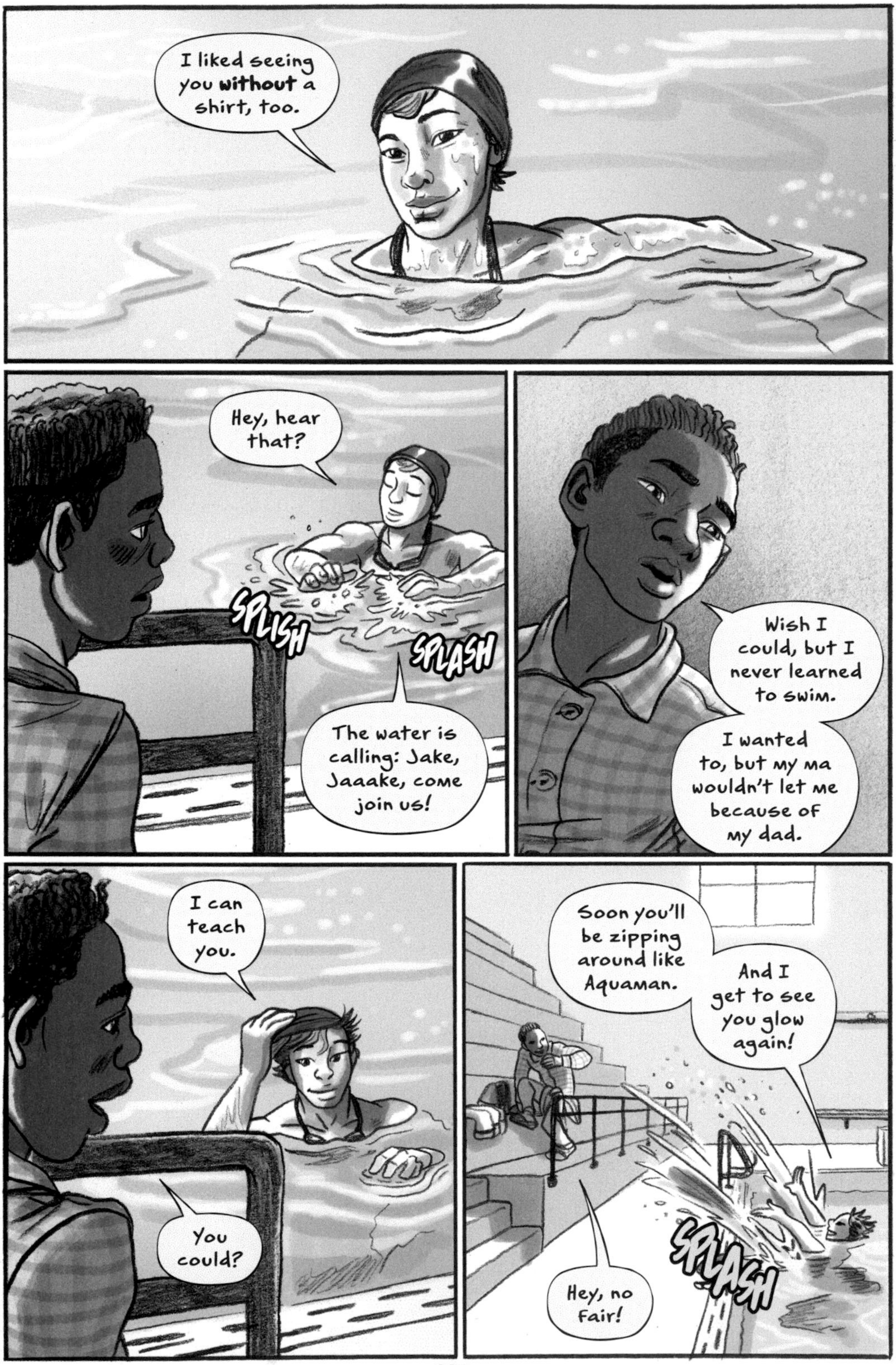
I liked seeing you **without** a shirt, too.
Hey, hear that?
SPLISH
SPLASH
The water is calling: Jake, Jaaake, come join us!
Wish I could, but I never learned to swim.
I wanted to, but my ma wouldn't let me because of my dad.
I can teach you.
You could?
Soon you'll be zipping around like Aquaman.
And I get to see you glow again!
SPLASH
Hey, no fair!

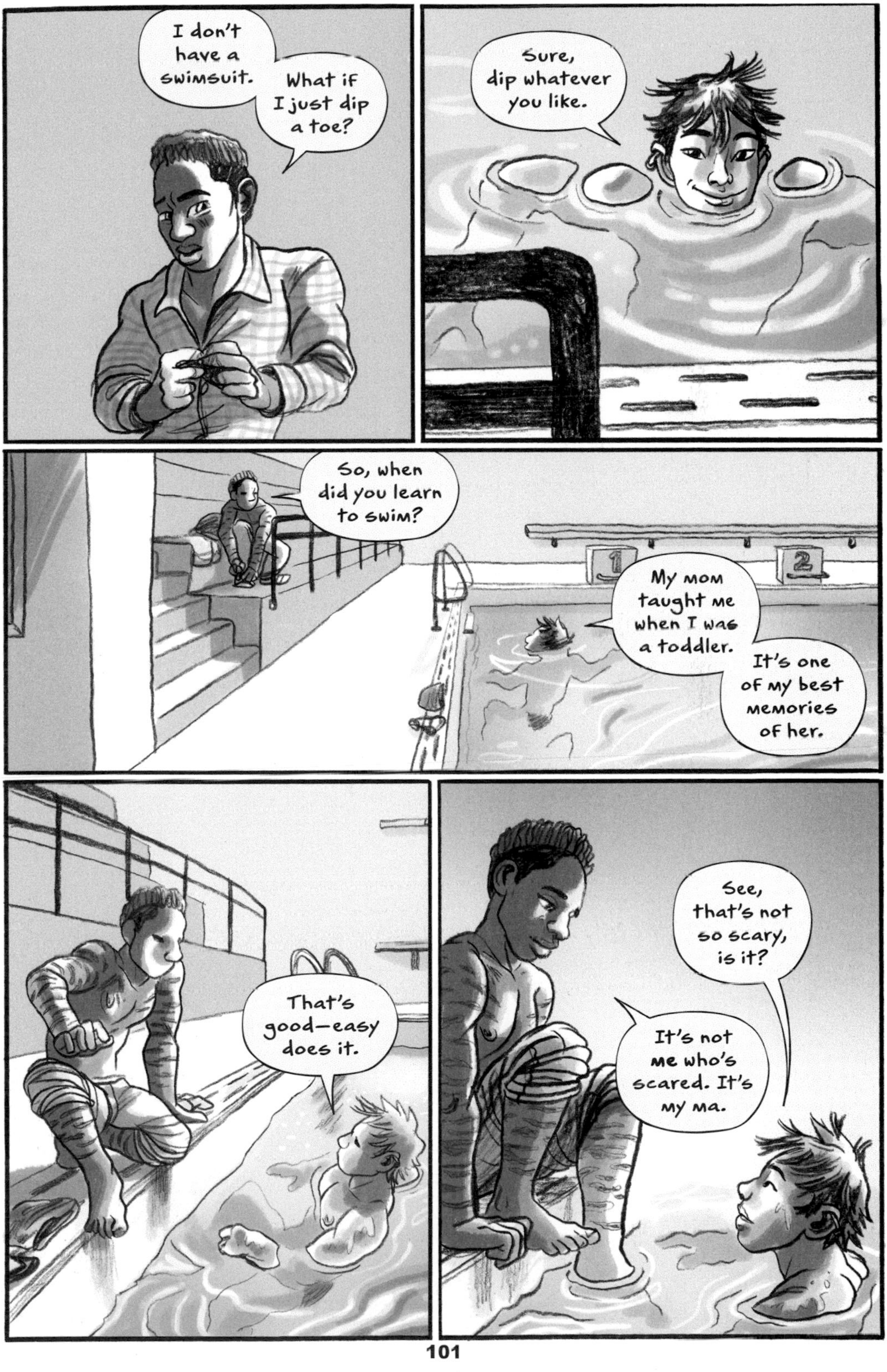
I don't have a swimsuit.
What if I just dip a toe?
Sure, dip whatever you like.
So, when did you learn to swim?
My mom taught me when I was a toddler.
It's one of my best memories of her.
That's good—easy does it.
See, that's not so scary, is it?
It's not me who's scared. It's my ma.

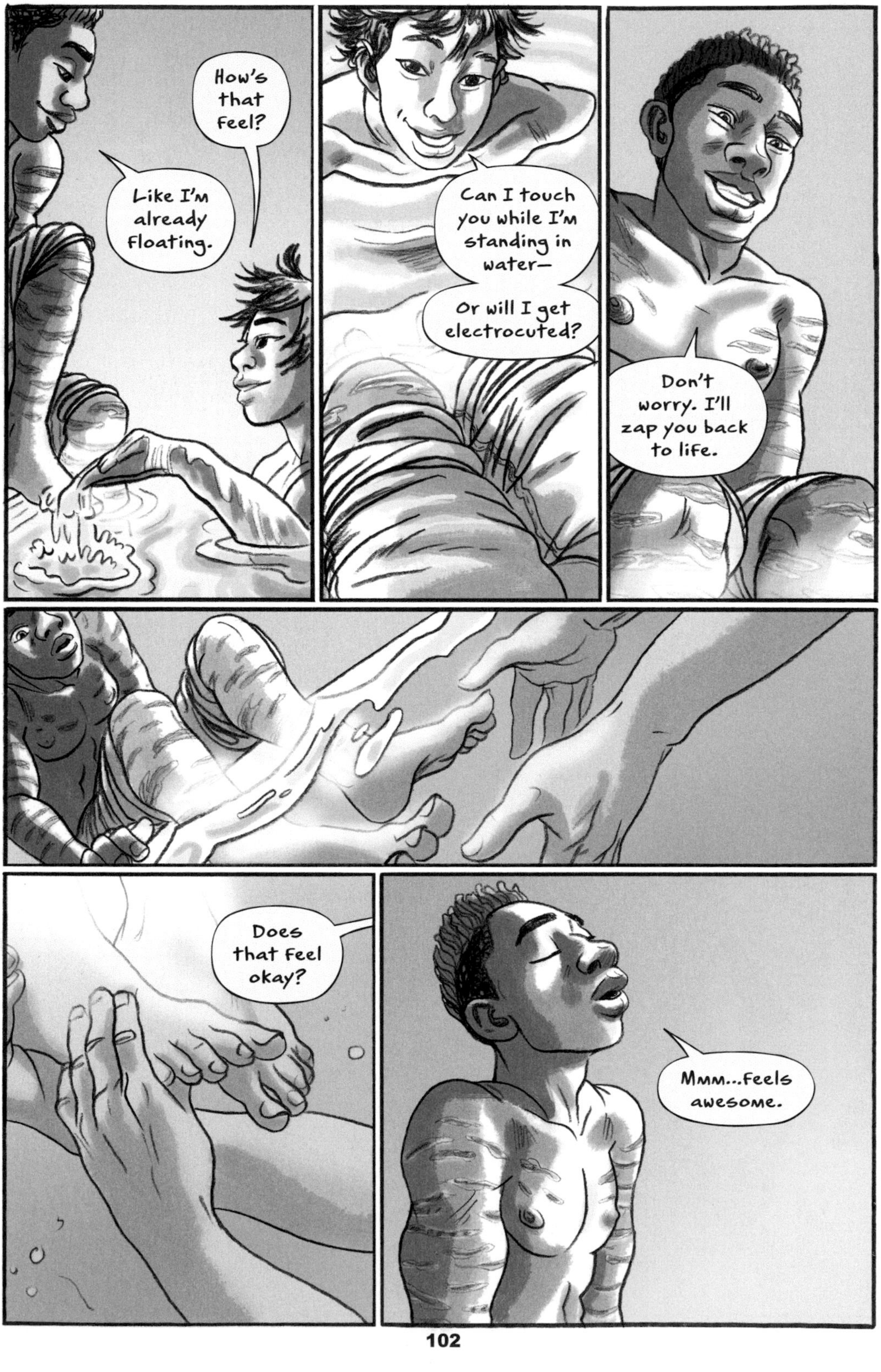
How's that Feel?
Like I'm already Floating.
Can I touch you while I'm standing in water—
Or will I get electrocuted?
Don't worry. I'll zap you back to life.
Does that Feel okay?
Mmm...Feels awesome.

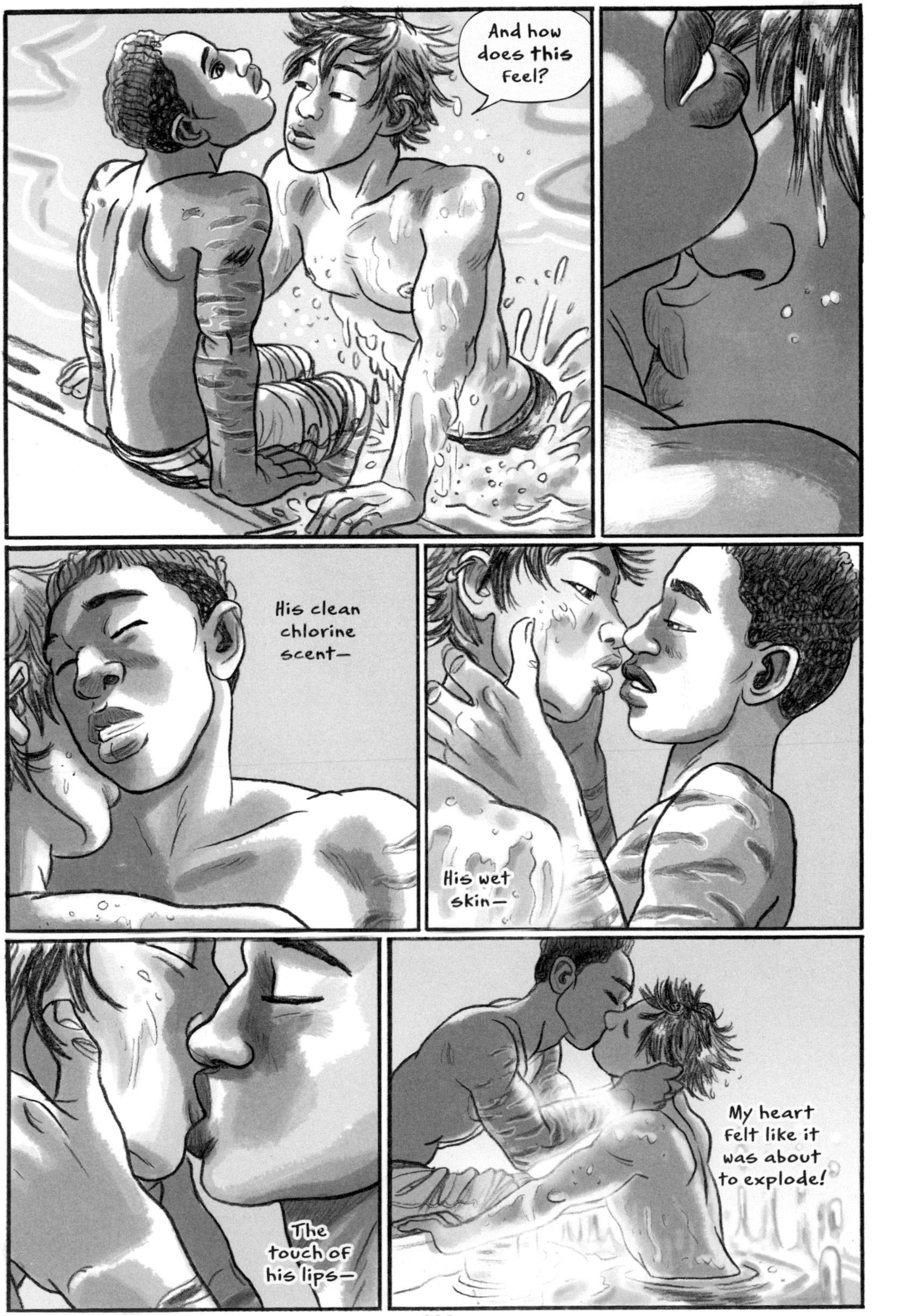
And how does this feel?
His clean chlorine scent—
His wet skin—
The touch of his lips—
My heart felt like it was about to explode!

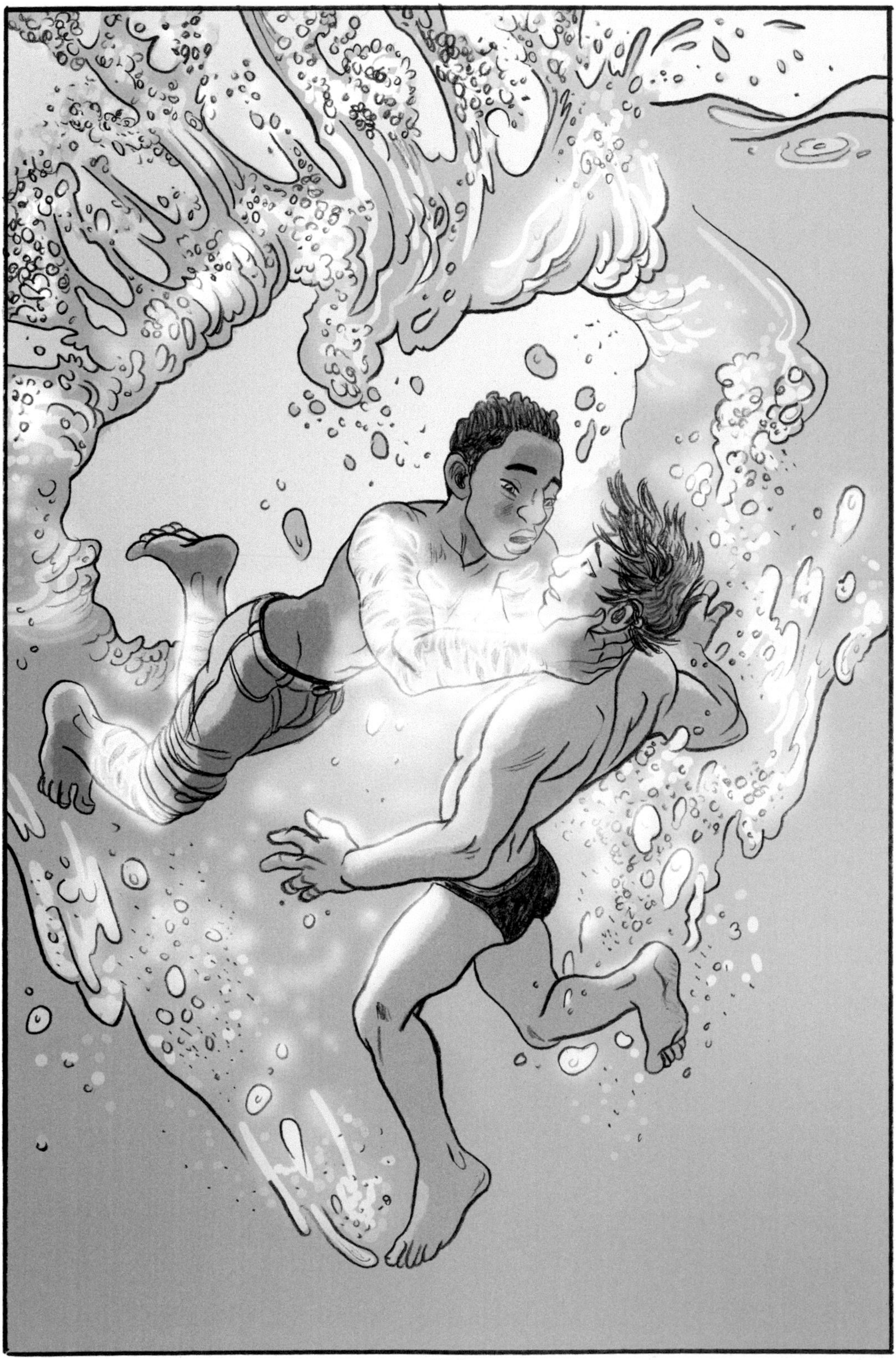

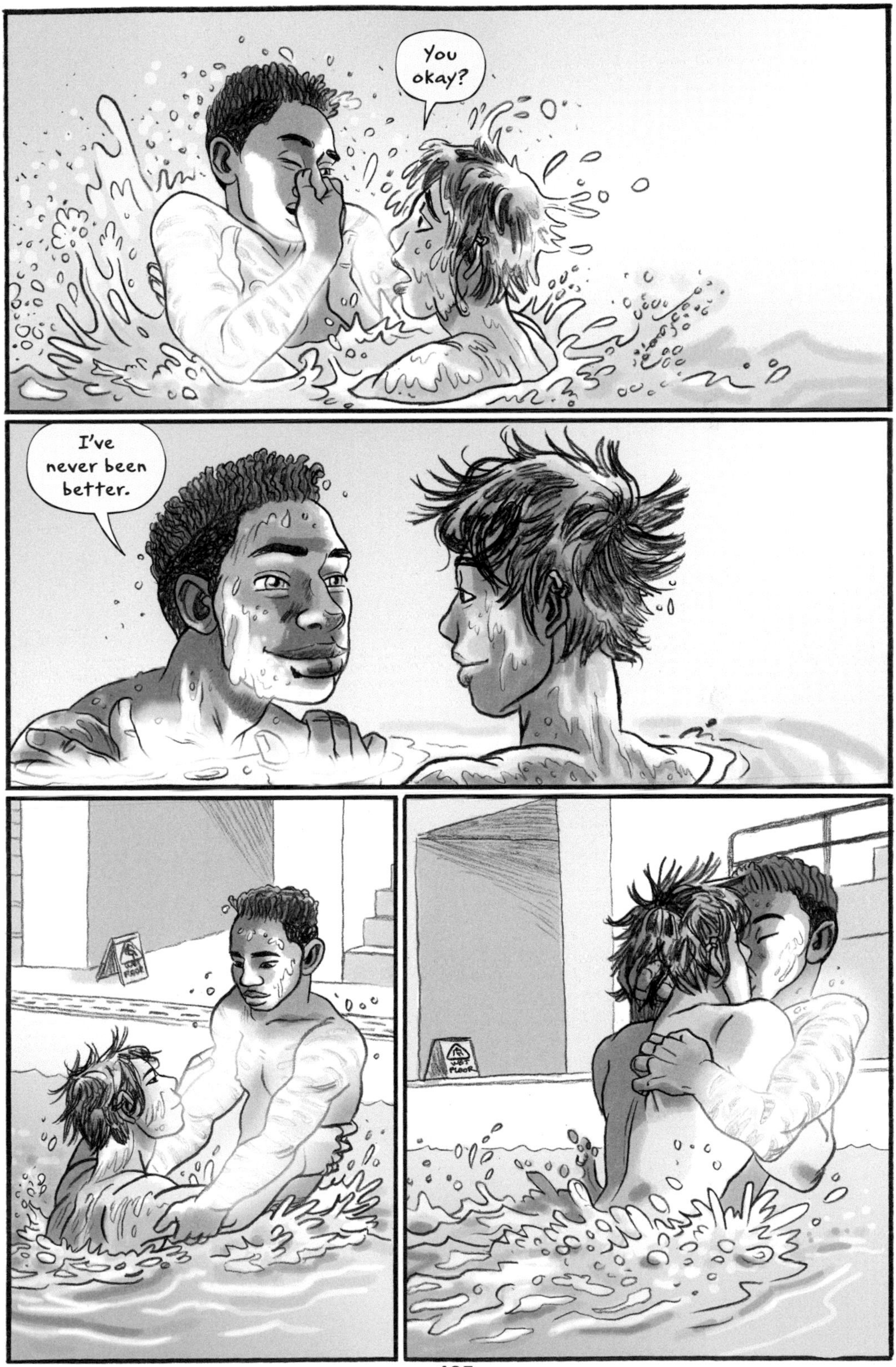
You okay?
I've never been better.
WET FLOOR
WET FLOOR

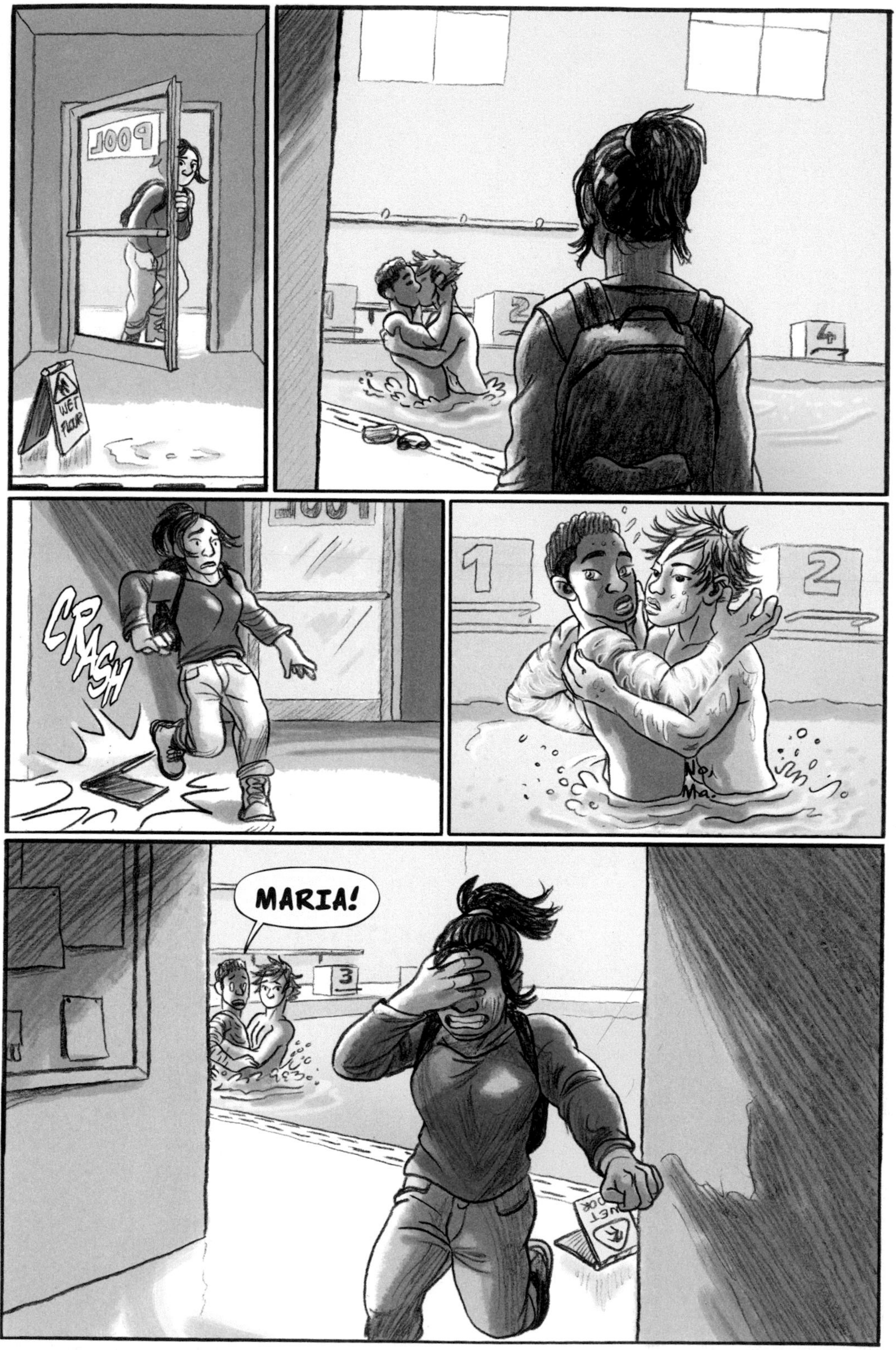
POOL
WET FLOOR
CRASH
MARIA!

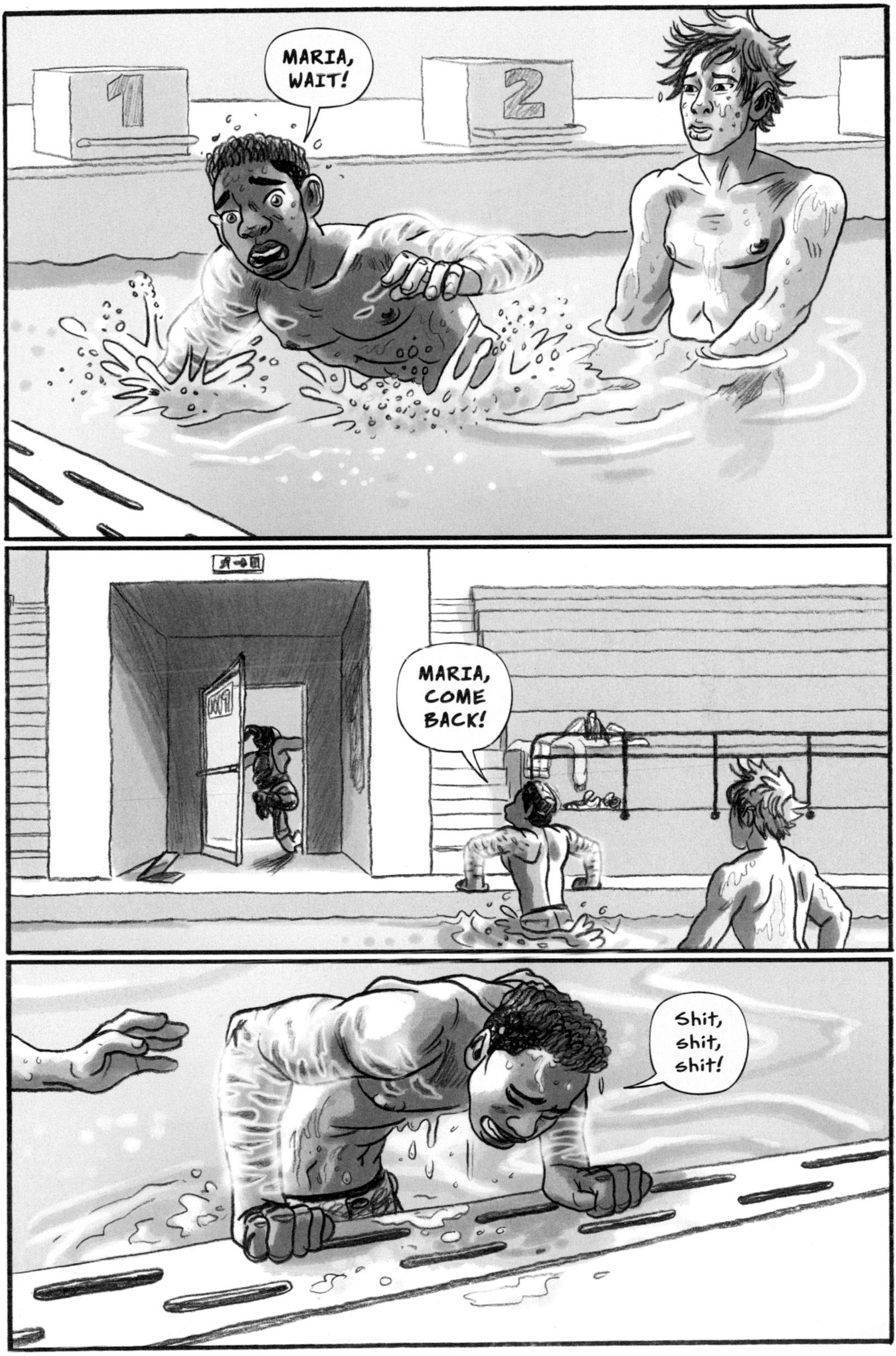

MARIA, WAIT!
MARIA, COME BACK!
Shit, shit, shit!

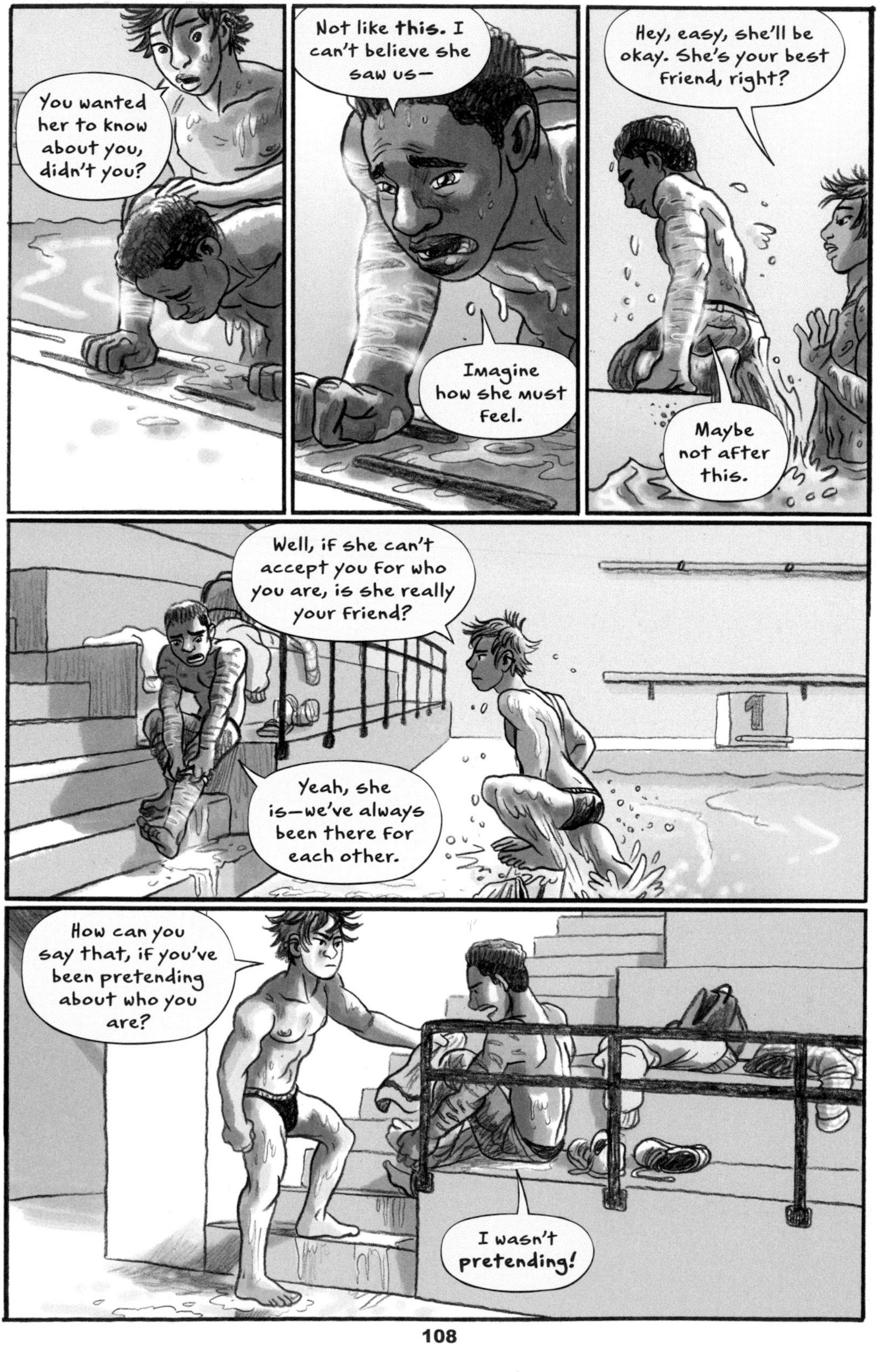
You wanted her to know about you, didn't you?
Not like this. I can't believe she saw us—
Imagine how she must feel.
Hey, easy, she'll be okay. She's your best friend, right?
Maybe not after this.
Well, if she can't accept you for who you are, is she really your friend?
Yeah, she is—we've always been there for each other.
How can you say that, if you've been pretending about who you are?
I wasn't pretending!

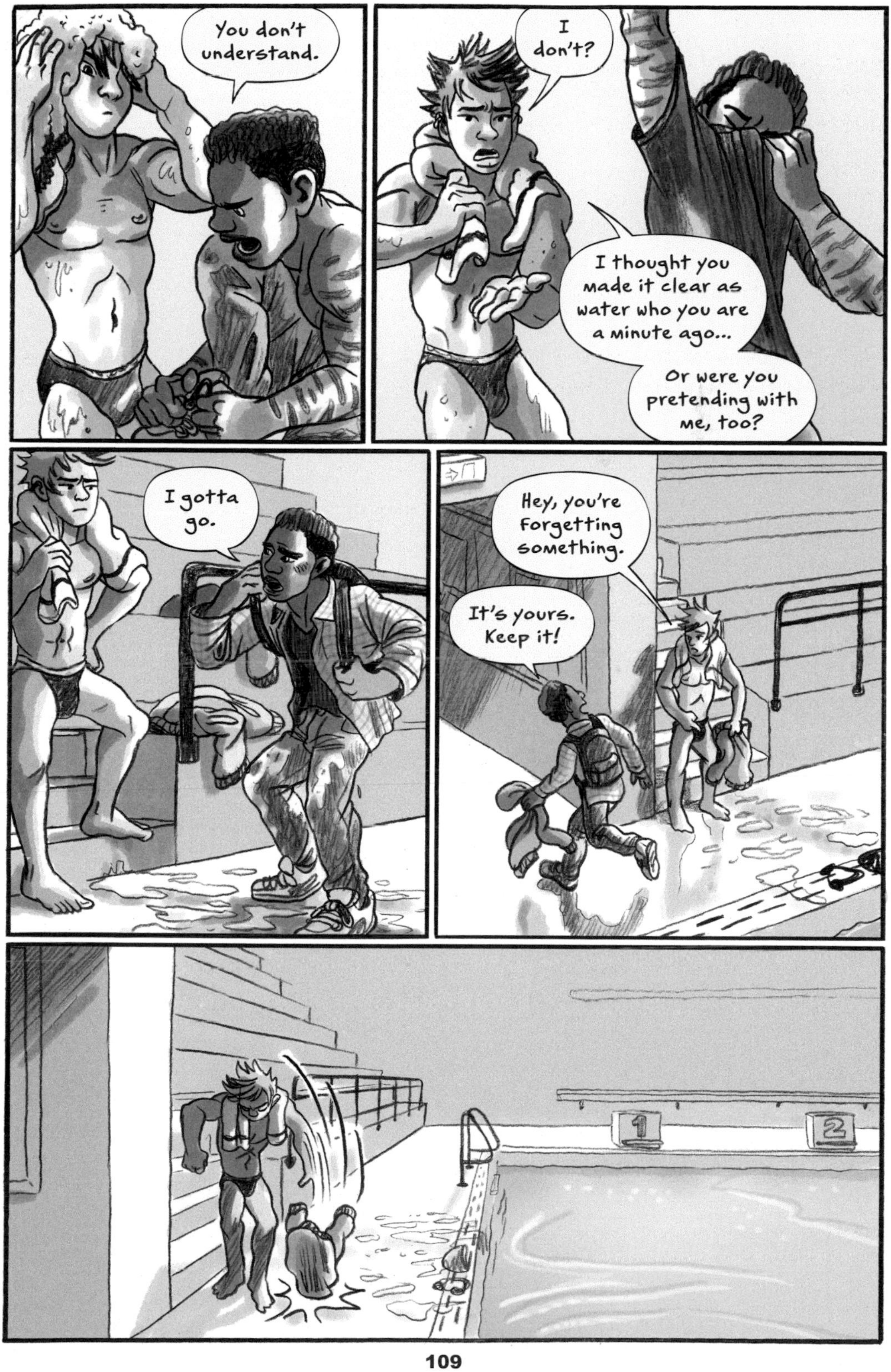
You don't understand.
I don't?
I thought you made it clear as water who you are a minute ago...
Or were you pretending with me, too?
I gotta go.
Hey, you're forgetting something.
It's yours. Keep it!

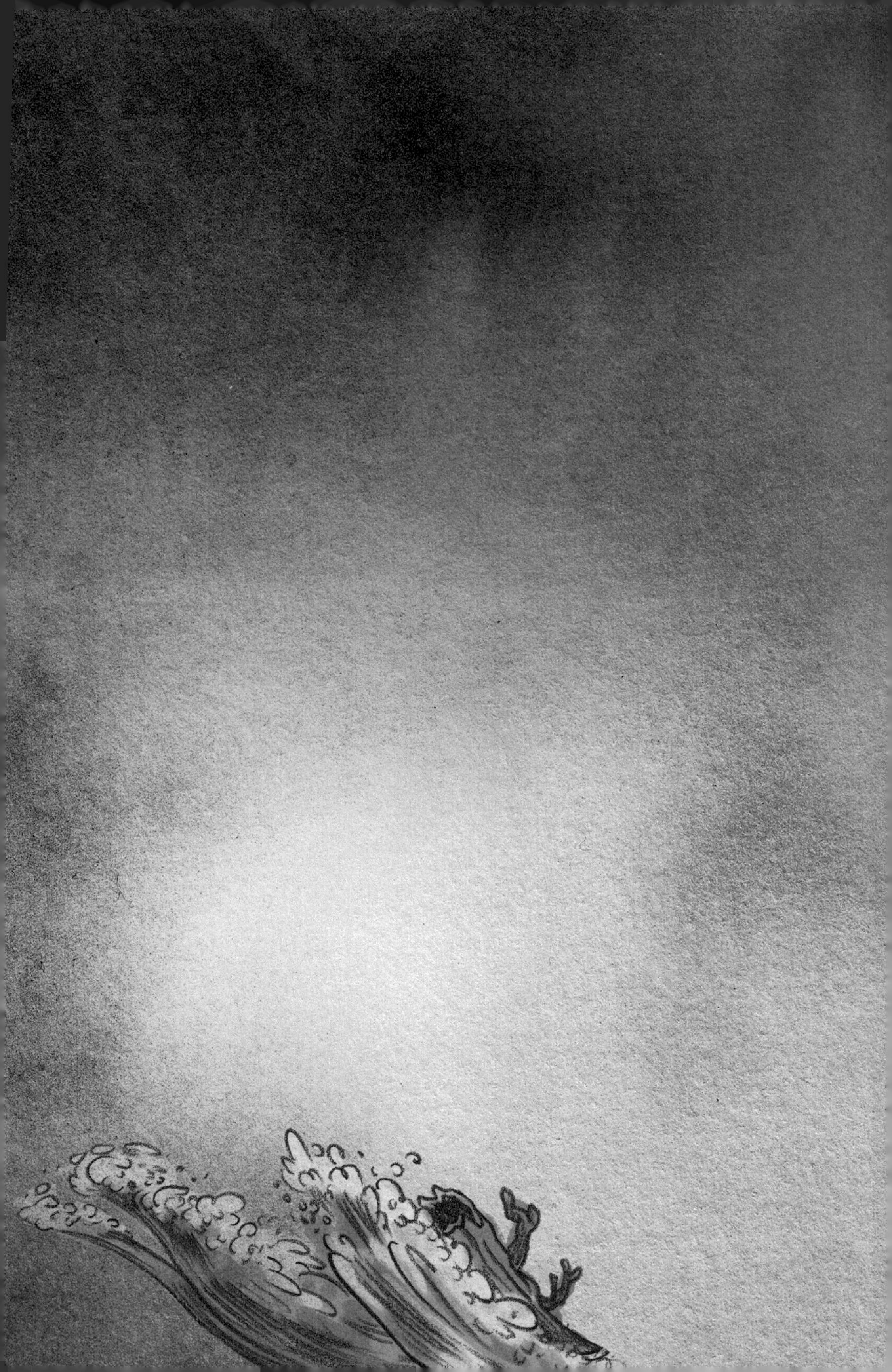

CHAPTER 3

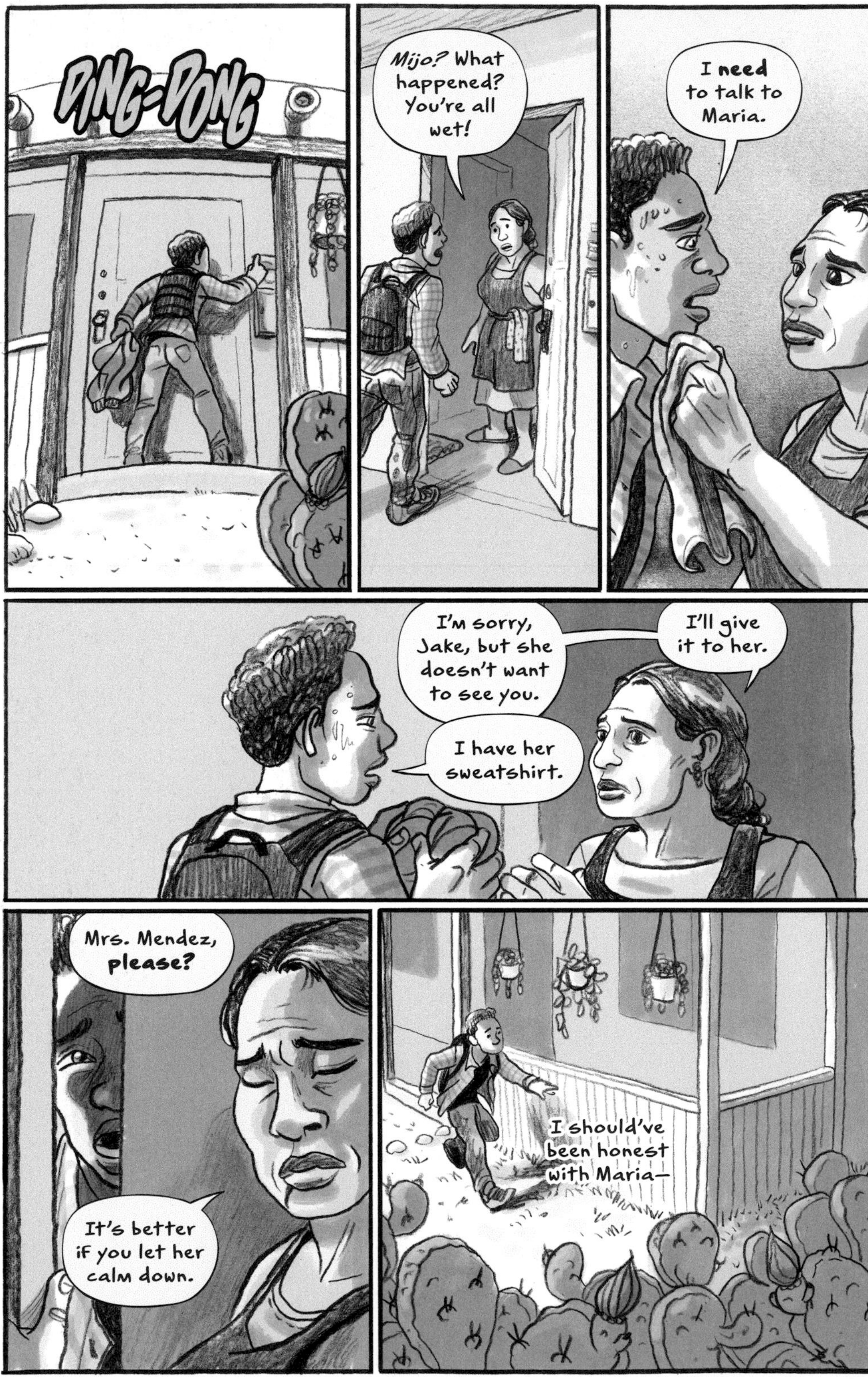
DING-DONG
Mijo? What happened? You're all wet!
I need to talk to Maria.
I'm sorry, Jake, but she doesn't want to see you.
I'll give it to her.
I have her sweatshirt.
Mrs. Mendez, please?
It's better if you let her calm down.
I should've been honest with Maria—

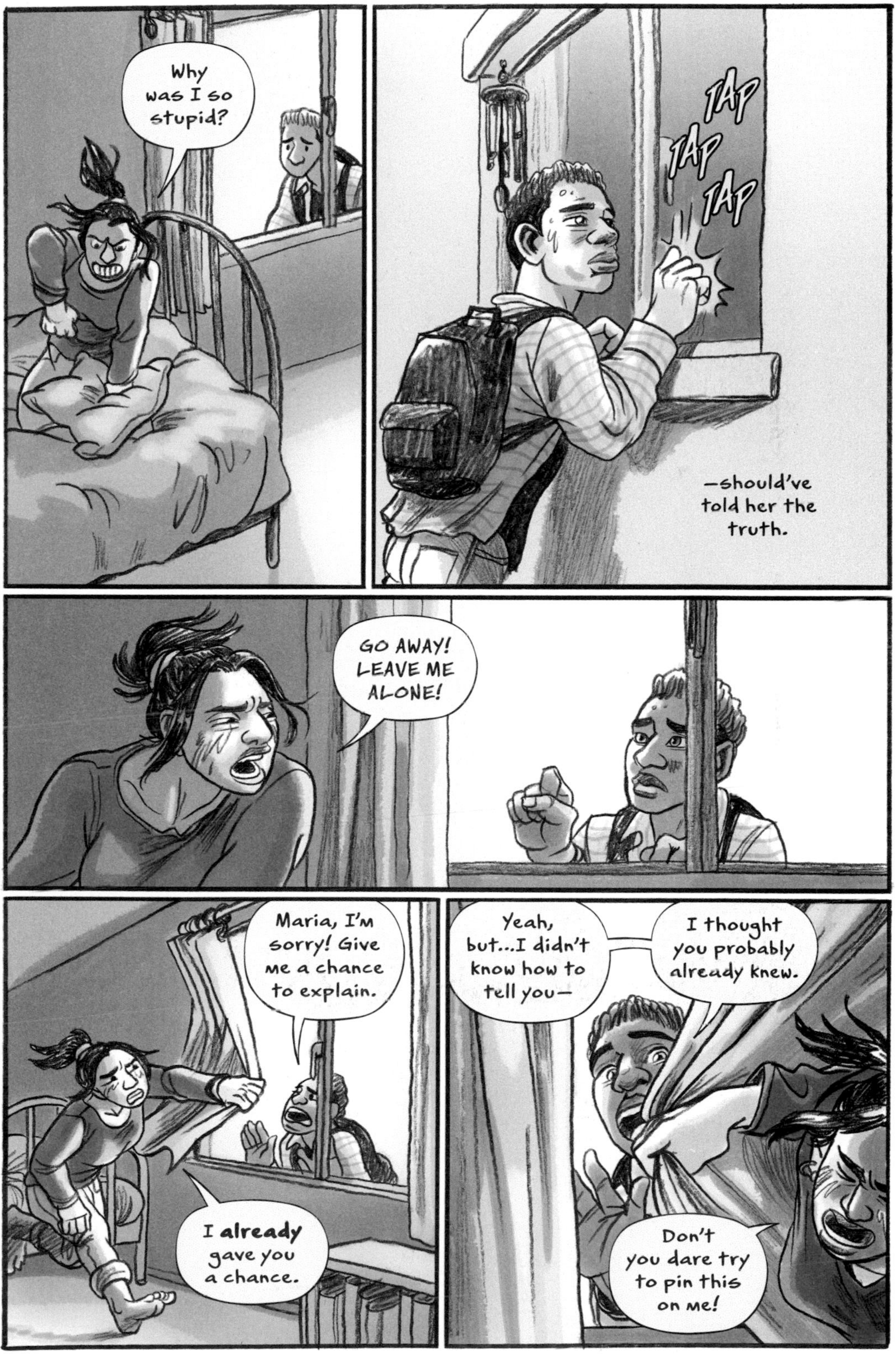
Why was I so stupid?
TAP TAP TAP
—should've told her the truth.
GO AWAY! LEAVE ME ALONE!
Maria, I'm sorry! Give me a chance to explain.
I **already** gave you a chance.
Yeah, but...I didn't know how to tell you—
I thought you probably already knew.
Don't you dare try to pin this on me!

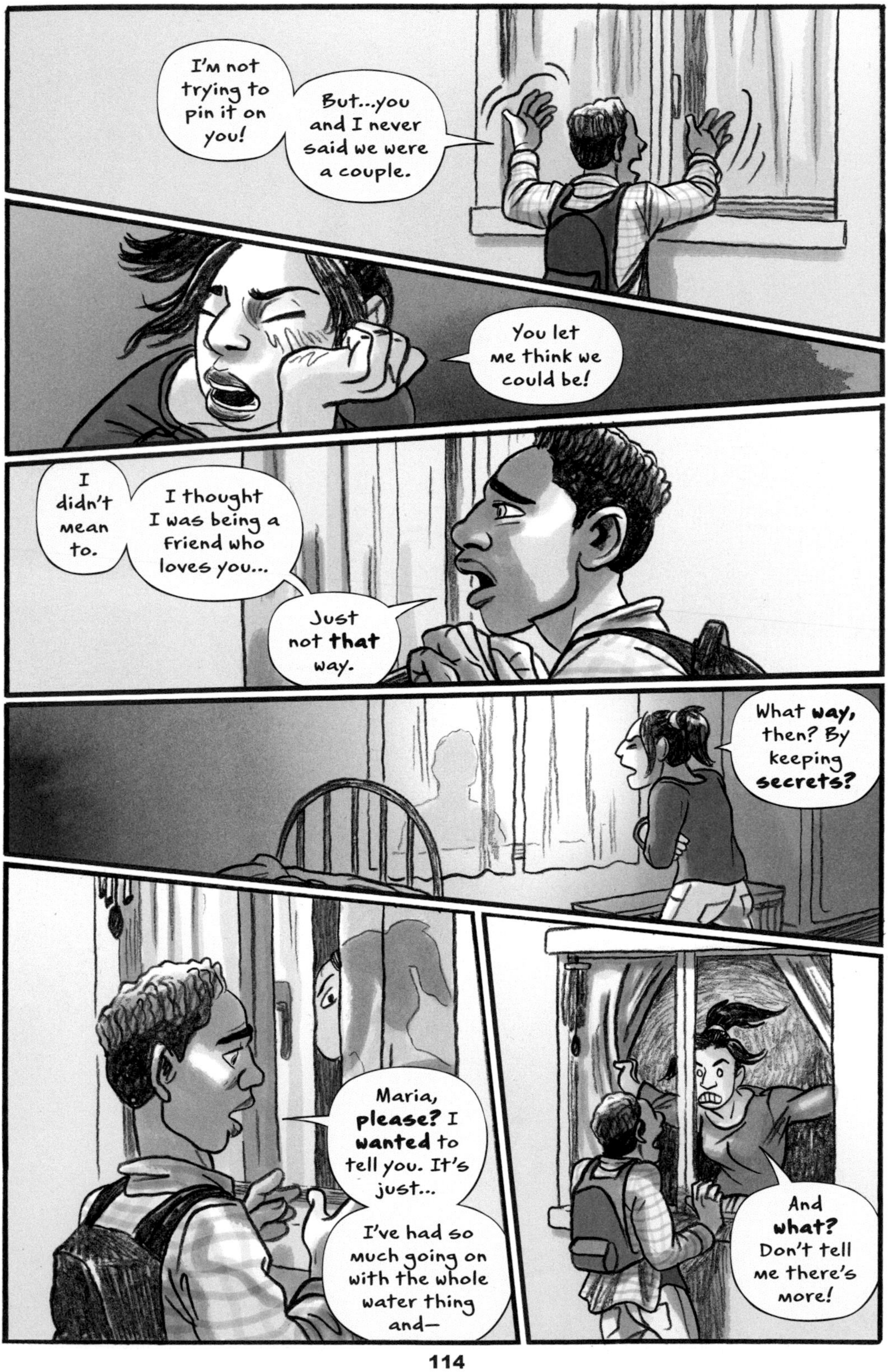
I'm not trying to pin it on you!
But...you and I never said we were a couple.
You let me think we could be!
I didn't mean to.
I thought I was being a friend who loves you...
Just not **that** way.
What **way,** then? By keeping **secrets?**
Maria, **please?** I **wanted** to tell you. It's just...
I've had so much going on with the whole water thing and—
And **what?** Don't tell me there's more!

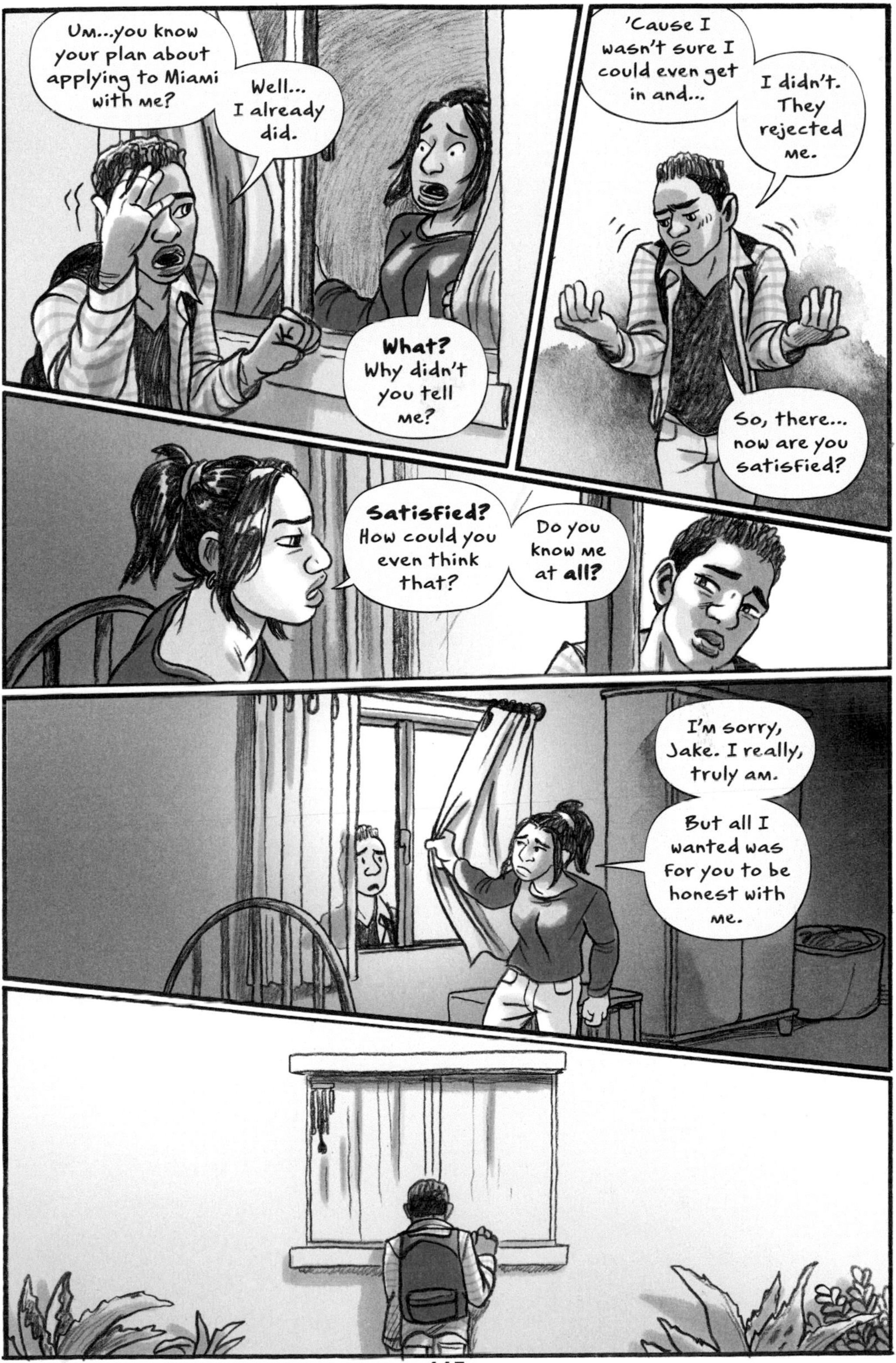
Um...you know your plan about applying to Miami with me?
Well... I already did.
What? Why didn't you tell me?
'Cause I wasn't sure I could even get in and...
I didn't. They rejected me.
So, there... now are you satisfied?
Satisfied? How could you even think that?
Do you know me at all?
I'm sorry, Jake. I really, truly am.
But all I wanted was for you to be honest with me.

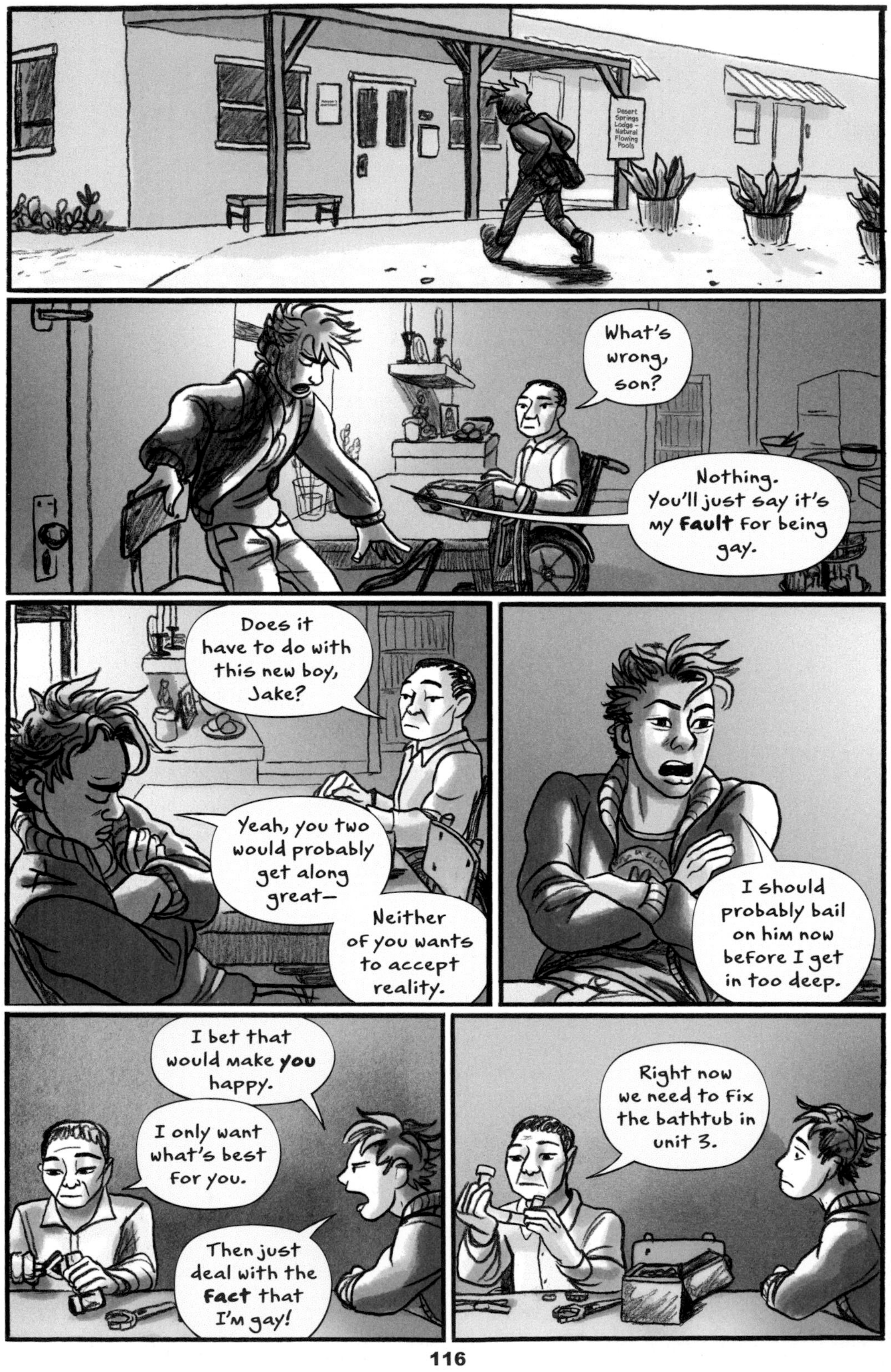
Desert Springs Lodge – Natural Flowing Pools
What's wrong, son?
Nothing. You'll just say it's my **fault** for being gay.
Does it have to do with this new boy, Jake?
Yeah, you two would probably get along great—
Neither of you wants to accept reality.
I should probably bail on him now before I get in too deep.
I bet that would make ***you*** happy.
I only want what's best for you.
Then just deal with the **fact** that I'm gay!
Right now we need to fix the bathtub in unit 3.

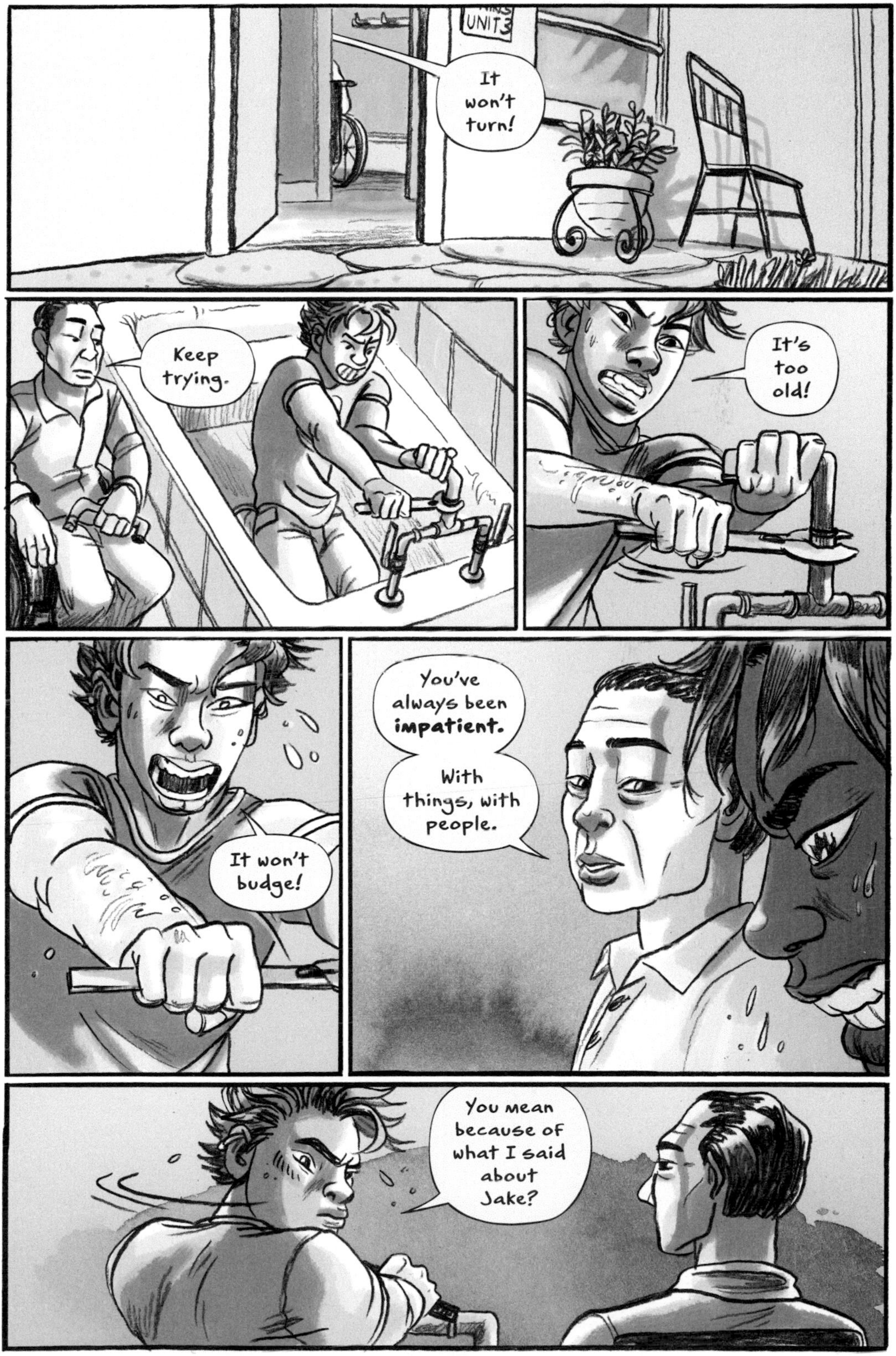
UNIT 3
It won't turn!
Keep trying.
It's too old!
It won't budge!
You've always been **impatient.**
With things, with people.
You mean because of what I said about Jake?

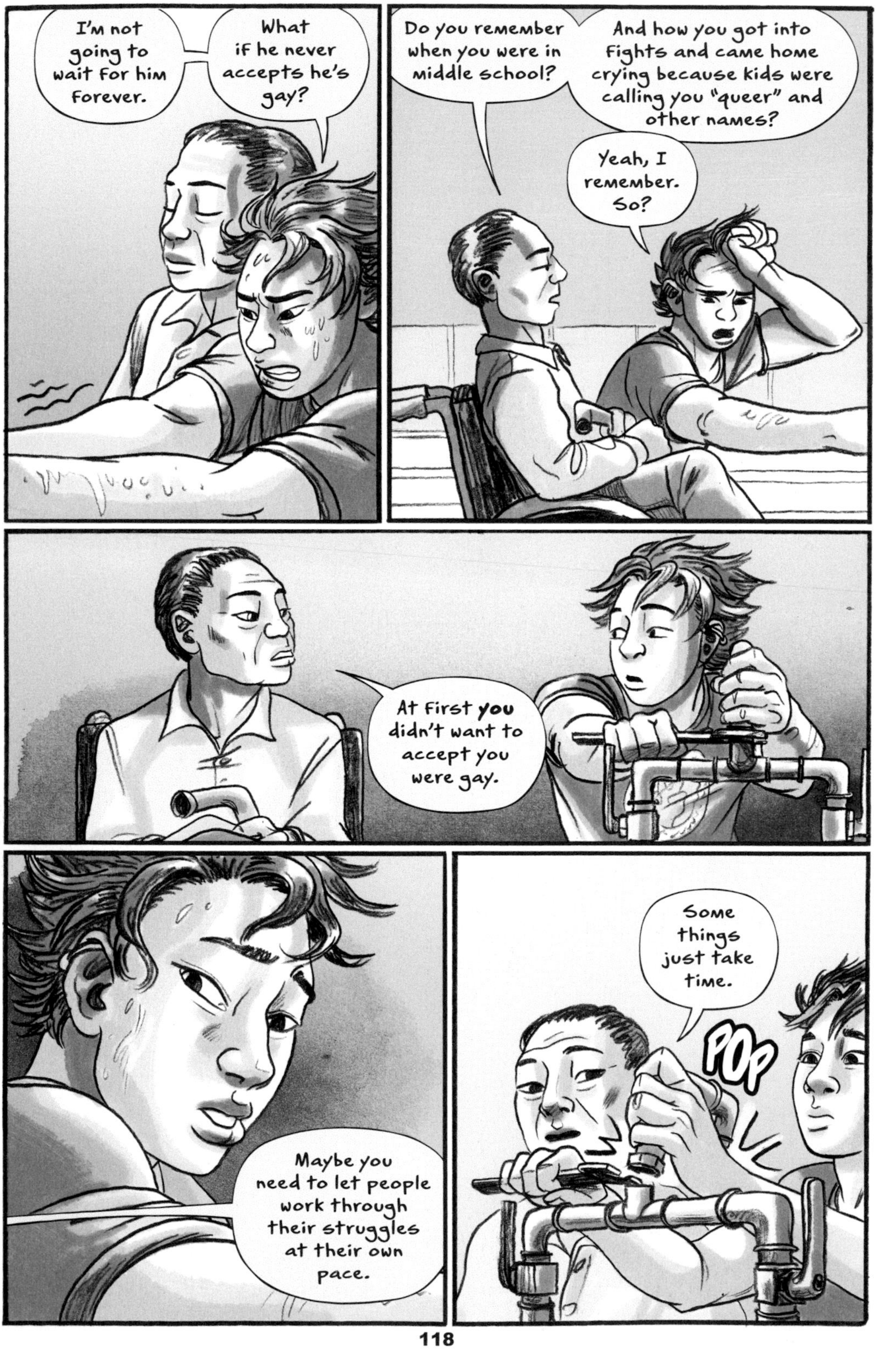
I'm not going to wait for him forever.
What if he never accepts he's gay?
Do you remember when you were in middle school?
And how you got into fights and came home crying because kids were calling you "queer" and other names?
Yeah, I remember. So?
At first you didn't want to accept you were gay.
Maybe you need to let people work through their struggles at their own pace.
Some things just take time.
POP

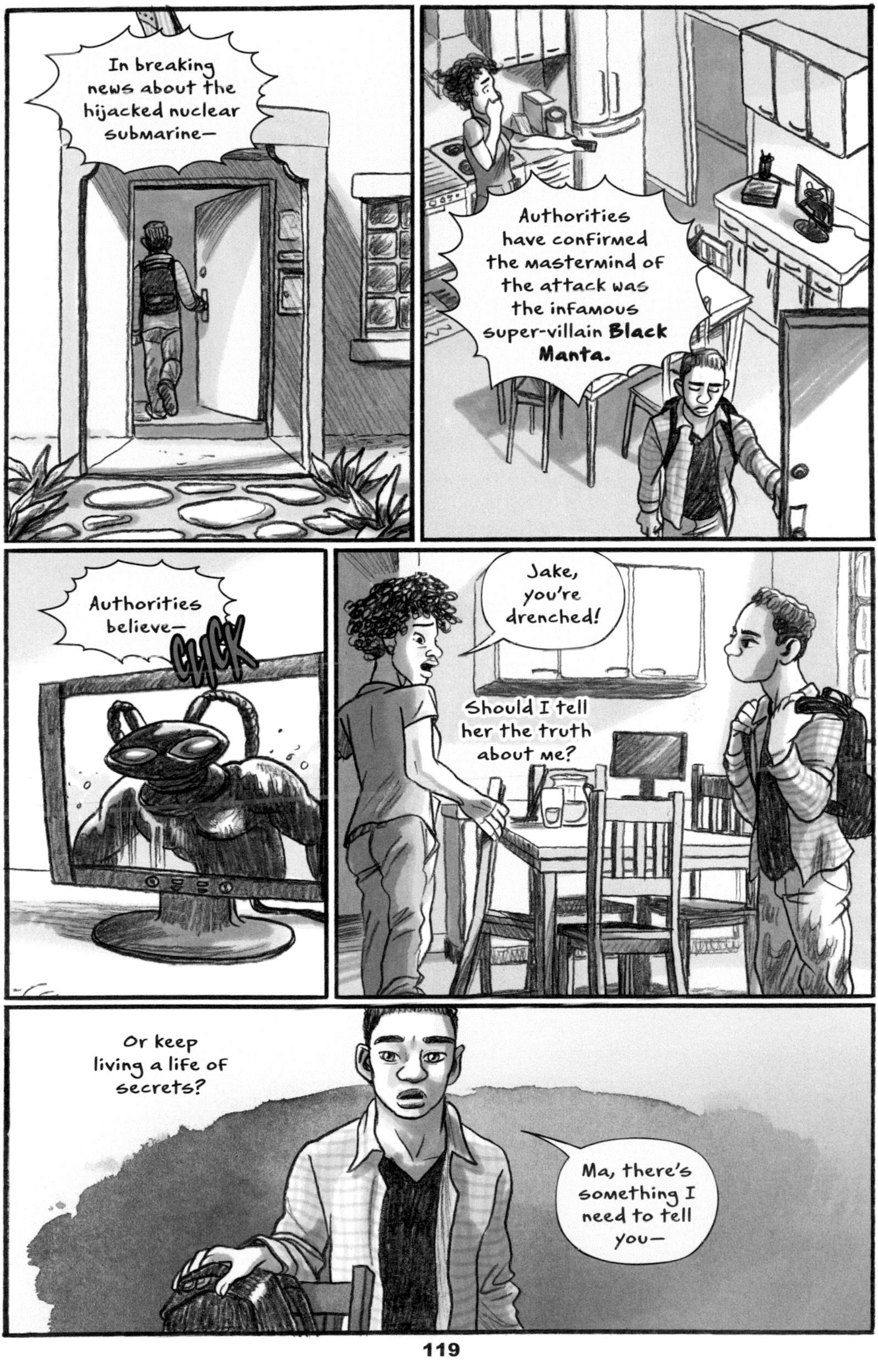
In breaking news about the hijacked nuclear submarine—
Authorities have confirmed the mastermind of the attack was the infamous super-villain **Black Manta.**
Authorities believe—
CLICK
Jake, you're drenched!
Should I tell her the truth about me?
Or keep living a life of secrets?
Ma, there's something I need to tell you—

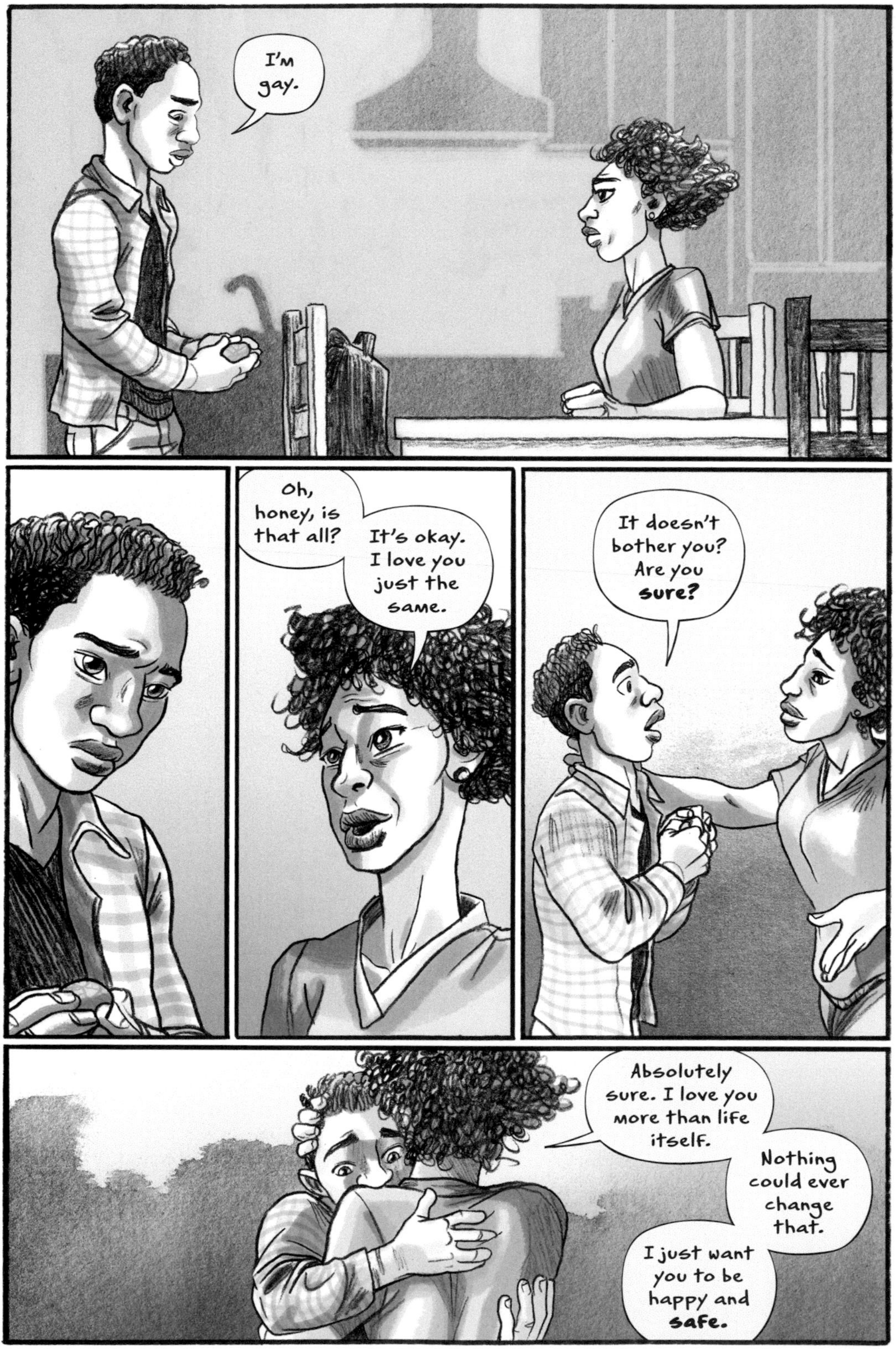
I'm gay.
Oh, honey, is that all?
It's okay. I love you just the same.
It doesn't bother you? Are you **sure?**
Absolutely sure. I love you more than life itself.
Nothing could ever change that.
I just want you to be happy and **safe.**

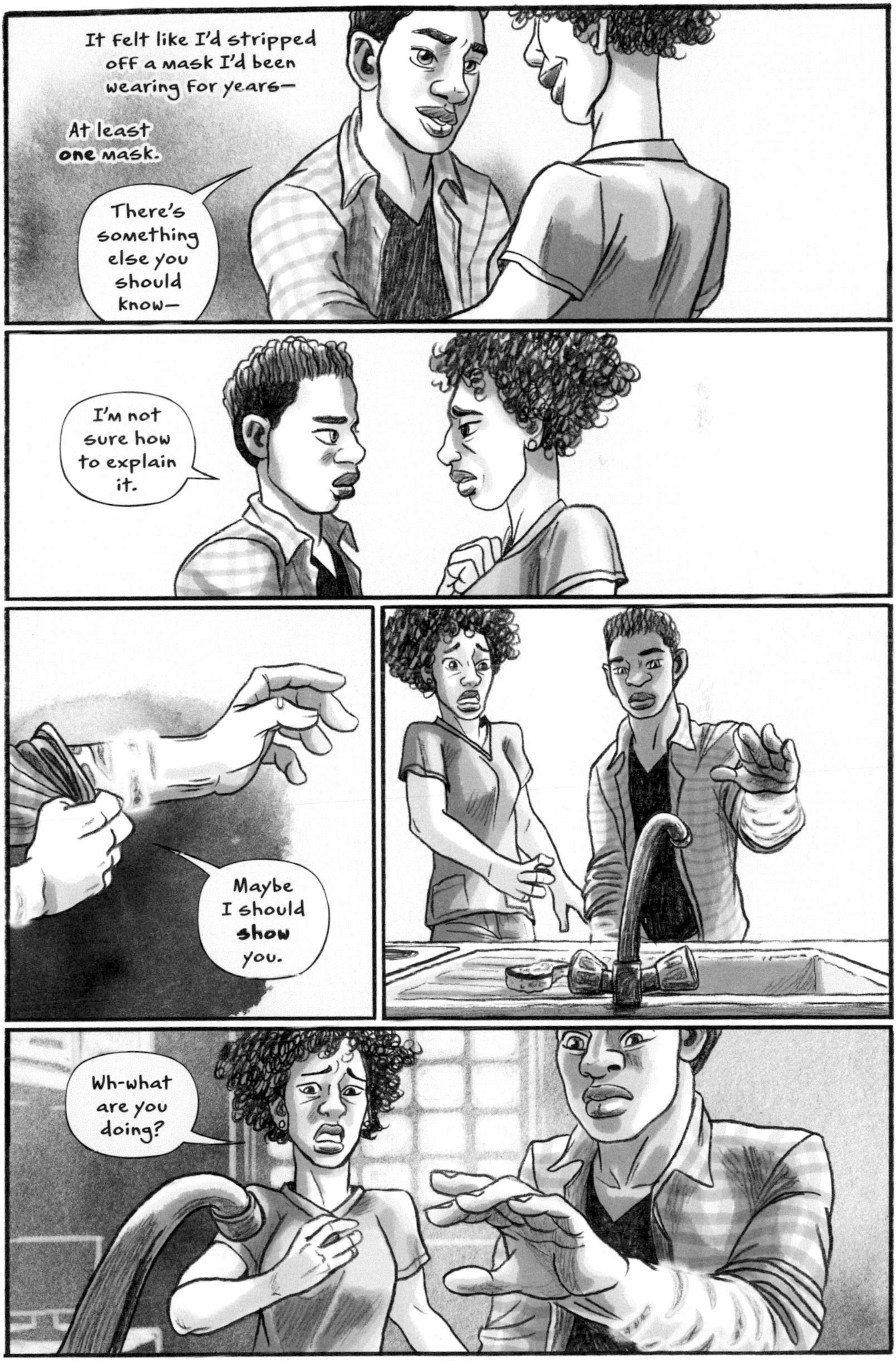
It felt like I'd stripped off a mask I'd been wearing for years—
At least **one** mask.
There's something else you should know—
I'm not sure how to explain it.
Maybe I should **show** you.
Wh-what are you doing?

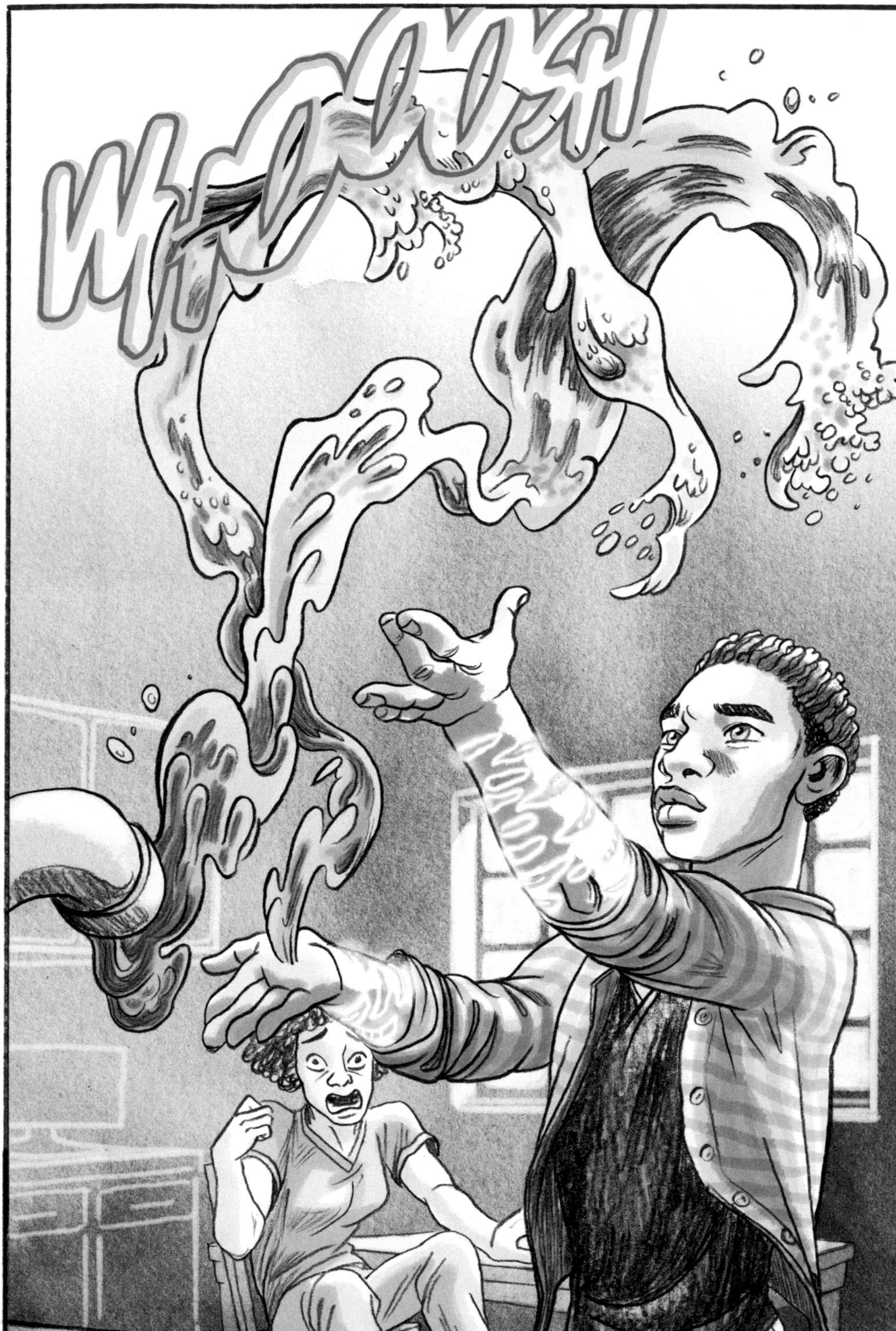
WHOOSH

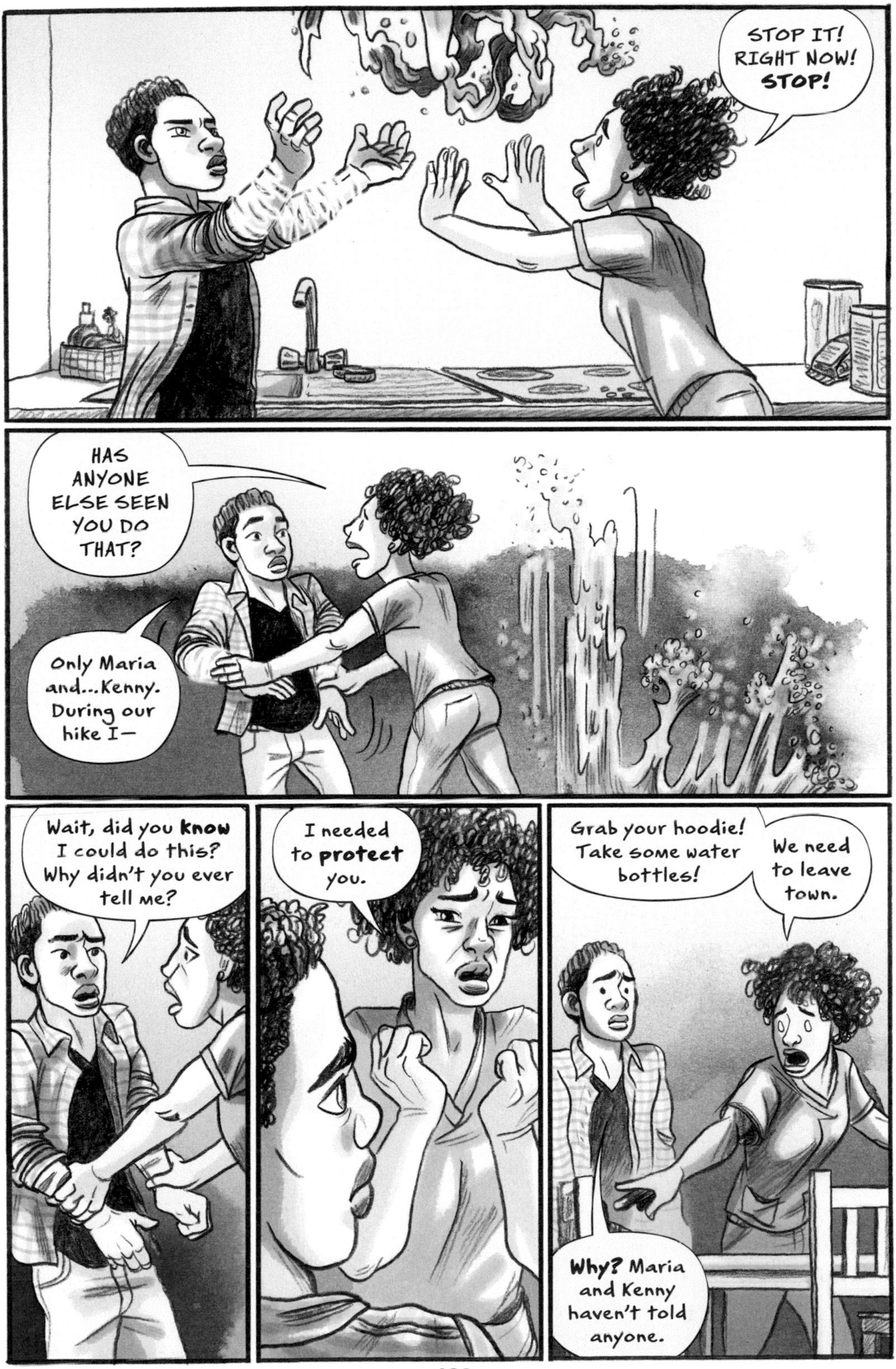
STOP IT! RIGHT NOW! **STOP!**
HAS ANYONE ELSE SEEN YOU DO THAT?
Only Maria and...Kenny. During our hike I—
Wait, did you **know** I could do this? Why didn't you ever tell me?
I needed to **protect** you.
Grab your hoodie! Take some water bottles!
We need to leave town.
Why? Maria and Kenny haven't told anyone.

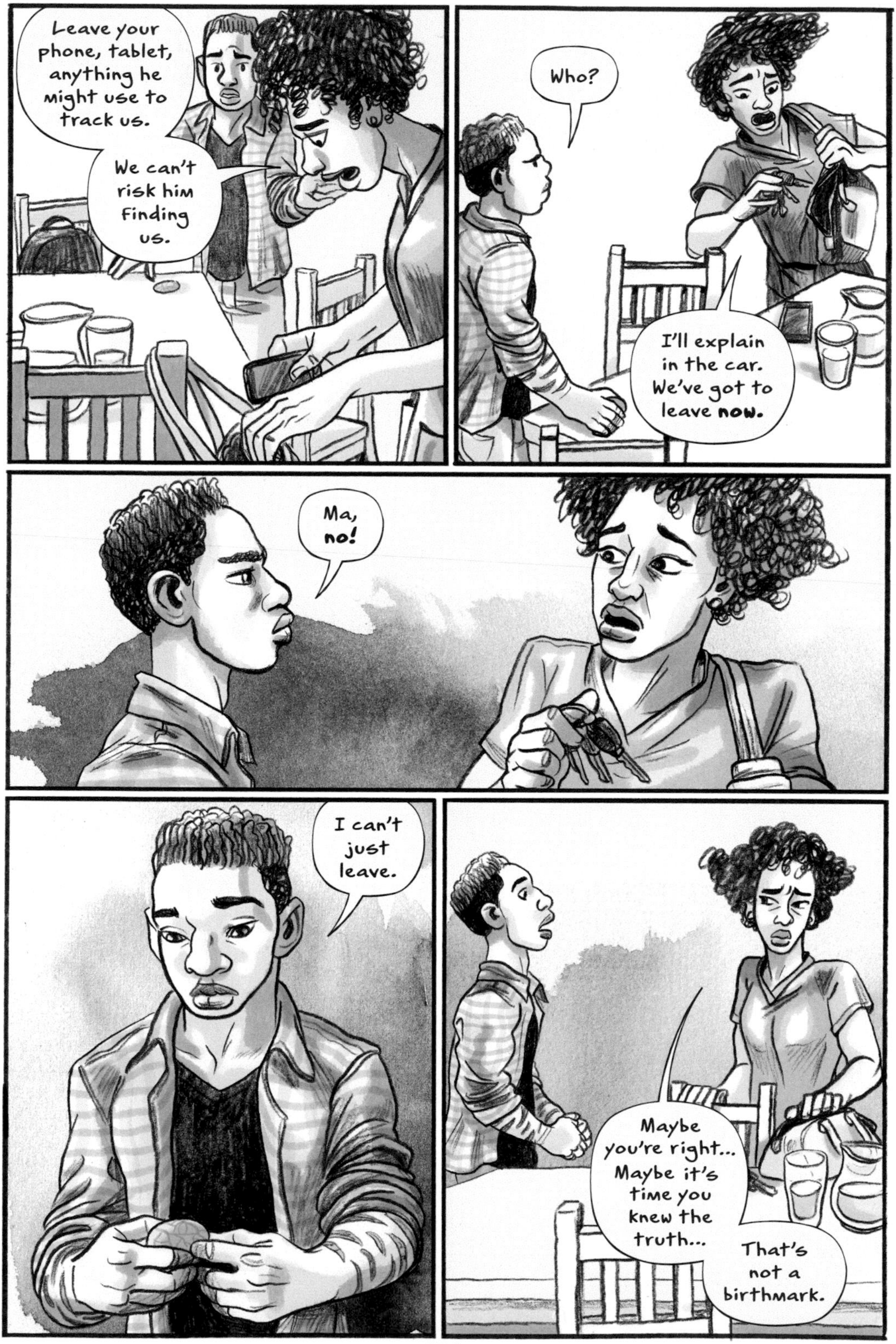
Leave your phone, tablet, anything he might use to track us.
We can't risk him finding us.
Who?
I'll explain in the car. We've got to leave **now.**
Ma, **no!**
I can't just leave.
Maybe you're right... Maybe it's time you knew the truth...
That's not a birthmark.

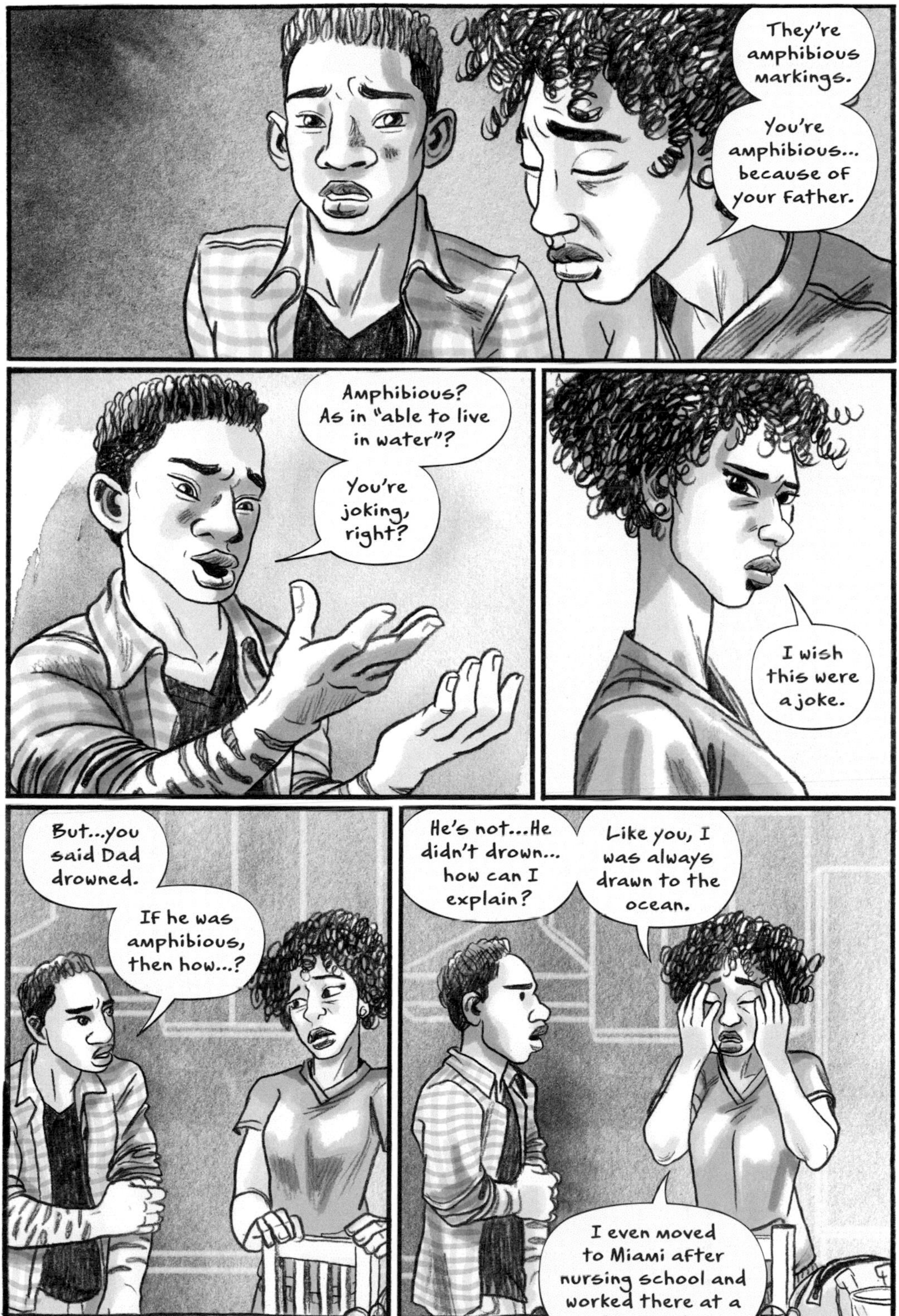
They're amphibious markings.
You're amphibious... because of your Father.
Amphibious? As in "able to live in water"?
You're joking, right?
I wish this were a joke.
But...you said Dad drowned.
If he was amphibious, then how...?
He's not...He didn't drown... how can I explain?
Like you, I was always drawn to the ocean.
I even moved to Miami after nursing school and worked there at a hospital—

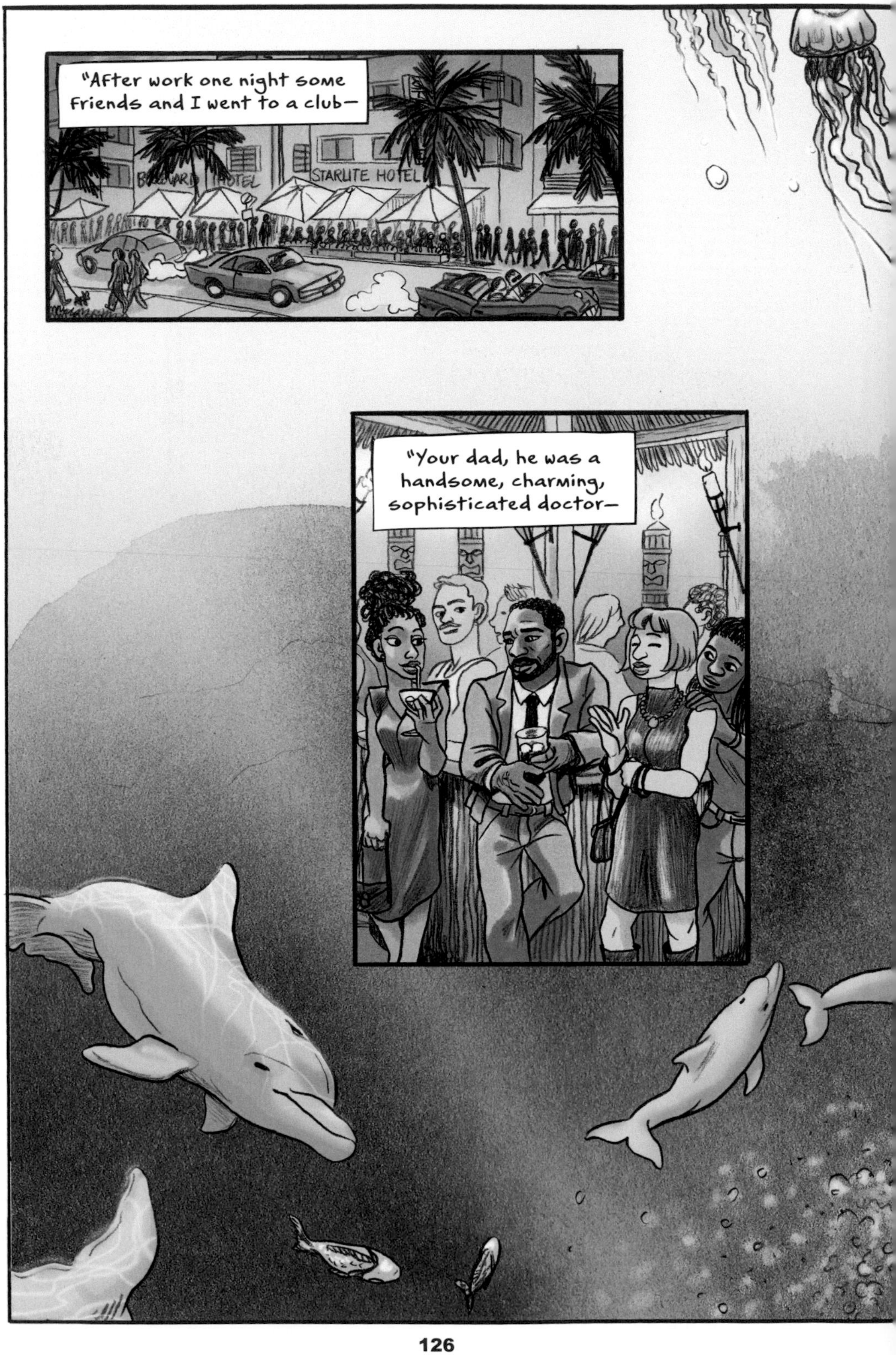
"After work one night some friends and I went to a club—
BOULEVARD HOTEL
STARLITE HOTEL
"Your dad, he was a handsome, charming, sophisticated doctor—

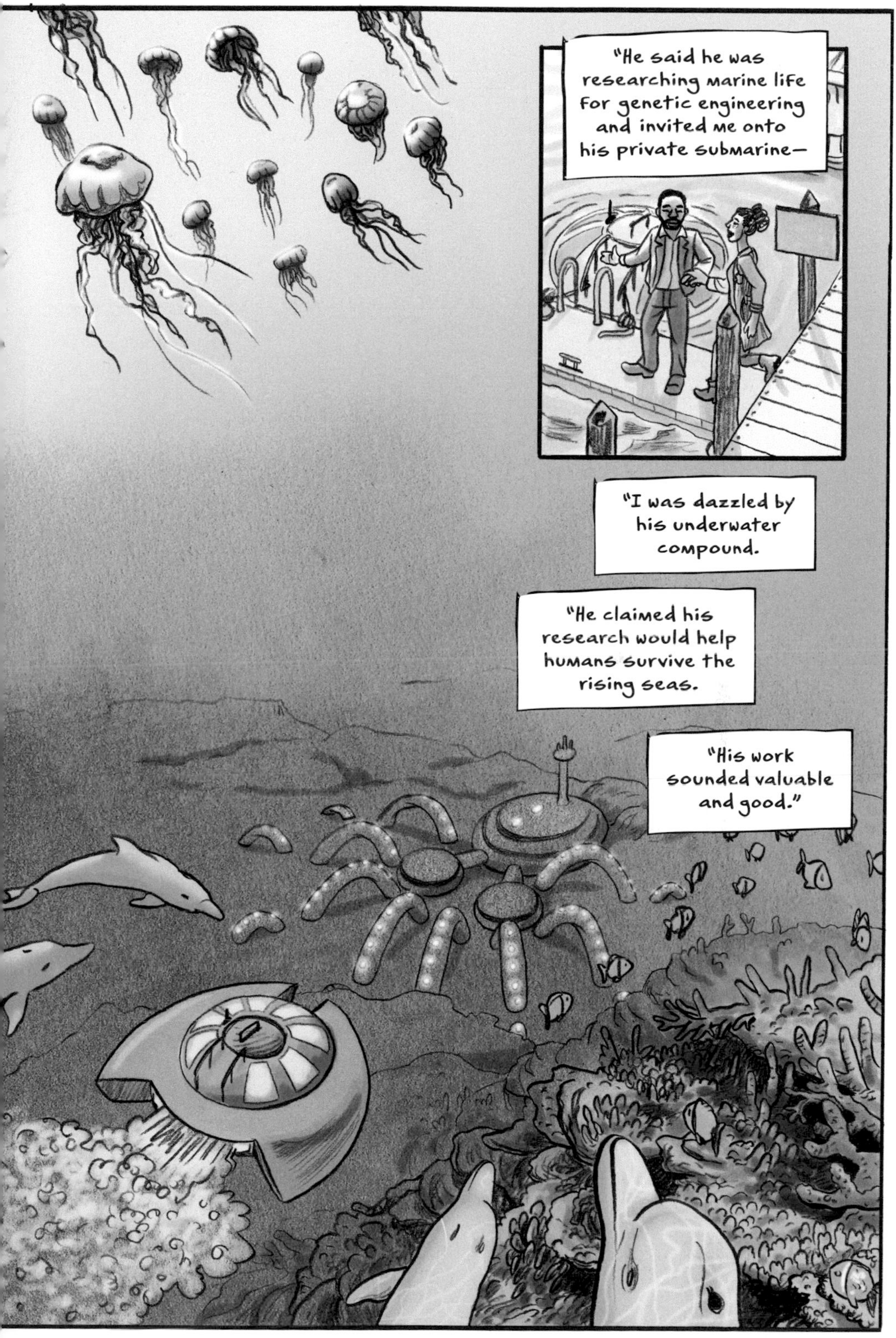
"He said he was researching marine life for genetic engineering and invited me onto his private submarine—
"I was dazzled by his underwater compound.
"He claimed his research would help humans survive the rising seas.
"His work sounded valuable and good."

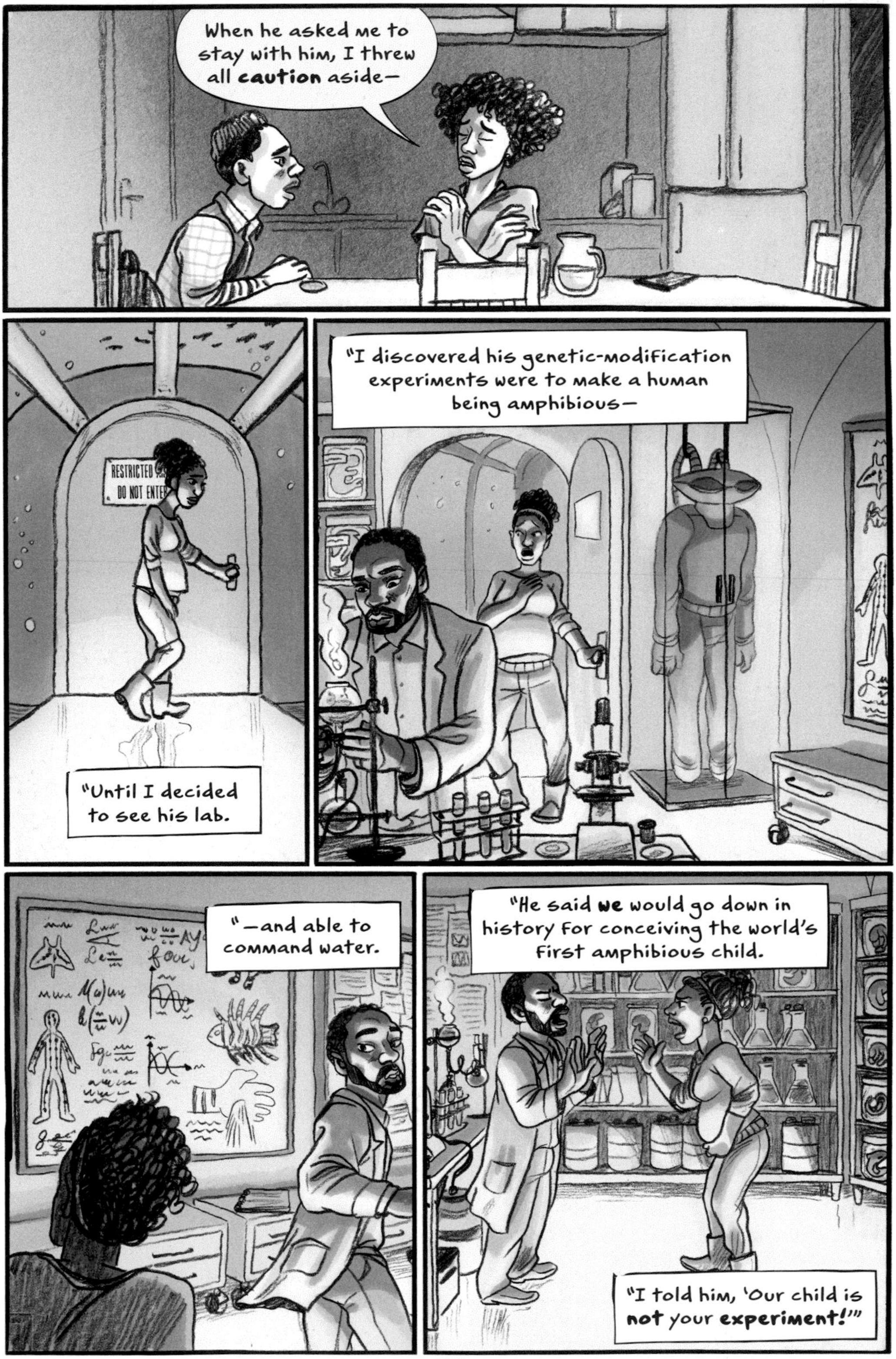
When he asked me to stay with him, I threw all **caution** aside—
RESTRICTED
DO NOT ENTER
"Until I decided to see his lab.
"I discovered his genetic-modification experiments were to make a human being amphibious—
"—and able to command water.
"He said **we** would go down in history for conceiving the world's first amphibious child.
"I told him, 'Our child is **not** your **experiment!**'"

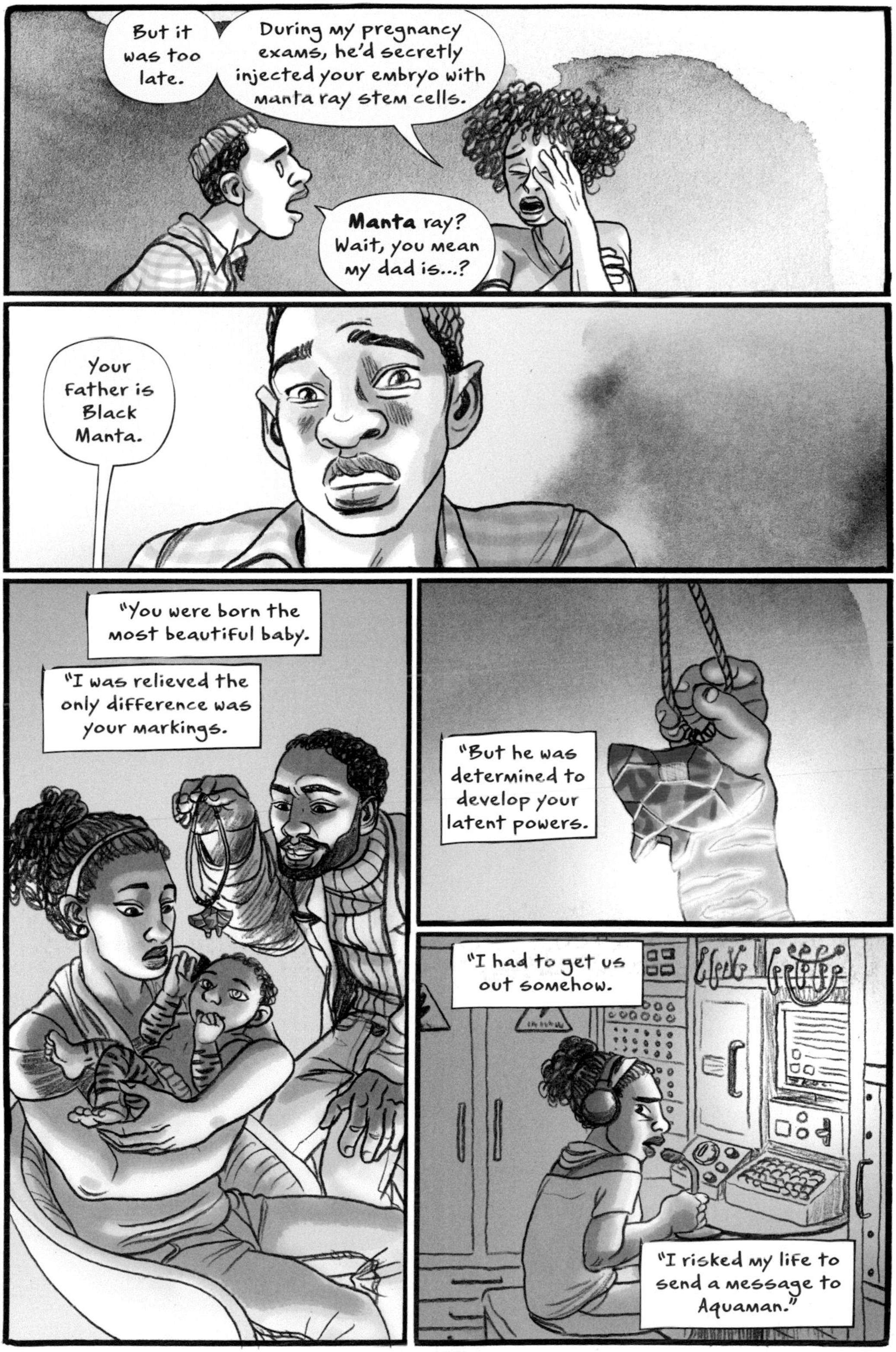
But it was too late.
During my pregnancy exams, he'd secretly injected your embryo with manta ray stem cells.
Manta ray? Wait, you mean my dad is...?
Your Father is Black Manta.
"You were born the most beautiful baby.
"I was relieved the only difference was your markings.
"But he was determined to develop your latent powers.
"I had to get us out somehow.
"I risked my life to send a message to Aquaman."

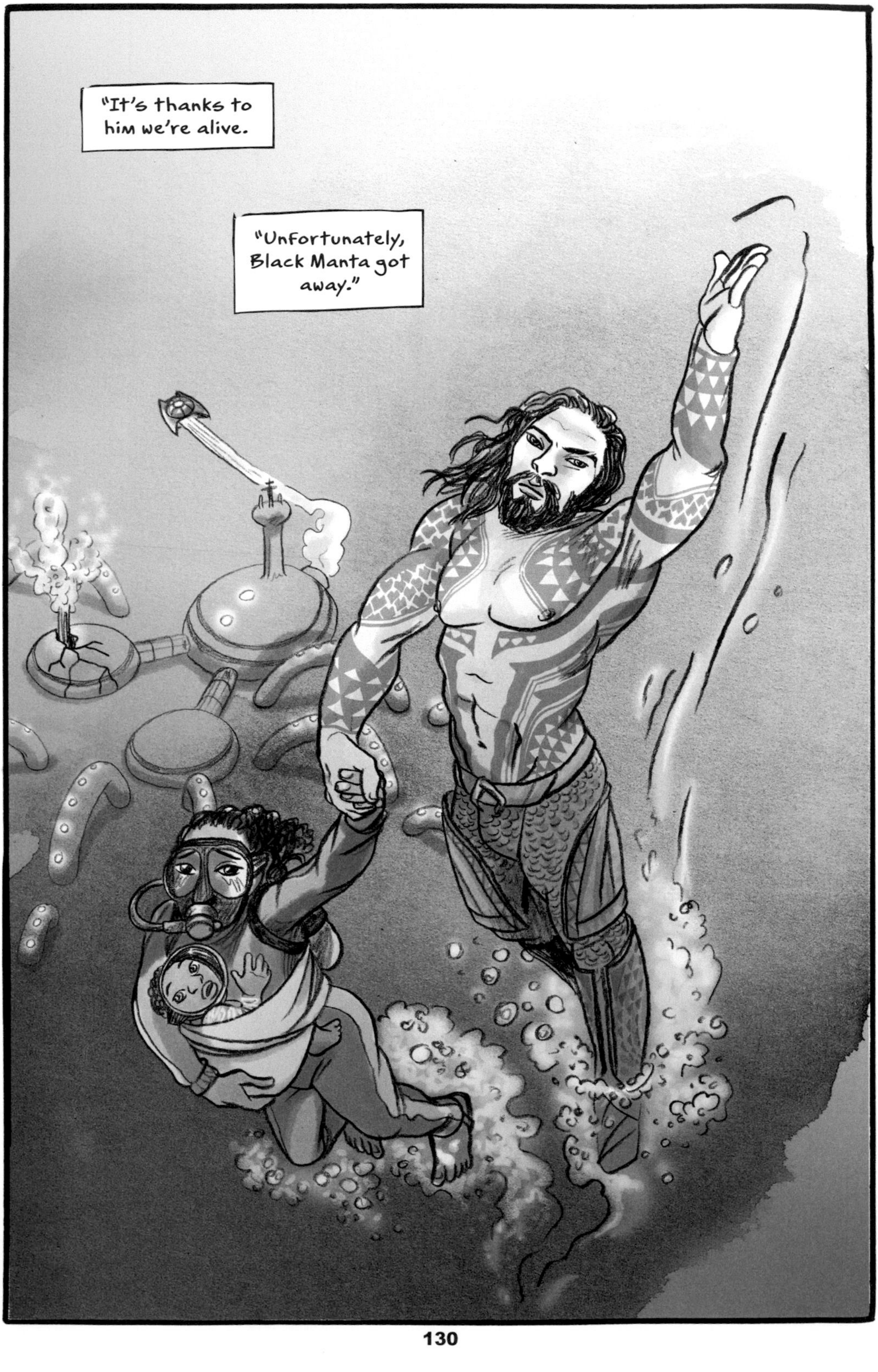
"It's thanks to him we're alive.
"Unfortunately, Black Manta got away."

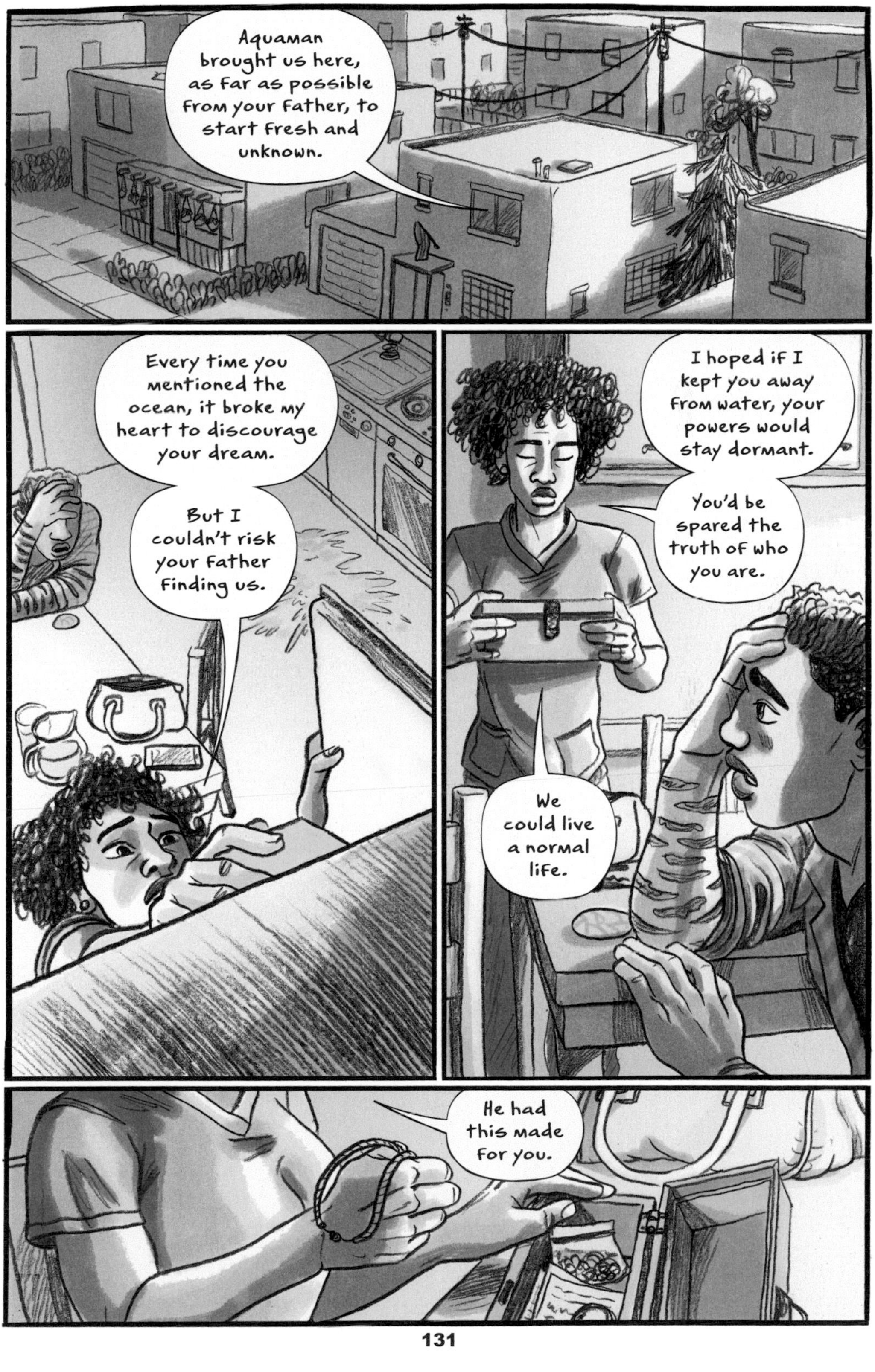
Aquaman brought us here, as far as possible from your father, to start fresh and unknown.
Every time you mentioned the ocean, it broke my heart to discourage your dream.
But I couldn't risk your father finding us.
I hoped if I kept you away from water, your powers would stay dormant.
You'd be spared the truth of who you are.
We could live a normal life.
He had this made for you.

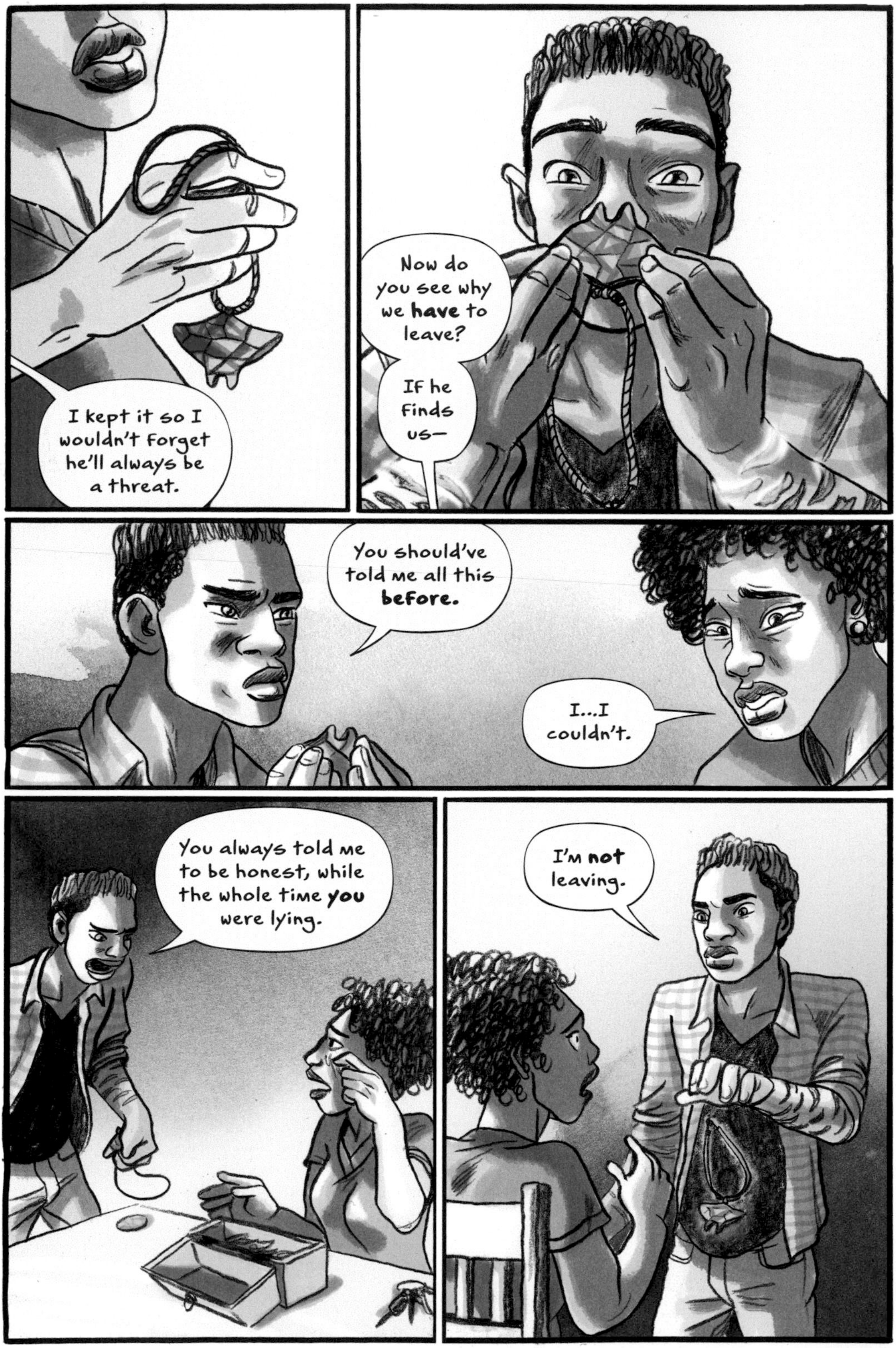
I kept it so I wouldn't forget he'll always be a threat.
Now do you see why we **have** to leave?
If he finds us—
You should've told me all this **before.**
I...I couldn't.
You always told me to be honest, while the whole time **you** were lying.
I'm **not** leaving.

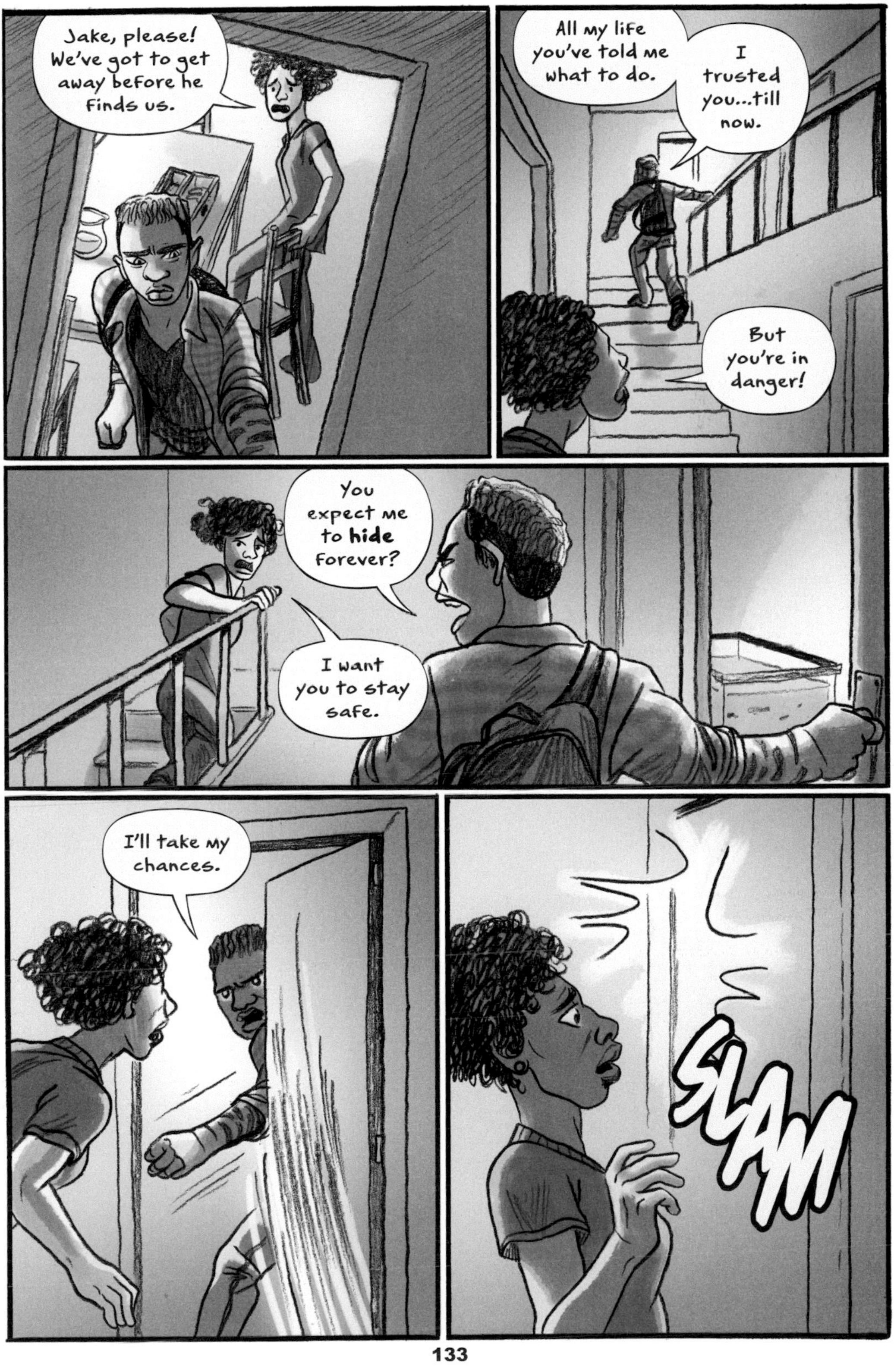
Jake, please! We've got to get away before he finds us.
All my life you've told me what to do.
I trusted you...till now.
But you're in danger!
You expect me to **hide** forever?
I want you to stay safe.
I'll take my chances.
SLAM

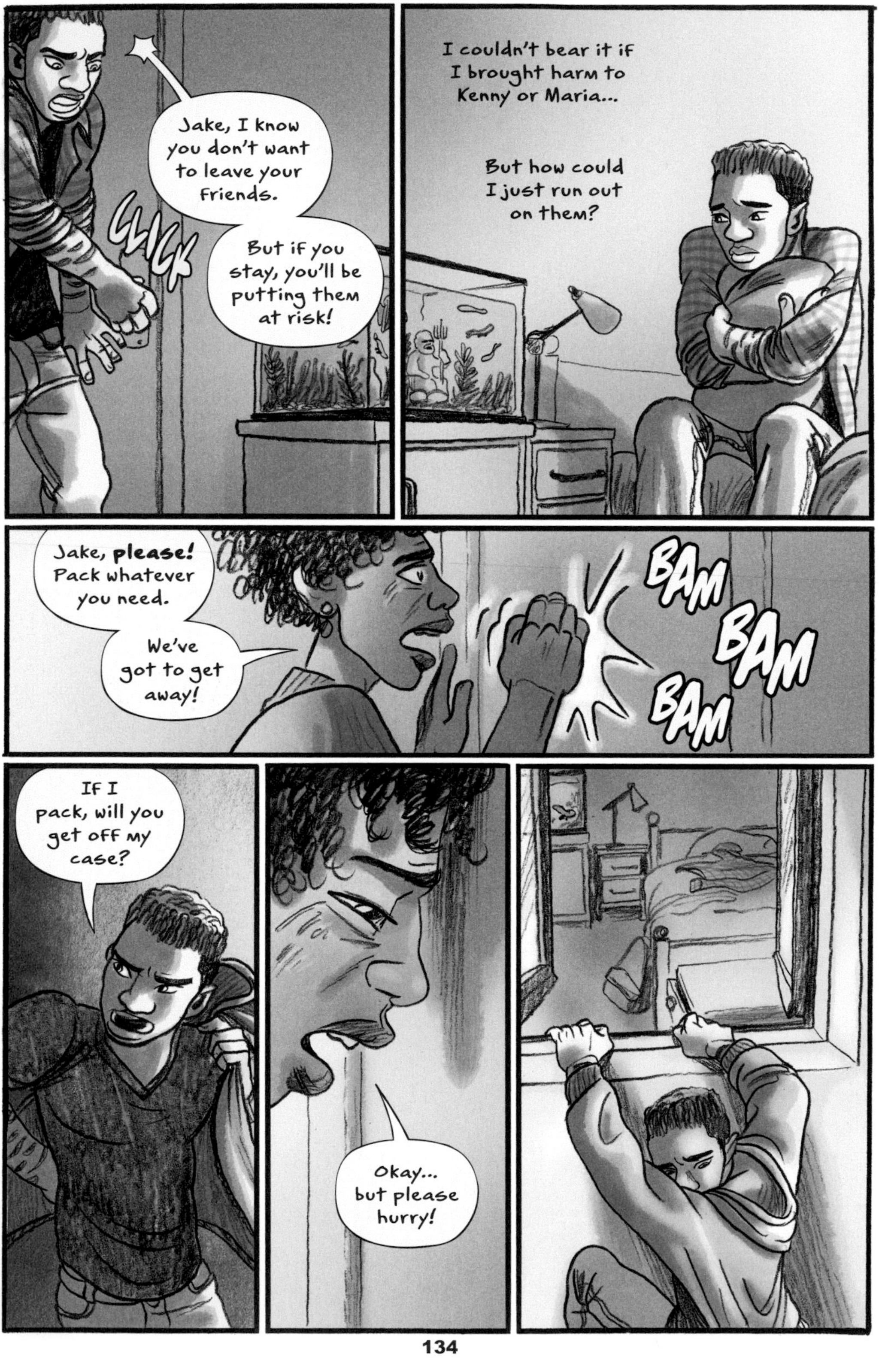
Jake, I know you don't want to leave your friends.
CLICK
But if you stay, you'll be putting them at risk!
I couldn't bear it if I brought harm to Kenny or Maria...
But how could I just run out on them?
Jake, please! Pack whatever you need.
We've got to get away!
BAM
BAM
BAM
If I pack, will you get off my case?
Okay... but please hurry!

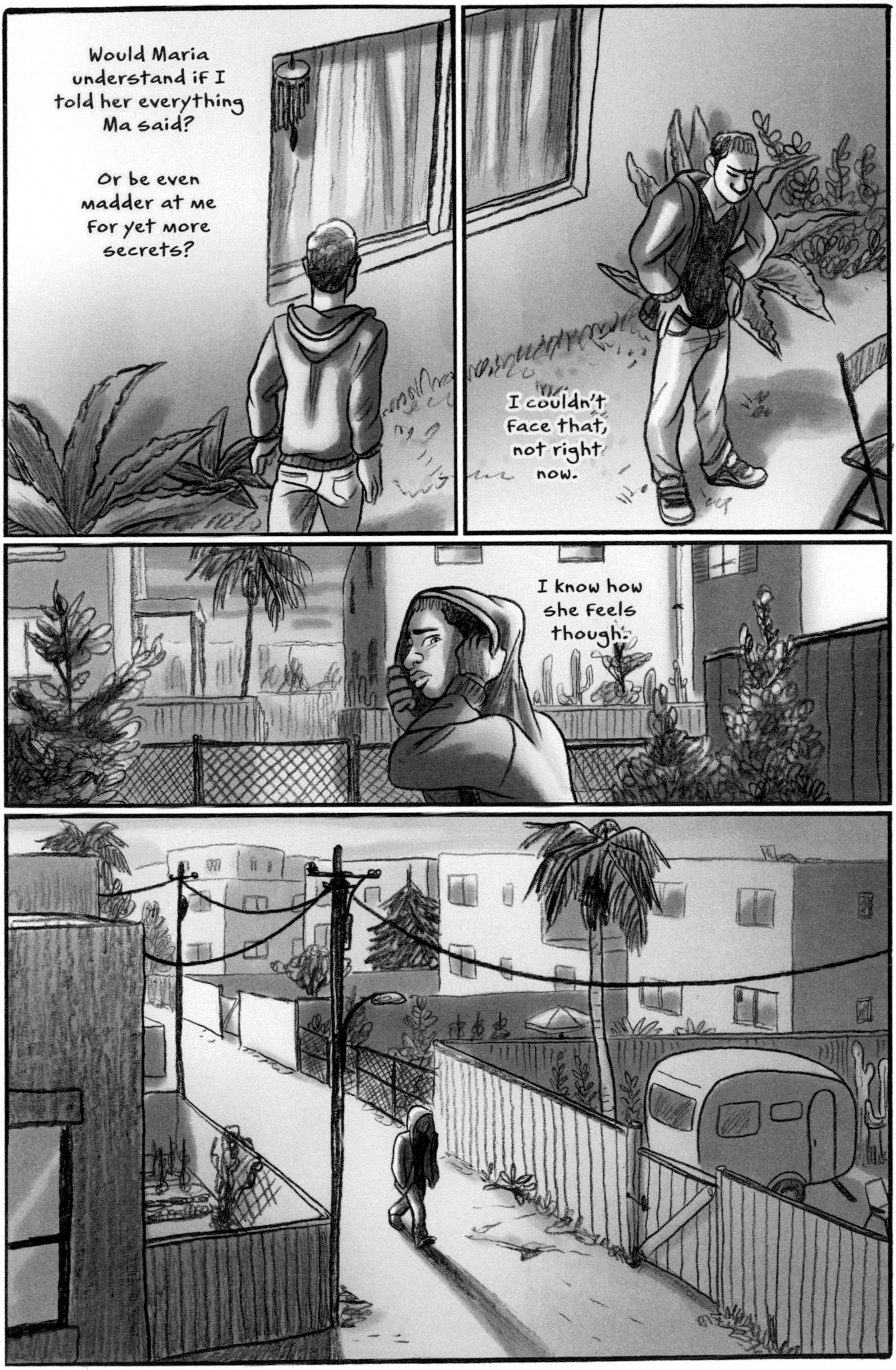
Would Maria understand if I told her everything Ma said?
Or be even madder at me for yet more secrets?
I couldn't face that, not right now.
I know how she feels though.

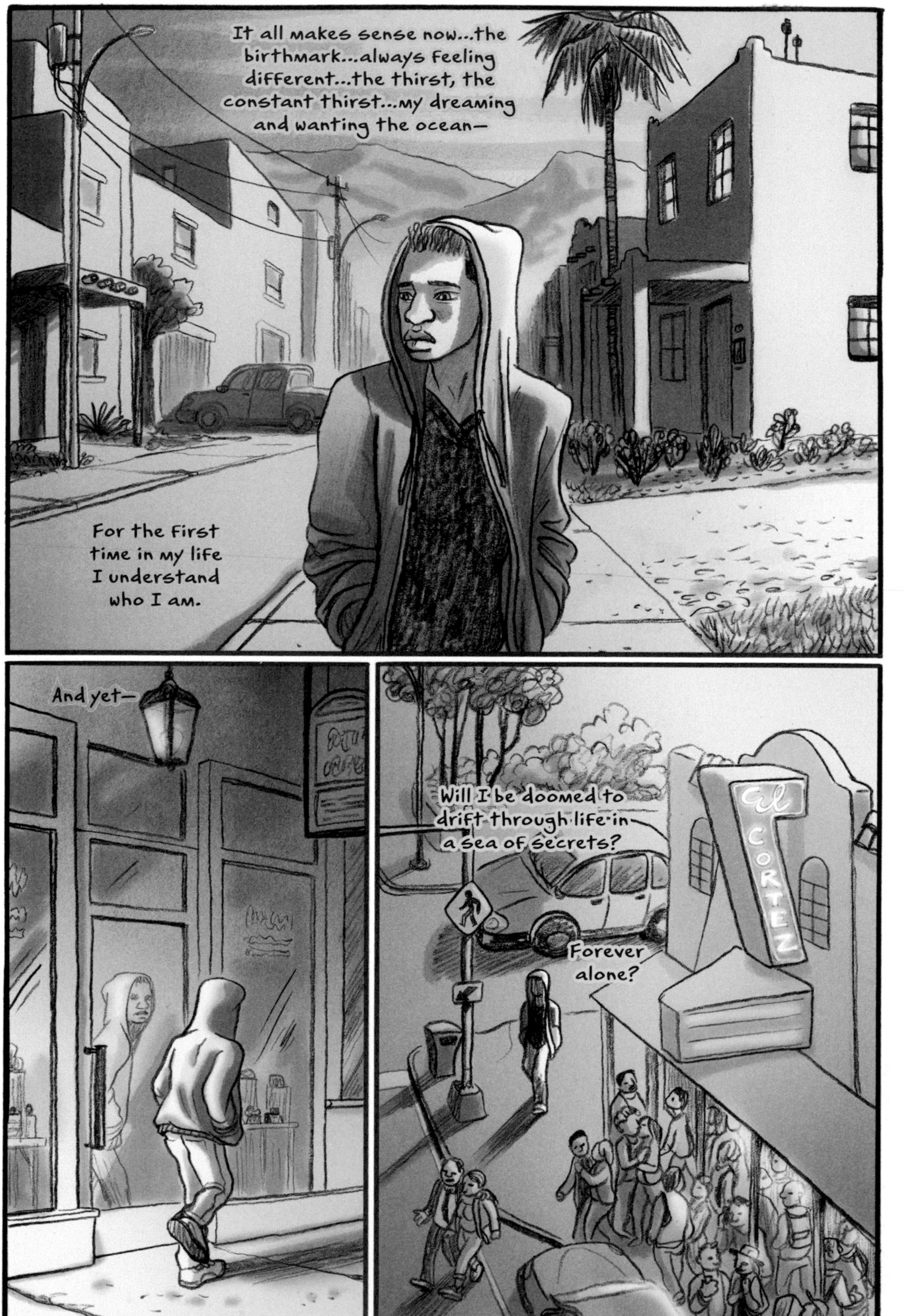
It all makes sense now...the birthmark...always feeling different...the thirst, the constant thirst...my dreaming and wanting the ocean—
For the first time in my life I understand who I am.
And yet—
Will I be doomed to drift through life in a sea of secrets?
Forever alone?
CORTEZ

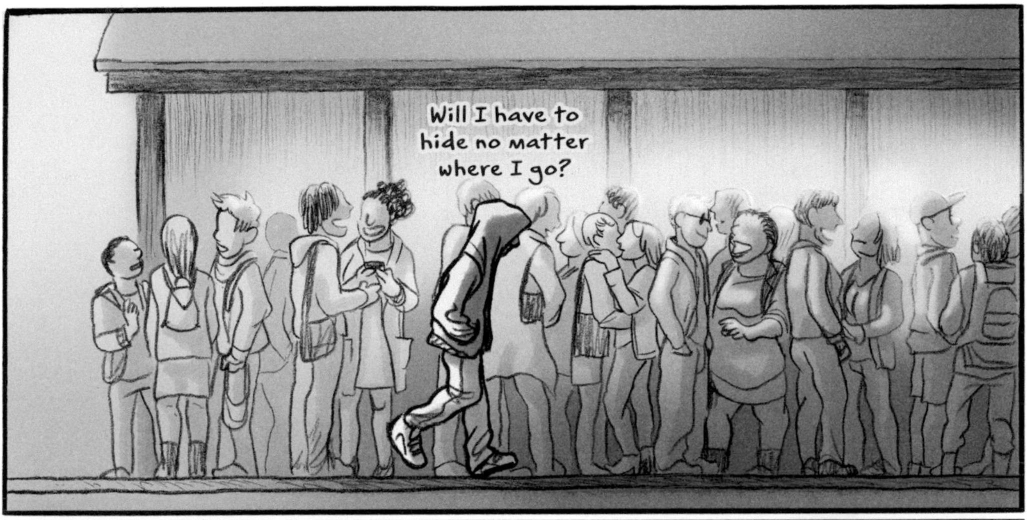
Will I have to hide no matter where I go?

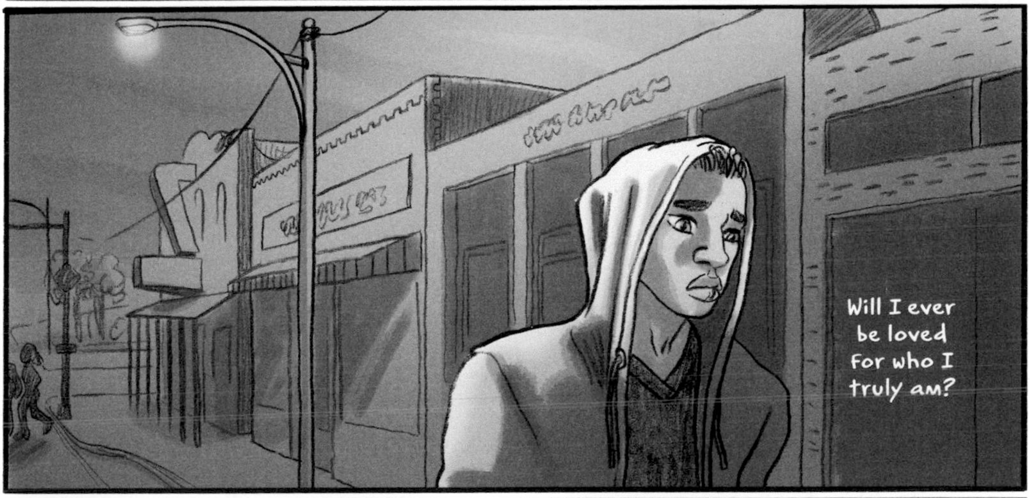
Will I ever be loved for who I truly am?

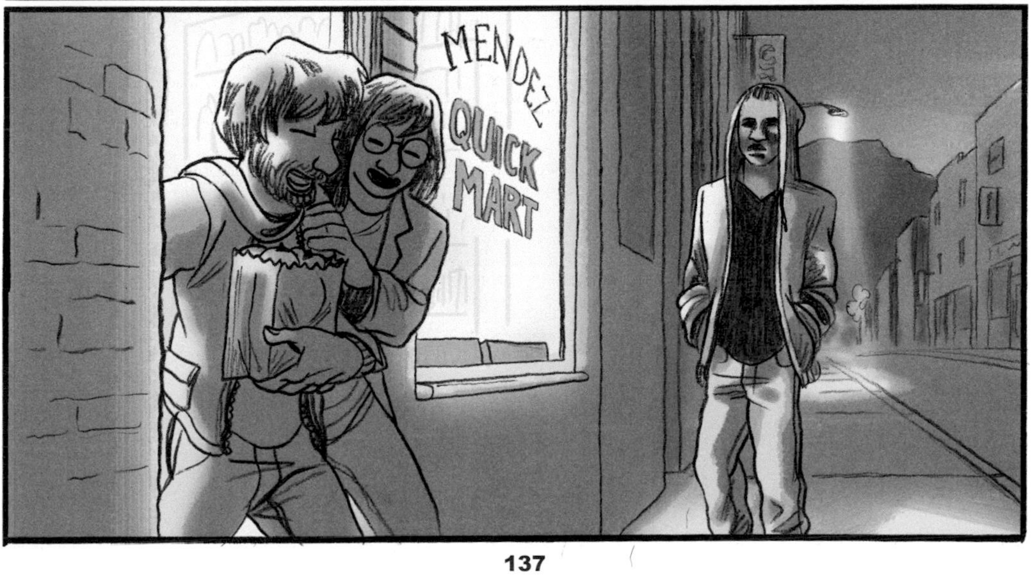
MENDEZ
QUICK MART

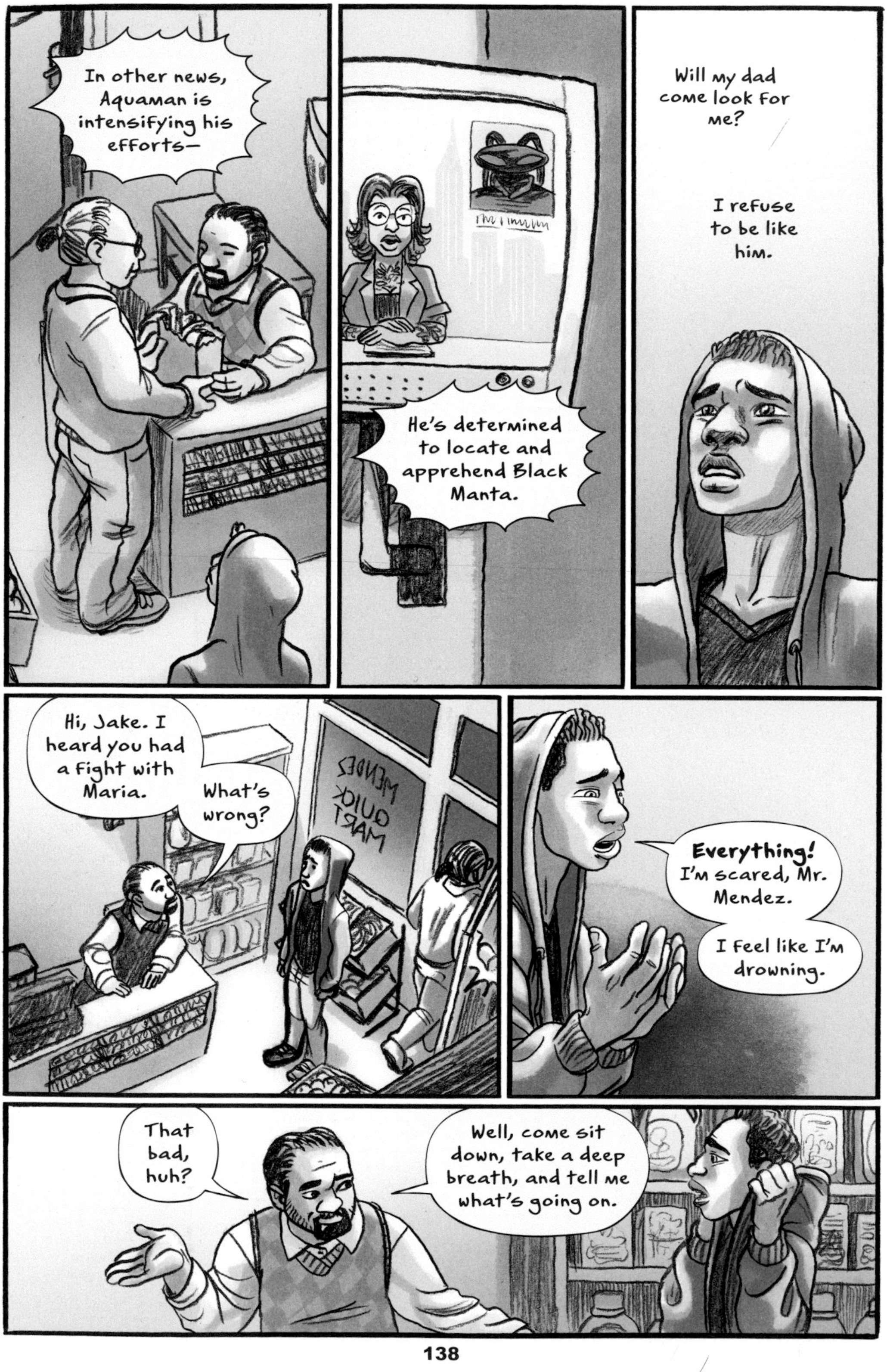
In other news, Aquaman is intensifying his efforts—
He's determined to locate and apprehend Black Manta.
Will my dad come look for me?
I refuse to be like him.
Hi, Jake. I heard you had a fight with Maria.
What's wrong?
MENDEZ QUICK MART
Everything! I'm scared, Mr. Mendez.
I feel like I'm drowning.
That bad, huh?
Well, come sit down, take a deep breath, and tell me what's going on.

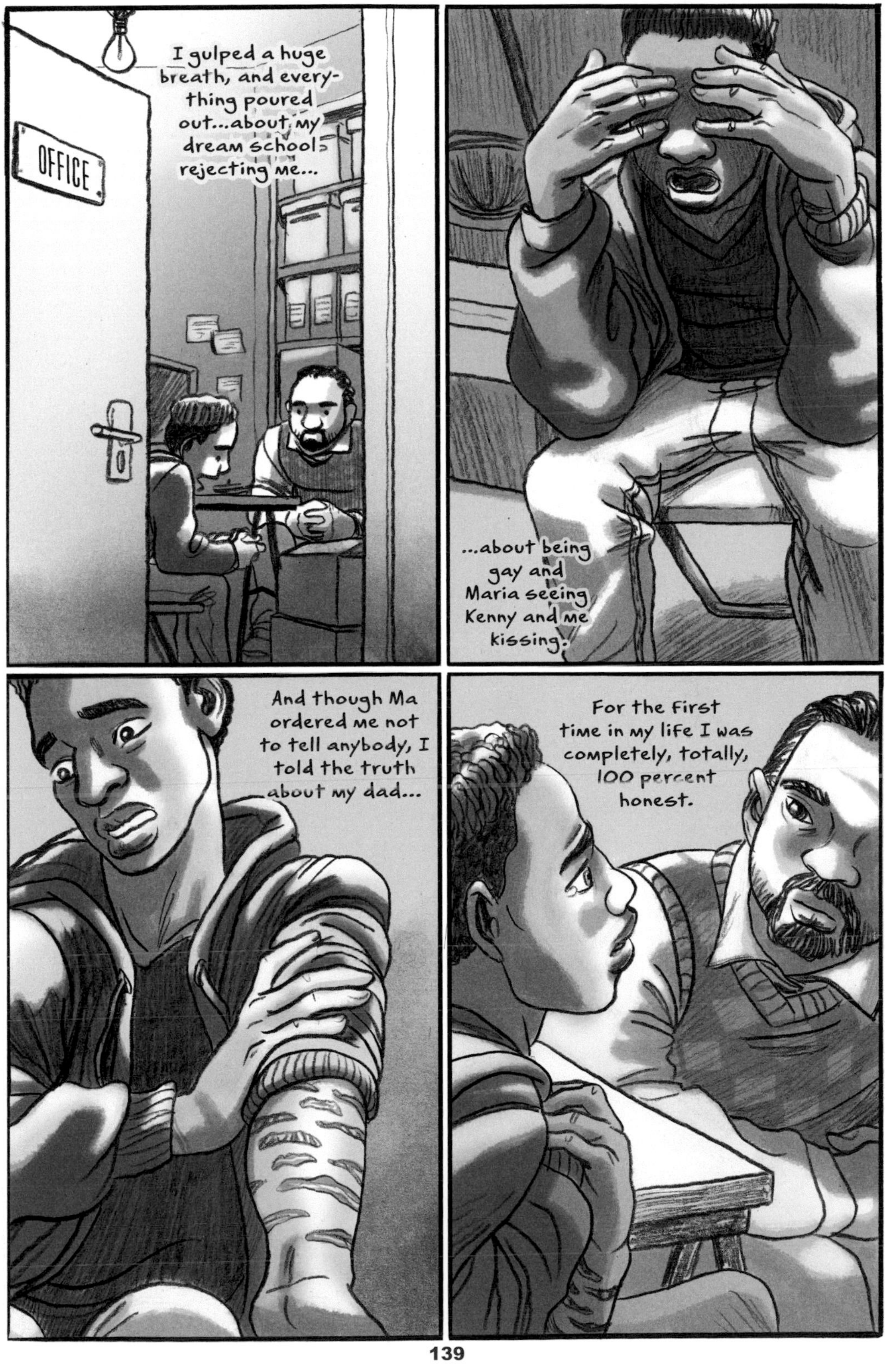
I gulped a huge breath, and everything poured out...about my dream school rejecting me...
OFFICE
...about being gay and Maria seeing Kenny and me kissing.
And though Ma ordered me not to tell anybody, I told the truth about my dad...
For the first time in my life I was completely, totally, 100 percent honest.

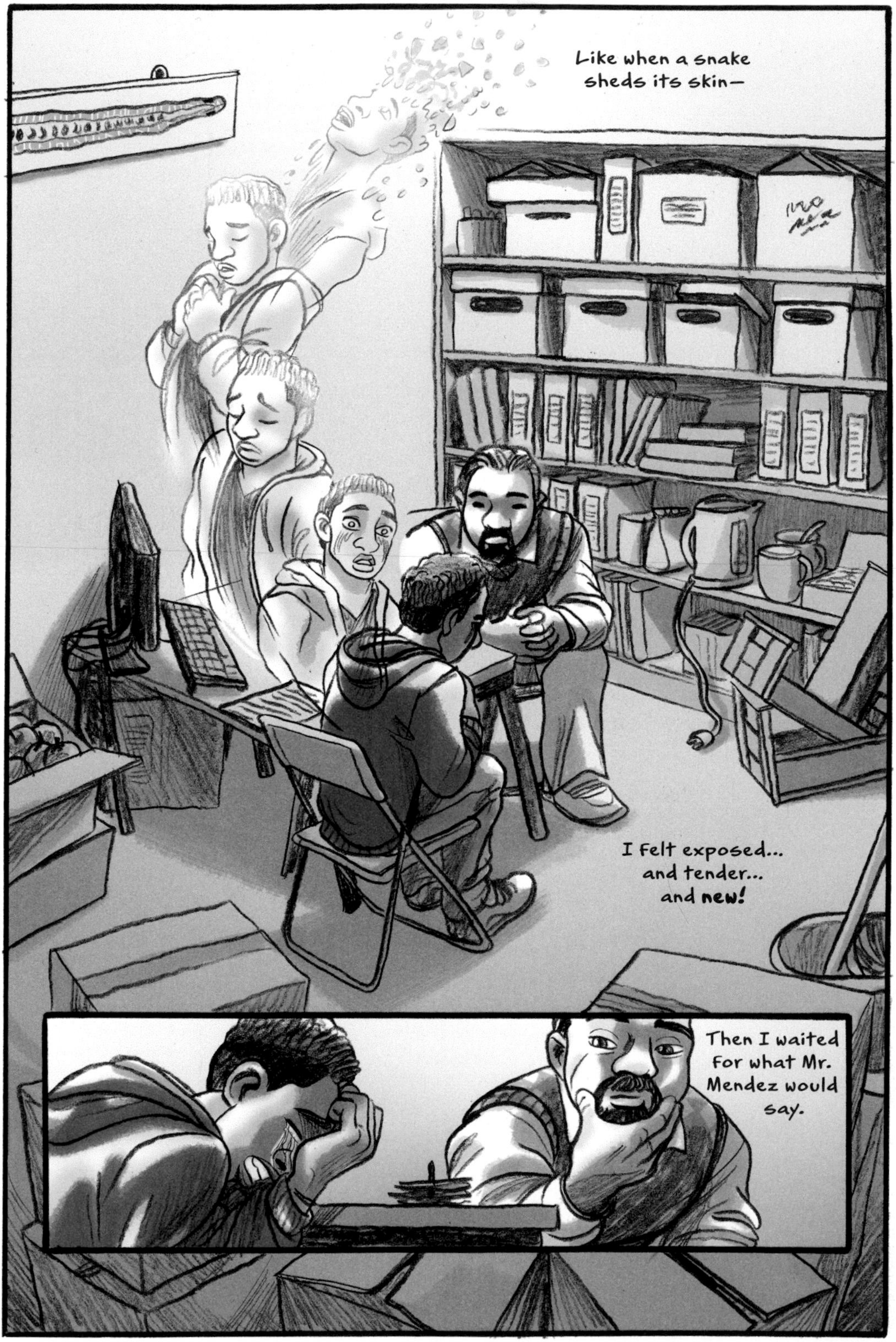
Like when a snake sheds its skin—
I felt exposed... and tender... and new!
Then I waited for what Mr. Mendez would say.

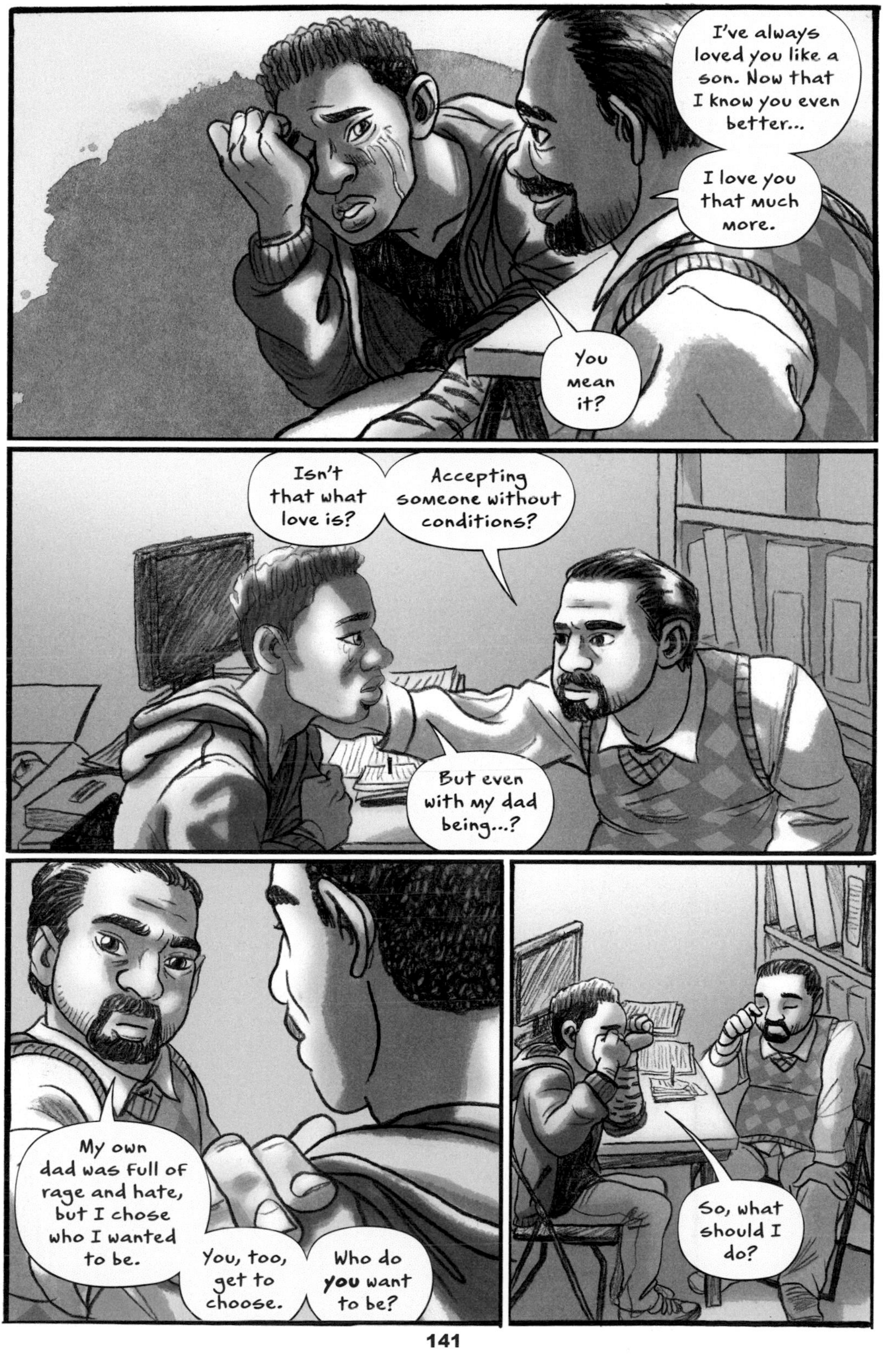
I've always loved you like a son. Now that I know you even better...
I love you that much more.
You mean it?
Isn't that what love is?
Accepting someone without conditions?
But even with my dad being...?
My own dad was full of rage and hate, but I chose who I wanted to be.
You, too, get to choose.
Who do **you** want to be?
So, what should I do?

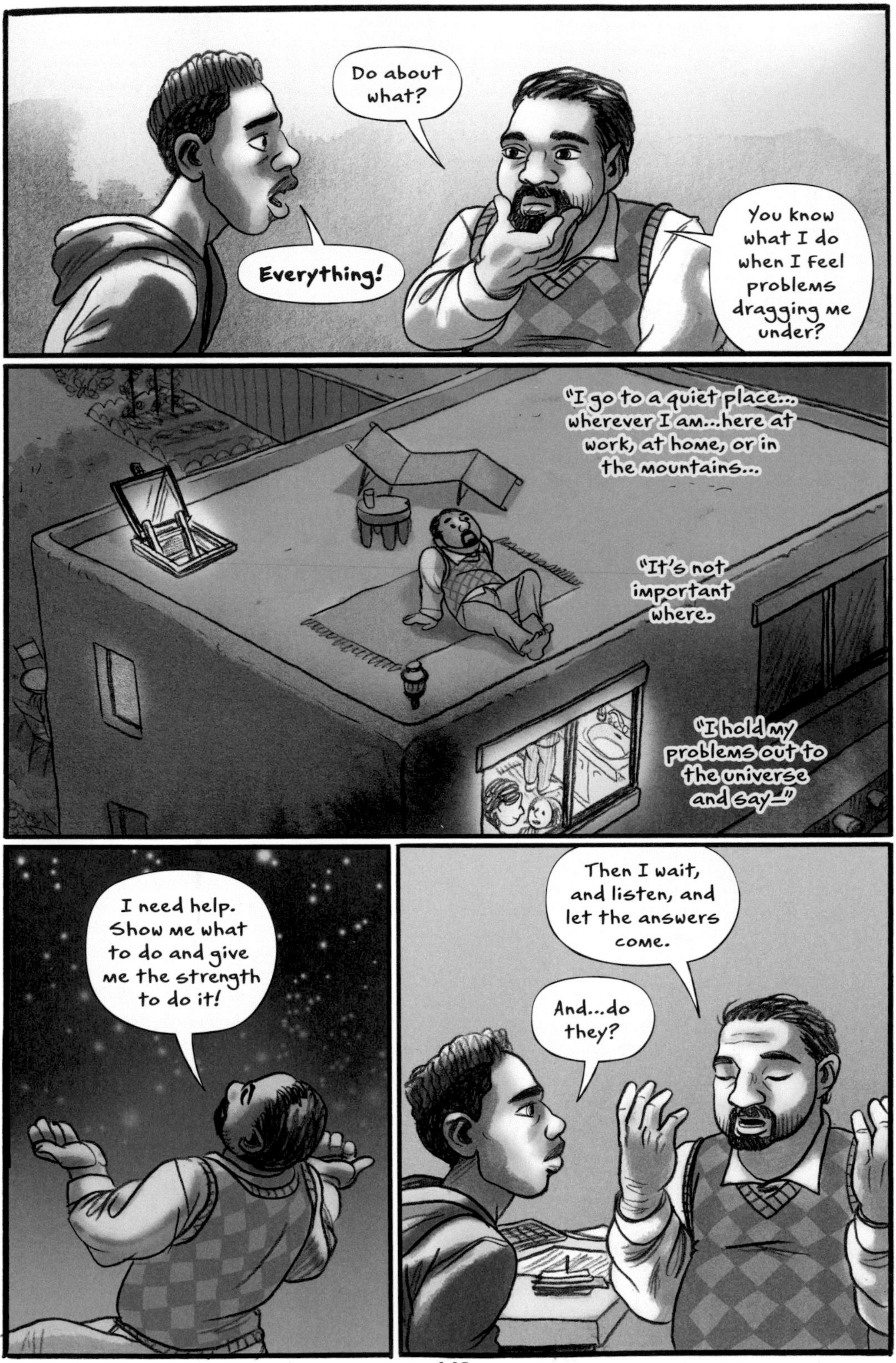
Do about what?
Everything!
You know what I do when I feel problems dragging me under?
"I go to a quiet place... wherever I am...here at work, at home, or in the mountains...
"It's not important where.
"I hold my problems out to the universe and say—"
I need help. Show me what to do and give me the strength to do it!
Then I wait, and listen, and let the answers come.
And...do they?

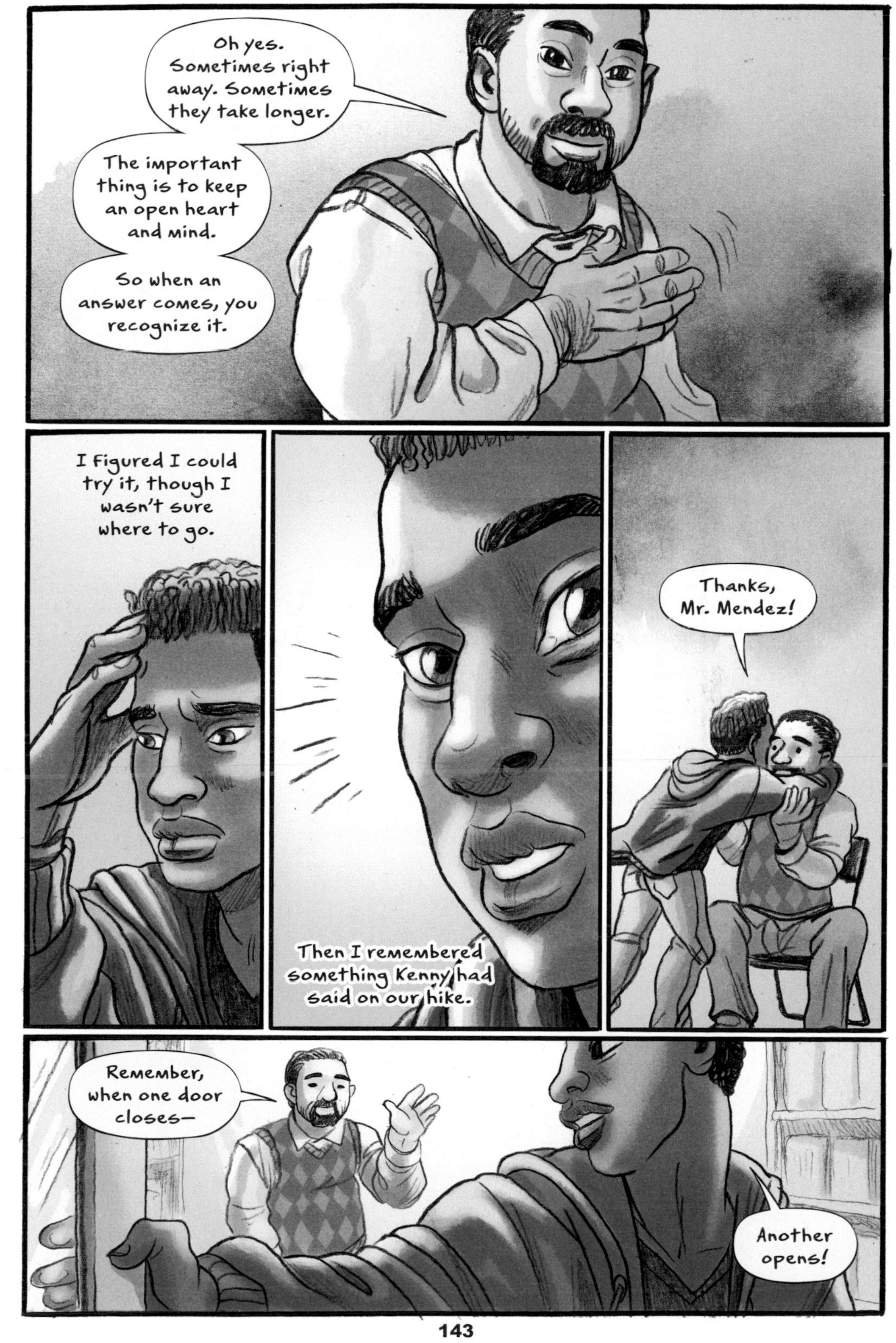
Oh yes. Sometimes right away. Sometimes they take longer.
The important thing is to keep an open heart and mind.
So when an answer comes, you recognize it.
I figured I could try it, though I wasn't sure where to go.
Then I remembered something Kenny had said on our hike.
Thanks, Mr. Mendez!
Remember, when one door closes—
Another opens!

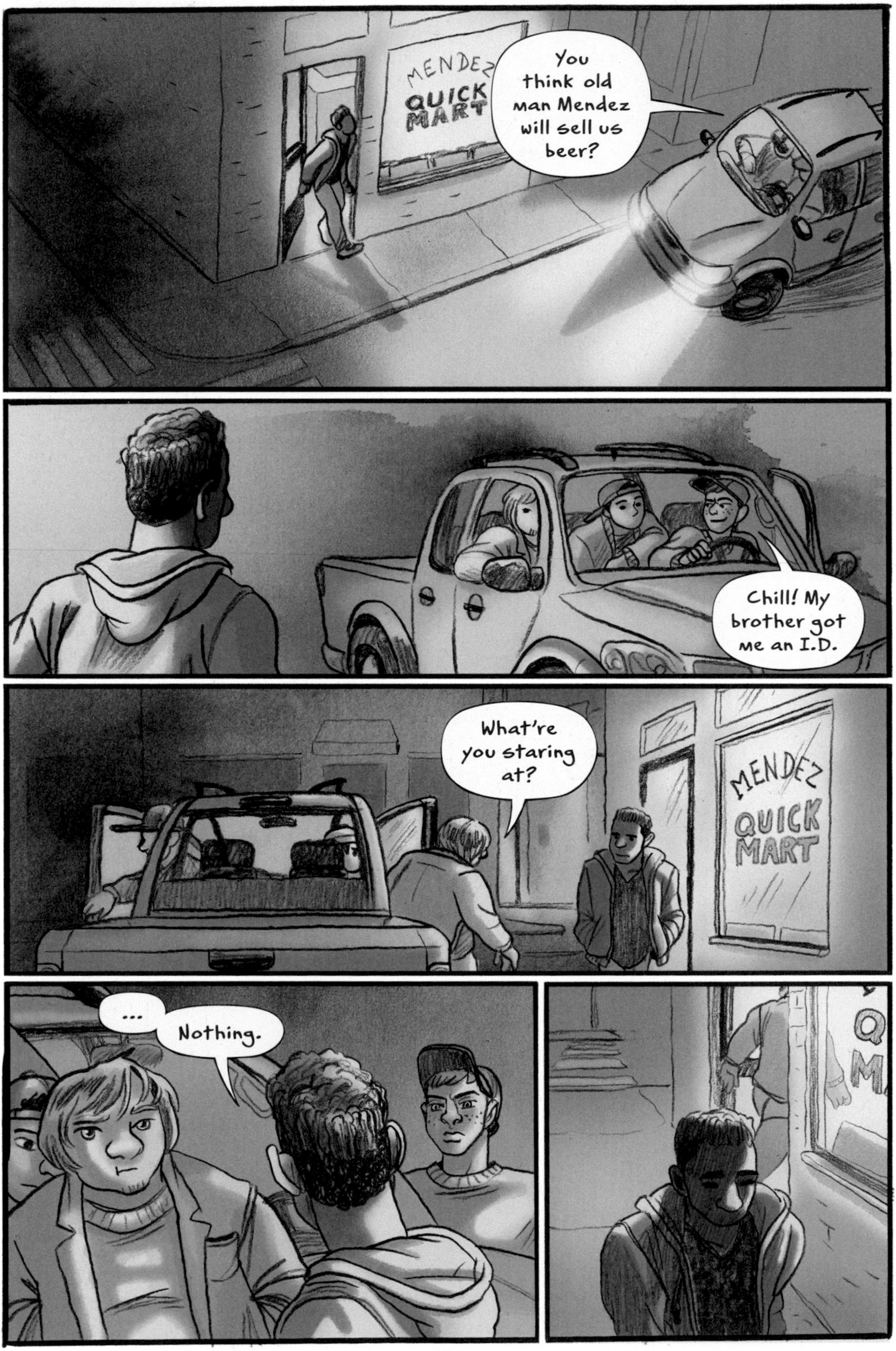
MENDEZ
QUICK MART
You think old man Mendez will sell us beer?
Chill! My brother got me an I.D.
What're you staring at?
MENDEZ
QUICK MART
...
Nothing.

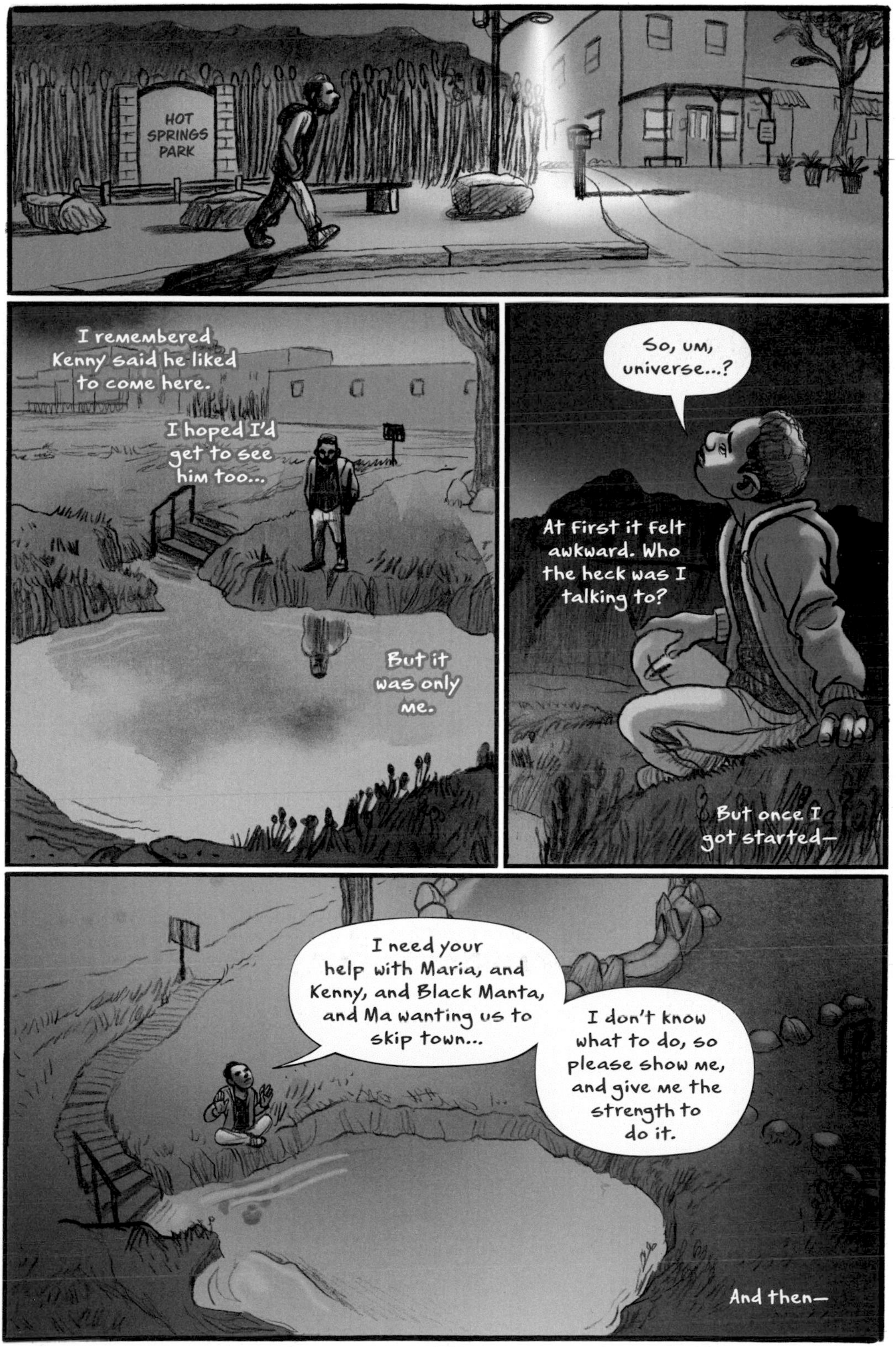
HOT SPRINGS PARK
I remembered Kenny said he liked to come here.
I hoped I'd get to see him too...
But it was only me.
So, um, universe...?
At first it felt awkward. Who the heck was I talking to?
But once I got started—
I need your help with Maria, and Kenny, and Black Manta, and Ma wanting us to skip town...
I don't know what to do, so please show me, and give me the strength to do it.
And then—

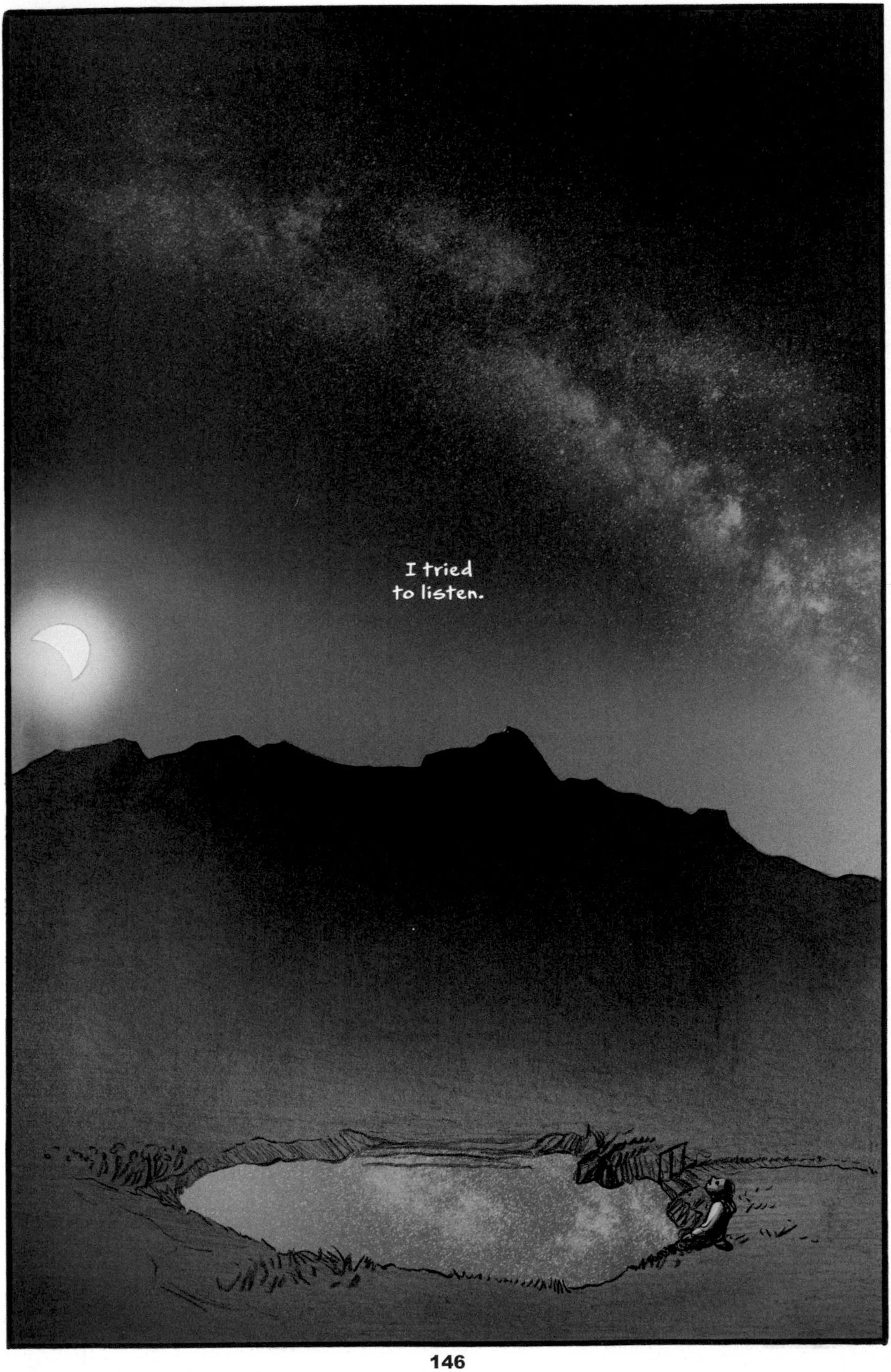
I tried
to listen.

CHAPTER 4

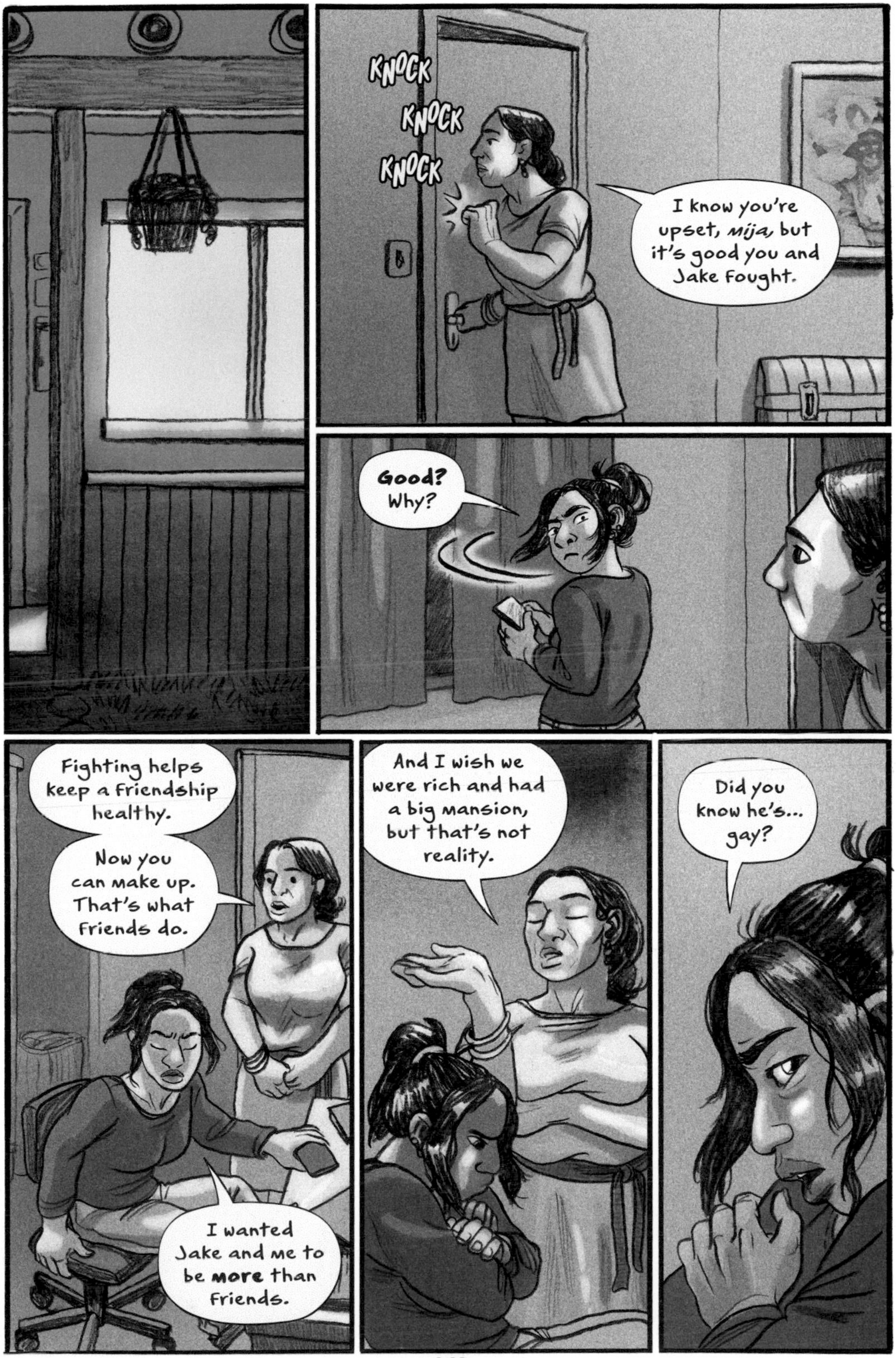

KNOCK
KNOCK
KNOCK
I know you're upset, *mija*, but it's good you and Jake fought.
Good? Why?
Fighting helps keep a friendship healthy.
Now you can make up. That's what friends do.
I wanted Jake and me to be **more** than friends.
And I wish we were rich and had a big mansion, but that's not reality.
Did you know he's... gay?

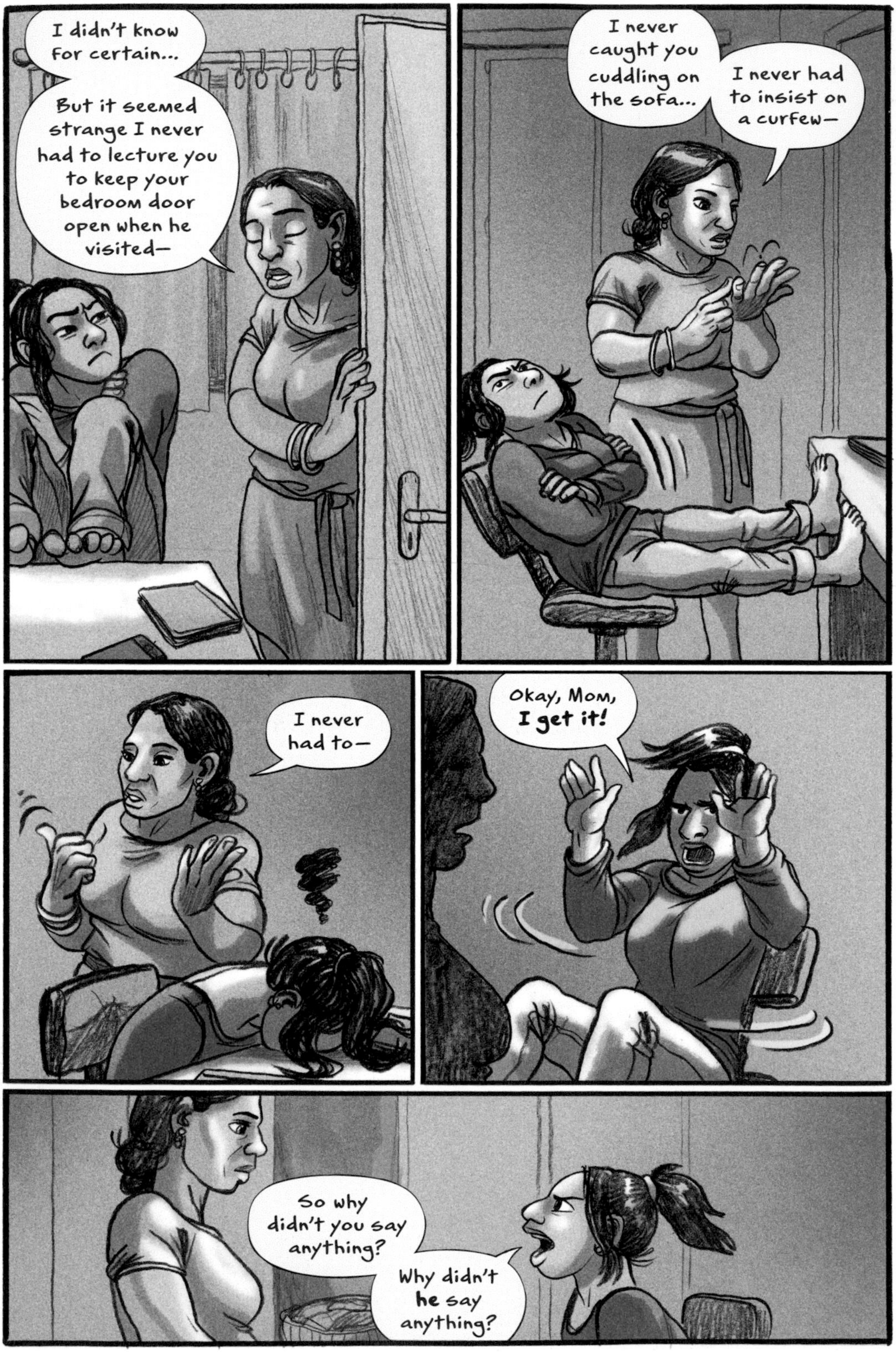
I didn't know for certain...
But it seemed strange I never had to lecture you to keep your bedroom door open when he visited—
I never caught you cuddling on the sofa...
I never had to insist on a curfew—
I never had to—
Okay, Mom, **I get it!**
So why didn't you say anything?
Why didn't **he** say anything?

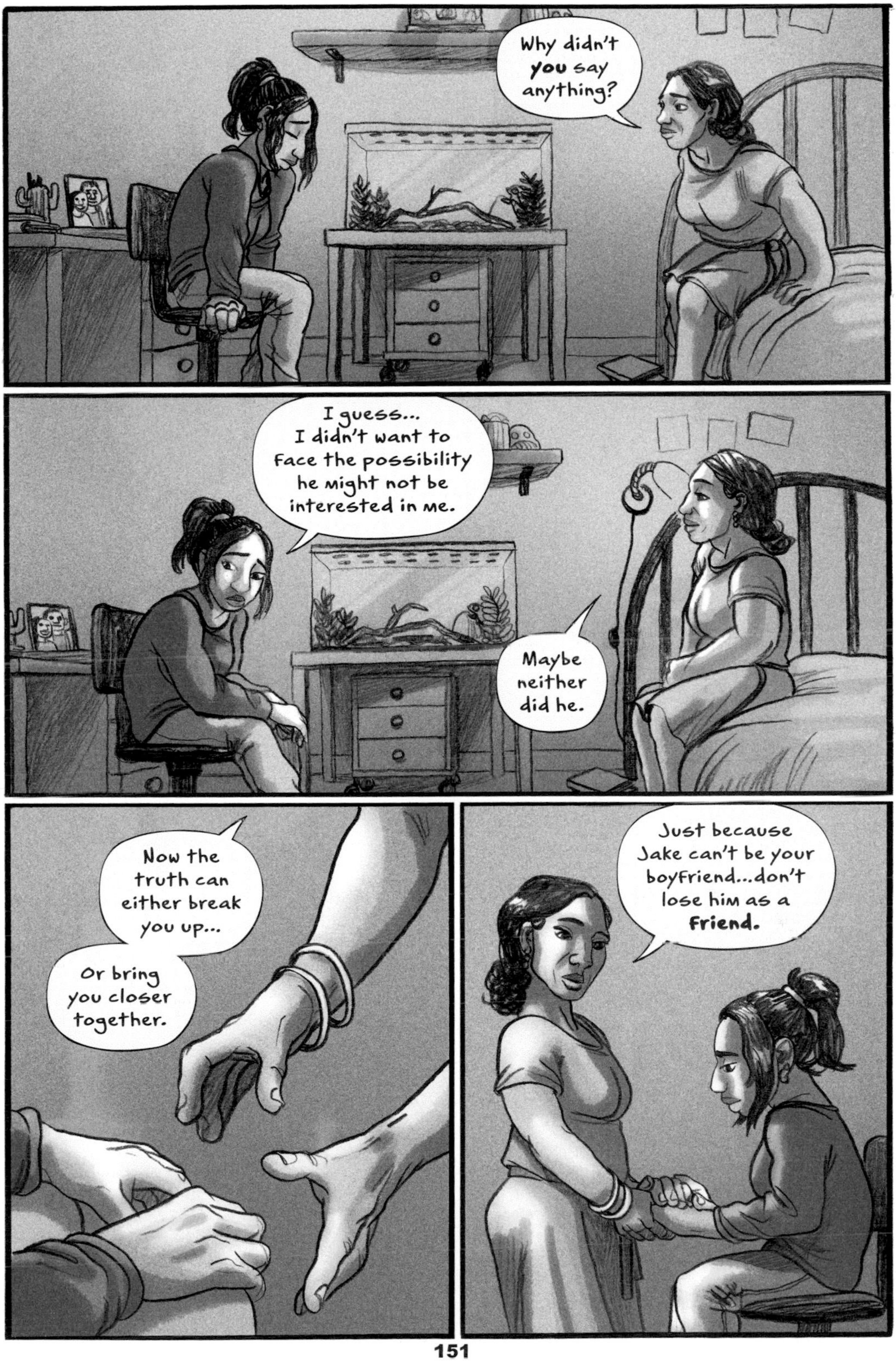
Why didn't **you** say anything?
I guess... I didn't want to face the possibility he might not be interested in me.
Maybe neither did he.
Now the truth can either break you up...
Or bring you closer together.
Just because Jake can't be your boyfriend...don't lose him as a **friend.**

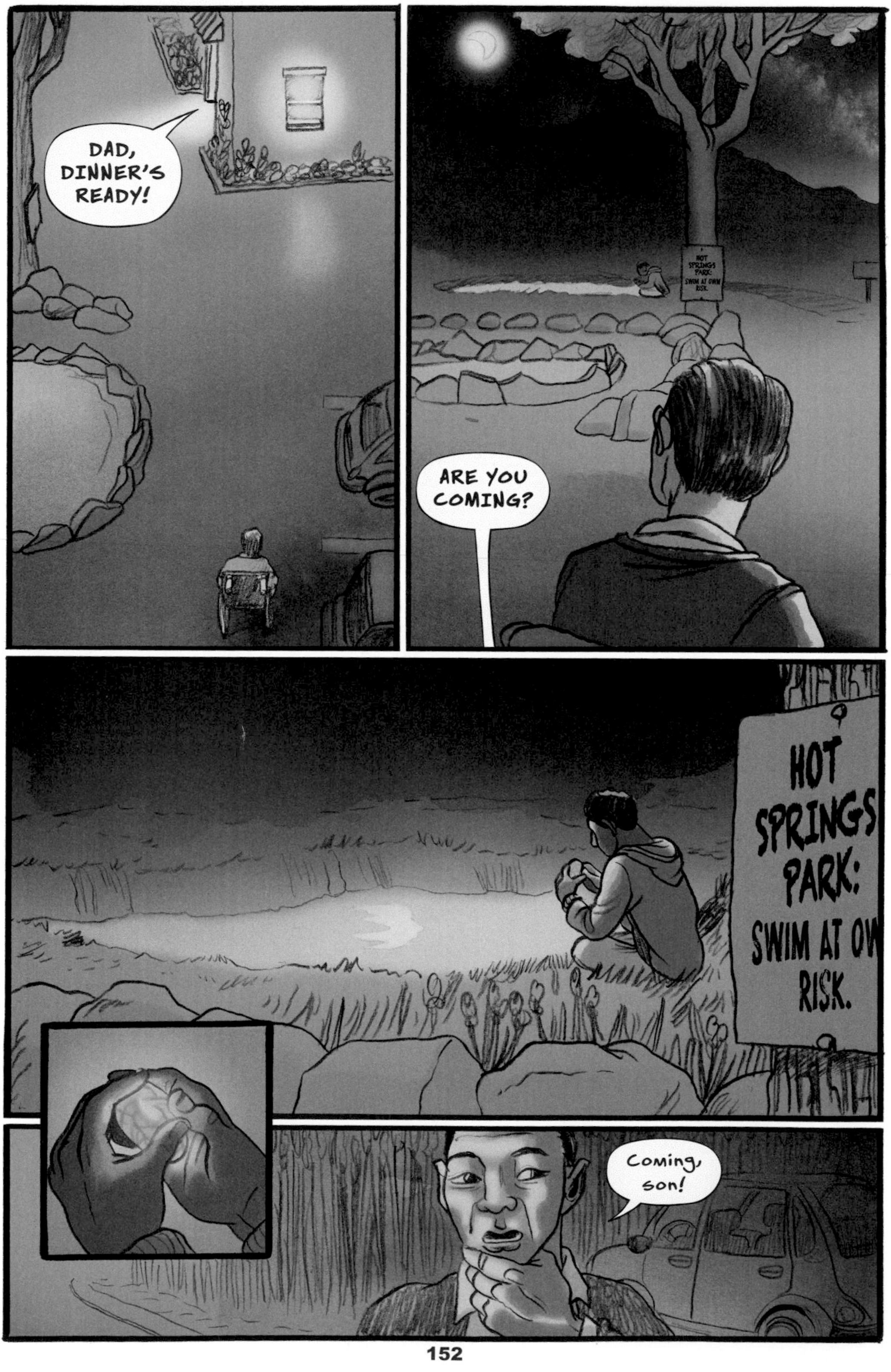
DAD, DINNER'S READY!
HOT SPRINGS PARK: SWIM AT OWN RISK.
ARE YOU COMING?
HOT SPRINGS PARK: SWIM AT OW RISK.
Coming, son!

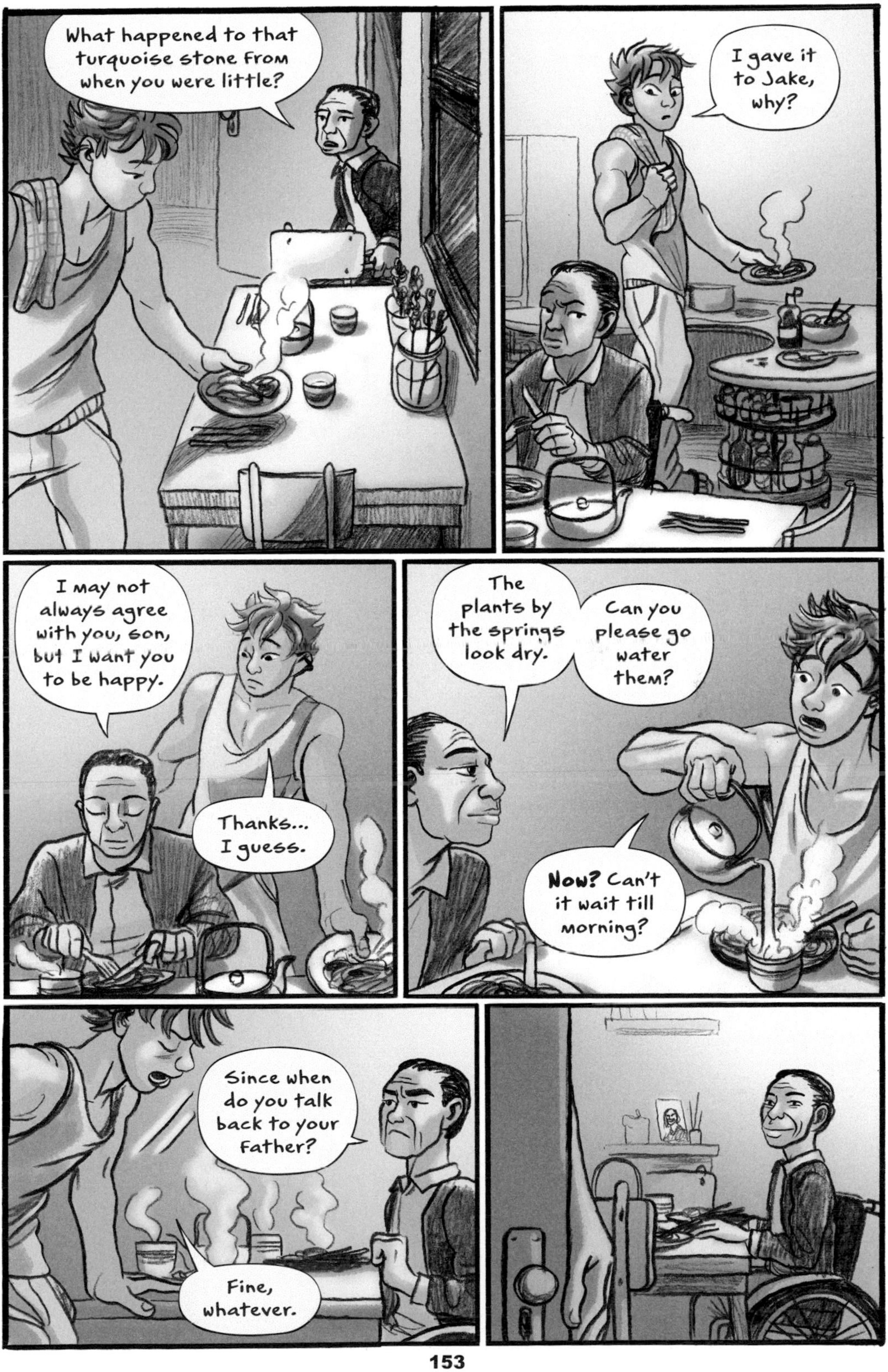
What happened to that turquoise stone from when you were little?
I gave it to Jake, why?
I may not always agree with you, son, but I want you to be happy.
Thanks... I guess.
The plants by the springs look dry.
Can you please go water them?
Now? Can't it wait till morning?
Since when do you talk back to your father?
Fine, whatever.

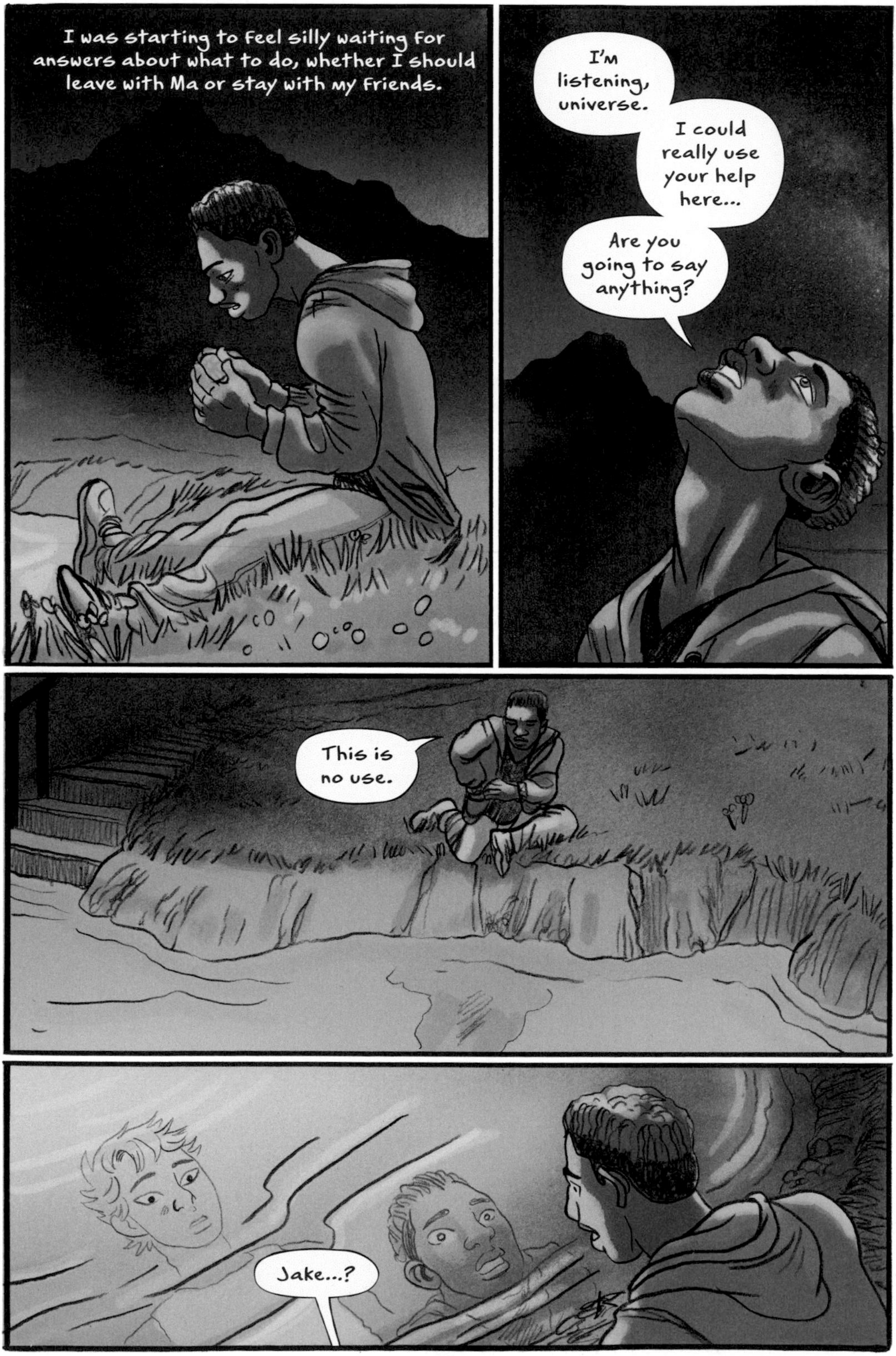
I was starting to feel silly waiting for answers about what to do, whether I should leave with Ma or stay with my friends.
I'm listening, universe.
I could really use your help here...
Are you going to say anything?
This is no use.
Jake...?

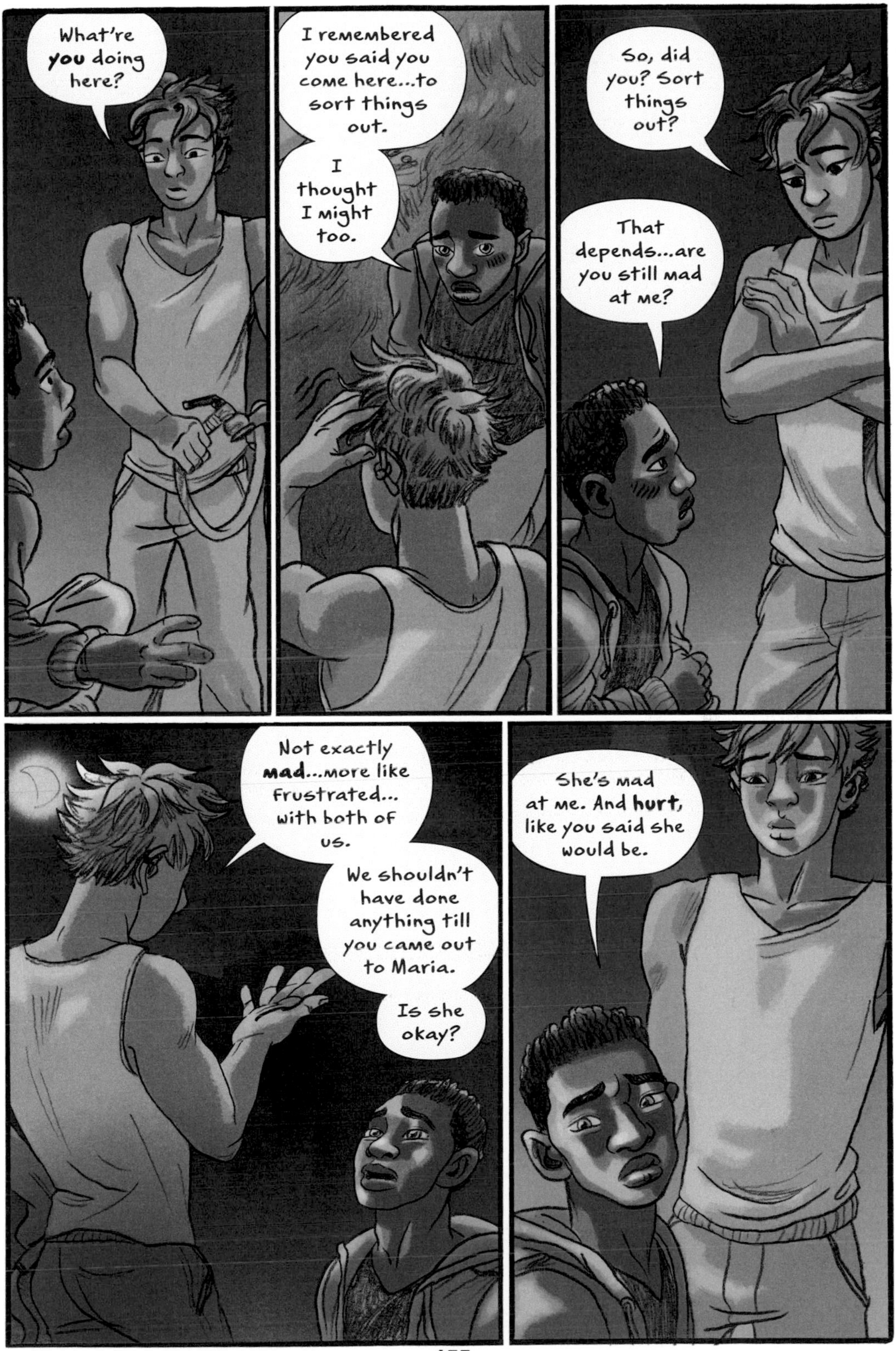
What're **you** doing here?
I remembered you said you come here...to sort things out.
I thought I might too.
So, did you? Sort things out?
That depends...are you still mad at me?
Not exactly **mad**...more like frustrated... with both of us.
We shouldn't have done anything till you came out to Maria.
Is she okay?
She's mad at me. And **hurt**, like you said she would be.

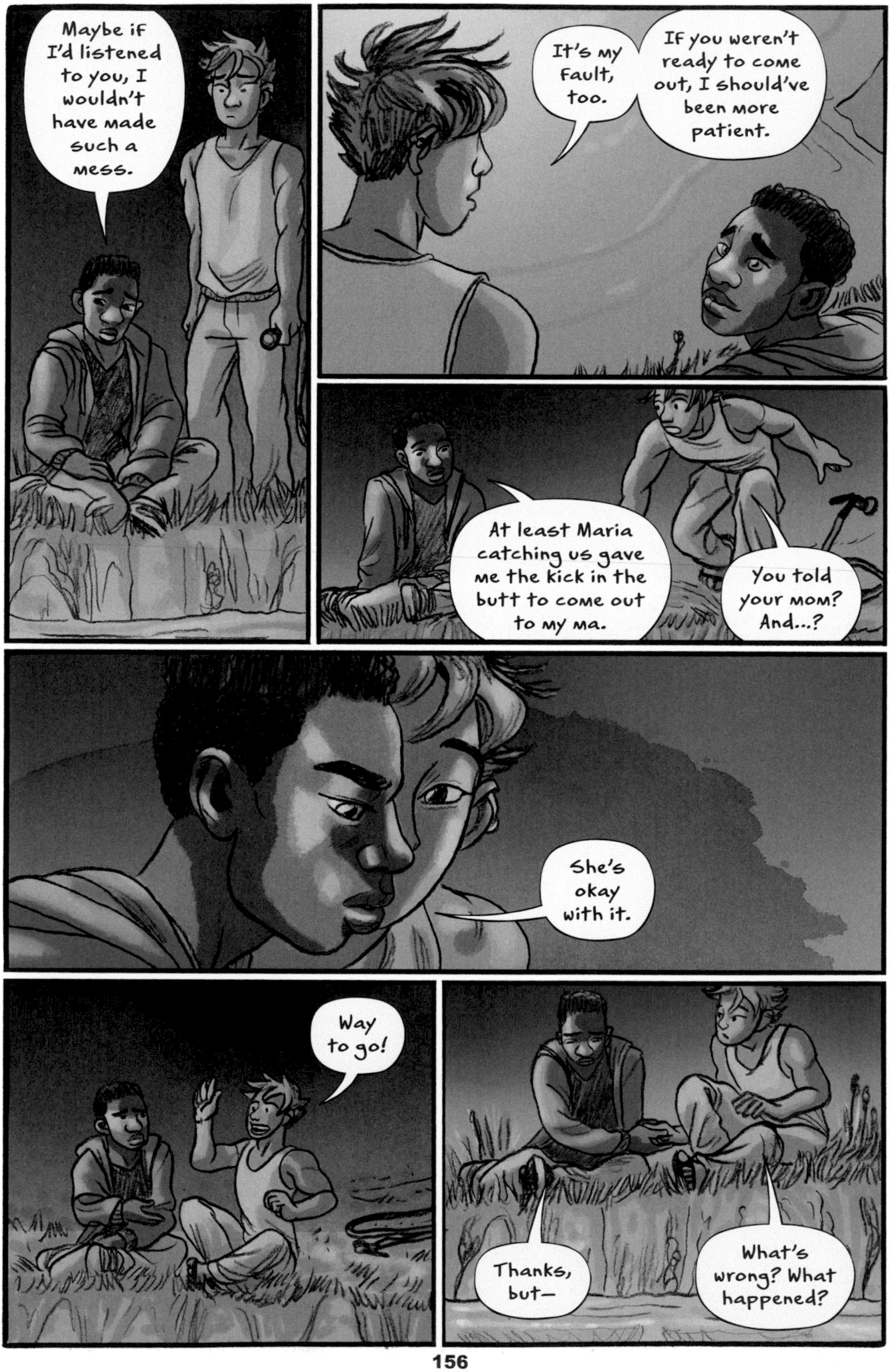

Maybe if I'd listened to you, I wouldn't have made such a mess.
It's my fault, too.
If you weren't ready to come out, I should've been more patient.
At least Maria catching us gave me the kick in the butt to come out to my ma.
You told your mom? And...?
She's okay with it.
Way to go!
Thanks, but—
What's wrong? What happened?

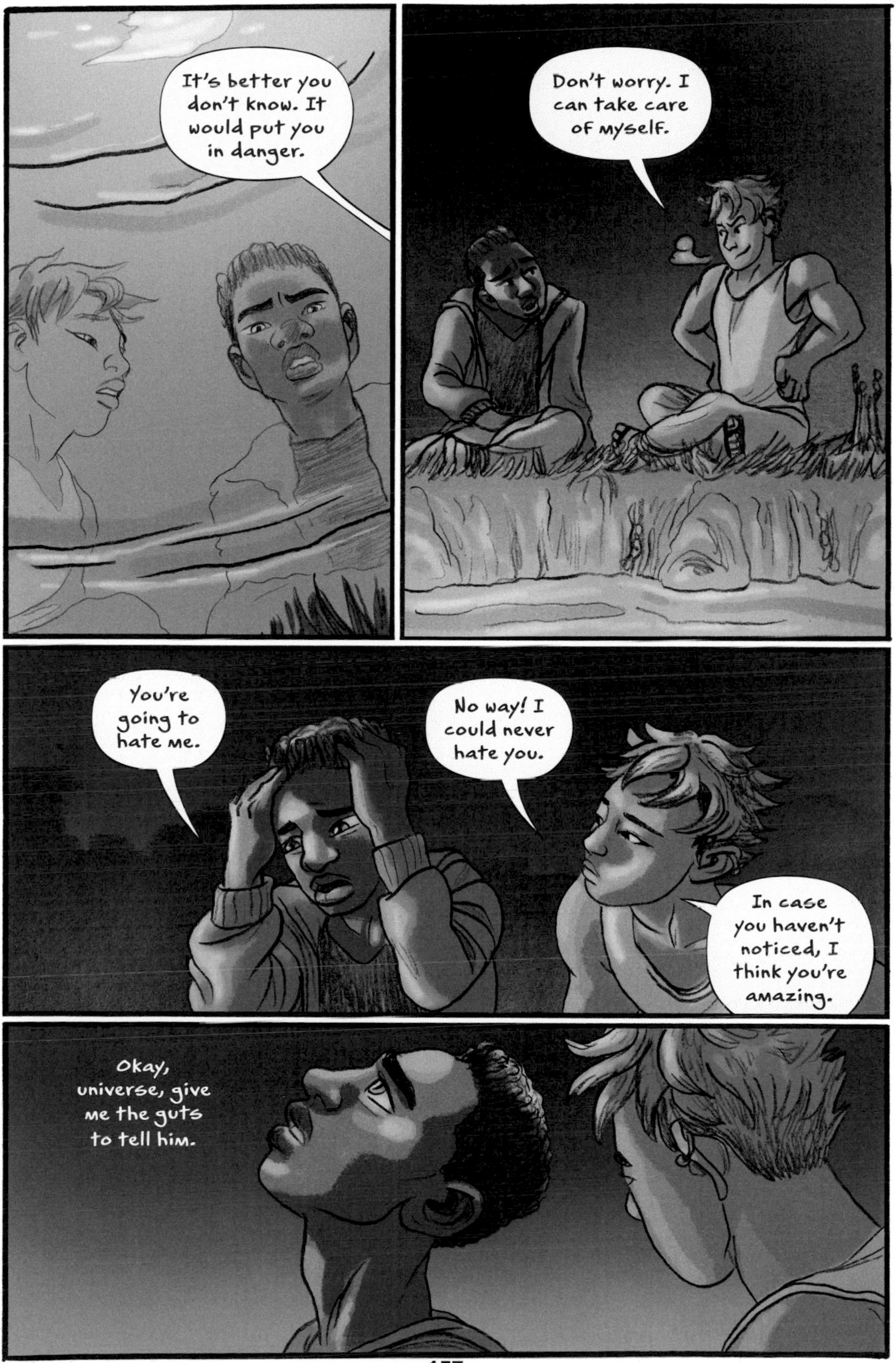
It's better you don't know. It would put you in danger.
Don't worry. I can take care of myself.
You're going to hate me.
No way! I could never hate you.
In case you haven't noticed, I think you're amazing.
Okay, universe, give me the guts to tell him.

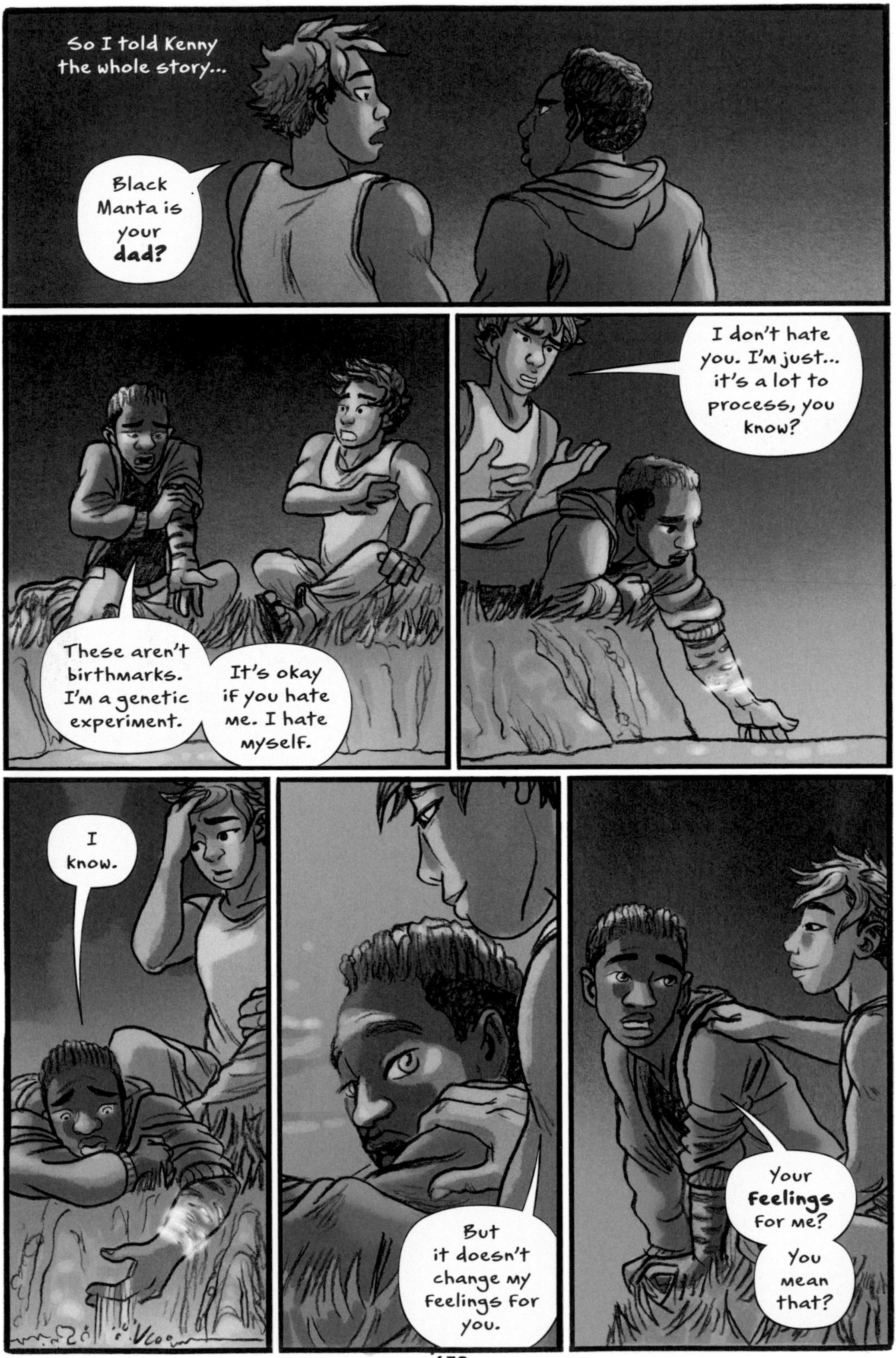
So I told Kenny the whole story...
Black Manta is your **dad?**
These aren't birthmarks. I'm a genetic experiment.
It's okay if you hate me. I hate myself.
I don't hate you. I'm just... it's a lot to process, you know?
I know.
But it doesn't change my feelings for you.
Your **feelings** for me?
You mean that?

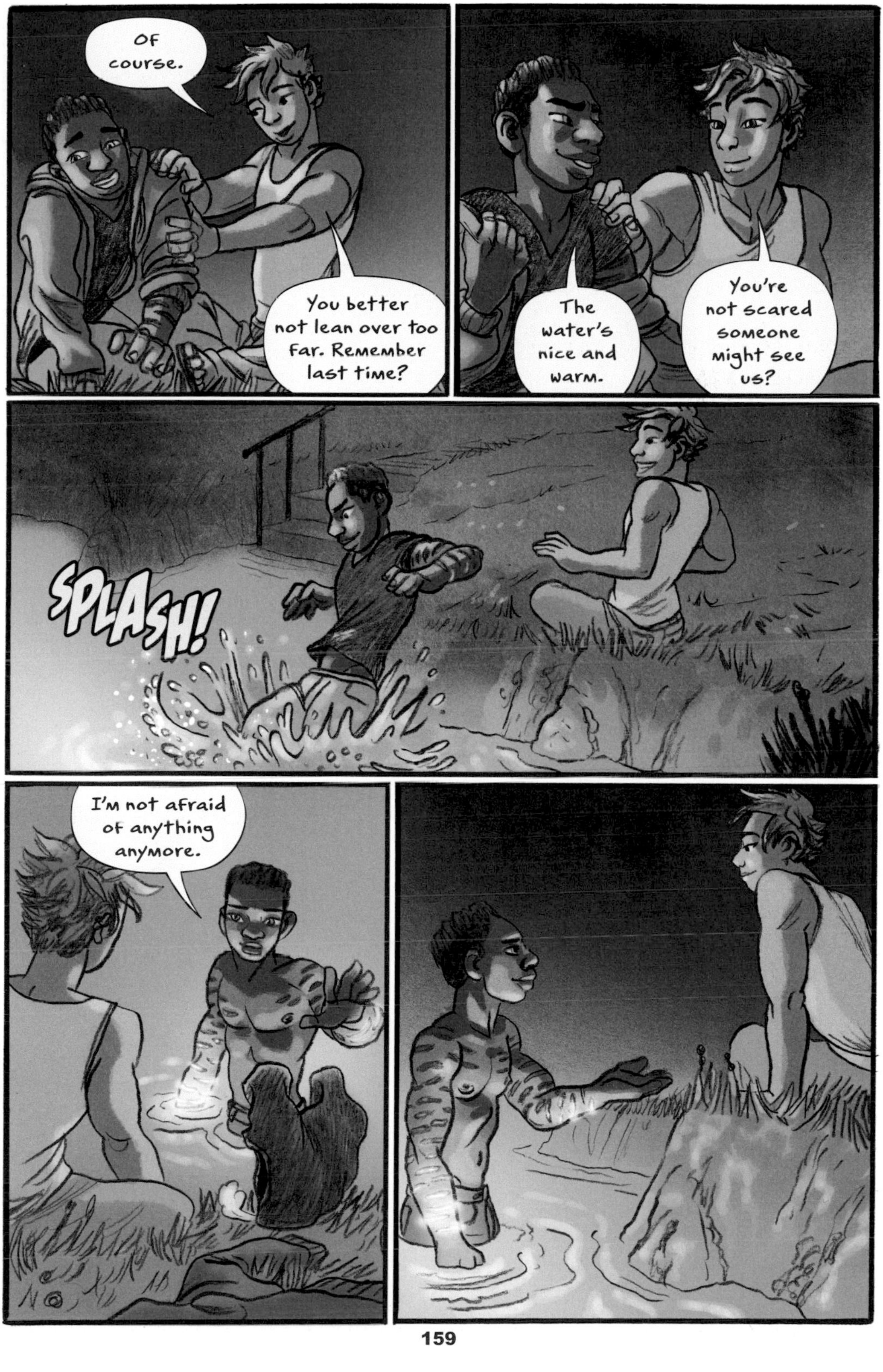
Of course.
You better not lean over too far. Remember last time?
The water's nice and warm.
You're not scared someone might see us?
SPLASH!
I'm not afraid of anything anymore.

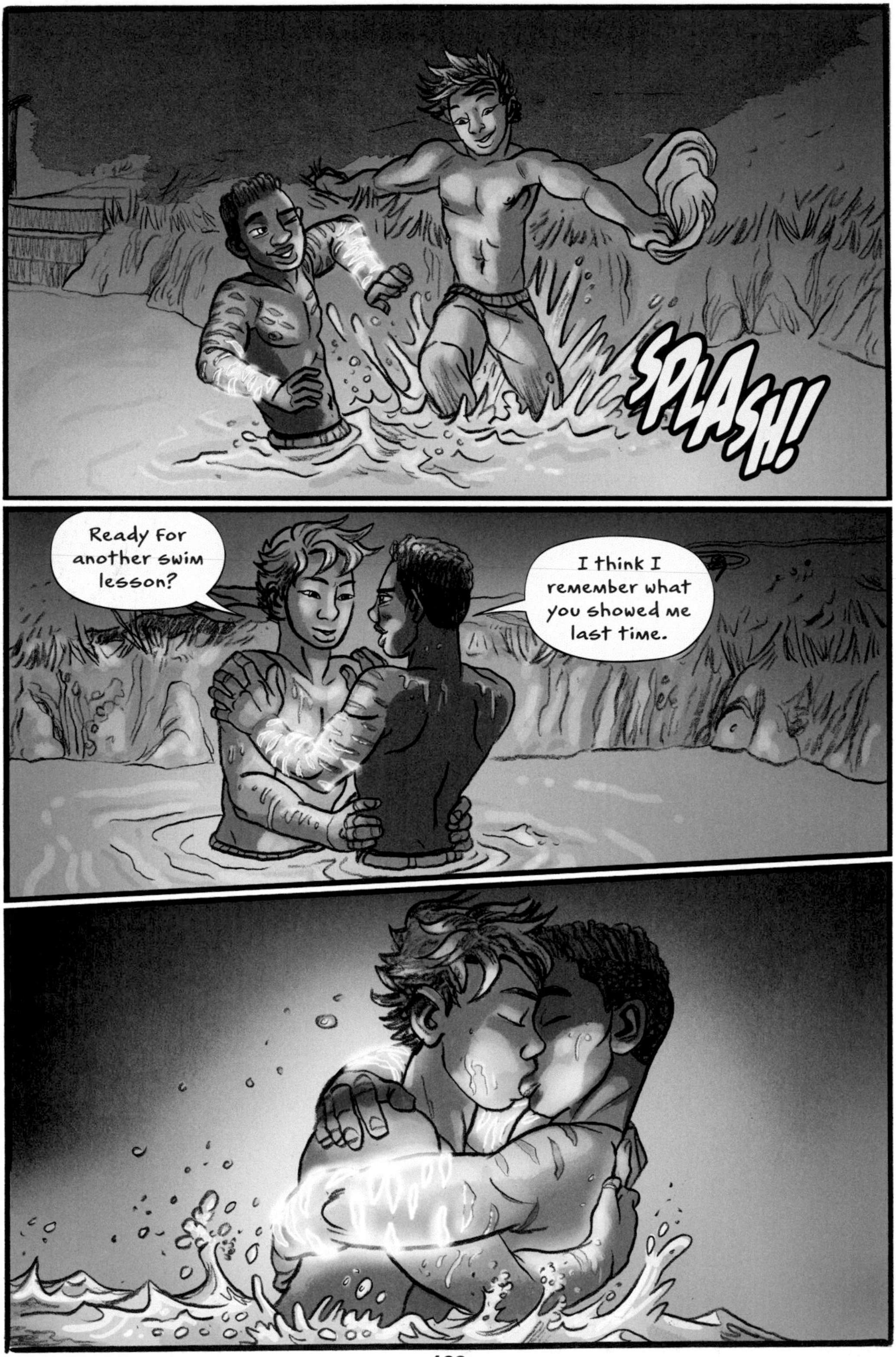
SPLASH!
Ready for another swim lesson?
I think I remember what you showed me last time.

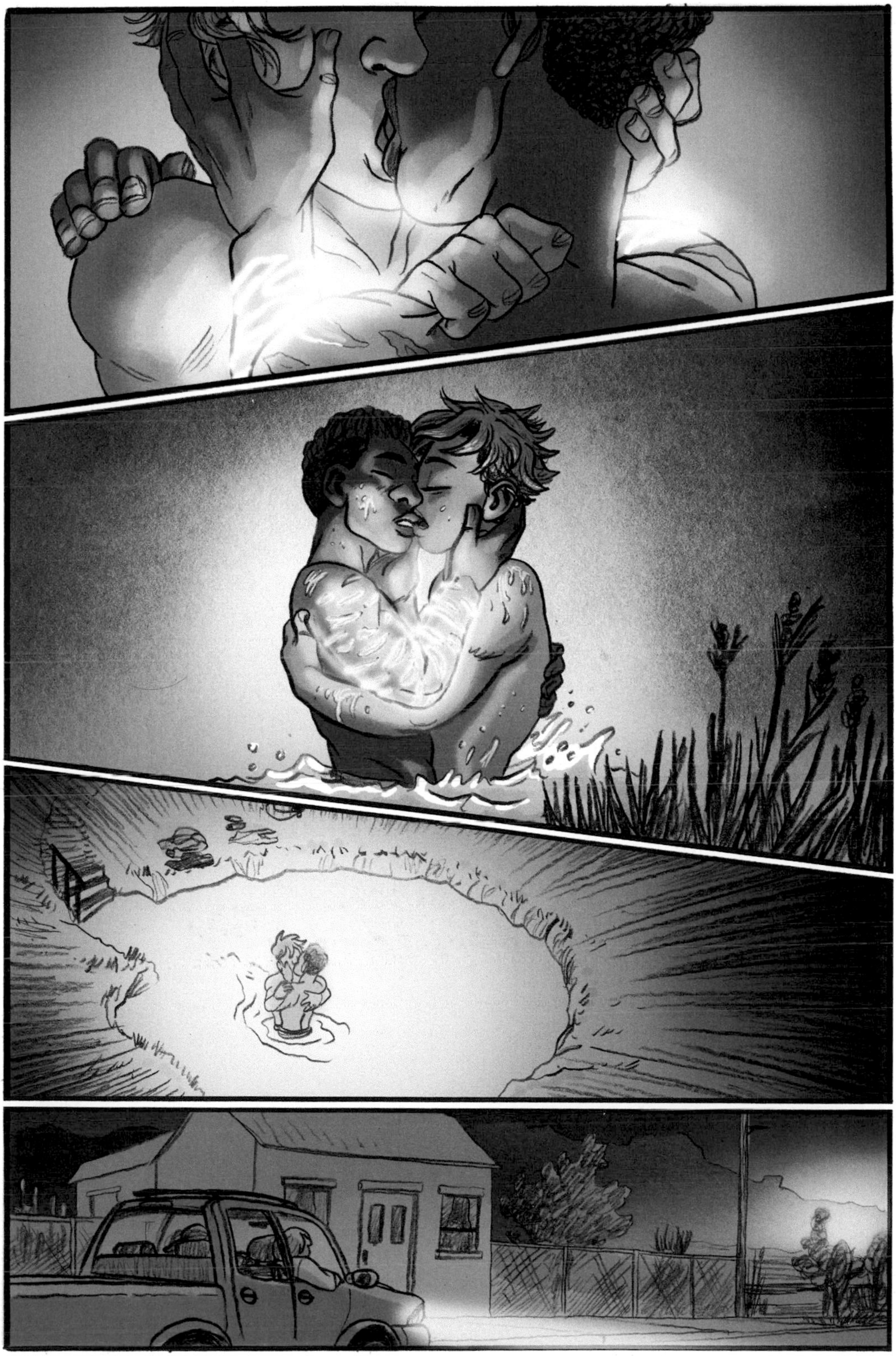

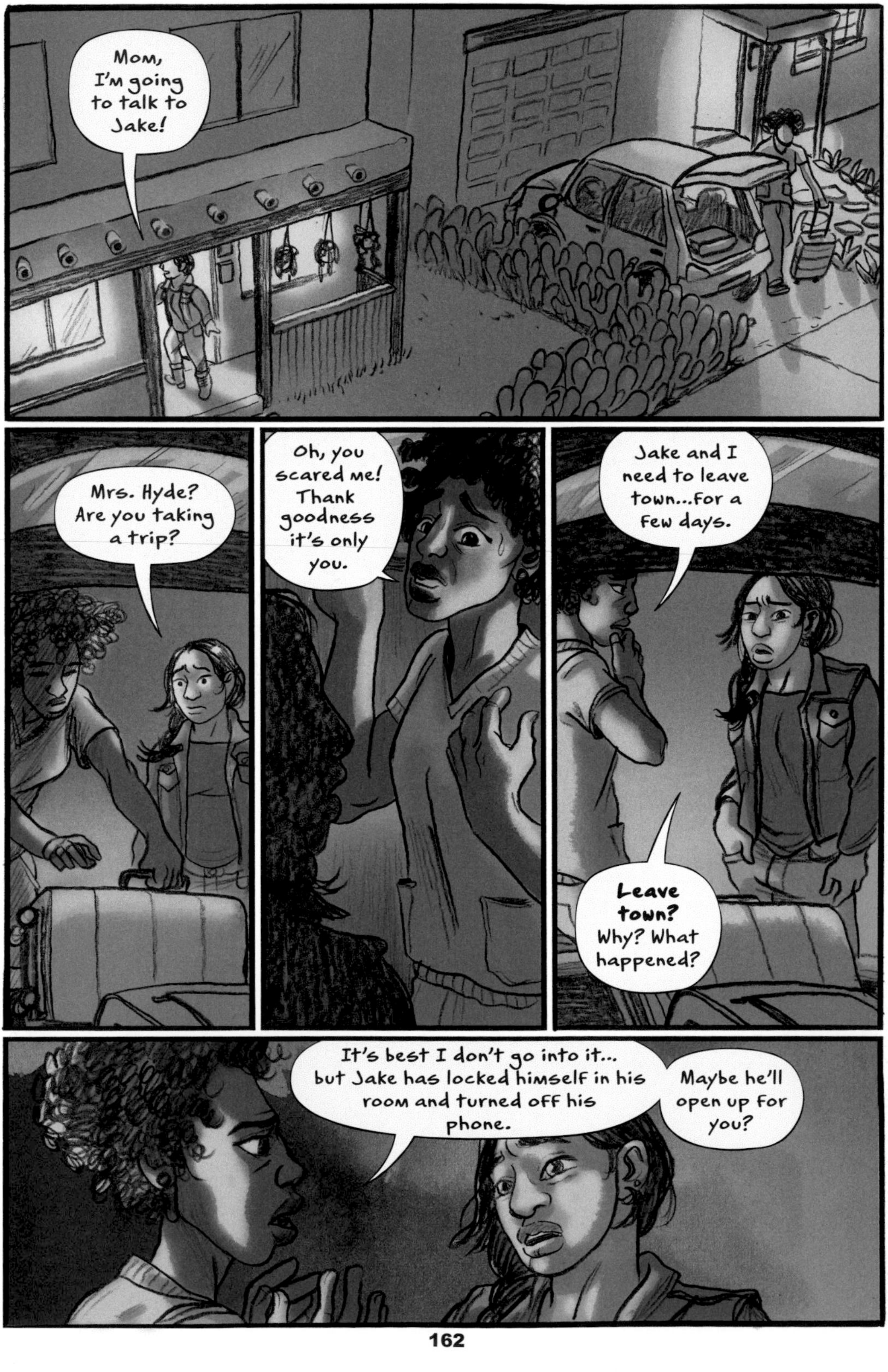

Mom, I'm going to talk to Jake!
Mrs. Hyde? Are you taking a trip?
Oh, you scared me! Thank goodness it's only you.
Jake and I need to leave town...for a few days.
Leave town? Why? What happened?
It's best I don't go into it... but Jake has locked himself in his room and turned off his phone.
Maybe he'll open up for you?

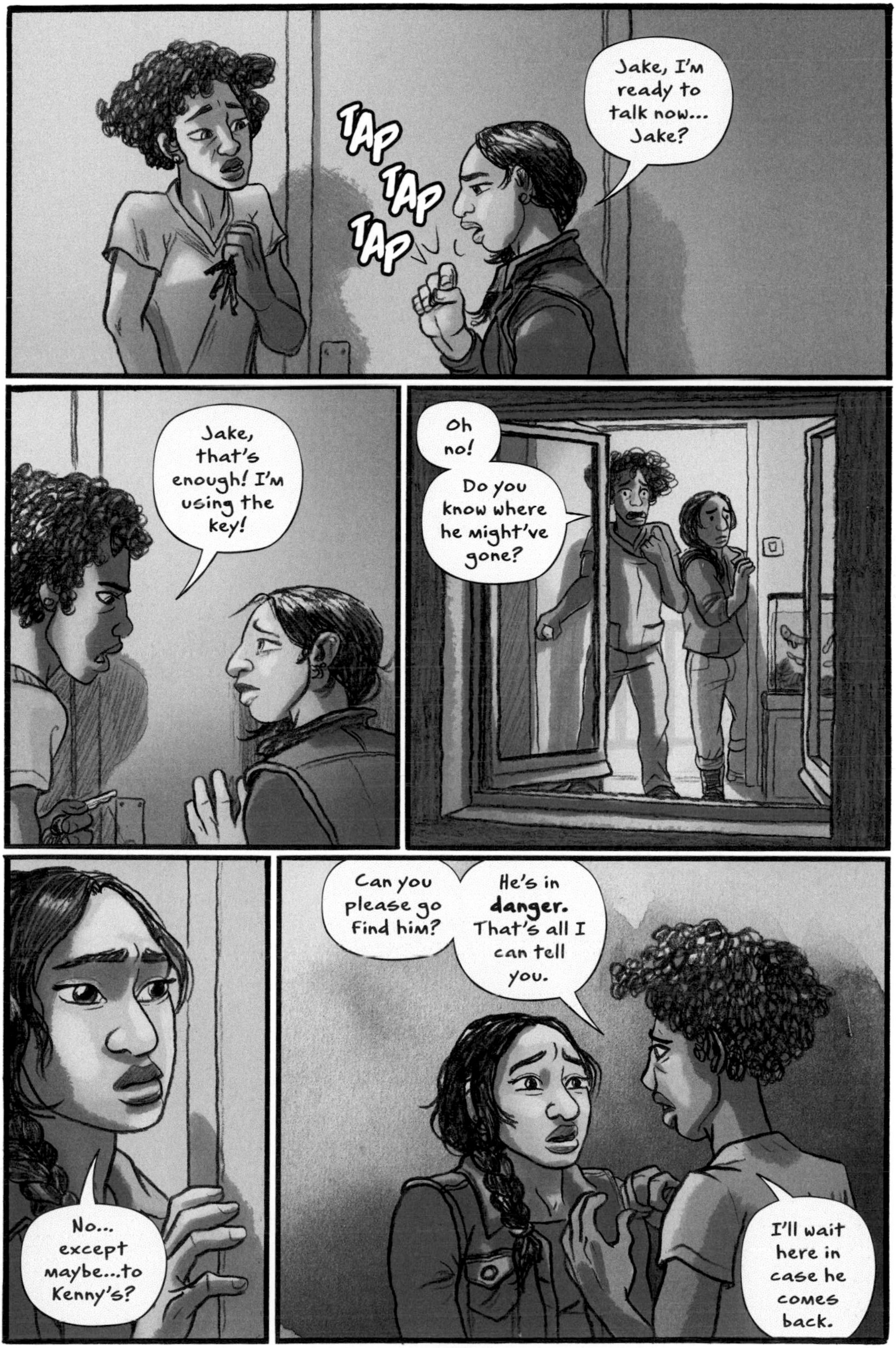
TAP TAP TAP
Jake, I'm ready to talk now... Jake?
Jake, that's enough! I'm using the key!
Oh no!
Do you know where he might've gone?
No... except maybe...to Kenny's?
Can you please go find him?
He's in **danger.** That's all I can tell you.
I'll wait here in case he comes back.

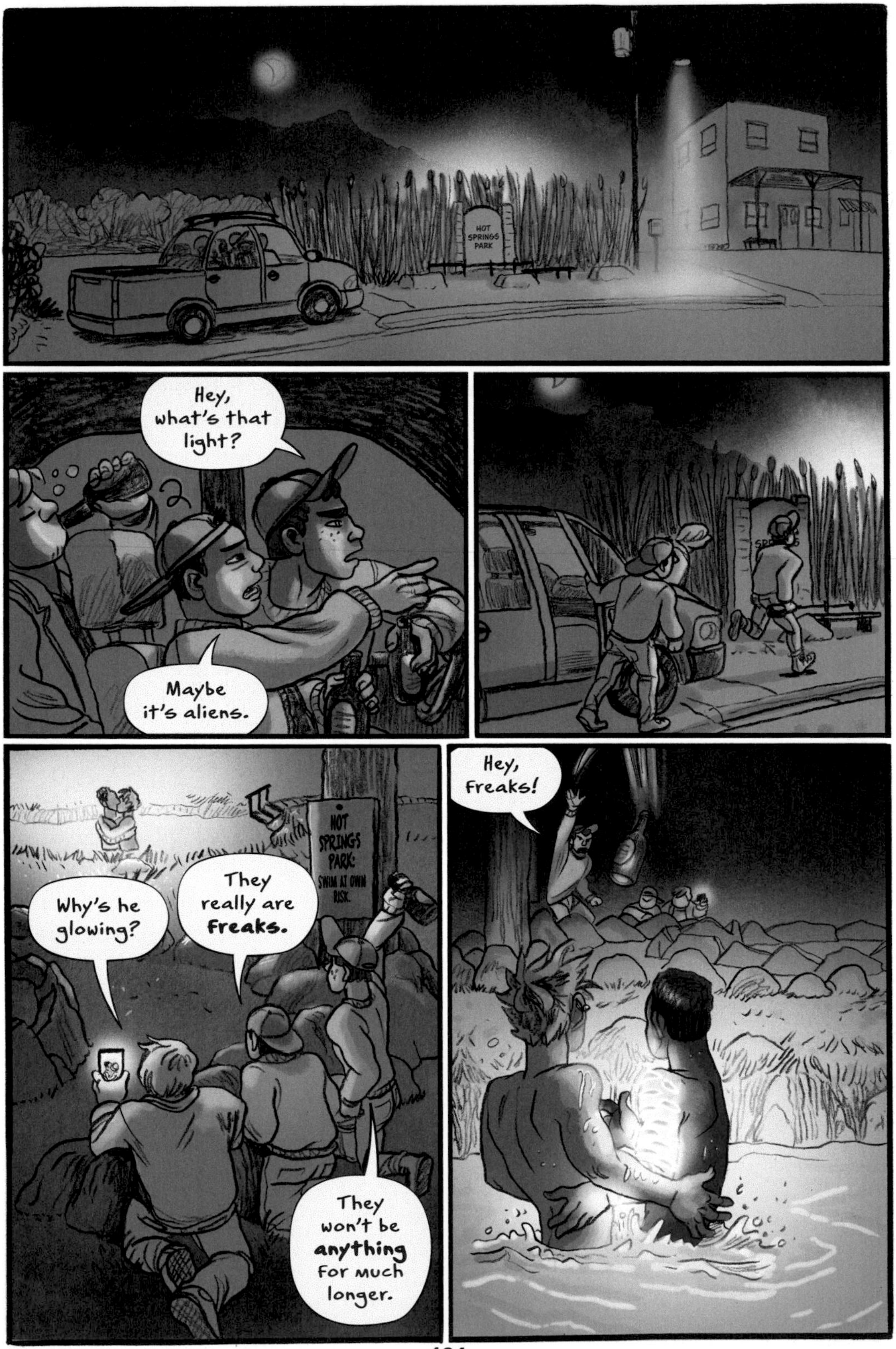
HOT SPRINGS PARK
Hey, what's that light?
Maybe it's aliens.
HOT SPRINGS PARK: SWIM AT OWN RISK.
Why's he glowing?
They really are Freaks.
They won't be anything for much longer.
Hey, Freaks!

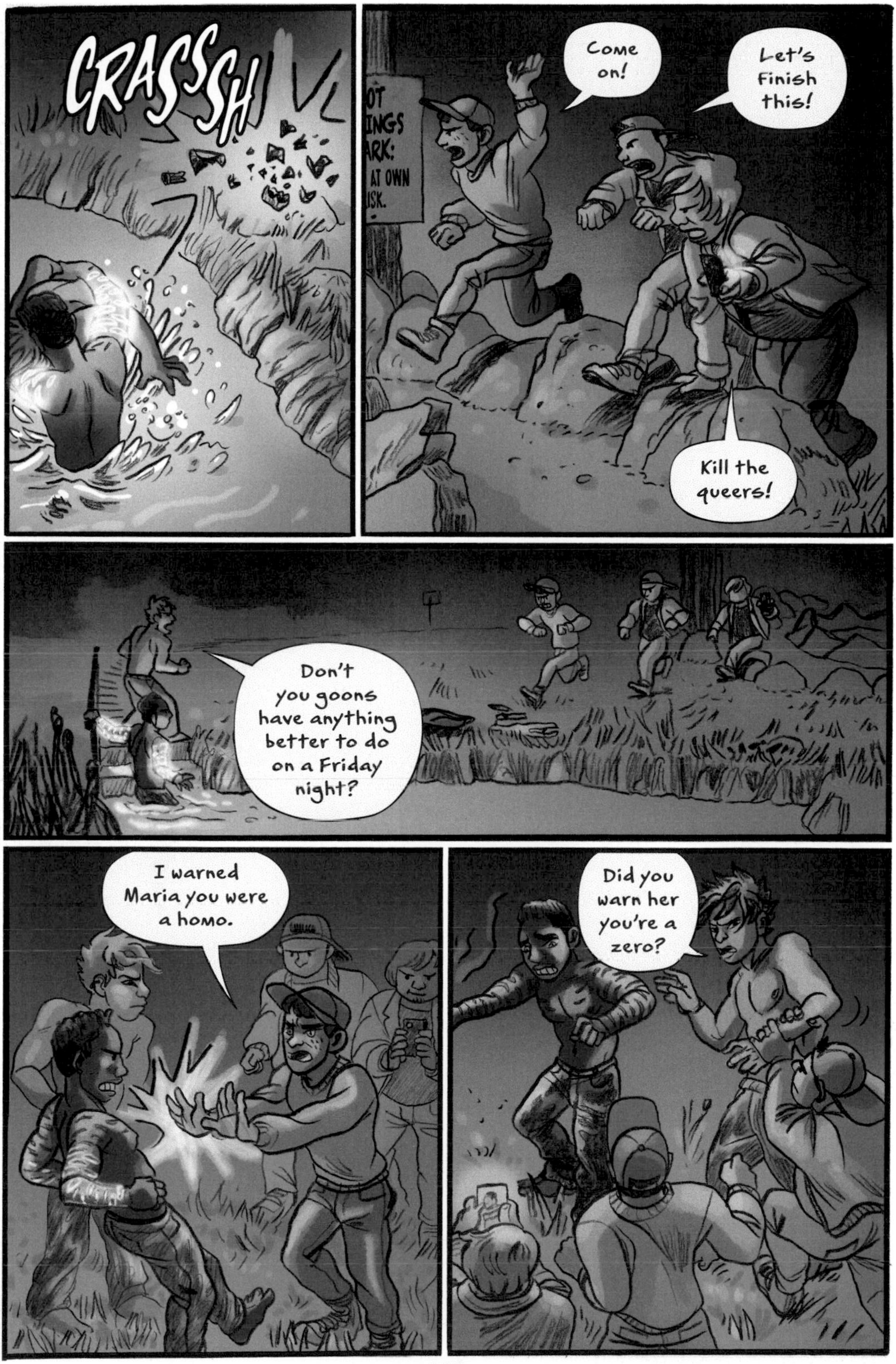
CRASSSH
Come on!
Let's Finish this!
Kill the queers!
Don't you goons have anything better to do on a Friday night?
I warned Maria you were a homo.
Did you warn her you're a zero?

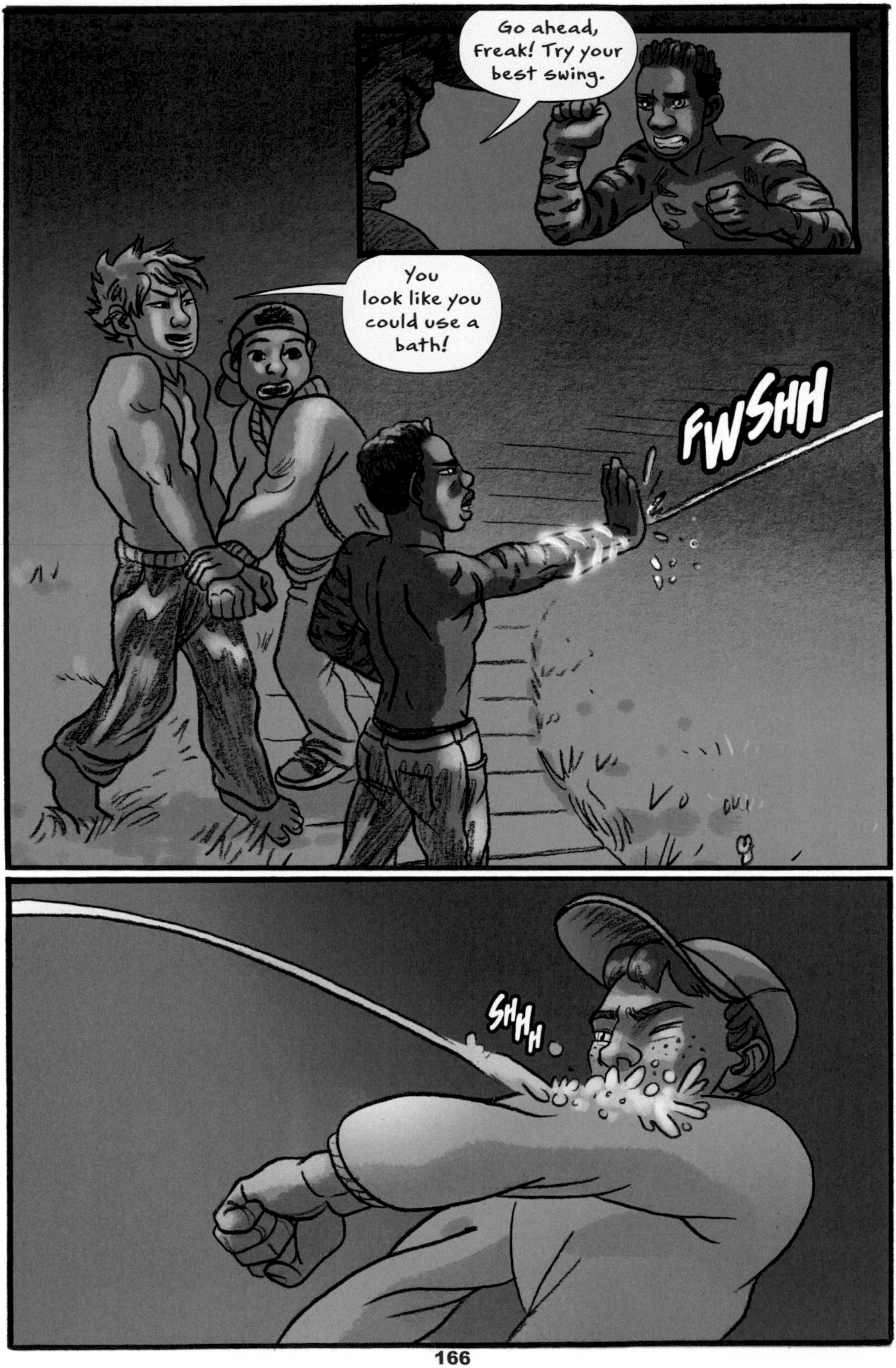
Go ahead, Freak! Try your best swing.
You look like you could use a bath!
FWSHH
SHHH

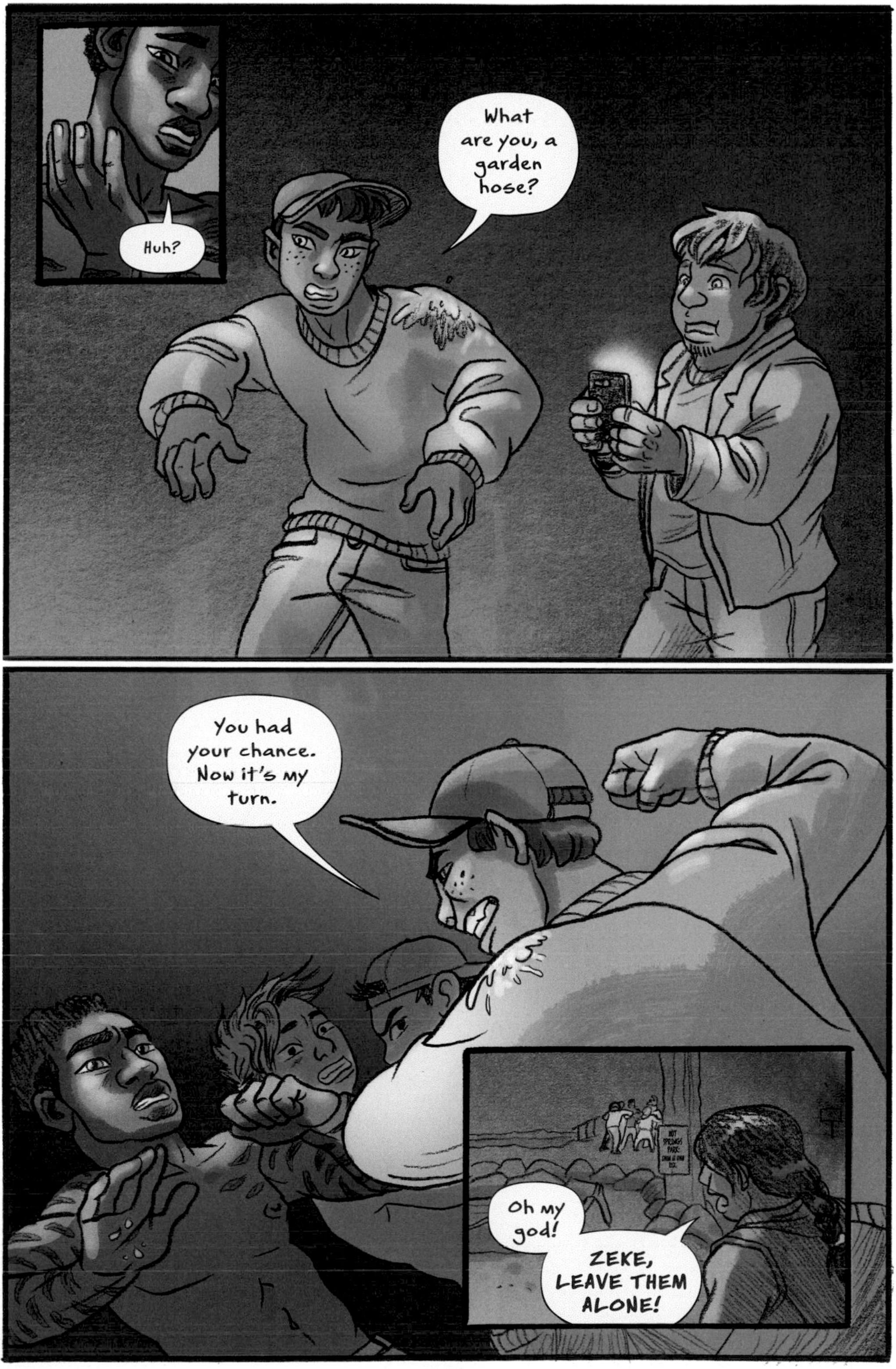
Huh?
What are you, a garden hose?
You had your chance. Now it's my turn.
Oh my god!
ZEKE, LEAVE THEM ALONE!

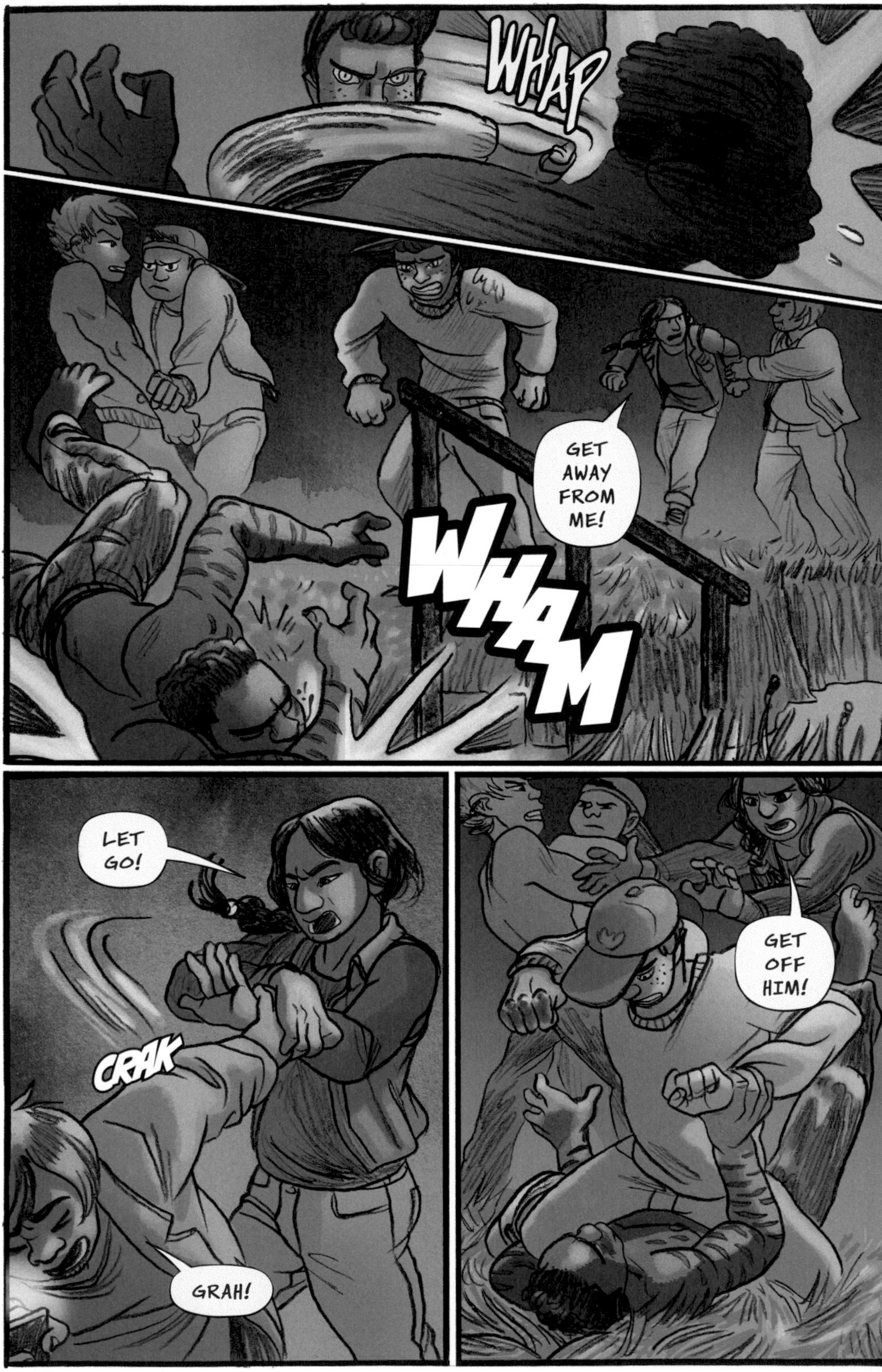
WHAP
GET AWAY FROM ME!
WHAM
LET GO!
CRAK
GRAH!
GET OFF HIM!

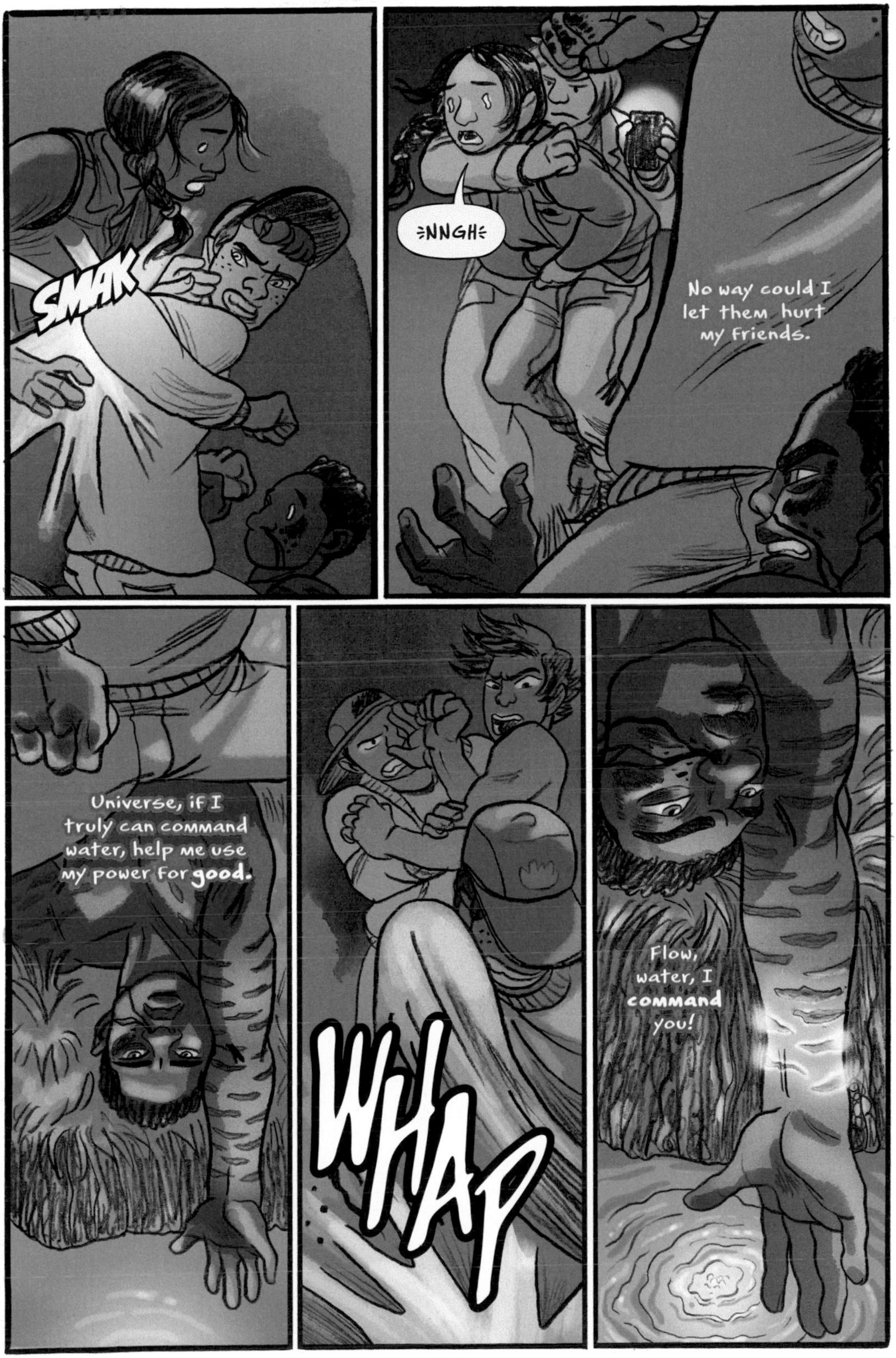
SMAK
NNGH
No way could I let them hurt my friends.
Universe, if I truly can command water, help me use my power for **good**.
WHAP
Flow, water, I **command** you!

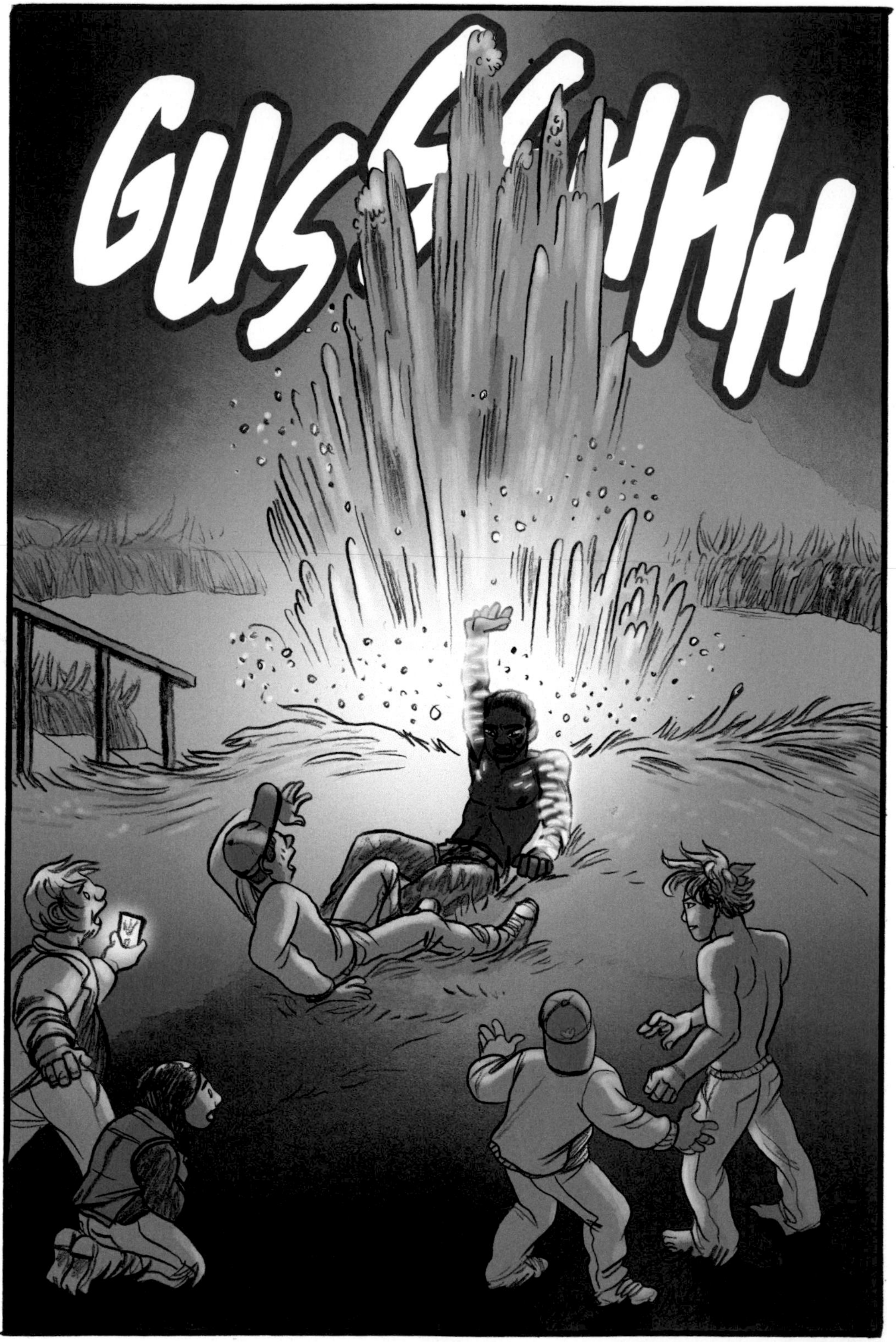
GUSHHHH

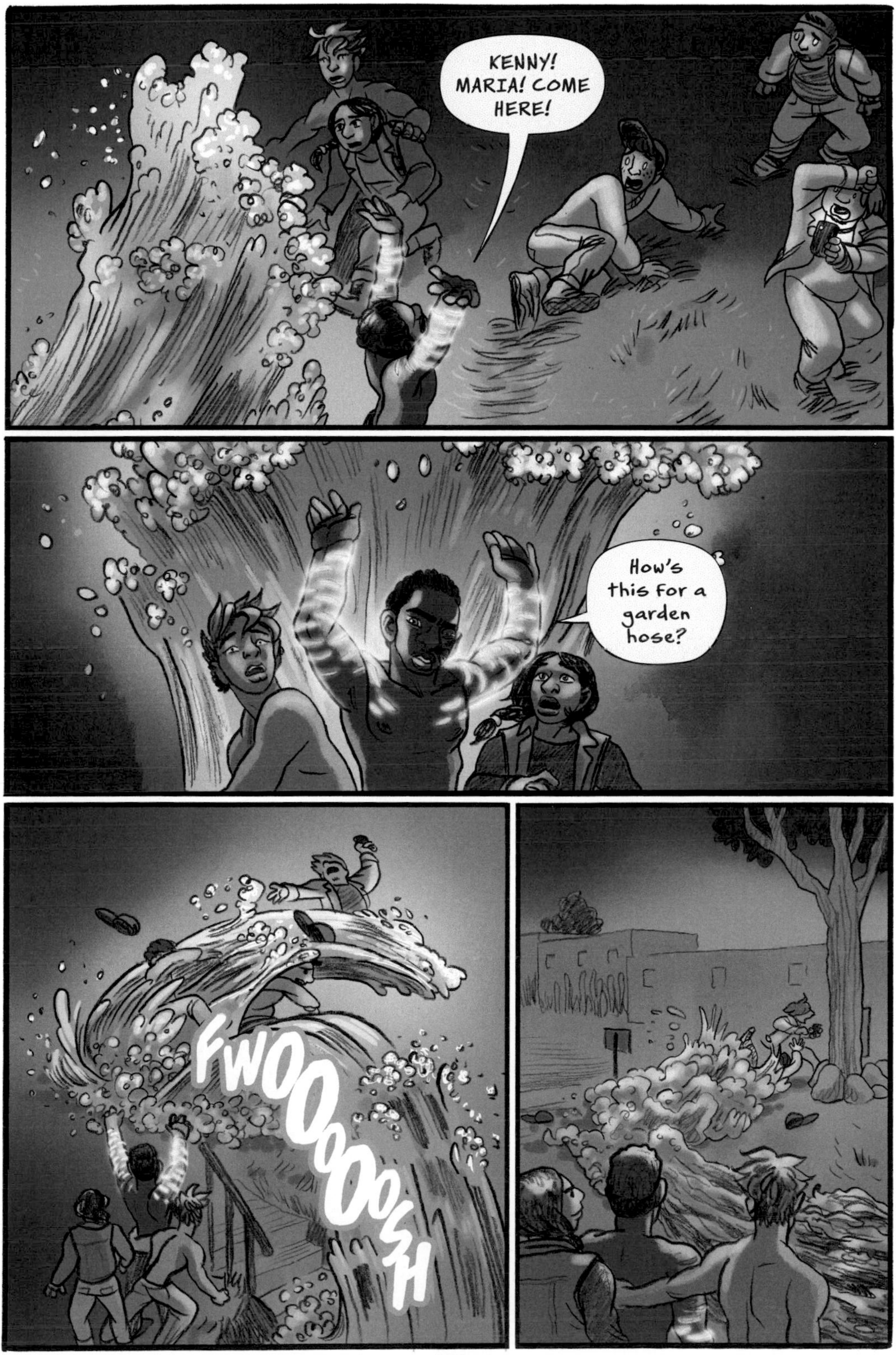
KENNY! MARIA! COME HERE!
How's this for a garden hose?
FWOOOOOOSH

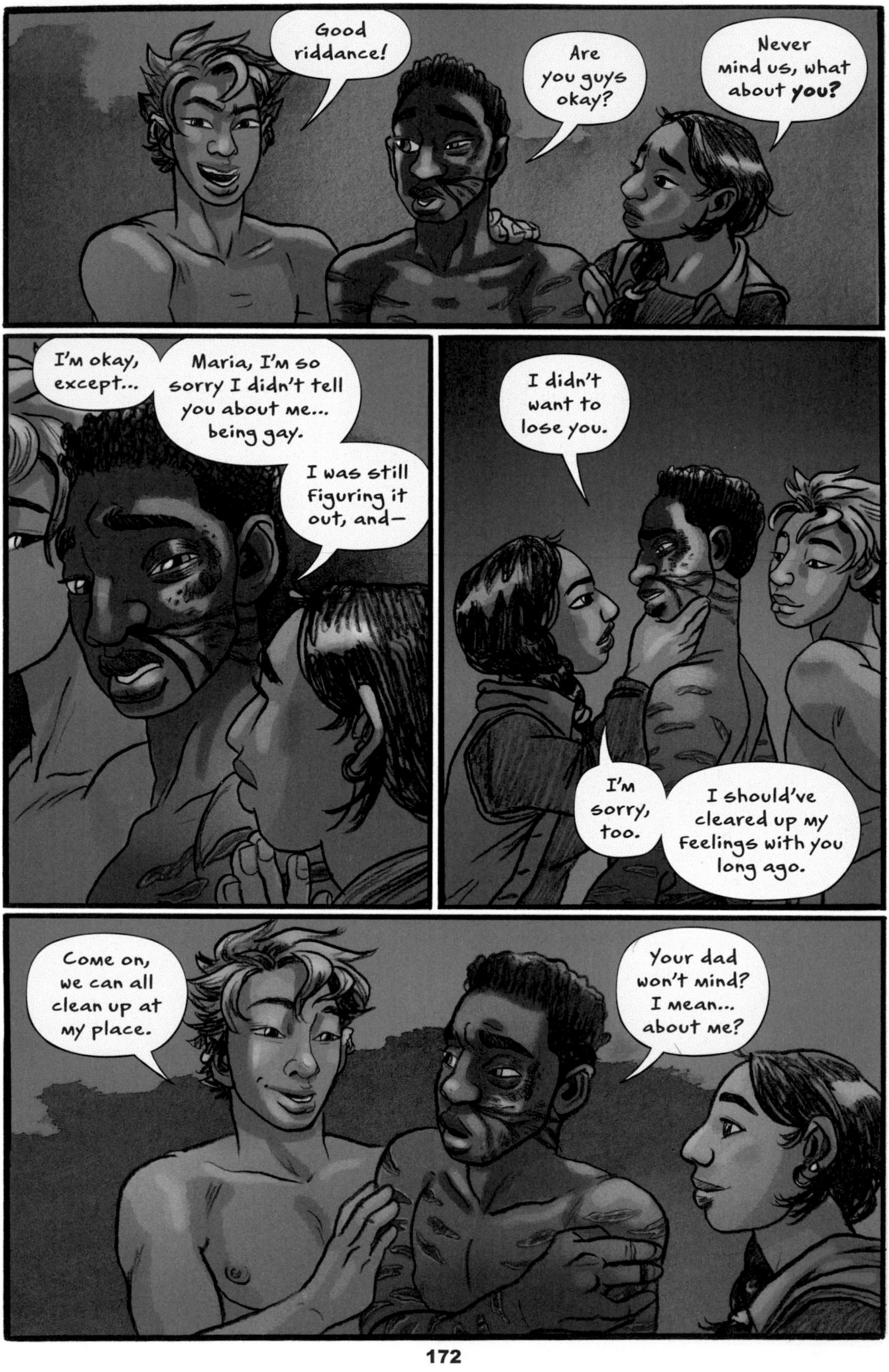
Good riddance!
Are you guys okay?
Never mind us, what about **you?**
I'm okay, except...
Maria, I'm so sorry I didn't tell you about me... being gay.
I was still figuring it out, and—
I didn't want to lose you.
I'm sorry, too.
I should've cleared up my feelings with you long ago.
Come on, we can all clean up at my place.
Your dad won't mind? I mean... about me?

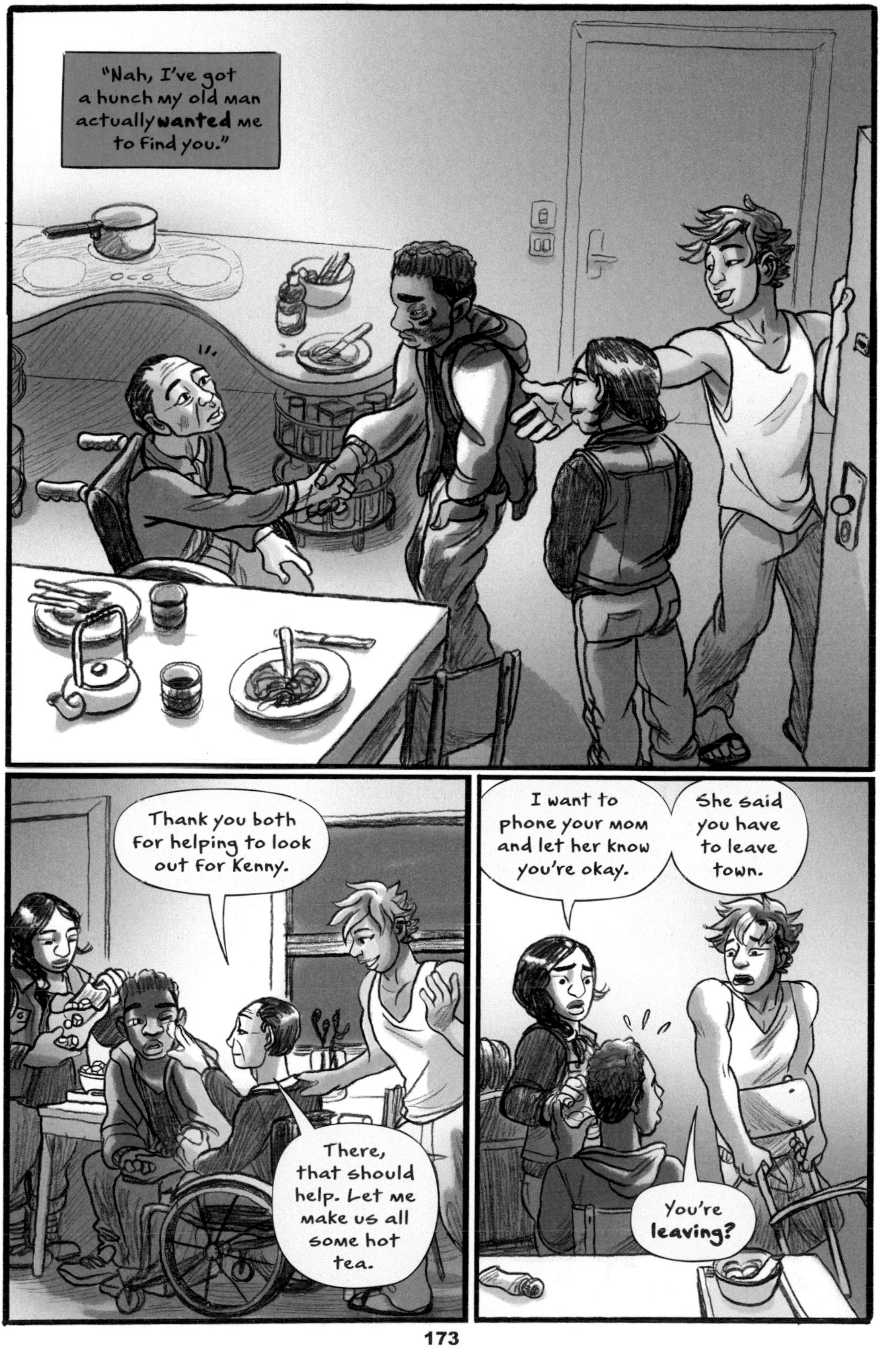
"Nah, I've got a hunch my old man actually **wanted** me to find you."
Thank you both for helping to look out for Kenny.
There, that should help. Let me make us all some hot tea.
I want to phone your mom and let her know you're okay.
She said you have to leave town.
You're **leaving?**

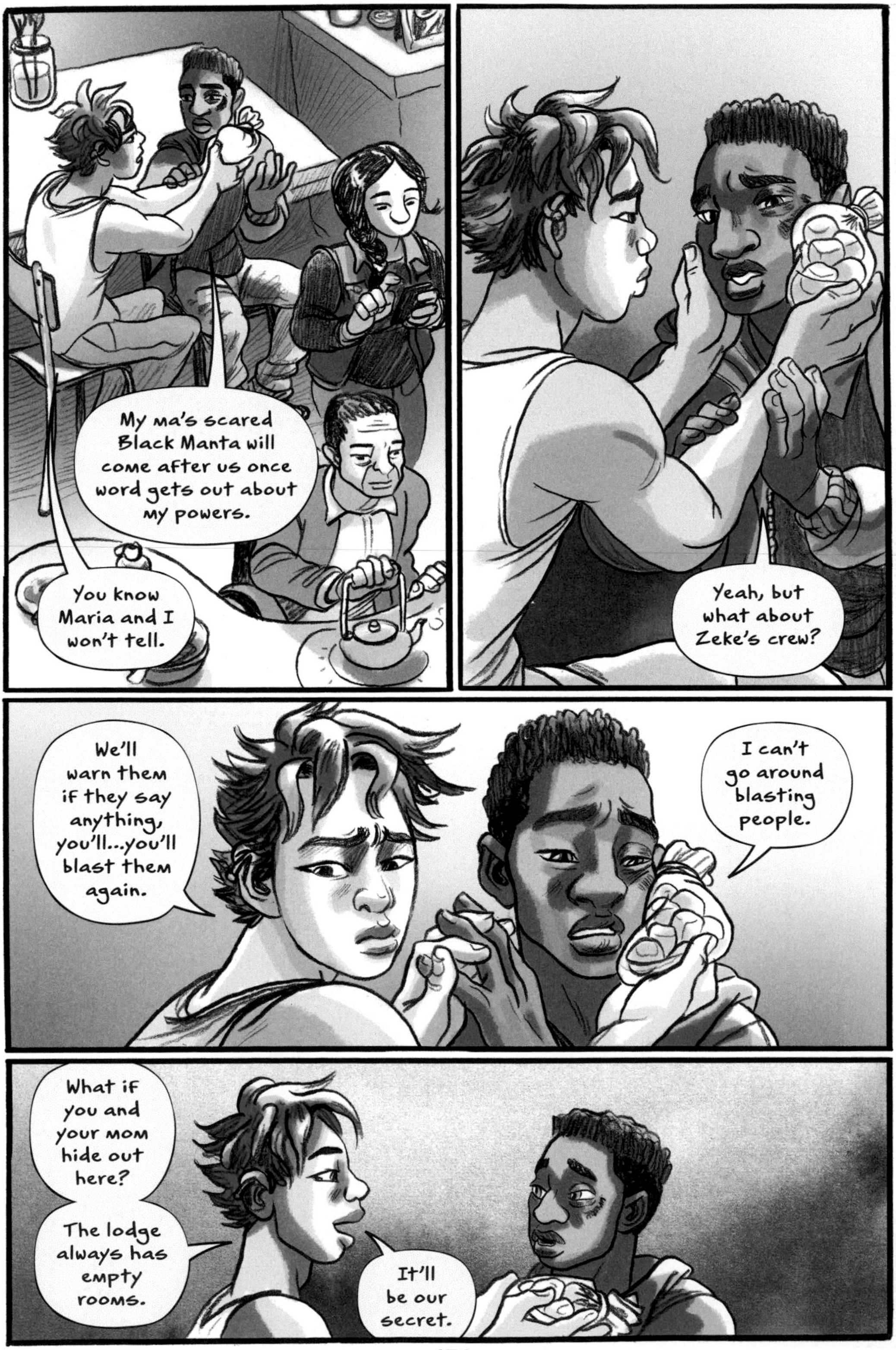

My ma's scared Black Manta will come after us once word gets out about my powers.
You know Maria and I won't tell.
Yeah, but what about Zeke's crew?
We'll warn them if they say anything, you'll...you'll blast them again.
I can't go around blasting people.
What if you and your mom hide out here?
The lodge always has empty rooms.
It'll be our secret.

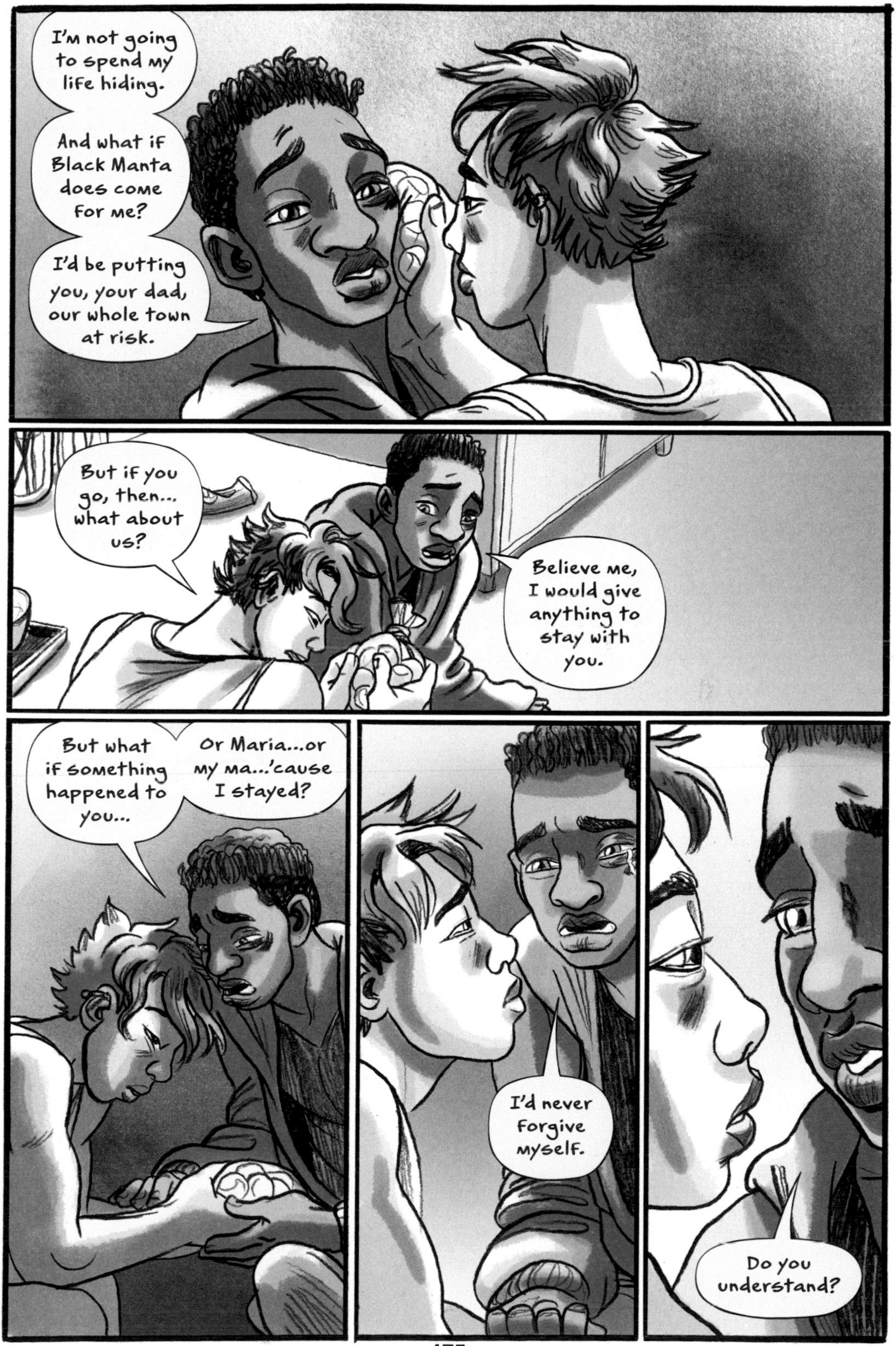
I'm not going to spend my life hiding.
And what if Black Manta does come for me?
I'd be putting you, your dad, our whole town at risk.
But if you go, then... what about us?
Believe me, I would give anything to stay with you.
But what if something happened to you...
Or Maria...or my ma...'cause I stayed?
I'd never forgive myself.
Do you understand?

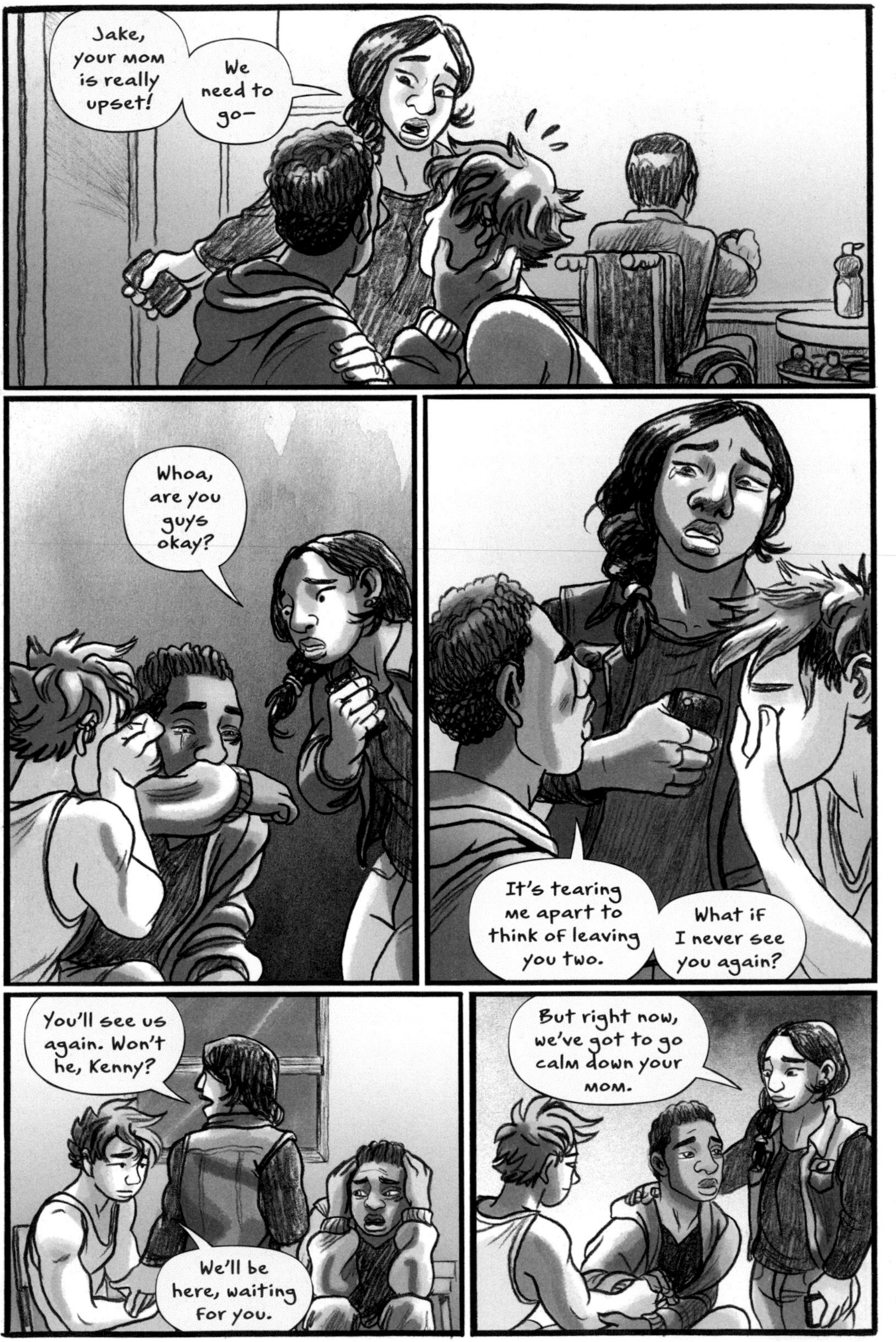
Jake, your MOM is really upset!
We need to go–
Whoa, are you guys okay?
It's tearing me apart to think of leaving you two.
What if I never see you again?
You'll see us again. Won't he, Kenny?
We'll be here, waiting for you.
But right now, we've got to go calm down your MOM.

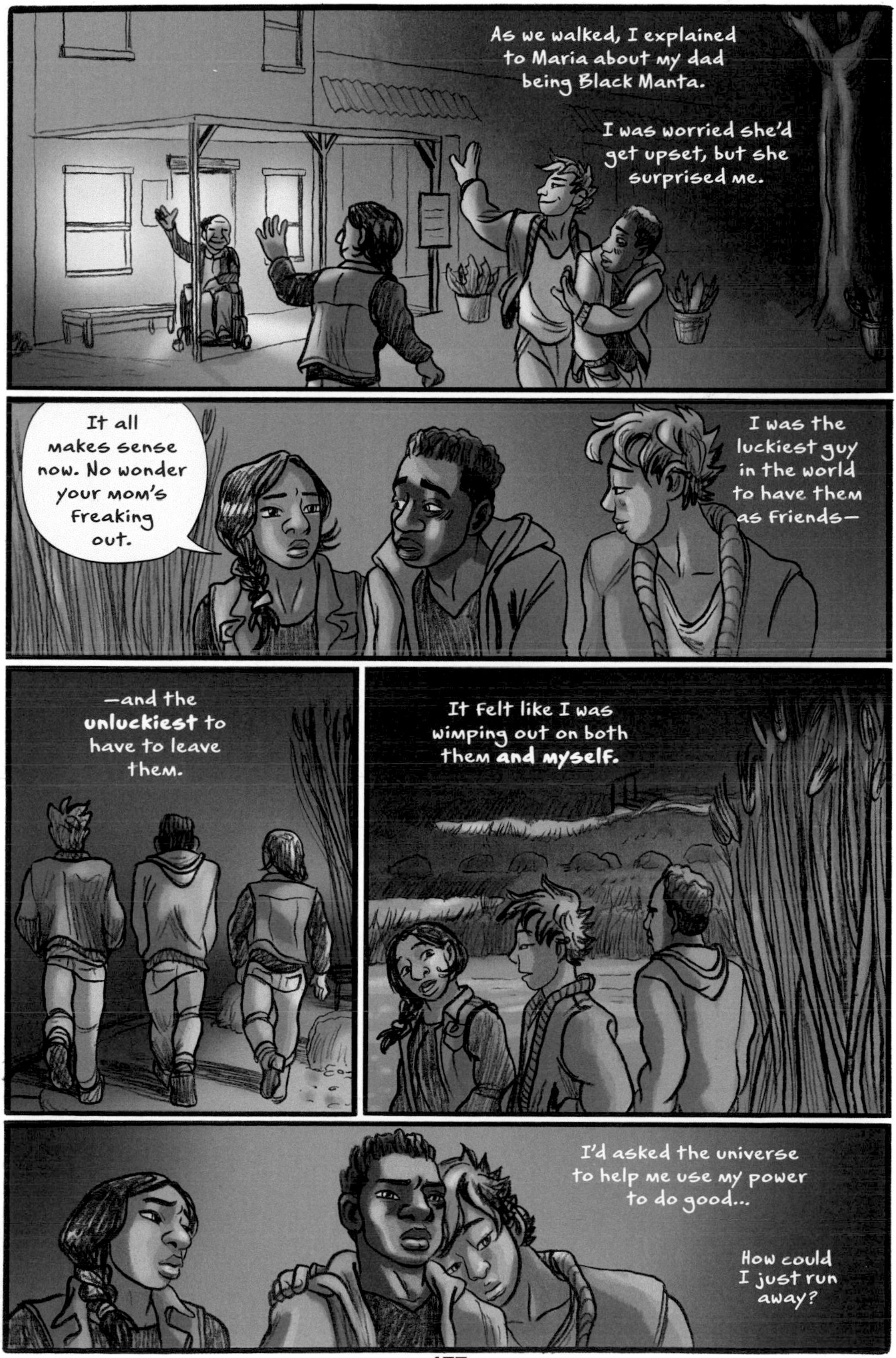
As we walked, I explained to Maria about my dad being Black Manta.
I was worried she'd get upset, but she surprised me.
It all makes sense now. No wonder your mom's freaking out.
I was the luckiest guy in the world to have them as friends—
—and the **unluckiest** to have to leave them.
It felt like I was wimping out on both them **and myself.**
I'd asked the universe to help me use my power to do good...
How could I just run away?

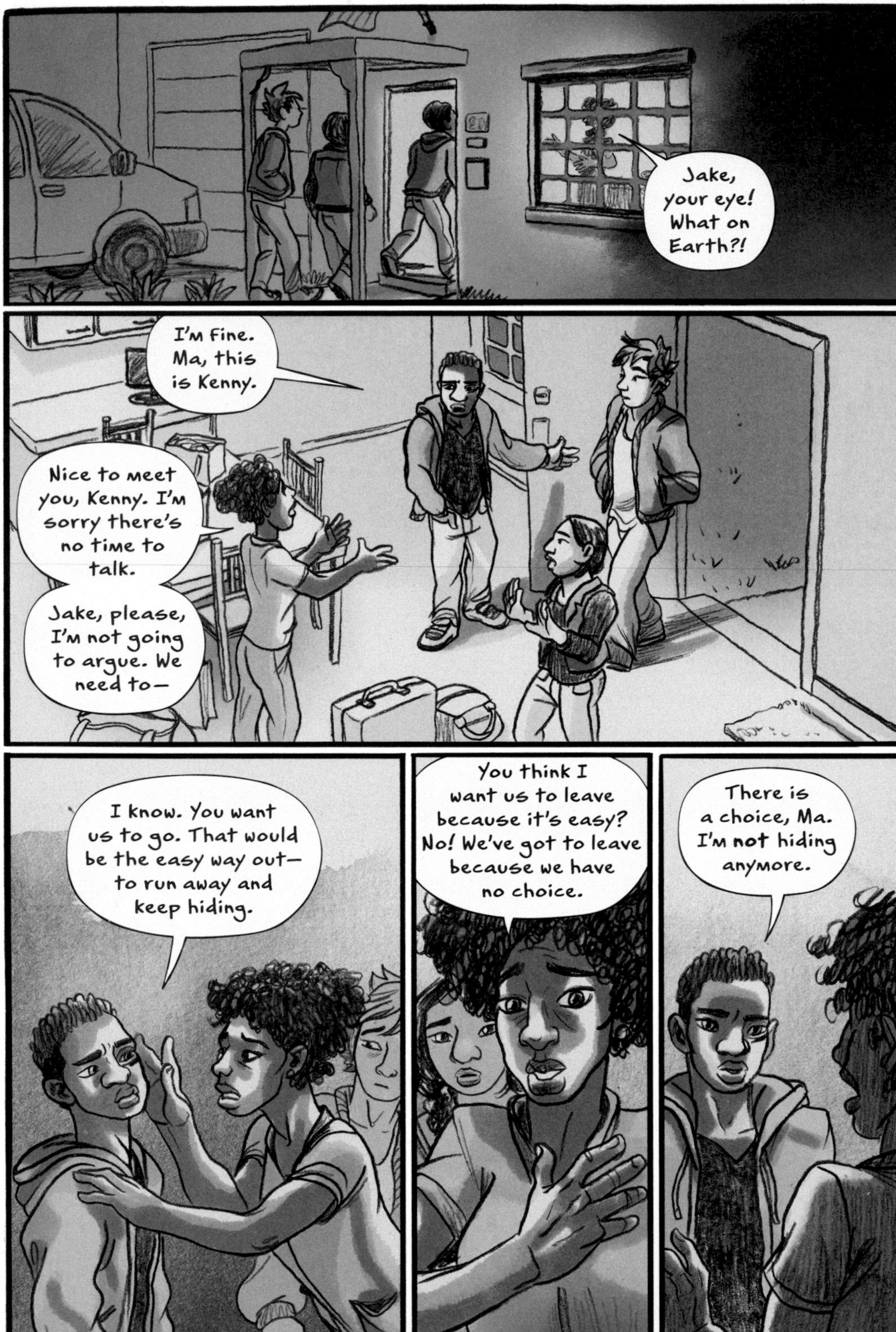
Jake, your eye! What on Earth?!
I'm fine. Ma, this is Kenny.
Nice to meet you, Kenny. I'm sorry there's no time to talk.
Jake, please, I'm not going to argue. We need to—
I know. You want us to go. That would be the easy way out— to run away and keep hiding.
You think I want us to leave because it's easy? No! We've got to leave because we have no choice.
There is a choice, Ma. I'm **not** hiding anymore.

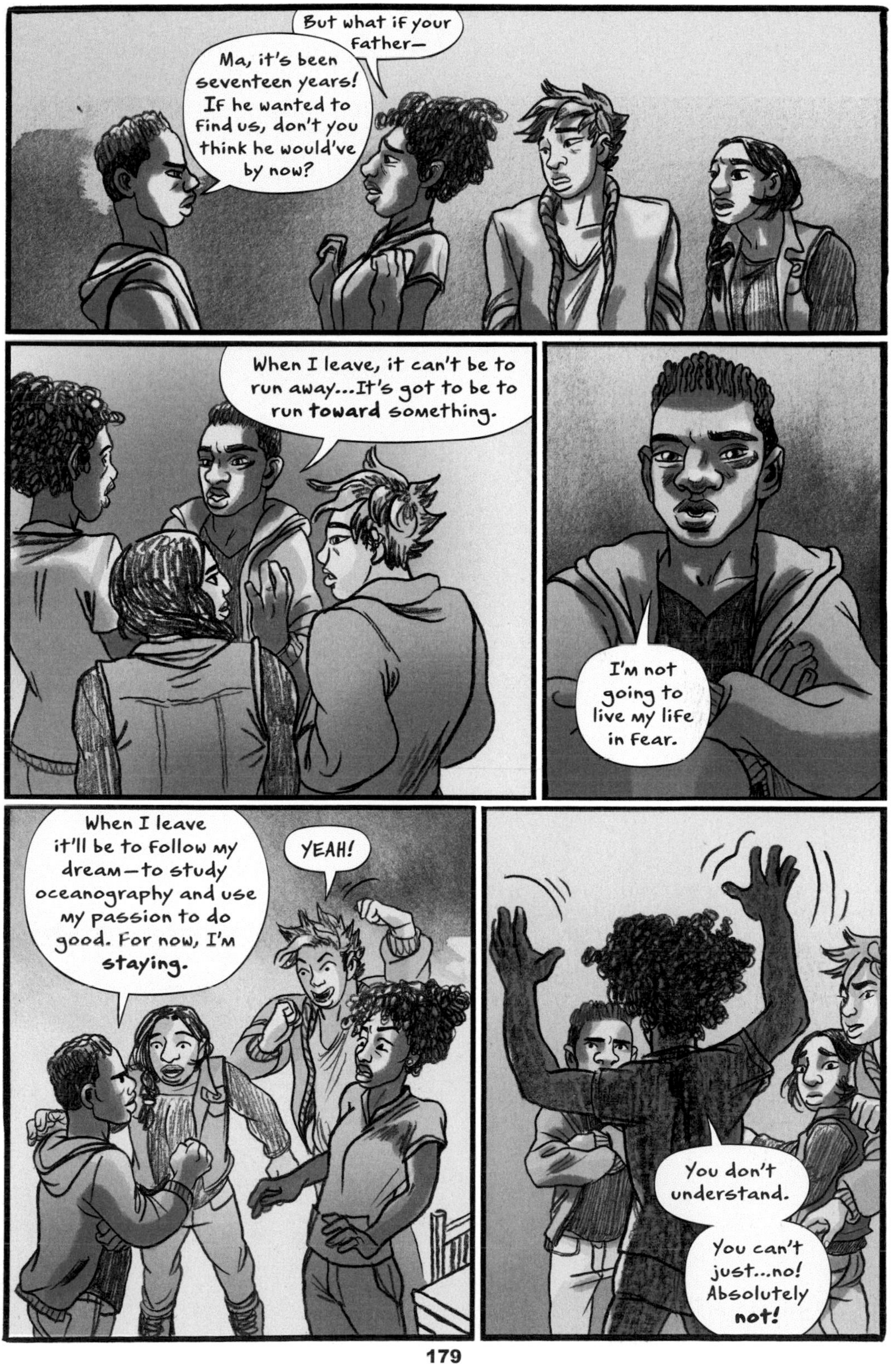
But what if your father—
Ma, it's been seventeen years! If he wanted to find us, don't you think he would've by now?
When I leave, it can't be to run away...It's got to be to run **toward** something.
I'm not going to live my life in fear.
When I leave it'll be to follow my dream—to study oceanography and use my passion to do good. For now, I'm **staying**.
YEAH!
You don't understand.
You can't just...no! Absolutely **not!**

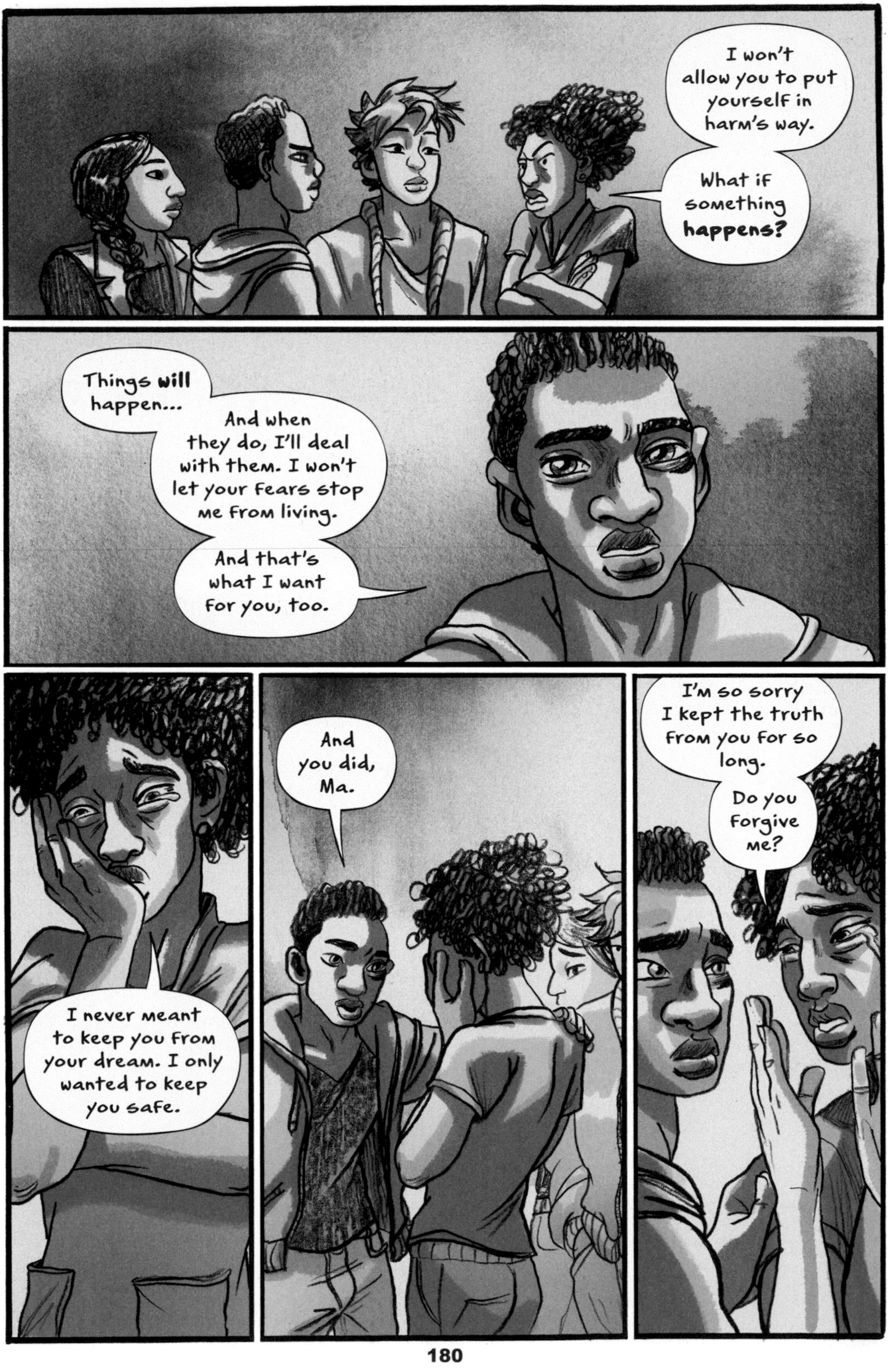
I won't allow you to put yourself in harm's way.
What if something **happens?**
Things **will** happen...
And when they do, I'll deal with them. I won't let your fears stop me from living.
And that's what I want for you, too.
I never meant to keep you from your dream. I only wanted to keep you safe.
And you did, Ma.
I'm so sorry I kept the truth from you for so long.
Do you forgive me?

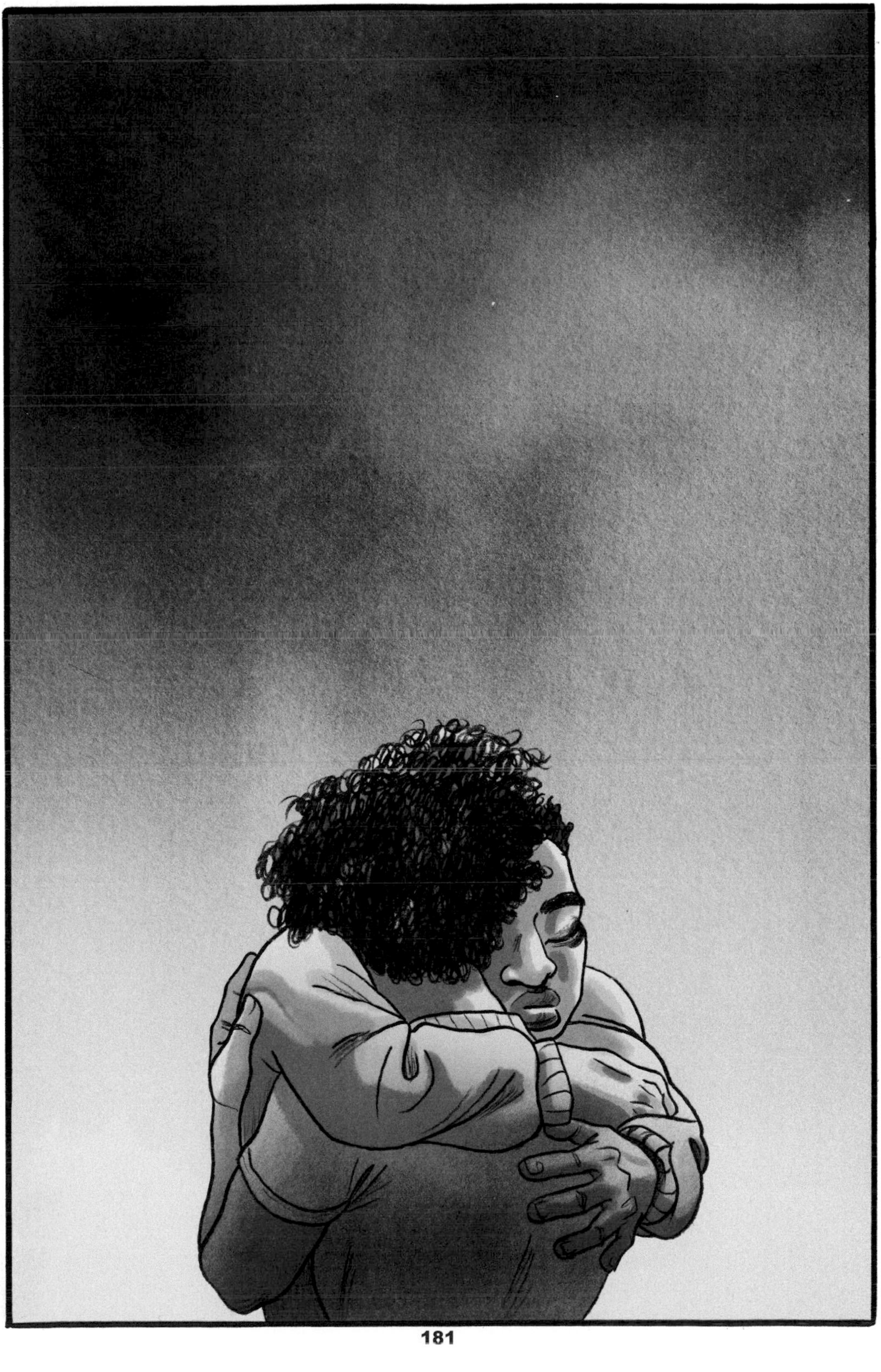

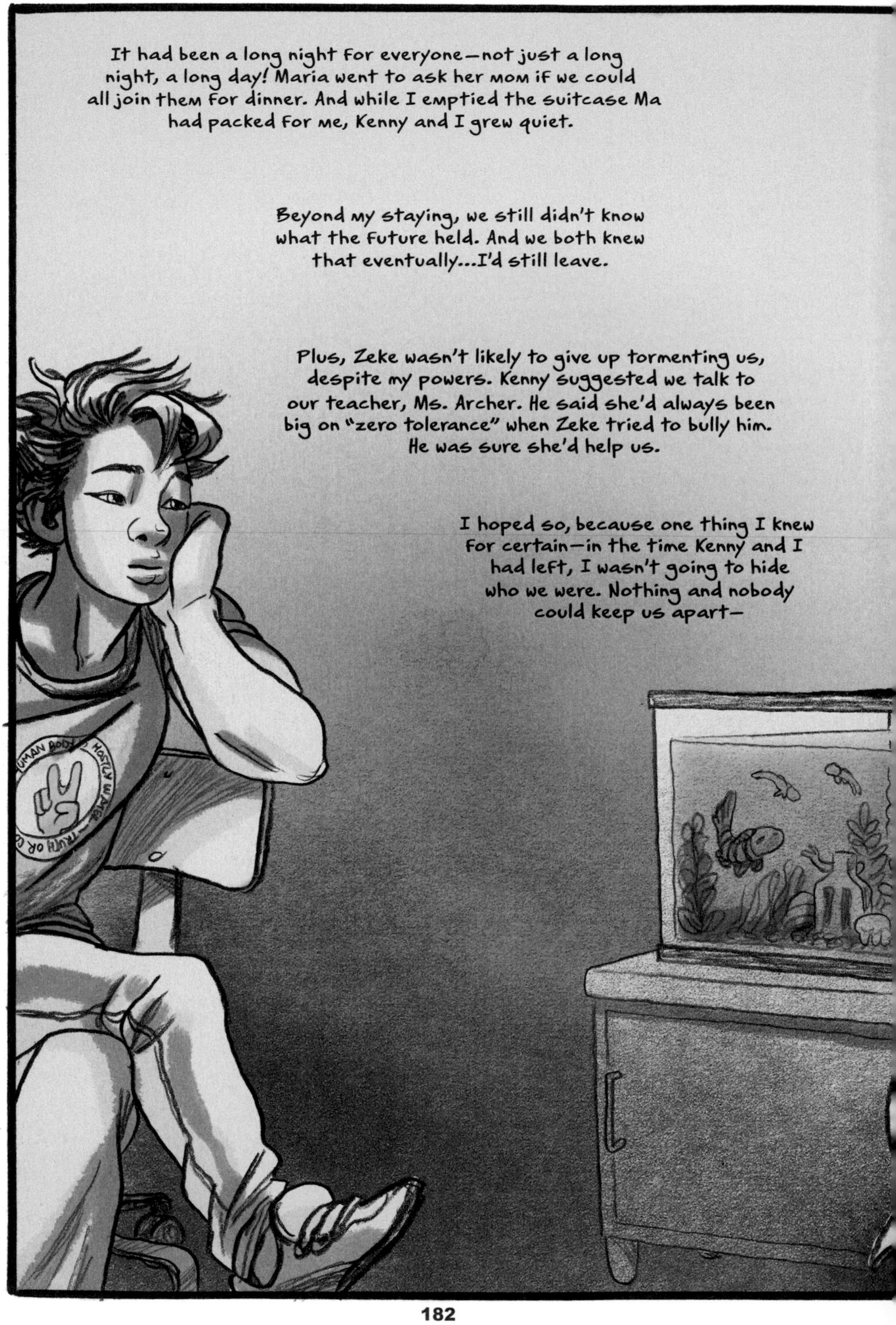
It had been a long night for everyone—not just a long night, a long day! Maria went to ask her mom if we could all join them for dinner. And while I emptied the suitcase Ma had packed for me, Kenny and I grew quiet.
Beyond my staying, we still didn't know what the future held. And we both knew that eventually...I'd still leave.
Plus, Zeke wasn't likely to give up tormenting us, despite my powers. Kenny suggested we talk to our teacher, Ms. Archer. He said she'd always been big on "zero tolerance" when Zeke tried to bully him. He was sure she'd help us.
I hoped so, because one thing I knew for certain—in the time Kenny and I had left, I wasn't going to hide who we were. Nothing and nobody could keep us apart—

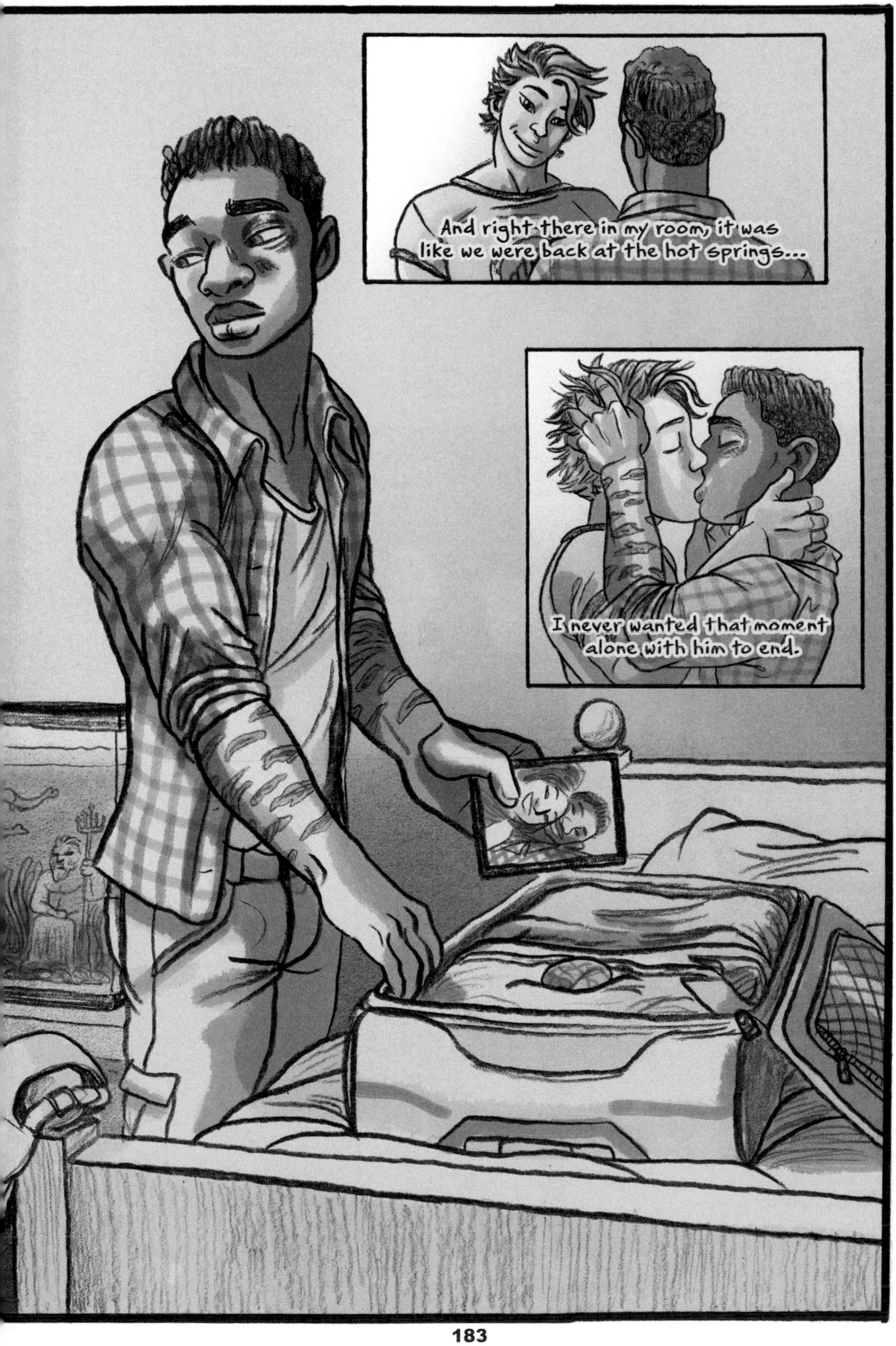
And right there in my room, it was like we were back at the hot springs...
I never wanted that moment alone with him to end.

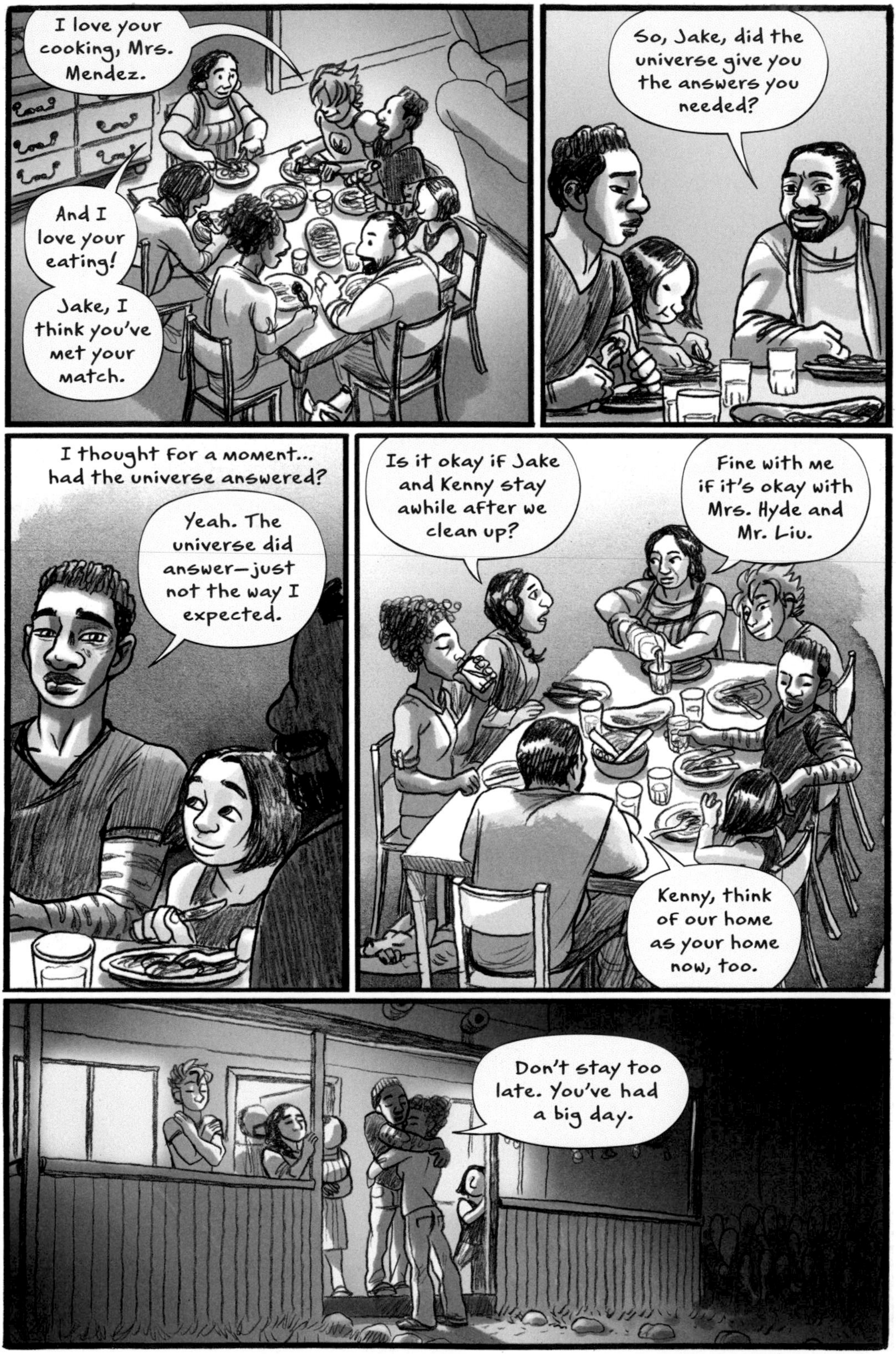

I love your cooking, Mrs. Mendez.
And I love your eating!
Jake, I think you've met your match.
So, Jake, did the universe give you the answers you needed?
I thought for a moment... had the universe answered?
Yeah. The universe did answer—just not the way I expected.
Is it okay if Jake and Kenny stay awhile after we clean up?
Fine with me if it's okay with Mrs. Hyde and Mr. Liu.
Kenny, think of our home as your home now, too.
Don't stay too late. You've had a big day.

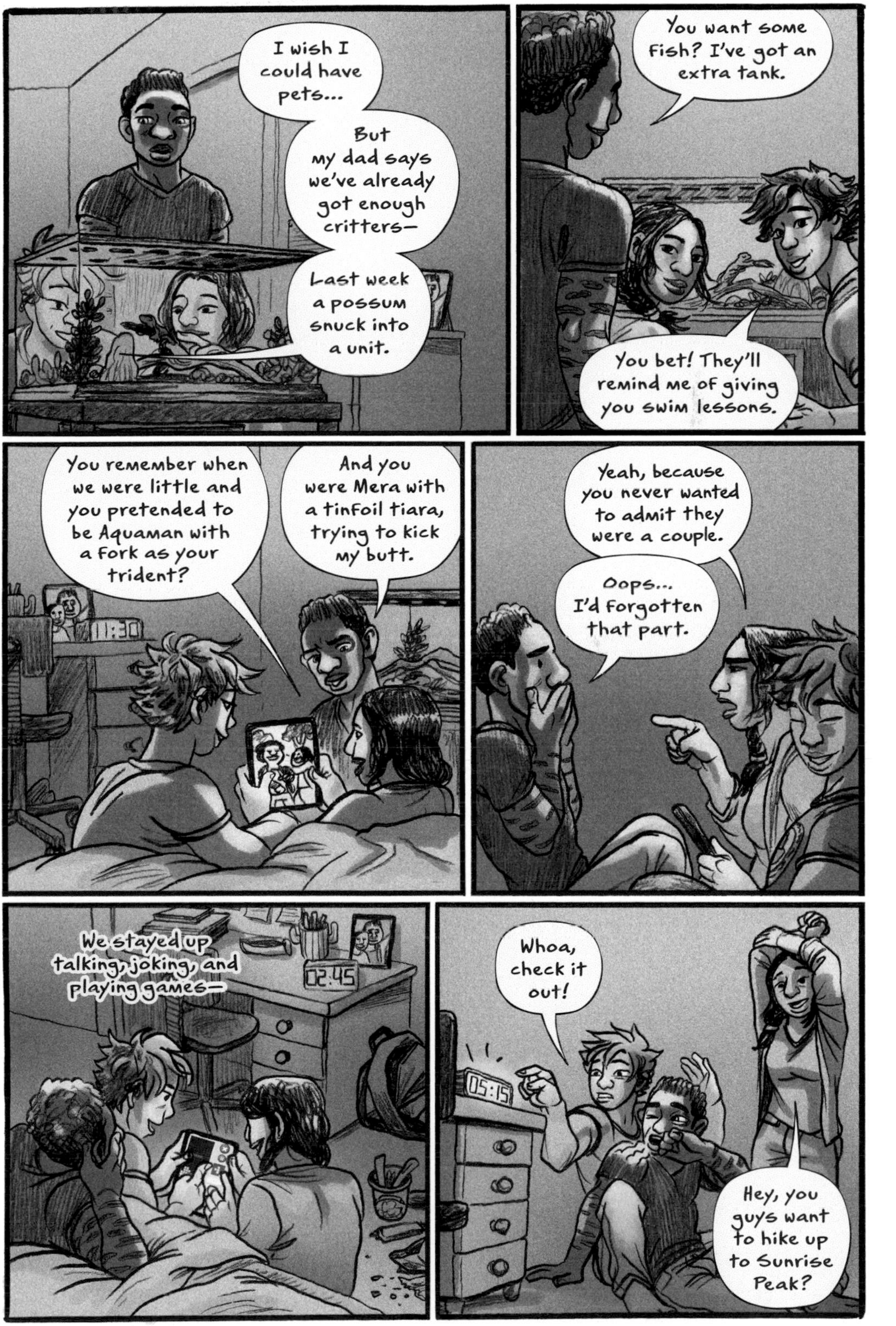
I wish I could have pets...
But my dad says we've already got enough critters—
Last week a possum snuck into a unit.
You want some fish? I've got an extra tank.
You bet! They'll remind me of giving you swim lessons.
You remember when we were little and you pretended to be Aquaman with a fork as your trident?
And you were Mera with a tinfoil tiara, trying to kick my butt.
11:30
Yeah, because you never wanted to admit they were a couple.
Oops... I'd forgotten that part.
We stayed up talking, joking, and playing games—
02:45
Whoa, check it out!
05:15
Hey, you guys want to hike up to Sunrise Peak?

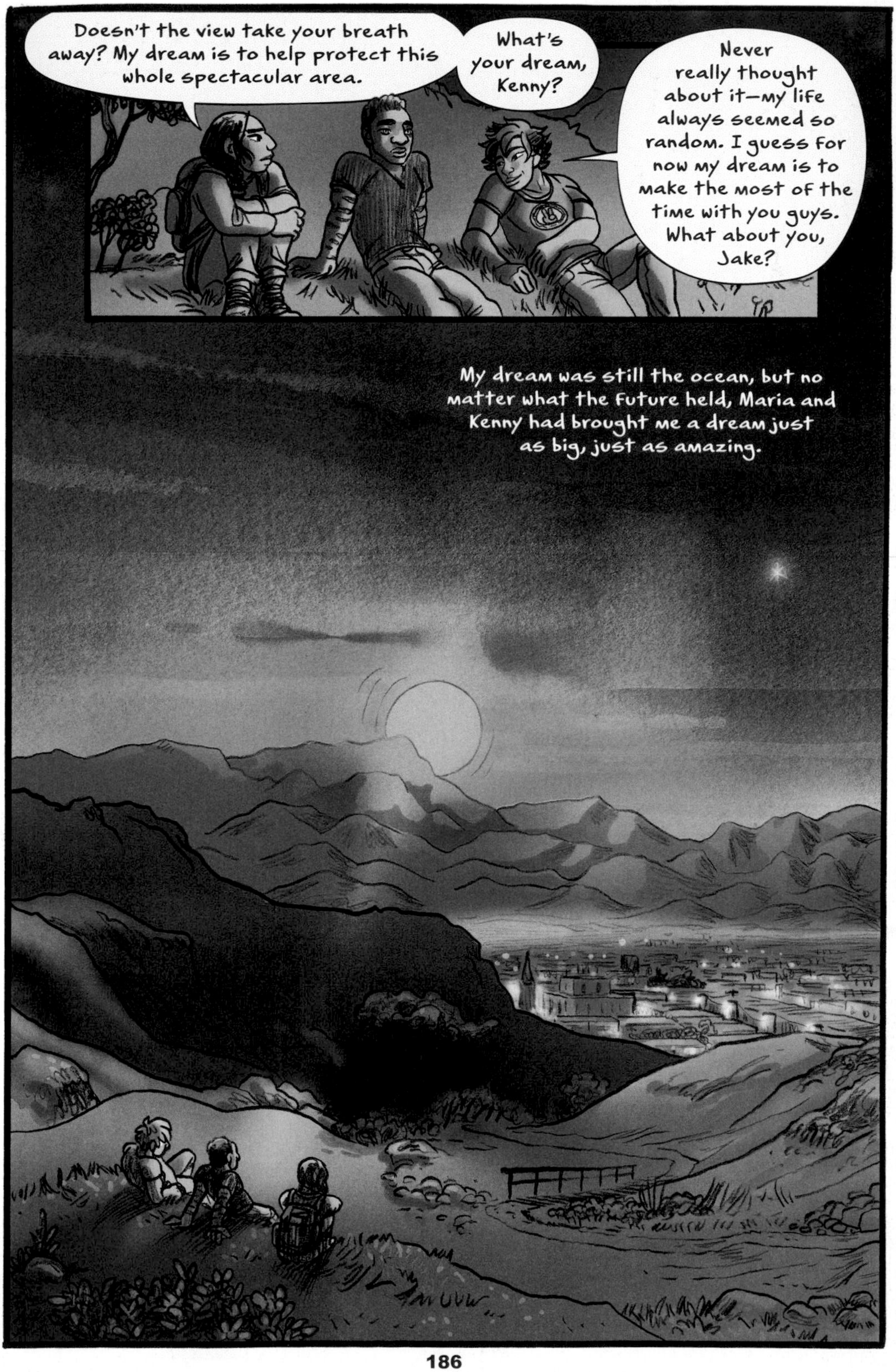
Doesn't the view take your breath away? My dream is to help protect this whole spectacular area.
What's your dream, Kenny?
Never really thought about it—my life always seemed so random. I guess for now my dream is to make the most of the time with you guys. What about you, Jake?
My dream was still the ocean, but no matter what the future held, Maria and Kenny had brought me a dream just as big, just as amazing.

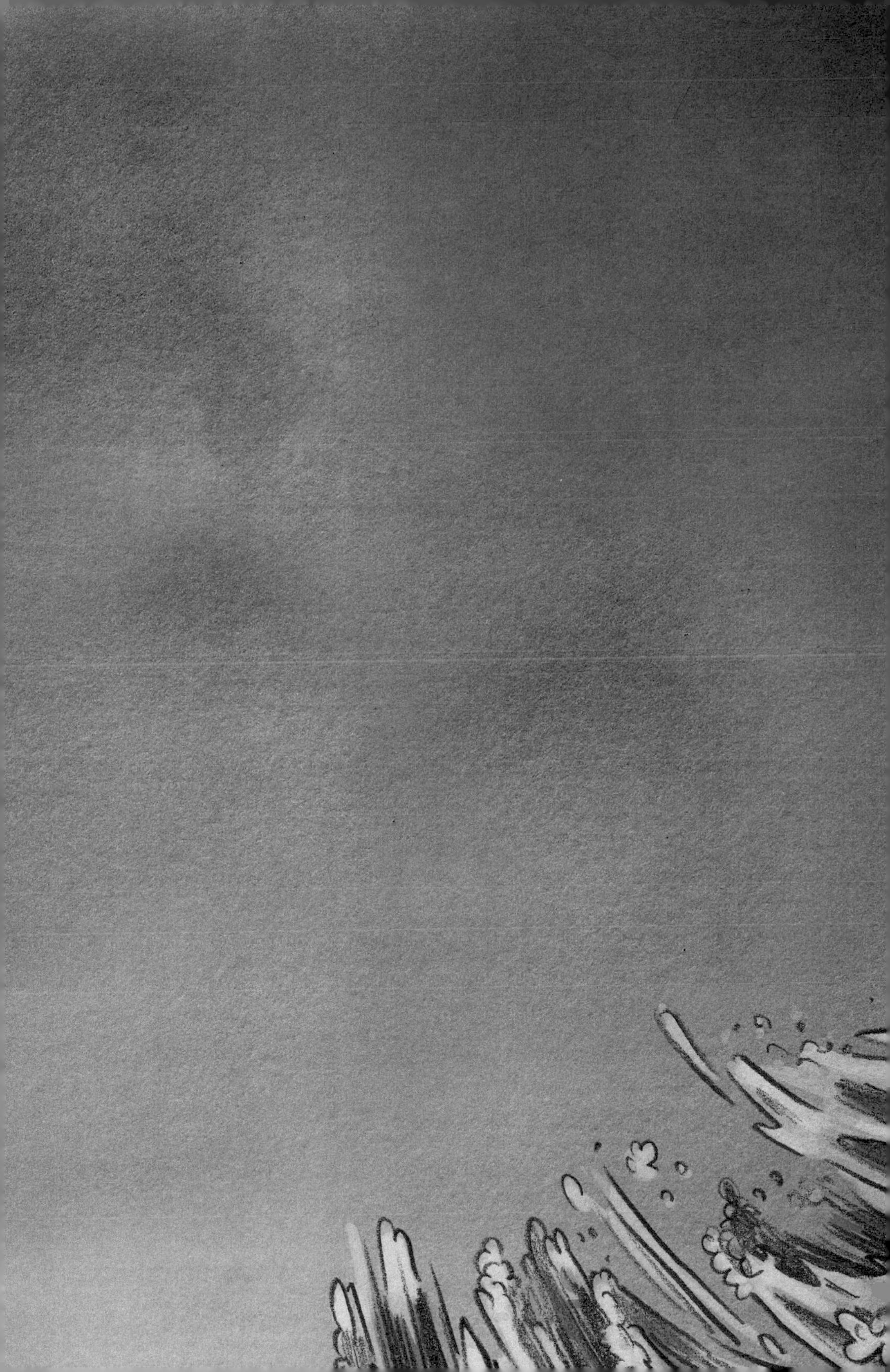

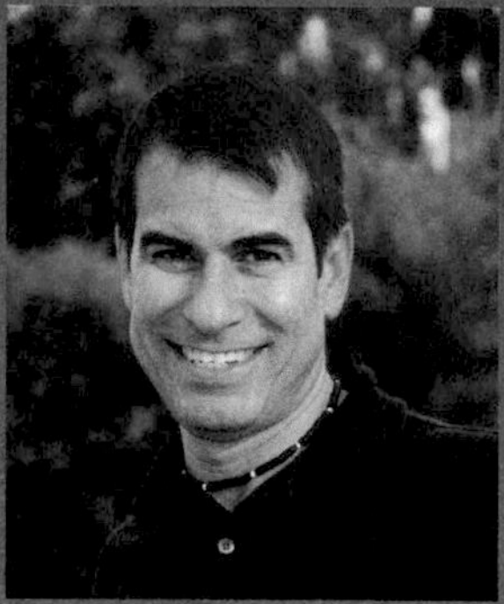

PHOTO BY BILL HITZ

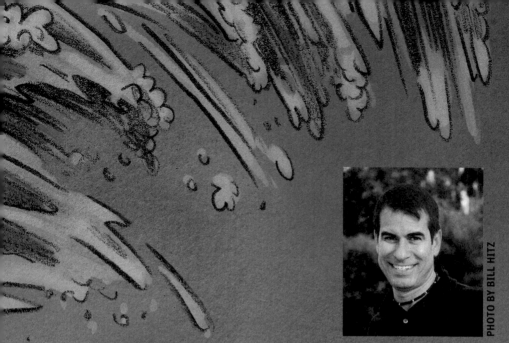

ALEX SANCHEZ has published eight novels, including the American Library Association "Best Book for Young Adults" *Rainbow Boys* and the Lambda Award-winning *So Hard to Say*. His novel *Bait* won the Tomás Rivera Mexican American Book Award and the Florida Book Award Gold Medal for Young Adult Literature. An immigrant from Mexico, Alex received his master's in guidance and counseling and worked for many years as a youth and family counselor. Now when not writing, he tours the country talking with teens, librarians, and educators about books, diversity, and acceptance. He lives in Penfield, New York and at www.AlexSanchez.com.

JULIE MAROH is a cartoonist, illustrator, feminist, and LGBTQIA+ activist from Northern France. They wrote and illustrated the graphic novel *Blue Is the Warmest Color*, about the life and love of two young lesbians, which was adapted into the 2013 Palme D'Or-winning film of the same name.

PHOTO BY JULIE MAROH

RESOURCES

If you, or a loved one, need help in any way, you do not need to act alone. Below is a list of resources that may be helpful to you. If you are in immediate danger, please call emergency services in your area (9-1-1 in the U.S.) or go to your nearest hospital emergency room.

The Trevor Project

The Trevor Project is the world's largest suicide prevention and crisis intervention organization for LGBTQ (lesbian, gay, bisexual, transgender, queer, and questioning) young people.

GLAAD

Leading the conversation. Shaping the LGBTQ media narrative. Changing the culture. That's GLAAD's work to accelerate acceptance.

The Jed Foundation

A nonprofit that exists to protect emotional health and prevent suicide for our nation's teens and young adults. Text "START" to 741-741 or call 1-800-273-TALK (8255). Website: jedfoundation.org

Safe Horizon

The largest provider of comprehensive services for domestic violence survivors and victims of all crime and abuse including rape and sexual assault, human trafficking, stalking, youth homelessness, and violent crimes committed against a family member or within communities. If you need help, call their 24-hour hotline at 1-800-621-HOPE (4673) or visit safehorizon.org.

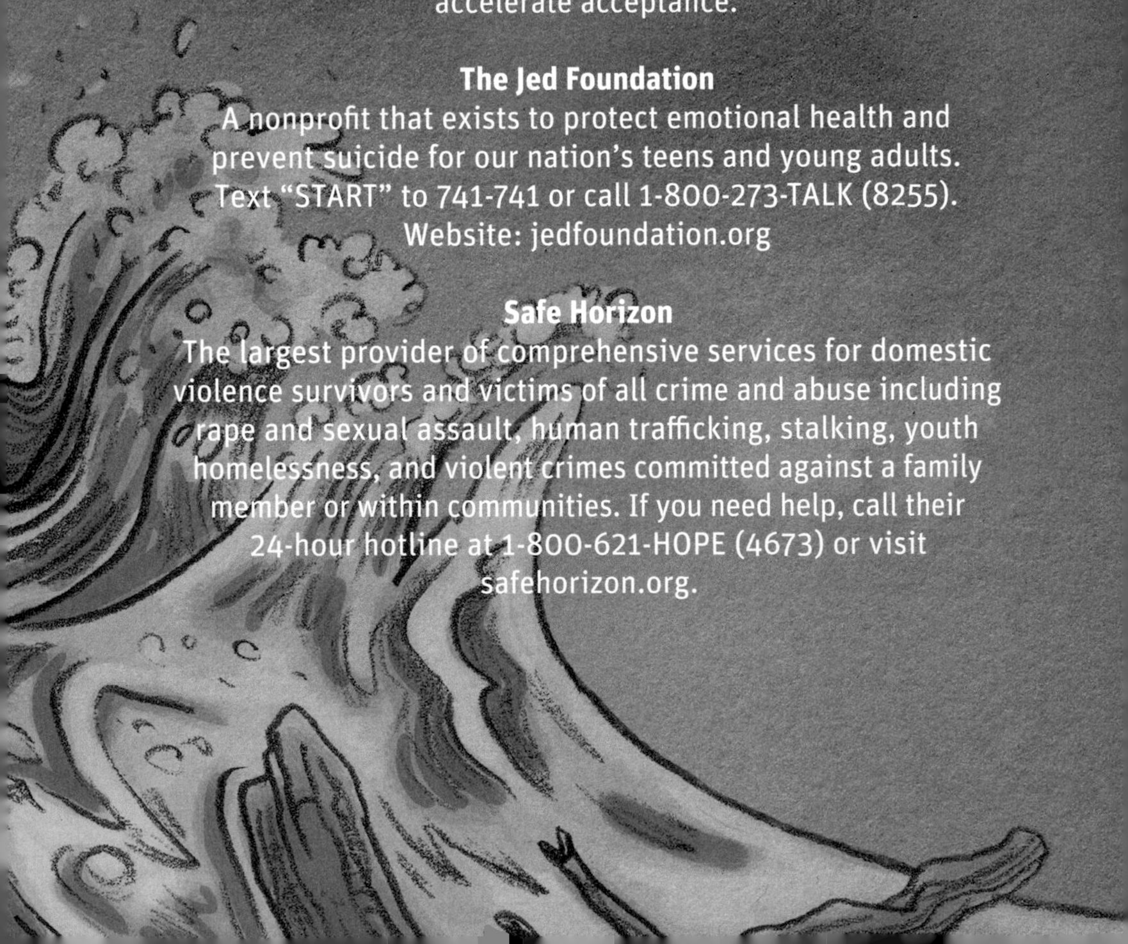

FROM
JULIE MAROH

Beyond the excitement to work on Jake Hyde's coming-out story, it was a personal joy and achievement for me to see this book released on the 10-year anniversary of *Blue Is the Warmest Color*. Ten years ago, my lesbian graphic novel arrived like a UFO in the comics industry, and its success has been so unpredictable. Many things have changed since then, for the LGBTQIA+ community as much as for our visibility and representation in comics and narratives in general. This hasn't occurred because of any sort of natural progress—a total political illusion—but thanks to the consistent work of activism, the courage of people coming out all around the world, and the support of allies. Clearly, we need to hold our ground. Homophobia, transphobia, and queerphobia remain lethal. Gays are tortured and deported in Eastern Europe and imprisoned under religious governments, trans women of color are the most vulnerable targets, and people of color represent more than 80 percent of victims reporting anti-LGBTQIA+ crimes. One of the biggest mass killings in the United States since 9/11 happened in the gay club Pulse in Orlando in 2016. Most of the victims were Hispanic people.

Jake comes out at a very challenging time, and as a teenager he probably struggles to see the sun on the horizon given what I just said. But since I'm twice his age, paddling about through gayness and transness since before he was even born, I'm allowed to play the old master Jedi and tell him, and every queer youth: the Force is strong in you! And it is strong also because it's all around you and shared by a powerful community. And it is getting better. We can make a difference, every day, by remaining true to our hearts. This is how we bring light and strength to our daily lives, and this is what I hope *You Brought Me the Ocean* will do too.

The year I was drawing this book was personally challenging for me. I wouldn't have been able to do it on my own. For their vital support and their love, I sincerely thank my queer family and folks. Thanks to my friends who posed for me and even looked after my body and energy when I thought I couldn't go on drawing. Thanks to Alex Sanchez for caring, listening, and for being the best sensitive mate I could dream of for sharing this adventure. Thanks to the team at DC who believed in this book in the first place and who entrusted it to us. We made it a reality all together, and it's been a radiant experience.

Thanks to my readers and followers for their love and enthusiasm, for making every story matter.

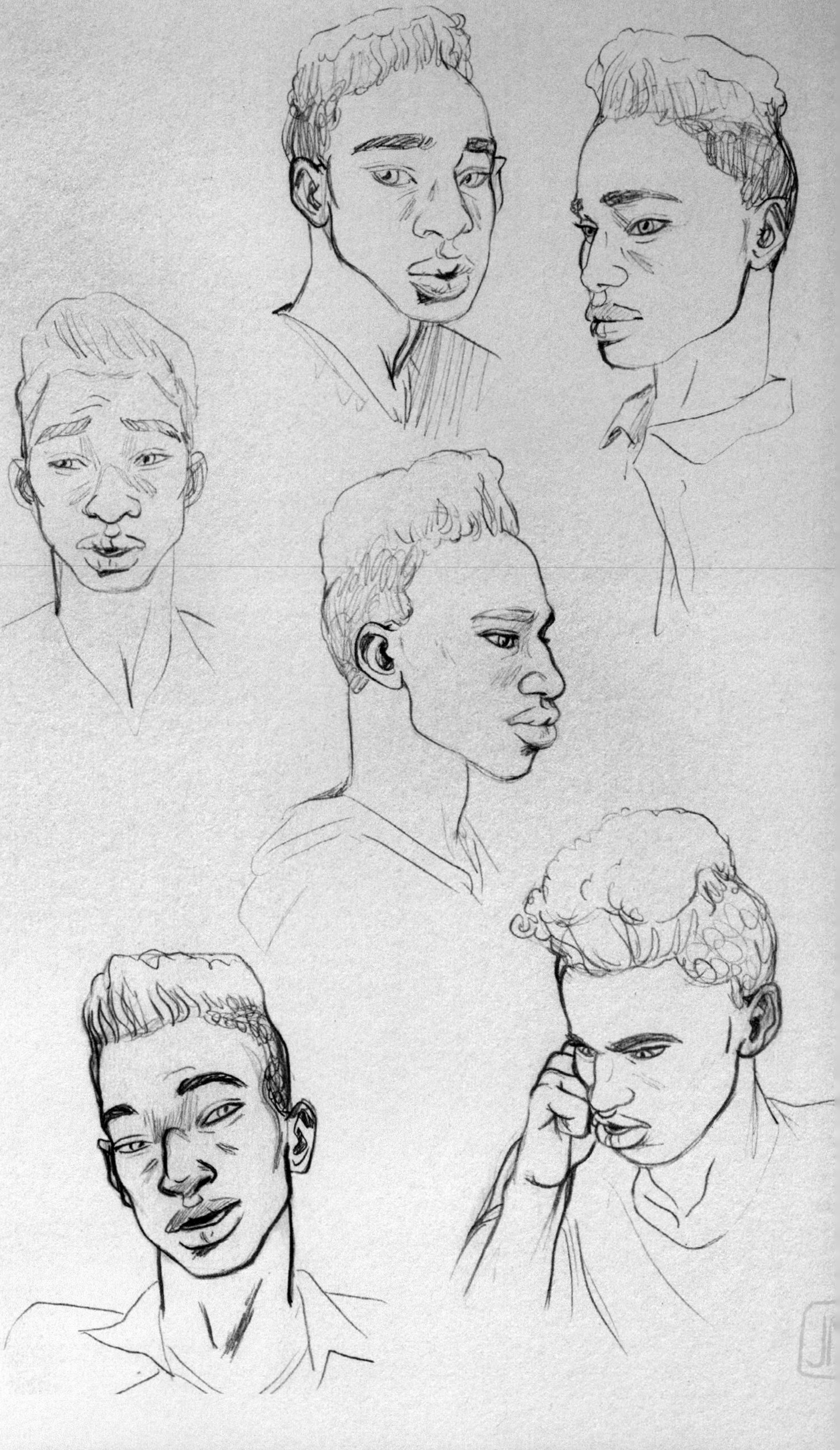

FROM THE PAGES OF JULIE MAROH'S

SKETCHBOOK

A master of visual storytelling and expressive, relatable characters, Julie Maroh brought Alex Sanchez's caring and compassionate cast to life, as proven by their charming and thoughtful character designs.

Starting with sketches of our hero, **Jake Hyde**, Julie captured his sweet and sensitive demeanor coupled with his self-consciousness.

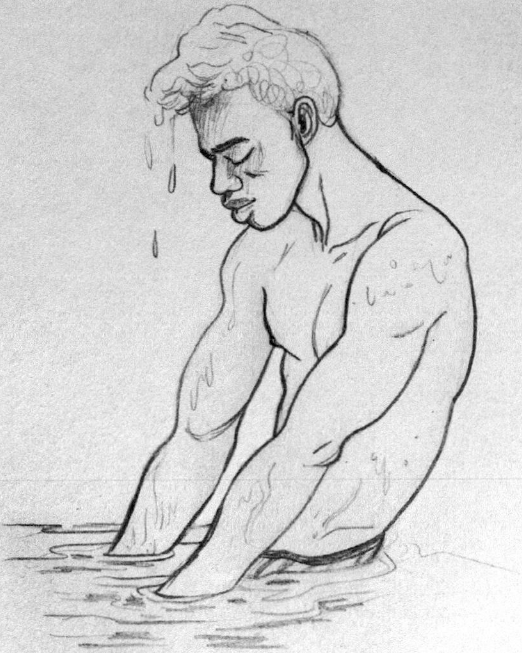

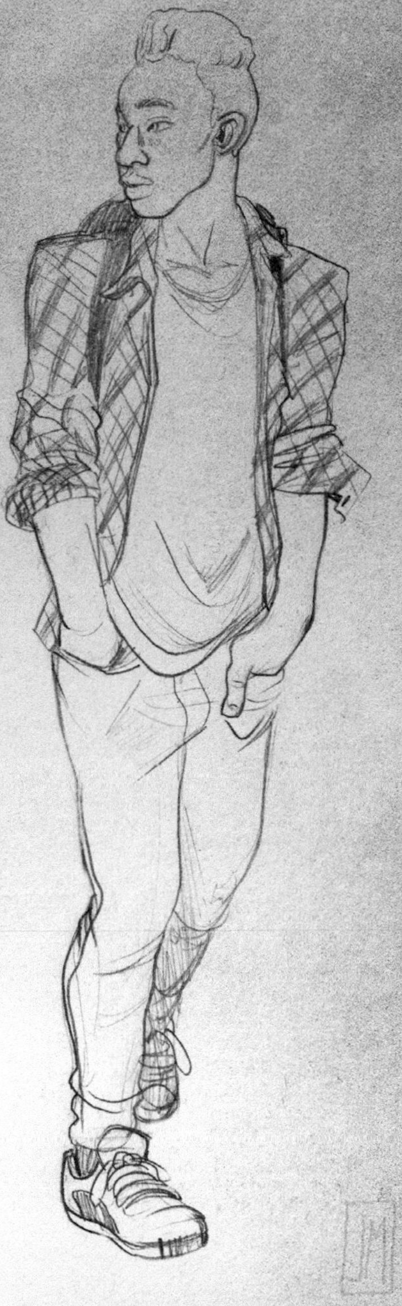

As a lover of the ocean, Julie pulled directly from nature to give Jake's markings a unique and authentic quality.

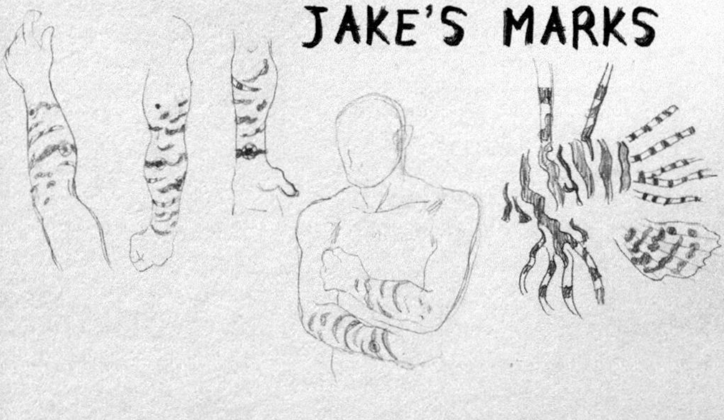
JAKE'S MARKS

Pterois volitans: also called red lionfish or fire fish, usually seen with red, maroon, and brown stripes (exactly the few colors used in the story), but this varies depending on its habitat.
Its personality is therefore similar to Jake's: exuberant but looking to blend into the landscape.

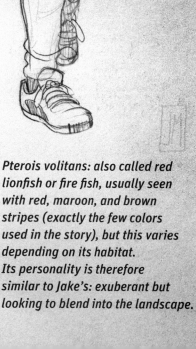

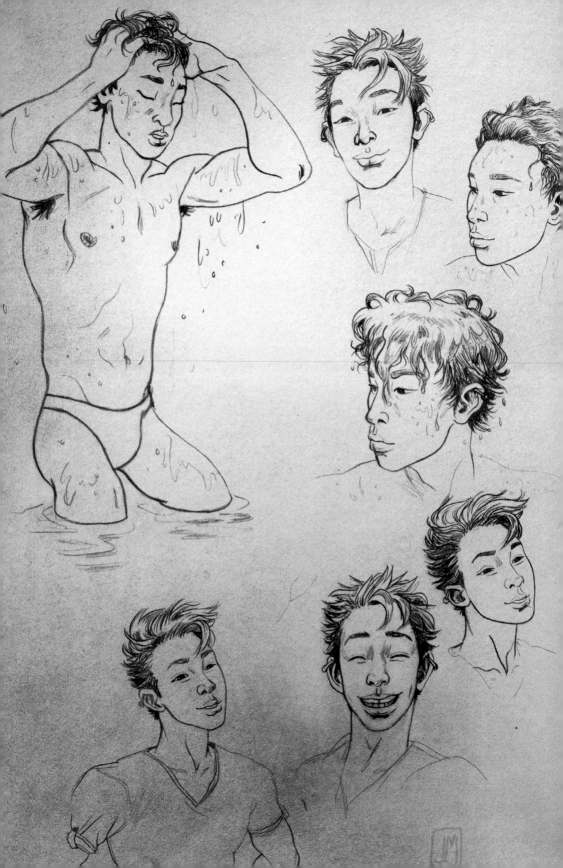

Jake's love interest, **Kenny Liu**, was given the extra-special treatment. It was important that Kenny be a combination of a rebel and a jock with a splash of *je ne sais quoi* to make him irresistible to Jake and the reader.

Julie was able to create immediate chemistry between Jake and Kenny on the page.

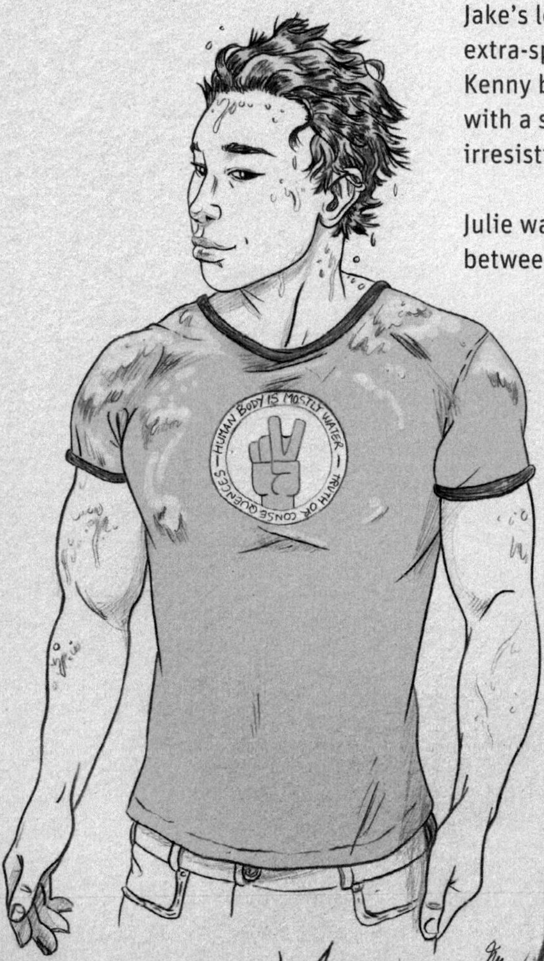
HUMAN BODY IS MOSTLY WATER
TRUTH OR CONSEQUENCES

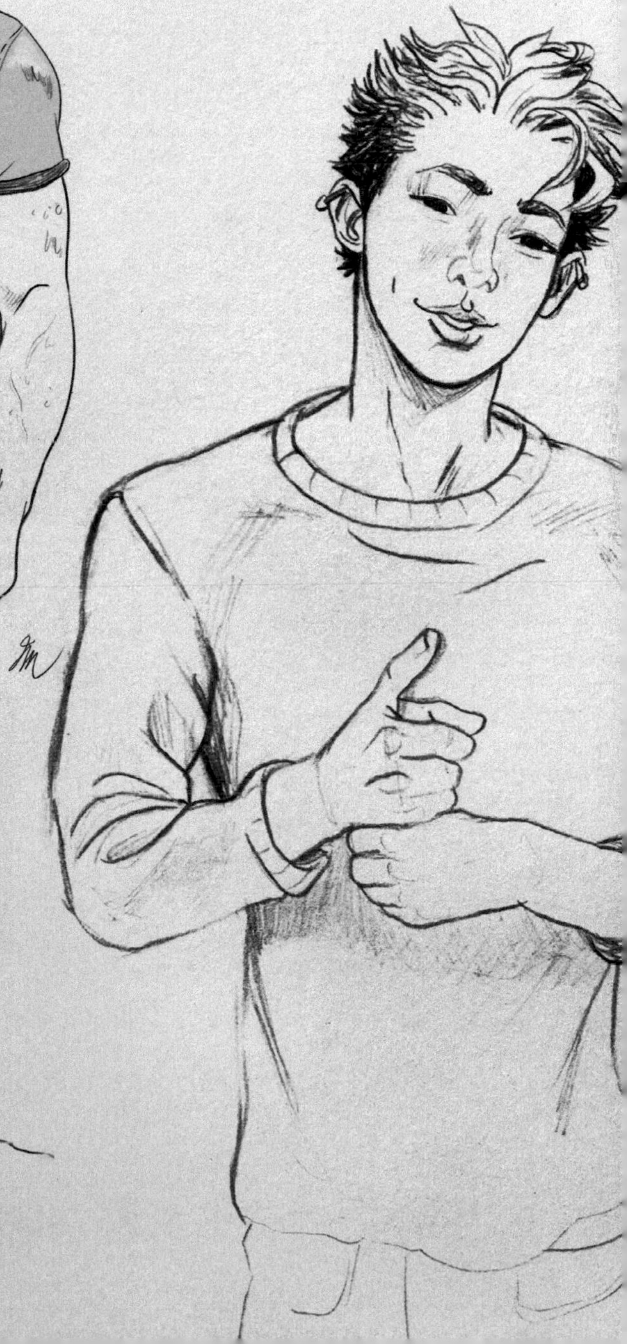

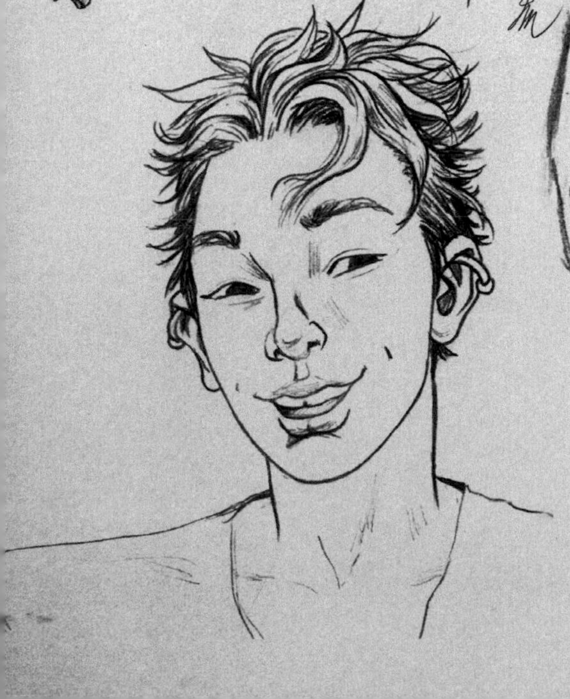

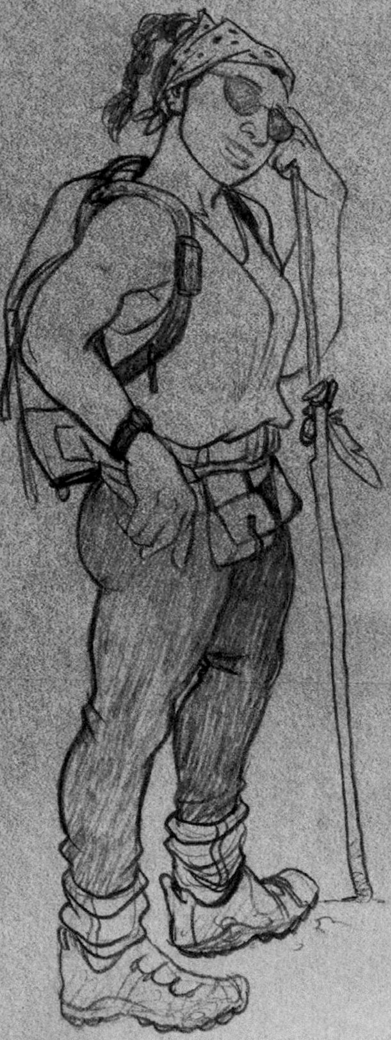

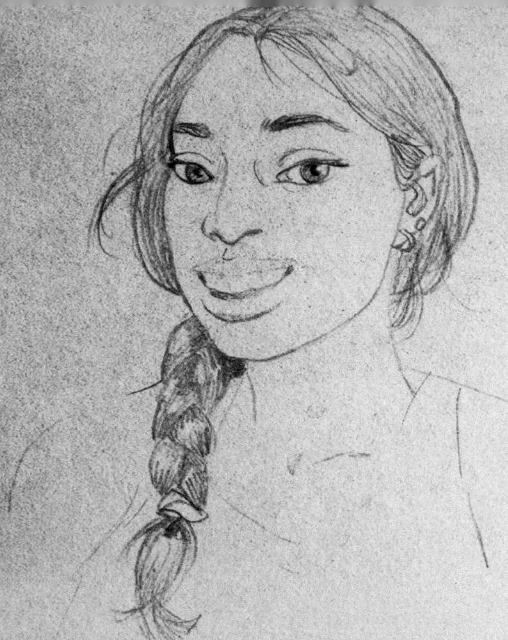

We wanted Jake's B.F.F., **Maria Mendez**, to be just as lovable as Jake and Kenny. Julie's craftsmanship really shows in these sketches; Maria's romantic and wistful personality shines through in just a few pencil strokes.

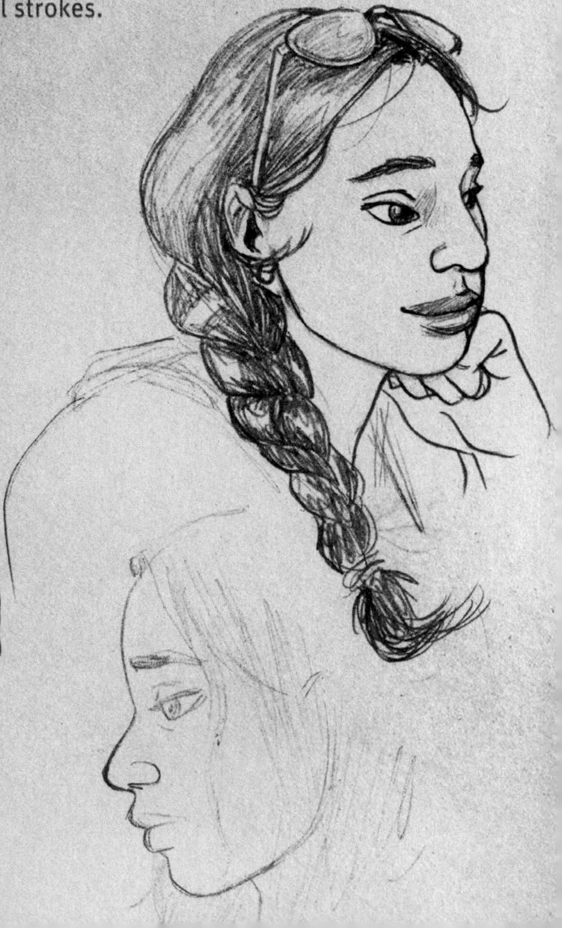

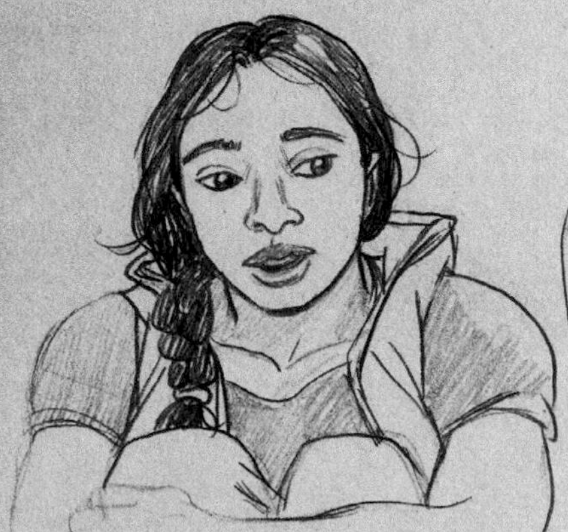

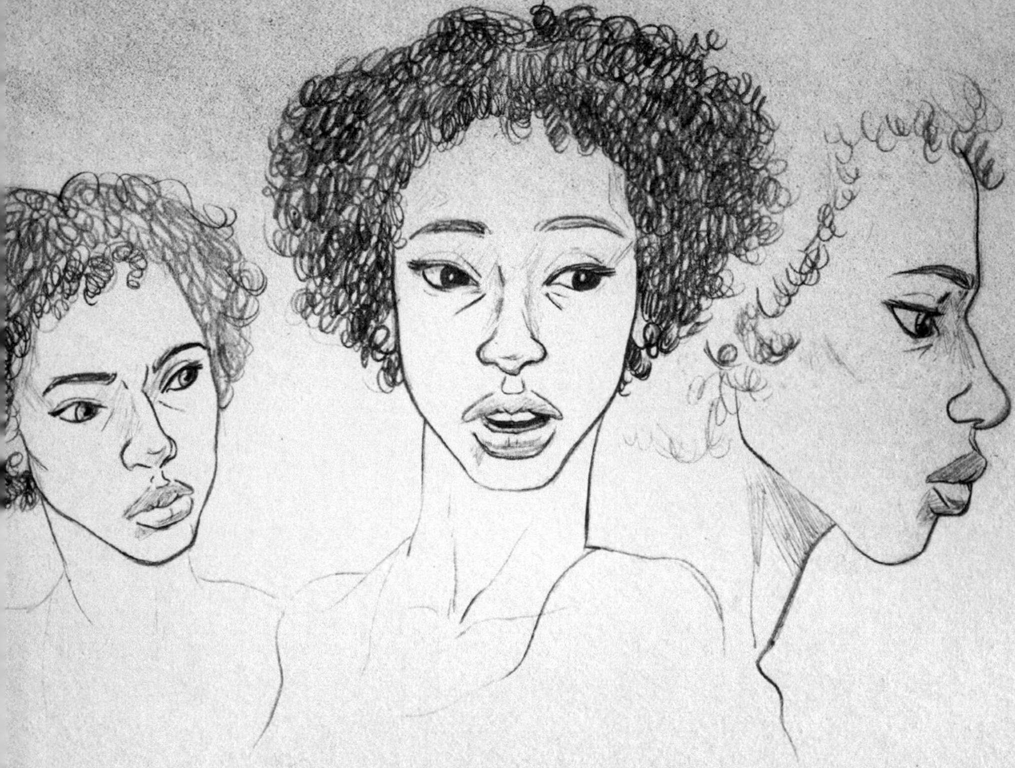

Mrs. Hyde, Jake's mom, has just as much nuance as the rest of the cast. It's easy to see that Jake got his sensitive nature from her.

Mr. Hyde, Jake's father, who unfortunately becomes the ecoterrorist known as Black Manta, was the perfect combination of handsome and sinister, with a touch of woundedness to make him feel real.

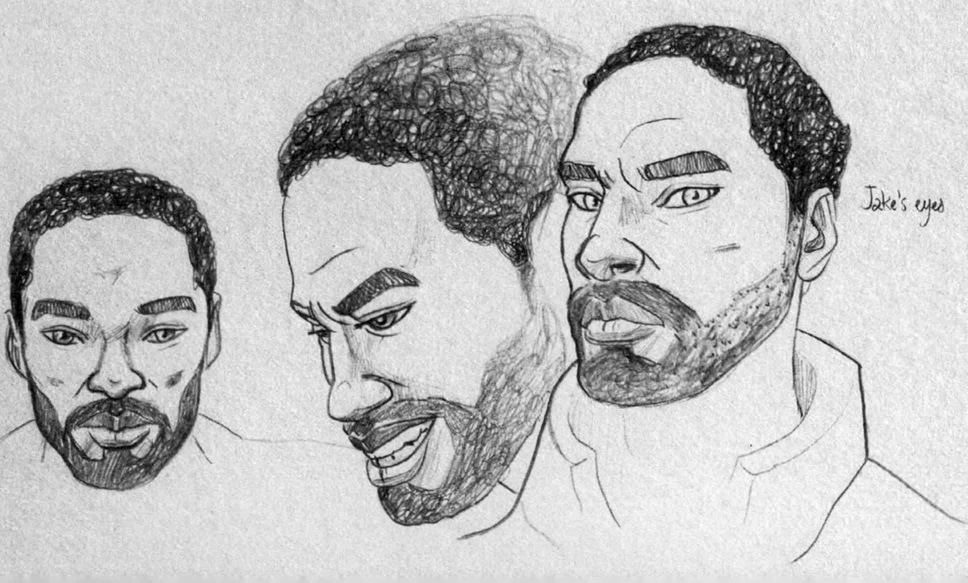
Jake's eyes

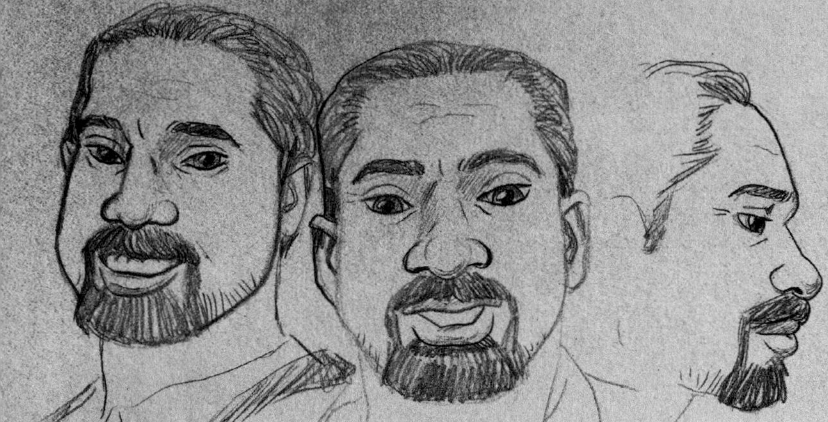

Maria's dad, **Mr. Mendez**, is the father Jake never had. You can see the kindness and compassion in his eyes, and it's not hard to see why Jake would seek him out for advice.

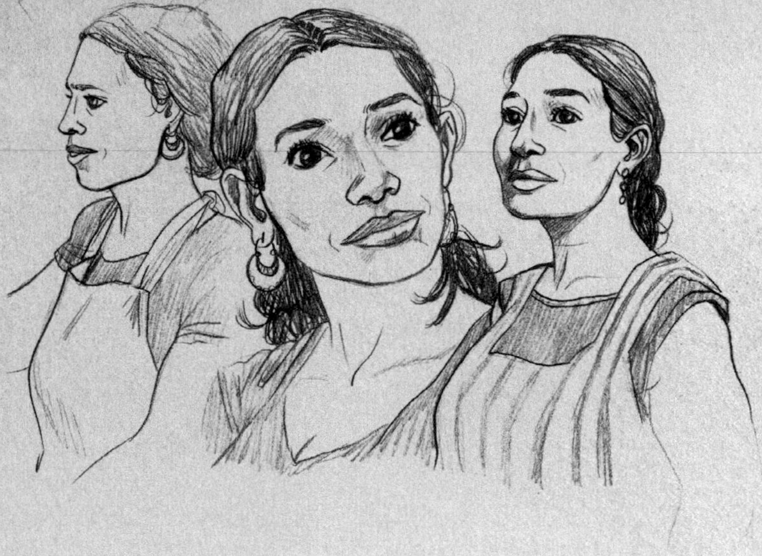

Maria's mother, **Mrs. Mendez**, is equally warm and loving but also capable of giving Maria the tough love she needs.

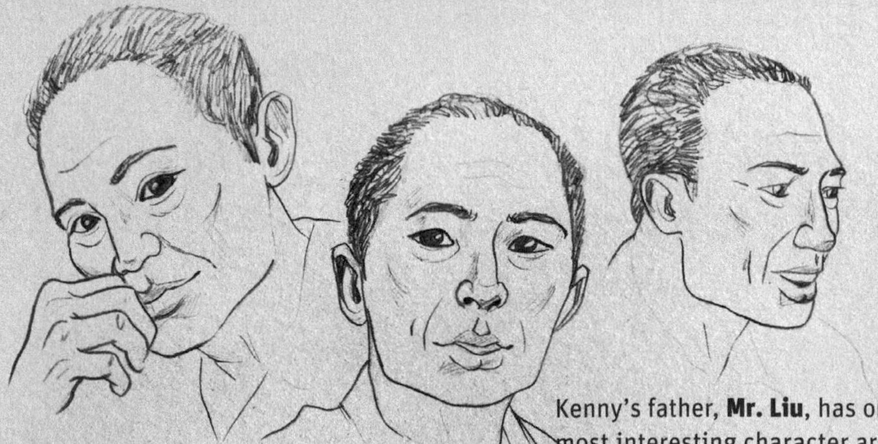

Kenny's father, **Mr. Liu**, has one of the most interesting character arcs in the story. He might hold too tightly at times to traditional family values, but he still has a few surprises up his sleeve.

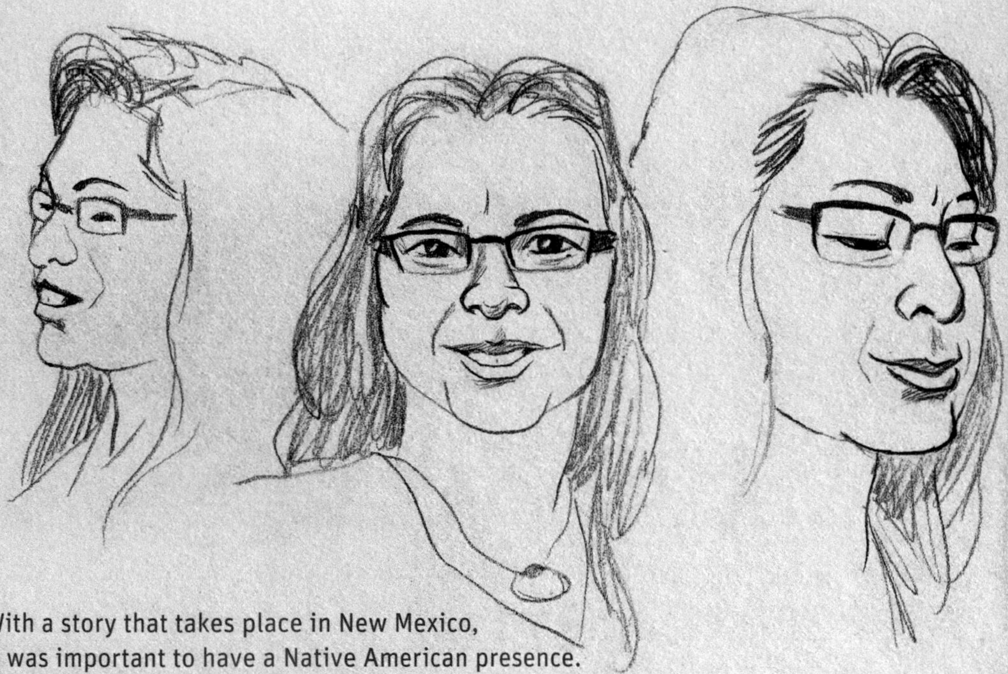

With a story that takes place in New Mexico, it was important to have a Native American presence. **Mrs. Archer**, Jake's favorite teacher, evolved from a character who was originally cut from the story. Julie wanted to depict someone with Hopi descent, and Alex had the perfect personal reference.

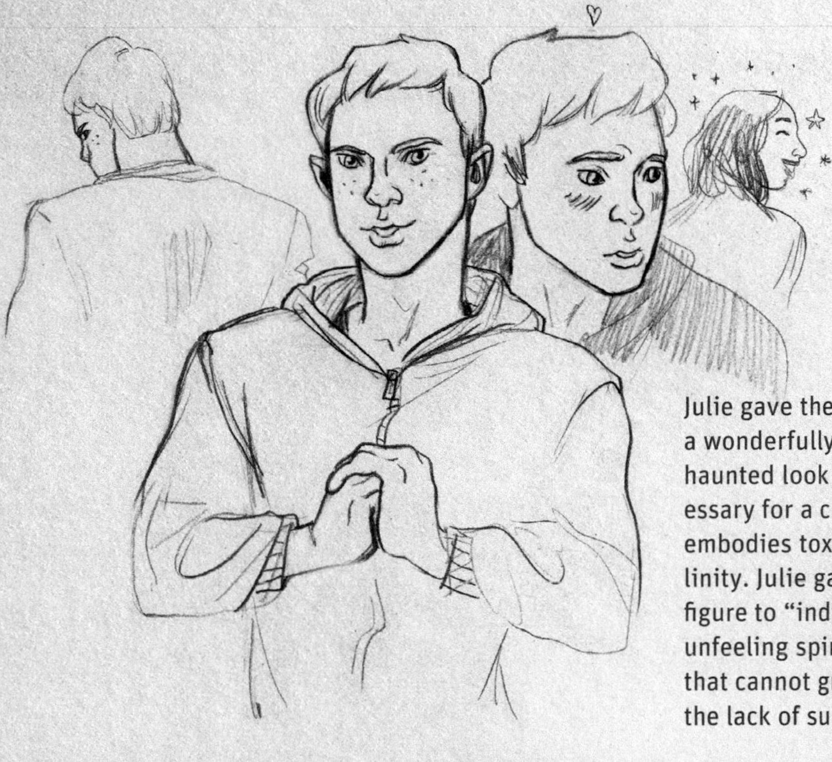

Julie gave the bully, **Zeke**, a wonderfully resentful and haunted look that was necessary for a character who embodies toxic white masculinity. Julie gave him a slender figure to "indicate a 'dry,' unfeeling spirit, like a plant that cannot grow properly for the lack of sun or water."

NEW YORK TIMES BESTSELLING AUTHOR

LAUREN MYRACLE

Victor and Nora

A GOTHAM LOVE STORY

ILLUSTRATED BY

ISAAC GOODHART

When brilliant, 17-year-old budding scientist Victor Fries falls for a dying girl, Nora Kumar, he has to make some hard choices about just what he'll do, and how far he'll go, for love.

New York Times bestselling author Lauren Myracle and artist Isaac Goodhart reunite in this gorgeous YA story, in stores fall 2020.

The Girl Who Refuses to Look Back

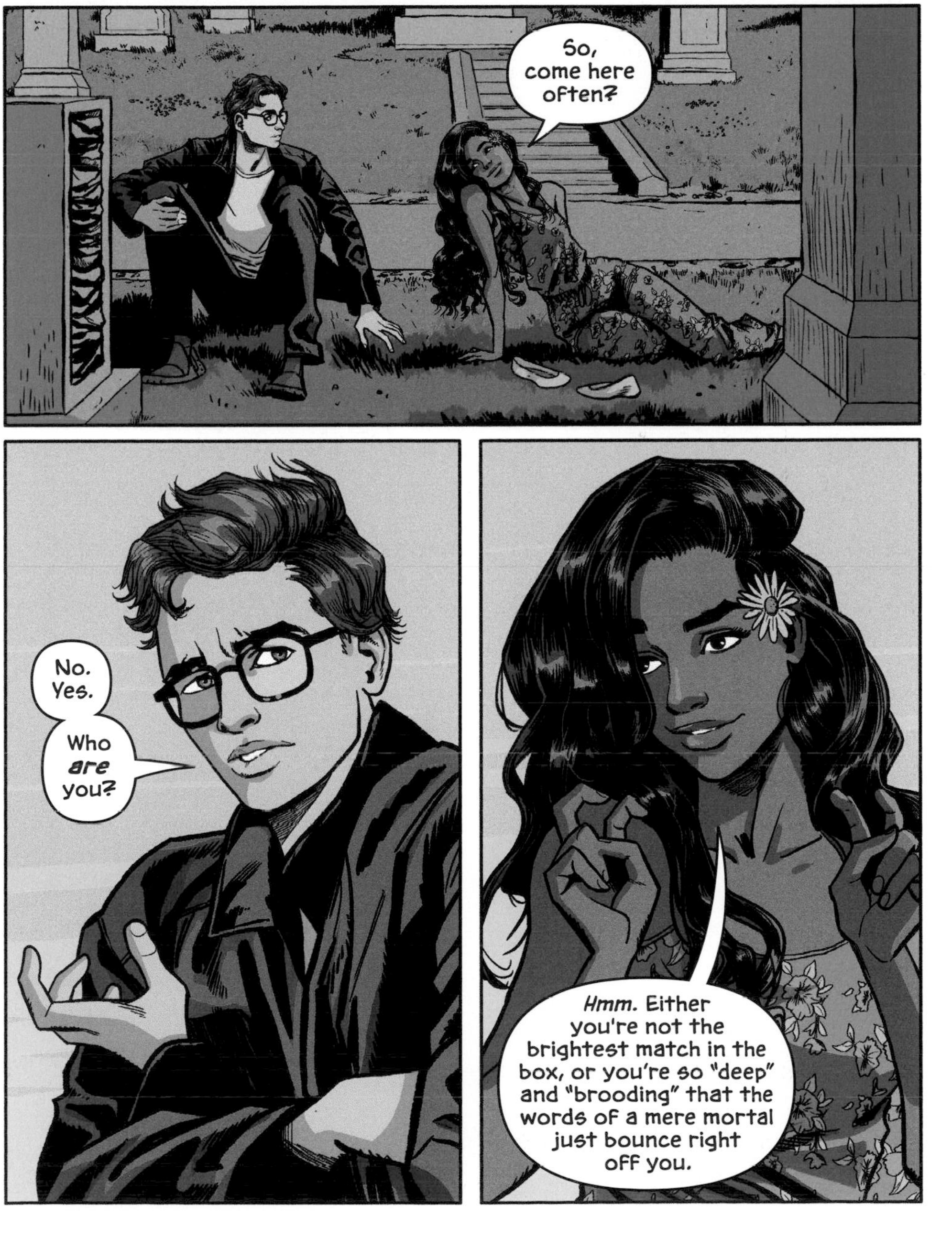
So, come here often?
No. Yes.
Who *are* you?
Hmm. Either you're not the brightest match in the box, or you're so "deep" and "brooding" that the words of a mere mortal just bounce right off you.

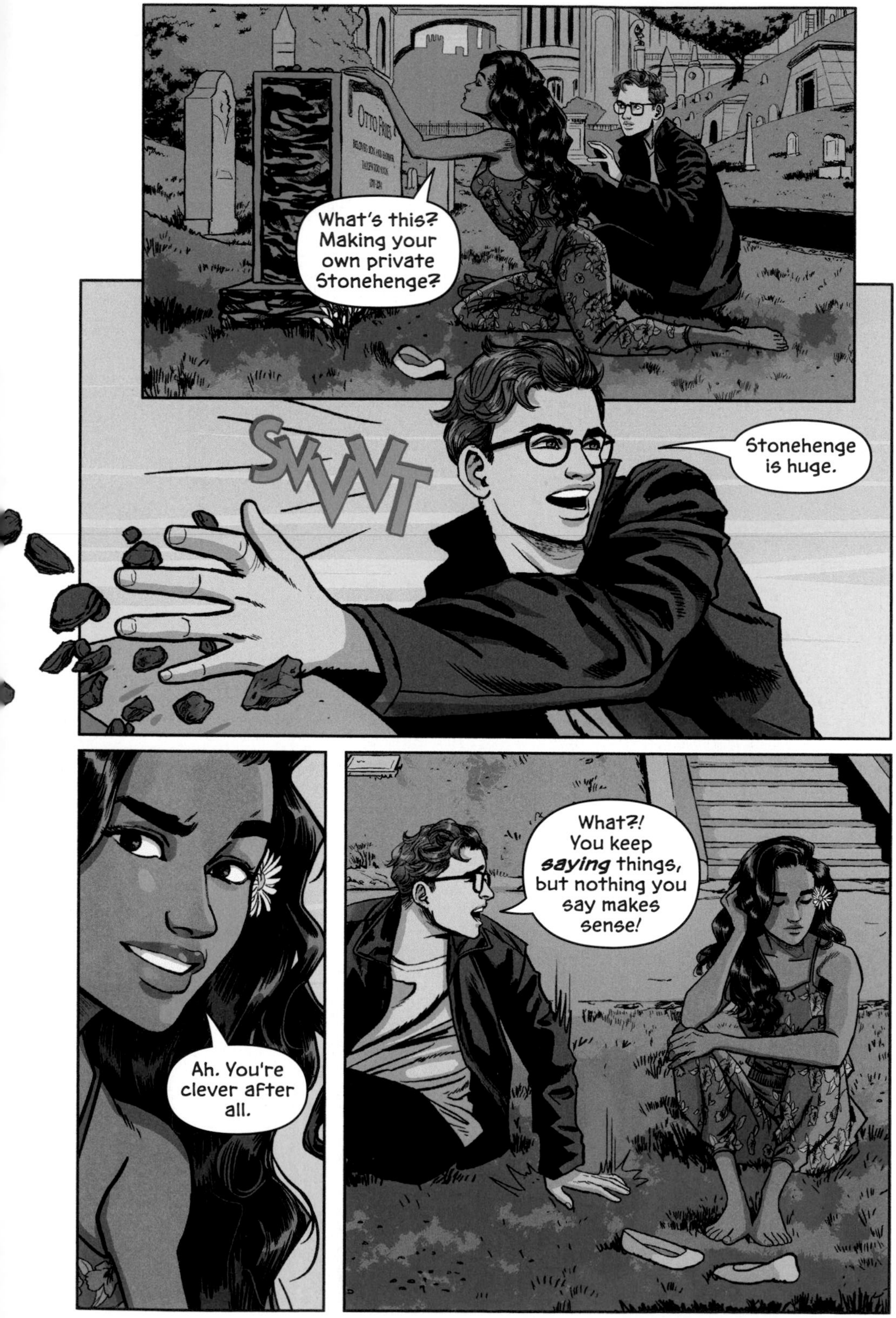

OTTO FRIES
What's this? Making your own private Stonehenge?
SVVVT
Stonehenge is huge.
Ah. You're clever after all.
What?! You keep *saying* things, but nothing you say makes sense!

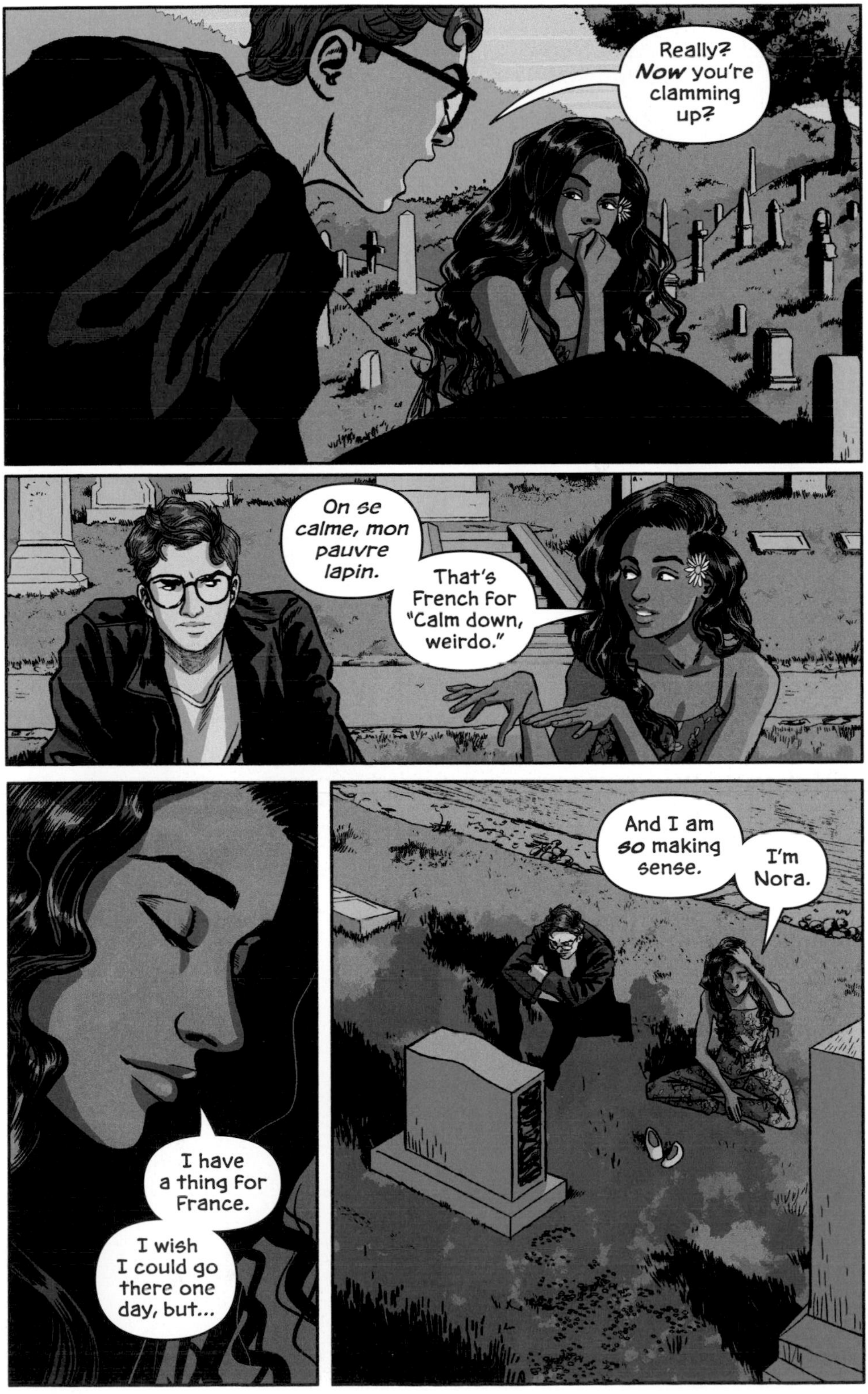
Really? Now you're clamming up?
On se calme, mon pauvre lapin.
That's French for "Calm down, weirdo."
I have a thing for France.
I wish I could go there one day, but...
And I am so making sense.
I'm Nora.

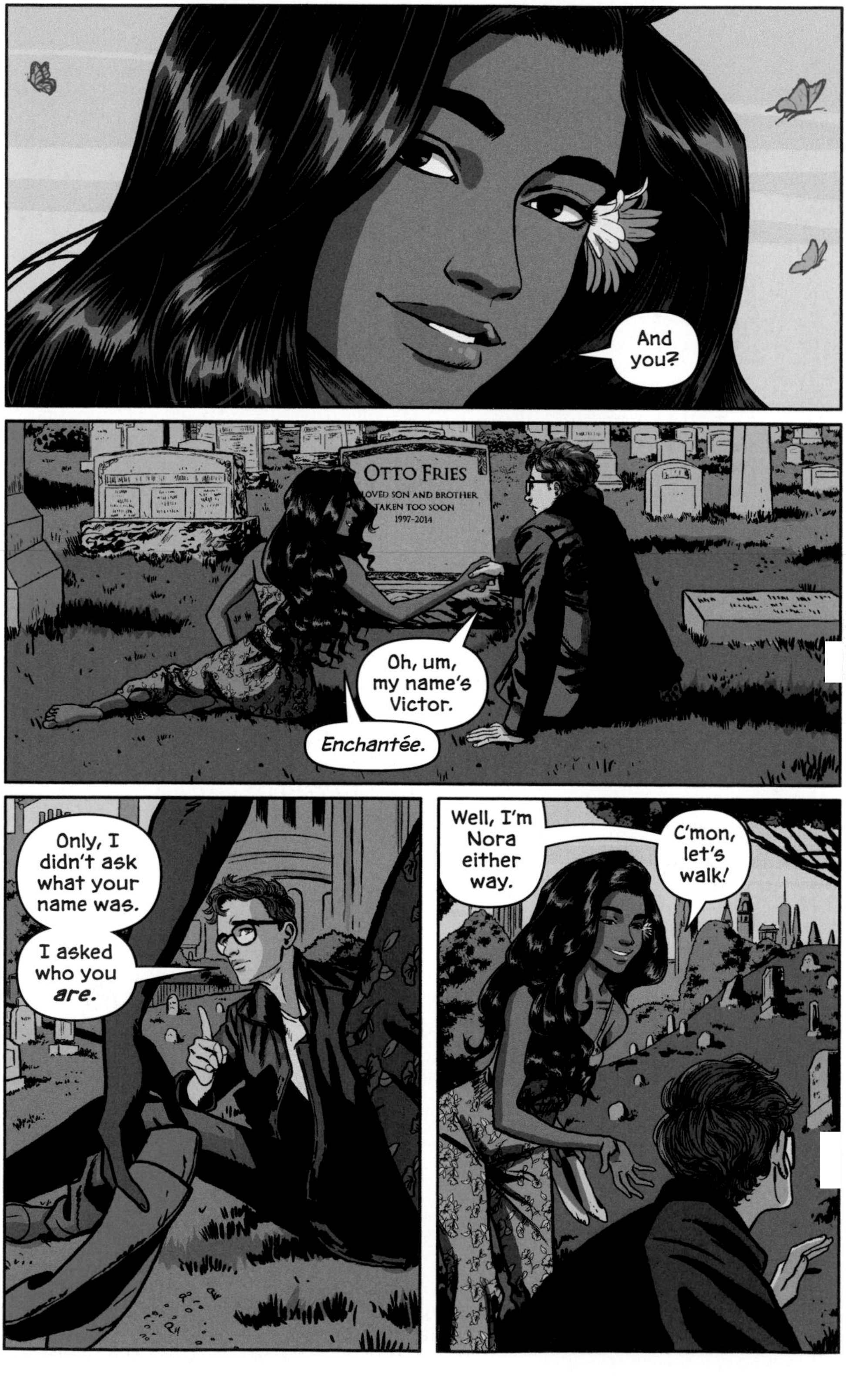

And you?
OTTO FRIES
LOVED SON AND BROTHER
TAKEN TOO SOON
1997-2014
Oh, um, my name's Victor.
Enchantée.
Only, I didn't ask what your name was.
I asked who you ***are.***
Well, I'm Nora either way.
C'mon, let's walk!

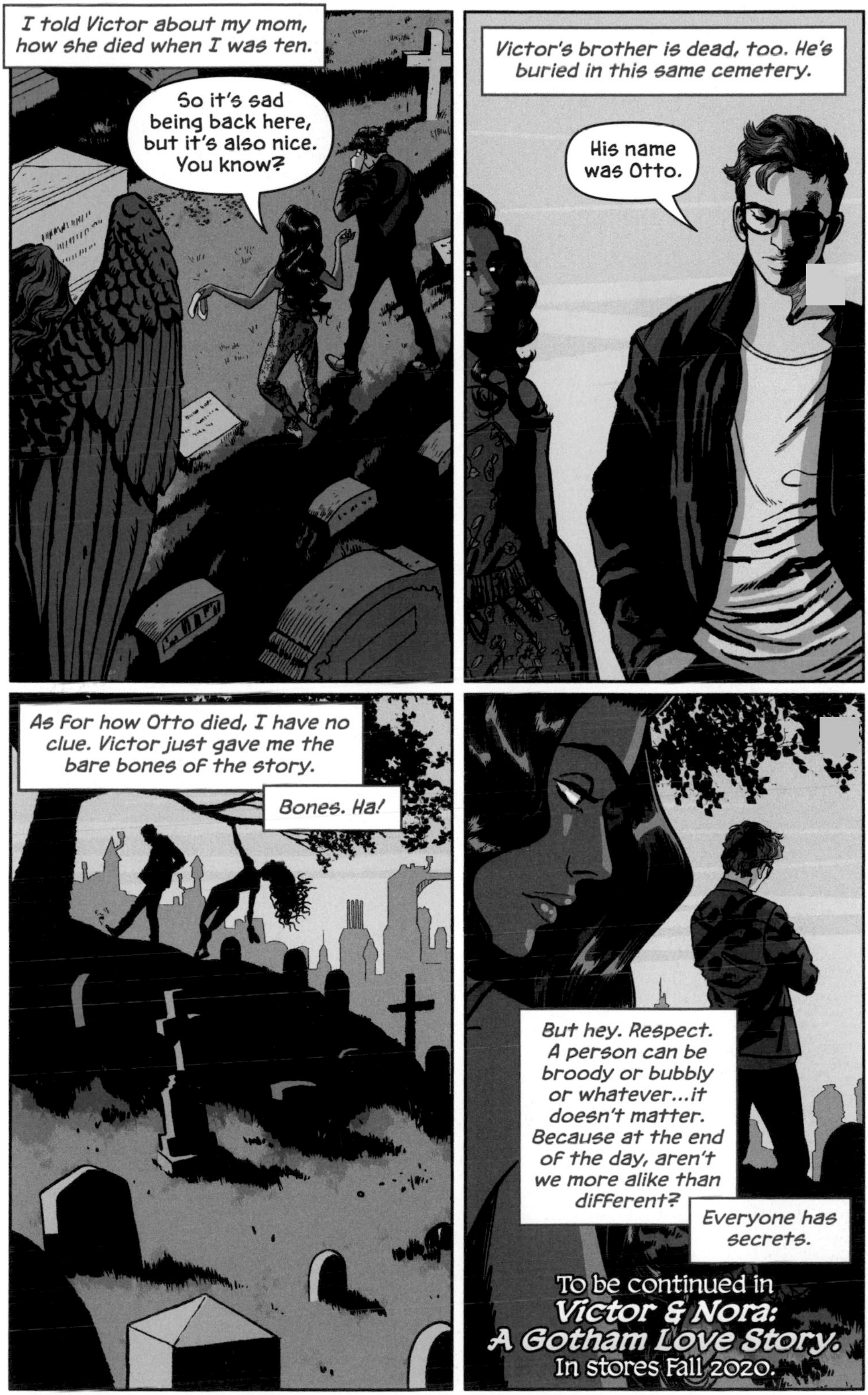
I told Victor about my mom, how she died when I was ten.
So it's sad being back here, but it's also nice. You know?
Victor's brother is dead, too. He's buried in this same cemetery.
His name was Otto.
As for how Otto died, I have no clue. Victor just gave me the bare bones of the story.
Bones. Ha!
But hey. Respect. A person can be broody or bubbly or whatever...it doesn't matter. Because at the end of the day, aren't we more alike than different?
Everyone has secrets.
To be continued in Victor & Nora: A Gotham Love Story. In stores Fall 2020.